With a sprinkling of fairy dust and the wave of a wand, magical things can happen—but nothing is more magical than the power of love.

Sea Spell
TESS FARRADY

As a child, Beth fell into the churning sea, only to be lifted gently out by a dark-haired youth with a knowing, otherworldly smile who then vanished into the mist. Somehow the young girl knew her elusive rescuer was a powerful, legendary selkie, who could become the love of her dreams...

Once Upon a Kiss
CLAIRE CROSS

For over a thousand years—so legend has it—the brambles have grown wild over the ruins of Dunhelm Castle. Many believed that the thorns were a sign that the castle was cursed, so no one dared to trespass—until an American hotelier decided to clear away the brambles himself, and found a mysterious slumbering beauty...

A Faerie Tale
GINNY REYES

According to legend, a faerie must perform a loving deed to earn her magic wand. So, too, must the leprechaun accomplish a special task before receiving his pot of gold. But the most mystical, magical challenge of all is ... helping two mortals fall in love.

A Faerie Tale

GINNY REYES

JOVE BOOKS, NEW YORK

If you purchased this book without a cover, you should be aware that this book is stolen property. It was reported as "unsold and destroyed" to the publisher, and neither the author nor the publisher has received any payment for this "stripped book."

MAGICAL LOVE is a trademark of Berkley Publishing Corporation.

A FAERIE TALE

A Jove Book / published by arrangement with
the author

PRINTING HISTORY
Jove edition / August 1998

All rights reserved.
Copyright © 1998 by Ginny Anikienko.
This book may not be reproduced in whole
or in part, by mimeograph or any other means,
without permission. For information address:
The Berkley Publishing Group, a member of Penguin Putnam Inc.,
200 Madison Avenue, New York, New York 10016.

The Penguin Putnam Inc. World Wide Web site address is
http://www.penguinputnam.com

ISBN: 0-515-12338-2

A JOVE BOOK®
Jove Books are published by The Berkley Publishing Group,
a member of Penguin Putnam Inc.,
200 Madison Avenue, New York, New York 10016.
JOVE and the "J" design are trademarks
belonging to Jove Publications, Inc.

PRINTED IN THE UNITED STATES OF AMERICA

10   9   8   7   6   5   4   3   2   1

A Faerie Tale

One

WOODBURY, PENNSYLVANIA—1899

"Please, Patrick, throw it in. *Now!*"

Stunned by his companion's plea, Patrick O'Toole froze.

"Please," Serena Keller repeated, her eyes tempting, beseeching . . . urgent. "For me."

Shaking his head to dispel his disbelief, Patrick frowned. "Are you sure? You *really* want this?"

Rosy lips pouted. A flush tinted high cheekbones. "Of course I do, Patrick. *Now!* Before someone comes along."

"Good God, Serena! Don't even mention it . . . imagine the gossip if we were caught."

"Oh, darling," she said, breathless, "don't get stuffy on me."

Shaking his head, Patrick flipped a silver coin skyward. He caught it, then eyed the flower-and-ribbon-bedecked well not two feet away. With another glance at the blond beauty at his side, he said, "For you, Serena. *Only* for you."

Feeling sheepish—ridiculous, actually—he closed his eyes. *I wish to find my one true love . . . soon!* He flicked

2   GINNY REYES

his thumbnail against the edge of the coin and sent it soaring. When he opened his eyes he saw a silver sparkle arch over the side of the stone well. Moments later, the *plink* of a splash rose from its depths.

"There! Are you happy?" he asked.

Smugness filled Serena's smile. She laced both hands around his arm and snuggled closer. "Deliriously."

With a swish of petticoats, she tugged him back toward Woodbury's town square where the May Day celebration was getting under way. *Women!* He'd never understand them, no matter how well he came to know them.

How could a well-educated, seemingly mature young lady like Serena Keller put faith in something as absurd as wishing at a well? Especially since she helped decorate the blasted thing herself! There was no more magic in that water-filled hole than . . . than . . . in a four-leaf clover.

Patrick ought to know. He was Irish, by damn! Magic and wishes and May Day were nothing more than old-time superstitions, and superstition never got a man anywhere. Discipline, hard work, determination—*there* lay all the luck a man needed. Wishing never brought about results.

Besides, he already knew who he would marry. As did Serena. Patrick hadn't yet proposed, because the ring he had ordered from a fine jeweler in Philadelphia hadn't arrived. The moment it did, he would make a beeline to Matthias Keller, the honorable Mayor of Woodbury, and ask for his daughter's hand in marriage. Wheedling, teasing, and rubbing up against him wouldn't win Serena that proposal she seemed so anxious to obtain a moment sooner. Everything at its own right time, he always said.

No amount of wishing at a May Day well could change his plans.

"Glorious!" exclaimed Annie Brennan, twirling around and around, arms raised to embrace May's warmth. In-

A FAERIE TALE

stinct told her she had just finished the painting she'd been working on all morning. After removing her blindfold, she studied the stand of willows, ashes, and oaks that had inspired her.

She again registered the impression of vibrant green foliage on earthy brown trunks—splashes of celadon, olive, and ivy topping spears of chestnut, chocolate, and sorrel. Daffodils dressed in yellow danced at the foot of the trees, echoing the glow of the freshly minted sun. A breeze sang its sweet chorus on the tender leaves overhead, and with every breath, Annie savored the essence of the season, the promise of spring.

Nature's splendor humbled her. No matter how diligently she tried to reproduce it, oils, brushes, and canvas always failed to duplicate the beauty of the Earth. Still, she kept trying to depict new and different scenes, experimenting with all imaginable means of creating a work of art.

This morning her feelings had bubbled so strongly at the welcome arrival of spring that she'd painted enthusiastically, blindly trusting the guidance of her other senses, anticipating a beautiful outcome.

Tingling with high hopes, Annie peered at her latest masterpiece. "Oh, dear."

Her *oomph* drained away. Unfortunately not all her artistic endeavors achieved success. The results of this latest attempt stole the enthusiasm she'd experienced since first feeling the heady rush of the new idea.

Once-white canvas now bore lumps of paint that reminded her of her swampy back walk after Tuesday night's downpour—at best. At worst, they resembled the droppings Fergus O'Shea, her burly tomcat, left at the same spot in the yard every blessed day. The only difference being that these blobs stunk of turpentine, and the others—well, of unmentionable, baser stuff.

Disgruntled, Annie collapsed on the small grassy rise where she'd set up her easel. "I wonder," she mused, "if

Botticelli had this much trouble getting it right?''

Lately her disappointment in her paintings tasted sharp and bitter. The lack of peers with whom to discuss the vagaries of art grew into a vast yearning, greater and more painful each day.

And there lay the reason she so wanted to achieve her fondest dream. The Artist's Haven. A place where like-minded folk could gather to create, surrounded by the support and encouragement of others following similar paths. Writers, poets, singers, sculptors . . . painters, too. All would be welcome at the Haven.

Then Annie would no longer be consigned to labor alone. The hated loneliness would surely abate.

All it took was money, and Annie had plenty—*if* she could only get her hands on what was hers.

But no. Patrick O'Toole, her stuffy banker—and the executor of Da's will—had other ideas about her inheritance. She grimaced, remembering. ''A trust,'' he'd said, insisting she put the bulk of her funds in a high-yield account and live off the resultant interest.

While Annie would never go hungry or homeless following Patrick's advice, she would also never achieve her dream. She needed ready cash to buy property, to stock supplies, to hire staff—to provide other artists with the means to follow their dreams without fear of imminent starvation or eviction.

But Patrick O'Toole stood squarely in her way. She found it strange that a man so young—Annie knew he couldn't be more than days past thirty—had such a boring outlook for the future.

She'd had no luck swaying him to her way of thinking. ''The luck of the Irish. Bah!''

The only kind of luck Annie ever had was the bad kind. She needed one of those fictitious leprechauns, complete with his pot of gold. Da's stories of Ireland had abounded with faeries, monsters, heroes, and mythical gods.

A FAERIE TALE

"Three lucky wishes," she whispered. She wasn't greedy. Three were enough.

Closing her eyes, she conjured a vision of one of the legendary fellows. He'd have a green-tinged complexion, pointed ears, and shiny silver-buckled shoes. A pot of gold rounded out her mental portrait. The image seemed so real that Annie reached out for the grinning man.

Her arms came up empty. As empty as she herself felt.

If only wishes came true. If only. . . .

"Oh, how I wish leprechauns were real."

With another pull up the rope that lowered the well's bucket into the water, Rosaleen Flynn finally saw the light of day. "Faith, and I thought I would never make it. I do believe His Majesty let things go a wee bit far this time."

Stretching, she caught hold of the stone wall around the well and pulled herself out. Dismayed by her latest magical failure, she sat on the warm stone and watched puddles form all around her.

Aye, she loved water—'twas the natural element for water faeries like herself—but when one dressed for a particular occasion and took great pains with one's appearance—including hair—having one's spell go awry didn't set too well. She shoved dripping blond locks off her forehead.

Rosaleen held King Midhir in high regard, as did all other Irish faeries. After all, he was the last ruler of the *Tuatha De Danann* and therefore the High King of faerie folk. But couldn't he have found someone to give her a wee bit of help casting her spell? Everyone in *Tyeer na N-og*—the Summerland, the Land of the Young, faerieland—knew Rosaleen had trouble making her magic work right. He should have known she'd be a tad off again. Her landing in the water fully dressed served no purpose. Besides, her godson, Patrick O'Toole, had already made his wish, and it had resonated through *Tyeer na N-og*. The wet wardrobe could have been avoided.

6   GINNY REYES

Now what should she do? Her May Day garb was ruined, and the Bealtaine bonfires wouldn't be lit until later in the evening. She couldn't very well wander around the festively decorated town of Woodbury while dripping wet. That would surely draw too much unwanted attention.

Irritated, she pulled the pins from her hair, twisted the mass into a rope, and squeezed out all the moisture she could. Then she set to work on her pale green silk spring frock.

"Oh, goodness!" exclaimed a woman from behind Rosaleen. "What on earth happened to you?"

Turning, Rosaleen responded with a wry grin. "I took a wee tumble in the well."

Dropping a rectangle of stretched white canvas and a brown leather case, the young woman hurried near. "Are you all right?"

"Aye. I just dented me dignity!"

With a good-natured chuckle, the stranger held out her hand. "I'm Annie Brennan, and I know all about dented dignity."

"Well, well, well . . . Annie Brennan, is it?" The familiar name caught Rosaleen by surprise. She studied the petite young lady. Thick black hair rebelled against the confines of pins, leaving wavy strands to frame a round, freckled face. Wide blue eyes sparkled merrily, open and friendly in their own scrutiny. "Might our dented dignities make us kindred souls, then? I'm Rosaleen Flynn."

"Looks like they might. What can I do to help?"

"Not much, unless you're willing to help me dry out and lend me something to wear."

"Is that all?" Annie asked, smiling. "Follow me. I was on my way home. I have plenty of towels, a warm kitchen, and, while they might be too short, I would be happy to lend you some clothes. You're visiting, right?"

Rosaleen wondered what Annie would think if she re-

A FAERIE TALE

vealed how much of a visitor she really was. She murmured a vague, "Mm-hmm."

Annie retrieved the items she had dropped. "For the May Day events?"

Rosaleen felt the urge to squirm. "Er . . . perhaps a wee bit longer."

"Where are you staying?"

Her discomfort grew. Rosaleen had never been good at prevaricating, but she thought it unwise to tell Annie the entire truth just yet. "Ah . . . I hadn't given it much thought."

"Would you like to stay with me?"

Annie's prompt offer caught Rosaleen by surprise. "Just like that?"

After a silent, head-to-toe scrutiny, Annie said, "You look fairly harmless, and I have more than enough room."

"Ye live alone, do ye?"

Sadness clouded Annie's bright blue gaze. "Mother died five years ago, and Father two."

"Ye miss them something frightful."

"Thank you for understanding."

"Well, and I do think we're kindred souls."

"Could very well be." Annie flashed her a smile, tipping her chin toward the street before them. "Come on, we're almost there."

"Here," Rosaleen offered, "let me help you carry something. 'Tis but the least I can do."

Annie handed over the leather case, a flush spreading over her freckle-frosted cheeks. "Take this."

The case weighed more than Rosaleen had expected. "Do you mind telling what you store here?"

"Paints," Annie mumbled, avoiding her gaze.

How peculiar. Up till now Annie had seemed open and straightforward. "You're an artist, then."

Rosaleen had to strain to hear her companion's response.

"Some would say no."

8 GINNY REYES

She frowned. "I didn't ask about some. What would *you* say?"

Annie's chin rose. "*I* say yes."

"Mmmmm. I love pretty things."

The chin dropped. "I doubt you would find my paintings pretty."

Rosaleen lifted an eyebrow, encouraging further explanation.

None seemed forthcoming.

"There!" Annie exclaimed minutes later, relief in her voice. She ran up the steps of a broad porch embracing the front and both sides of a white frame house. "We're home. Follow me."

Later that afternoon, after Annie had offered Rosaleen practically every item of clothing she owned, and the two women had laughed at their disparate heights, they hastily added a flounce to the hem of one of Annie's skirts. Then, both freshly groomed—Annie in china blue dimity, Rosaleen in mint mousseline—and anticipating the day's continued enjoyment, they left the Brennan house, heading for the square.

A hum of excitement filled the air, and the two women let the sound guide their steps. Before they went more than ten paces, an emerald blur darted between the Maguire home and that of the Breuers. "Did you see that?" Annie asked Rosaleen.

"See what?"

"Why . . . I'm not sure. Something green just dashed between those two houses."

Rosaleen glanced where Annie pointed but then shrugged. "There's nothing there."

"Hmmm . . . don't see it now, either. But I saw *something*, I just don't know what."

Rosaleen sent Annie a slow, suggestive wink. " 'Tis May Day, ye know. Must have been a faerie. They love to come out and dance."

Annie smiled. "You sound just like my father. The Irish do love their faeries. Still, I can't say I ever saw one."

Rosaleen's throaty laugh brought Annie to a halt. "Don't be so sure, lass."

"Oh, stop, Rosaleen! I'm too old for faerie tales. Besides, I heard them all on Da's lap when I was a babe. You can't tease me with the hope of magic."

But, oh, how Annie wished for a touch of magic in her life.

Since wishing never brought anything about, Annie squared her shoulders and resumed walking toward the center of town. "Let's hurry. We wouldn't want to miss the entertainment."

Rosaleen followed without another comment.

On their way, they passed a number of Woodbury's residents. "Afternoon, Mrs. Maguire," Annie called.

"Ah, childie, you look like a piece of the sky, you do!" exclaimed the plump lady. "And who's your pretty friend?"

Annie glanced at her companion. "This is Rosaleen Flynn. Rosaleen, this is Bridget Maguire, one of my late mother's closest friends."

Mrs. Maguire patted her considerable breast. "Aye, I miss Eileen, I do."

A prickle of tears stung Annie's eyes. Despite the passing of five years, the mention of her mother's name was enough to bring back pain. "So do I," she murmured.

"There, there, sweet. Didn't mean to make you weepy. Not today. Don't you know the May Day's for feasting, rejoicing, and frolic?"

Annie squared her shoulders. "That it is. Come along, Rosaleen! I'd like to see what they have going on at the square."

With a sideways glance at her new friend, Annie felt a mild tweak of envy. Rosaleen was so lovely. . . .

Indeed she was the most beautiful woman Annie knew.

10 GINNY REYES

The swirled moonglow-colored hair atop her head added to Rosaleen's already willowy stature. Exotically tilted jade eyes peered out from behind dark brown lashes, contrasting with her roses-and-pearls complexion. A slow, wide smile riveted the attention of all who viewed it, as Annie observed each time a gentleman tipped his hat in greeting.

Beefy Mr. Bremmerhausen, Woodbury's much appreciated butcher, presented a case in point. As he approached the two women, Annie identified the exact moment he noticed Rosaleen. His pale blue eyes bugged out, he ripped off his hat, revealing a shiny red pate, and his cascade of chins quaked as he gulped in admiration. "*G—gut* after . . . er . . . noon."

Annie squashed a chuckle. "Mr. Bremmerhausen, this is Rosaleen Flynn. Rosaleen, Mr. Bremmerhausen, our butcher."

That lush smile again illuminated her friend's face. " 'Tis a pleasure, I'm sure."

The butcher harrumphed, his cheeks burning redder still. "*Das ist all mein, Fräulein. Gut* day." With a bouncy bow, he continued on his way.

Biting her lips to avoid laughing, Annie caught Rosaleen's wicked wink. "If I hadn't already decided to like you," she informed her friend, "I'm afraid I would have to hate you."

A frown drew Rosaleen's brows close. "And why would ye be after doing that?"

Annie's laugh pealed out. She waved helplessly in Mr. Bremmerhausen's direction. "We could start with the effect you have on everyone you meet. Then we could mention how pretty you are. Is it *always* like this?"

"Thank you for the compliment, I'm sure, but what do you mean, 'like this'?"

"You mean . . . you don't know?"

"Annie Brennan! What are ye talking about?"

Annie's jaw dropped. "You don't think Mr. Bremmer-

A FAERIE TALE

hausen usually stammers, do you?'' When Rosaleen retained her bewildered look, Annie exclaimed, ''You truly don't know!''

Rosaleen raised an eyebrow.

''Why . . . you're plumb gorgeous!''

''Ah, stop your fooling, Annie. I'm fair ordinary.''

Just then, an adolescent on a bicycle rode by, his neck craning as he stared at Rosaleen, openmouthed. Seconds later, he crashed into Ethel Pilford, Woodbury's pinch-faced postmistress.

''You watch where you go on that contraption, Rupert Reichardt!'' spit out Miss Pilford. ''And while you're at it, you impertinent pup, chase those thoughts straight out of your head! You are far too young to be looking at ladies with *that* on your mind. Harrumph!''

Annie chuckled again. ''Explain Rupert's response, Miss Ordinary.''

A suspicion of roses glowed on Rosaleen's fair cheeks. ''Sure and I don't know what made the boy run down that poor lady.''

''Oh, honestly, Rosaleen! It was *you*. He couldn't help but notice how pretty and graceful and . . . and . . . *beautiful* you are. You're so fortunate.''

''I wouldn't know why,'' Rosaleen answered. ''I look much like the others back in—'' She caught herself up short before saying more than she should.

Annie waited, finally prompting, ''Back where?''

Rosaleen's green eyes skipped from tree, to house, to street. ''Ah . . . back where I come from . . .'' Then she waved at the wreath-topped, beribboned tree in the center of the square. ''Aye! Back where I come from we decorate a Maypole for Bealtaine, too.''

''Beelteen?'' Annie asked.

''Aye. That's the old name for the May Day, ye know.''

''Old name?''

''Just so,'' she answered, her lips again tilting into her

remarkable smile. "The Bealtaine Sabbat marks a change in the life of the Goddess and God."

Annie frowned. She'd never heard any of this, and her parents had been Irish as poteen. "Who are this Goddess and God?"

Rosaleen's smile bore a touch of wistfulness. "The Great Earth Mother and her Horned Consort, the Ancient Ones everyone honored before Patrick brought his faith to Eire."

"Oh . . . godless pagans."

"Aye, pagans, but not godless."

Annie shrugged. "If you say so." Turning, she caught the scent of fresh oatcakes. "Hmmm . . . doesn't that smell good? I'm famished! Follow me."

Annie took off in a hurry, knowing Rosaleen would follow in her slow, fluid way. Pity she had never been the smooth and elegant sort. Instead, she always hurtled head-long toward her goal—

"Ooooph!" she cried as she crashed into a wall of warm navy serge. "So sorry."

"*Miss* Brennan."

Oh, dear! She'd done it again. As if her desire to establish the Artist's Haven hadn't been enough to persuade Patrick O'Toole of Annie's questionable judgment, at this very moment he stood before her, miles taller, lips clamped, narrowed eyes glaring.

It occurred to her then that Patrick would make a splendid model for a painting of Fionn MacCumhall, the legendary warrior god of Ireland. He was certainly handsome enough, looked ferocious enough, and his powerful body resembled that of a battle-seasoned warrior's enough, too.

A titter at his side caught her attention, putting an end to her ridiculous fantasy.

Oh, ick! What abominable taste the man had. He was escorting arrogant Serena Keller to the town's celebration.

Annie tipped her chin up. Way up. "I did apologize, *Mr.* O'Toole."

A FAERIE TALE

His square jaw tightened. Freshly shaved skin rippled with the movement, drawing Annie's attention to the line of cheekbone, clearly defined by the taut flesh. And his eyes . . . eyes that rich an amber had no right to stare so coldly. In fact, that golden gleam in the irises always made her think of flames, hot and lively.

"Come along, darling," purred Serena, vining both arms around his, smothering the image of fire in Annie's imagination. "Let's leave the *youngsters* to their games. We have more . . . adult matters to attend to."

Annie's temper jerked to life. "Why, Serena Keller! What a silly thing to say. You know perfectly well your birthday comes ten days after mine."

Serena's icy gray eyes raked Annie from head to toe. "The difference lies in one's attitude."

A foul epithet burned on the tip of Annie's tongue, but with the man who held her future in his unimaginative, humdrum hands escorting Serena, Annie had to call on every bit of her determination to stifle the ugly word. She turned back to Patrick. "Did you read over my proposal as you said you would, Mr. O'Toole?"

The young banker shook his head and frowned again. "This is *not* the time or place for this discussion, Miss Brennan. We have an appointment scheduled for next Wednesday. In my office. At eleven o'clock."

Annie's mischievous side hungered to give the too-serious man a cocky salute. Her lonely, yearning side urged her to go along with his dictates.

Loneliness won out.

Annie sighed. "Very well, Mr. O'Toole. Wednesday morning it shall be."

A curt nod acknowledged her capitulation. Serena dragged him off toward the gazebo in the square, where Annie could see the unpleasant young woman's father, Woodbury's pompous mayor, holding court.

"Faith, and what sourness!" exclaimed Rosaleen in their wake.

"Mm-hmm." Annie ground her teeth. *Ooooh!* She was so angry, she had to cross her arms over her chest to keep from chasing Serena and scratching out her stone-cold eyes. Wednesday would not come any too soon. She gave a final glare at the two who had dampened her earlier festive mood.

There! She'd seen it again. That strange flash of deep emerald, as if someone had whipped around the stall where Mrs. Krieger sold the delightful painted tops her husband carved. But now all Annie could see was a group of boys who were busy admiring the Kriegers' wares.

She couldn't be going crazy, could she?

Annie closed her eyes then opened them immediately when her mind conjured up the image of Patrick and Serena, heads together in conversation. Would she ever persuade Patrick to grant her control of her money before she turned twenty-five—as Da's will prescribed? She'd wither away if she had to wait seven more years.

Could a person actually die of loneliness?

Sometimes Annie feared she might.

Would she ever open her Artist's Haven?

It occurred to her that instead of treating this as a business venture, perhaps she would find more success by appealing to the banker's mercy. Everyone had a measure of mankind's gentler feelings. Didn't they?

Annie sighed. It all boiled down to whether stuffy Patrick O'Toole hid a heart in that big, solid body of his.

The wheels in Annie's head turned over her problem so assiduously that she missed most of what Rosaleen said next. She frowned. How strange. She could have sworn the Irish girl murmured something about magic, Patrick, and *her.*

But before Annie had a chance to ask Rosaleen to repeat herself, Rosaleen exclaimed, "Faith, and I have me work cut out for me!"

Two

Patrick watched Serena ascend the steps of the gazebo to help her father launch the May Day festivities. Being the mayor's daughter, she was expected to participate, but he wished she hadn't insisted on his company for the entire day. A mountain of work clamored for his attention at the office, and more would be added to it Monday morning.

Besides, why did Woodbury require such frequent excuses to celebrate minor holidays? Easter wasn't long past, and the town had made the most of that with a parade, rabbits, egg hunts, and baked goods of all sorts. Now they were at it again, this time with a Maypole, dancing, bonfires, a King and Queen of the May, and the liberal consumption of mead.

According to ancient Irish tradition—many of the town's residents descending from Irish immigrants—Woodbury observed the rebirth of the fertile time of the year on May Day, anticipating the bounty to be coaxed from the land by man's labors.

Patrick believed a man's harvest would be greater if he worked steadily rather than if he took time to prance around the town square.

Since childhood he had heard about the horrors of Ireland's Great Famine of '47. He knew of the hunger, the

16 GINNY REYES

walking carcasses, the millions of dead. He'd been told of those who were forced to emigrate, many of whom died in the attempt. His mother's family had dwindled to a cousin and her, the others starving while landlords demanded the last of the corn or oats as their due.

Little Margaret Mulligan lived to tell the tale, thanks to a Quakeress who, moved by the tragedy, took in the orphaned two-year-old and helped her weather the storm.

But Ma hadn't learned. She had married an idealist, then suffered for it. A fiery Fenian, Sean O'Toole got himself arrested after a meeting of ardent nationalists in the fall of 1869. Pregnant with Patrick, Margaret became a widow when, after an enthusiastic lashing by his jailers, Sean died, his last breath expended on a cheer for Ireland.

Margaret emigrated to America, joining the cousin who also survived the famine. Patrick never knew his patriotic father, only painful poverty and the disdain of Americans for the Irish.

Not until his mother married Guenther Mertz and the family moved to the hills of Pennsylvania did matters improve. If nothing else, hard-working, practical Guenther had ensured they never knew lack again.

Patrick learned the lesson well. Hard work, with a keen eye on common sense, led to a man's success. His position at the bank and his upcoming marriage into the well-connected family of Woodbury's mayor were choices he had made for concrete reasons. Patrick refused to see again the haunted look that had aged his mother's features prematurely.

"Ladies and gentlemen!" Matthias Keller called out in his stentorian voice. "We are ready to begin this year's May Day celebration."

Patrick sighed. It was just as well. The sooner the events got under way, the sooner he could go home.

"As usual," the mayor continued, "we shall start by crowning our king and queen. Every year we select distinguished citizens of Woodbury who will bring honor

A FAERIE TALE

and respect to the position. This year's sovereigns will do no less.''

A familiar laugh and a rustle of skirts at his right caught Patrick's attention. That Annie Brennan! Flighty and fanciful as they came. Just by looking at her one could tell she thrived on the hoopla of the day. And why not? She was a dreamer, so impractical that she wanted to establish an Artist's Heaven or some such nonsense with the fortune her father left her. Patrick saw where the notion of holiday royalty would appeal to one cursed with a fey nature. His idealistic mother had also loved holidays and traditions and all they stood for.

Then Serena spoke. ''It is my pleasure to crown this year's King of the May. And I must tell you, Woodbury has chosen well.''

The smile she sent him jabbed Patrick with unease.

She continued, her voice a purr. ''This year's king is one of our most respected citizens—hard-working, honest, and a fine figure of a man.''

Feminine laughter broke out through the crowd.

The determined glint in Serena's gray eyes turned Patrick's unease to fear. He began to sidle away.

''He's far too modest, too, ladies and gentlemen,'' she cried in a rush. ''I present to you, Patrick O'Toole, our King of the May!''

Patrick's gut lurched. This was awful, he thought, as everyone turned and fixed curious stares on him. The crowd drew closer, cutting off all hope of escape. Moments later, Serena approached, bearing the ivy-and-twig circlet she intended to use as his crown.

He took a step back.

Feminine hands shoved him forward.

''Oooh, Serena!'' cooed a woman at his left. ''You're so right. See how splendid a blush looks on him!''

Patrick frowned, seething inside. He would have to speak to Serena about this, make his stance clear. She was *never* to do anything so . . . so . . . preposterous again before consulting with him.

Serena laid a proprietary hand on his chest. "Of course it does, Elizabeth. *Everything* about Patrick is splendid."

"Oooooh!" crooned the female throng.

Just when he had thought matters couldn't get worse. Patrick's temples pounded with humiliation. He resented Serena's insinuation. She was clearly staking her claim, but she should be more careful with her methods. He didn't want his future wife's reputation tarnished when he hadn't even come close to attempting what she suggested. He had taken a scant handful of kisses—unsatisfying ones, at that.

She commanded his attention with a whisper. "Lean down. I can't crown you while you stand so stiff and tall. Help me, please."

"*I* should help *you* with this farce?"

A frown and a pout clouded Serena's expression. "There you go again! Why must you be so stuffy, Patrick? You're only thirty years old!"

Clenching his jaws, Patrick submitted, suspecting matters would only worsen if he didn't yield to her wishes.

As soon as the crown lay upon his brow, clapping broke out.

"Well, now," boomed Mayor Keller above the ovation, "we need a fitting queen for our fine king, do we not?"

A rowdy male cheer filled the air.

Patrick rolled his eyes. Surely everyone knew the mayor would crown his darling daughter.

Matthias Keller droned on, regardless. "Woodbury has chosen an excellent queen this year. Daughter of one of our most prominent families, she is known to one and all for her cheerful nature, her willingness to help whenever and wherever help is needed, and her talents—too many to enumerate—are legendary."

Serena preened, arms twined around Patrick's. Then,

A FAERIE TALE 19

without releasing his arm, she waggled her fingers at her father.

"Ladies and gentlemen!" the mayor announced. "It is my distinct honor to crown Annie Brennan as Woodbury's Queen of the May!"

Expressions of delight rose from every throat.

That is, from every throat except the one belonging to the woman with a death grip on Patrick's left arm.

"How could you, Father?" Serena wailed, her reproach drowned by cheers.

Patrick supposed he ought to comfort her, but at that moment, he only felt dread. He would have to spend the remainder of the day at Annie Brennan's side—the single, solitary thing that might be worse than enduring the upcoming silliness.

He supposed there were less desirable companions than Annie. He didn't know a soul who could claim boredom in her company. But boredom didn't scare him; it was Annie herself he feared.

Well, not feared, either. Patrick wasn't scared of a giddy girl who'd had the good fortune to be born into a well-to-do family. Somehow, each time they met, Annie managed to wriggle under his skin. Her tendency to do nothing according to tried-and-true methods, nothing normal, nothing ordinary, disturbed him. Then, too, she . . . bubbled. Chattered. And she had the most unsettling way of punctuating her conversation with strokes and pats for her listener.

Those soft, warm hands unnerved him each time they touched him. Heaven only knew what today's heightened excitement would make her do! He did not want to find out.

But he would.

And he didn't have long to wait.

In a flurry of blue skirts, Annie appeared at his side. "Oh, Patrick—er, Mr. O'Toole!" she exclaimed, her sapphire eyes sparkling. "Isn't this thrilling?"

20   GINNY REYES

That was another thing. Those eyes. They made him feel . . . *something* each time she turned them on him. They affected him so much, he refused to identify what that something might be.

"Patrick will do," he said, knowing sooner or later he would regret the familiarity he offered.

Annie flashed her dimpled smile. "Very well, too, I should say! It's a lovely man's name."

More feminine laughter surrounded them.

He regretted it, all right. Patrick clenched his jaw again.

Then Annie shocked him by placing her hands on his right arm, rising to the very tips of her toes, leaning her warm weight against him, and landing a soft, tender kiss on his cheek.

"Oooooh!" The women sighed.

"Wheeee!" The men whistled.

Dazed by the sting of awareness set off by her lips, Patrick heard Annie congratulate him but couldn't dredge up a better response than, "Mmmmm . . ."

Plastering herself against his other side, Serena made a strange, seething sound deep in her throat.

Good grief! What had he done to deserve this? More to the point, what would he have to do to survive it?

The band in the gazebo burst into song. Mayor Keller approached Annie, bearing a braided honeysuckle crown. As soon as he set the woven blossoms on Annie's black hair, another cheer rose from those around them.

Congratulating his king and queen, Mayor Keller led Patrick and Annie to the decorated Maypole in the center of the square. The tall pine was shorn of branches nearly the whole way up. A tuft of greenery had been left at the top, and a grapevine wreath was attached to the trunk below the remaining limbs. Numerous red and white ribbons streamed down from the wreath. Accepting his fate, Patrick grasped a red strip of satin as Annie took a white.

The music grew louder, and the crowd began clapping in time to the tune. Mayor Keller pushed Patrick forward,

A FAERIE TALE

21

bobbing his chin in the direction he should go. Patrick had never felt so inadequate in his life. He had never spared a thought to dancing around a Maypole, much less actually doing so. He had no idea what to do.

As a compromise, he began a shuffling walk, noting the exuberant jig Annie performed on the opposite side of the tree. If she weren't such a wholesome sort, one might take her for a woodland sprite.

She skipped and swayed.

She twirled and bobbed.

She kicked her legs out enthusiastically, and with each step she took, her skirts frothed, giving Patrick tantalizing glimpses of well-turned ankles. With a wave, she beckoned the spectators to join the dance.

As others took their places, ribbons in hand, Patrick sighed his relief. At least he would no longer be on display before the entire town. He could perhaps fade into the mob who now worked to weave a red-and-white pattern around the trunk of the tall tree.

Every so often he caught glimpses of Annie's blue dress, her smile, her twinkling eyes. She fit right in, he thought. He could just imagine her insisting on a permanent Maypole at her blasted Artist's Heaven. He could also envision her poor father turning in his grave at the thought of what his daughter meant to do with the money he had worked so hard to acquire.

Then Patrick spotted trouble brewing just beyond the circle of dancers. Red-faced, Serena stood before her father, gesturing forcefully. Yet another measure of dread landed in the pit of his gut. He would doubtless hear no end to the supposed indignity she had suffered when the mayor failed to crown her Queen of the blasted May.

His desire to escape grew to prodigious proportions.

The sprite in blue again danced into his line of vision, laughing as her curvy body did justice to the music.

Annie's response to the celebration so enthralled him that he paused in his shabby imitation of a dance. The

22　　　　　　　　GINNY REYES

woman to his rear bumped into him, murmured a vague, "Sorry," and waited for him to proceed. Patrick took another step, stumbled, staggering against the woman before him. He cursed in frustration.

How long could a dance last? How long did he have to exhibit his ineptitude?

Before today, Patrick had never thought he needed something as impractical as a rudimentary knowledge of the social art of dancing. But he did, a fact that grew glaringly obvious as he pitched and lurched along, while even the youngest of tots romped smoothly around the Maypole.

He had never taken the time to learn. He'd been too determined to establish his career, to ensure himself a livelihood, to avoid the horrors his family had once endured. He'd had no time for frivolity, for entertainment, and for the first time in his life, Patrick wondered what he had been missing.

He glanced again at his queen, then caught sight of the admiration reflected in the expressions of the young men awaiting their turn to dance at the edge of the circle. He frowned. Some of those stares bordered on salacious.

With another look at Annie, he noticed the passion in her movements, the total involvement of her firm, young body in her actions. Her arms rose and fell gracefully, lifting her full breasts beneath her blue bodice. That soft quiver of flesh riveted his gaze, and he wondered if she even wore a corset. Just the possibility that she might not smacked of freedom, of bohemian wantonness. An artist's natural sensuality.

He swallowed.

Hard.

Then she dipped in a shallow curtsy. Her narrow waist bent, contrasting deliciously with the roundness of her hips. He had never before realized Annie Brennan was so . . . so womanly. He'd always viewed her as an irrepressible child.

A FAERIE TALE

But the woman living the music was no child.

When Annie turned her back his way, Patrick's breath caught in his throat. The sway of her bottom commanded masculine attention, and in horror he realized his trousers were growing tight where they should hang loosely.

Annie? Annie Brennan had captured the attention of his libido?

Worse yet, Patrick's libido was responding. Avidly!

In plain view of everyone he knew.

He was hard as a rock, for goodness sake! When would the music ever stop?

When would Annie's enticing dance come to an end?

Suddenly the square thrummed with silence. Patrick dropped his satin ribbon as if it burned as hot as its hue. He rammed his fists into his front pockets. "*About time*." he muttered and slunk away from the revelers.

Standing beyond the edge of the crowd, Patrick's body felt afire. How could this happen to him? He had always kept himself under strict control, and his body had rarely betrayed him. Yet here he stood, clenching his teeth to keep from chasing after a flighty female he had never considered the least bit attractive.

But she was. Blast her, anyway!

Without conscious effort, the image of Annie's lush body giving itself to the music shot through his head, vividly illustrating how attractive a woman Annie Brennan really was. How would he ever concentrate on the intricacies of her father's will when she came to his office on Wednesday? He suspected he would have the devil of a time countering her foolish plans for her money. Especially if all he could think about were the secrets veiled by her simple garments.

Without warning, something catapulted into Patrick's back, stealing his breath. He stumbled. He coughed. His arms windmilled in an effort to regain his balance. "What the—"

"Ah, by gum and by golly! 'Tis sorry, I am, Your

24   GINNY REYES

Highness,'' proclaimed a heavily brogued man's voice, still far too close to Patrick's back for comfort.

When the coughing stopped, he waved and said, "I'll be fine, thank you. And please drop that Highness nonsense.'' Turning, Patrick found himself facing a stranger in a deep emerald suit and a wine-red waistcoat trimmed with gold thread.

"Aye, and you're a wee bit troubled, nay?"

Patrick chuckled wryly. "Some."

"Must be a lady doing the troubling."

Patrick didn't bother to reply.

The colorful Irishman grinned. "Mayhap 'tis two of them.''

Patrick narrowed his eyes. "How would you know?"

Green eyes twinkled. " 'Tisn't much Eamon Dooley misses, me lad! I watched the crowning and the dancing.''

Heat filled Patrick's cheeks. Just how much had the observant Mr. Dooley seen? "I'm not one for dancing in the town square.''

"Nor for a couple of dueling beauties, I'd say! Even if you do seem . . . *lathered up* by at least the one.''

The gent had seen too much. "Yes, well, some things can't be helped.''

Eamon chuckled. "And you wouldn't want to help them, either, lad. You can trust Eamon Dooley on that, you can.''

"This is one case where I would. She's the last woman who should catch my eye.''

" 'Twasn't just your eye she caught," Eamon crowed.

The chat had lasted long enough. "If you'll excuse me—''

"And here she comes again."

Patrick groaned. He had lost the opportunity to shake off the sharp-eyed Mr. Dooley, and yes, the object of his discomfort was headed his way.

"Patrick!" Annie called. "There you are. Mayor Keller wants us present for the tapping of the cask of mead.''

A FAERIE TALE 25

Helpless to avoid it, Patrick found his attention riveted to the sassy sway of Annie's skirts. Something in the way she moved did shocking things to his composure. And he had to spend the rest of the day at her side?

What about Serena? His soon-to-be fiancée. The woman who had never aroused in him even the slightest of tingles. The woman he intended to—*would* marry, dammit .

"I'll . . . er . . . be there," he muttered.

Annie smiled radiantly. "Isn't this fun?"

" 'Tis a lovely day for Bealtaine," agreed the beautiful blonde at her side. Patrick wondered who the woman was.

"Ahem!" offered Eamon, obviously fishing for an introduction.

Patrick cast him a sideways glance and found the man's deep green eyes fixed on Annie's fair companion. Good to see he wasn't the only one "lathered up" by a woman.

"Annie," he said, "this is Mr. Eamon Dooley . . ."

Patrick's voice trailed off. Who *was* this fellow, anyway? He had never seen him before. "Say, Dooley, you don't hail from these parts, do you?"

Never taking his gaze from Annie's friend, Eamon shook his head.

Patrick frowned. "Well, where *are* you from?"

"Eire."

"I already knew *that*," Patrick said. "Since my acquaintance is so taken with your friend, Miss Brennan, why don't you do the honors?"

Annie chuckled and shot a knowing look at her companion. "Patrick O'Toole, Mr. Dooley, this is my new friend, Rosaleen Flynn. She is also from Ireland but will be visiting me for a while."

The beauteous Rosaleen extended a hand to her dazed admirer. Eamon took it, clicked together the heels of his silver-buckled black boots, then with much ceremony, bent over and kissed the lady's fingers. Her lips widened slowly—seductively—into a stunning smile. Eamon looked sucker-punched.

" 'Tis a pleasure to meet you," Rosaleen said in a throaty voice.

Eamon roused himself from his stupor. He winked. "Nay, the pleasure . . . why, 'tis all mine, I'm sure!"

"I see you found your tongue," Patrick murmured.

"Never lost it, lad," Eamon countered.

"Could have fooled me."

"Mr. O'Toole," Annie said, "you didn't finish introducing me to Mr. Dooley."

Embarrassed, Patrick faced her, and found his gaze snared by the reproach in her sapphire eyes. "Ah . . . I'm sorry . . . er, Miss Brennan." How did she always manage to do it? Just by looking at him with those expressive eyes, Annie turned him into a stammering fool. "Eamon, this is Annie Brennan, today's Queen of the May."

Eamon dropped Rosaleen's hand. His head spun toward Annie. He narrowed his green eyes, studying her for a moment. Then in a courtly manner, he bowed, extending his hand. "Miss Annie Brennan, 'tis an honor to meet you."

Annie placed her fingers on Eamon's palm, and Patrick waited for the sure-to-come kiss. But Eamon surprised him by merely shaking Annie's hand.

Something inside Patrick loosened, and only then did he realize he had dreaded the moment Eamon's lips would land on the confounded Miss Brennan's hand. What was wrong with him today?

"Er . . . didn't you say the mayor wanted us for something?" he asked Annie.

"Oh, my, yes!" With a pat to Eamon's hand, Annie turned her attention back to Patrick. "Everyone expects us to have the first taste of the mead. But we should hurry. I'm sure we've made them wait."

In her characteristic way, Annie reached out and took Patrick's hand. The warmth of that soft skin hit him the way it usually did, curling through him, sparking off twinges of awareness. Cursing himself for a fool, he admitted that he liked the sensations Annie set off in him, no matter how inappropriate they were. He allowed her to lead him through the crowd.

As they made their way to where the cask of mead was ready for tapping, Patrick heard Eamon comment, "Sure and 'tis a fine couple they make."

Rosaleen responded, "Aye, Mr. Dooley. They're a fine match indeed."

What was wrong with those two, anyway? He and Annie weren't a couple, and they would never make any match at all. Serena Keller was the woman for him. Even if for the day's celebration he had ended up with Annie Brennan as his queen.

It was only make-believe. Only for one day.

Three

A short while later, each carrying a full cup of mead, Patrick and Annie strolled toward a bench beneath the canopy of a spreading maple.

"Awfully warm for May, isn't it?" Annie asked after sitting and smoothing her skirt.

Patrick replied with a vague, "Mmm . . ."

She tried again. "The mead is excellent, don't you think?"

He took a long draught from his beverage. "Mm-hmm."

Oh, dear! Here she had the perfect chance to persuade Patrick to her way of thinking about the Artist's Haven and she couldn't get him to answer even the most innocuous of questions. Annie doubted she would get another opportunity half so good as this.

"I wish I had my oils and canvas," she ventured, glancing sideways at him. "I think the sky, the sun, the trees, and the ladies' spring frocks would make a lovely painting, don't you?"

With another surreptitious peek at Patrick, Annie noticed the narrowing of his eyes. *Uh-oh!* "I'm always on the alert for scenes that might make interesting compositions," she hurried to say. "My art lives with me each moment of every day."

A FAERIE TALE

A frown framed his narrowed eyes.

Setting her cup of mead by her feet, Annie gathered more steam. "You know, Mr. O'Toole—"

"Patrick."

"Wha—Oh! Yes, of course," she said, surprised to get that much out of him. For a moment, she'd feared he might never utter another word. "You did ask me to call you Patrick."

He nodded, then took yet another swallow of his drink.

So he chose silence again. And the mead. Perhaps she ought to wait until the ale did its job. A mellow banker might not be such a bad thing. Then she saw trouble heading their way.

A mutinous look on her Teutonic features, Serena Keller was clearly a woman on a mission. And that mission boded ill for Annie.

"Well, and here you are, Annie, Patrick," said Rosaleen as she came around the bench.

"How do you like our May Day celebration?" Annie asked her new friend, mourning the lost opportunity. At her side, Patrick stood and offered Rosaleen his seat.

" 'Tis a fine cask of mead your town is tapping, Annie, lass," offered Eamon from the other side of the bench. "I see you and the boyo here taking nips of it, too. Fine ale, I say."

Serena stopped her advance about ten paces away, her expression reminiscent of storm clouds. Glancing from Rosaleen to the multicolored Eamon and back at Rosaleen again, Annie wondered if their sudden appearance had caused Serena's halt. If so, she welcomed their arrival. "Where did you two come from? I didn't see you while the mayor poured the mead."

"We took ourselves a wee slow walk to get acquainted, you know," answered Eamon. "Sure and 'tis a pleasure to go a-walking with a fair *cailin* on a May Day afternoon."

30 GINNY REYES

Annie smiled. "And Rosaleen is an especially fair one."

Eamon's puckish features grew serious. "Aye, Annie, lass, that she is."

A soft blush appeared on her friend's cheeks. The blond girl smiled, and Eamon again donned that dazed look he wore when he had first set eyes on her.

"Stop your flattering, Eamon Dooley," chided Rosaleen despite her smile.

"Ah, but 'tisn't in vain I speak, *ma vourneen*. 'Tis but the truth I tell." Eamon slapped Patrick on the back. "Isn't it, boyo?"

Patrick choked on his mouthful of mead. "Ah . . . er, yes. You're right, you're right." He turned to Annie. "What is he talking about?"

Annie laughed, stood, then took Patrick's empty cup. "Not paying attention, I see. Perhaps you've had enough."

Patrick straightened, donning his usual dignified expression. "Do you accuse me of over-imbibing, Miss Brennan?"

"Oh, for goodness' sake, Patrick! You tell me."

"Of course not, I—I was just . . . thinking of something else."

Annie cast a pointed look at Serena. "I'd say it was some*one* else you were thinking about."

Patrick's cheeks reddened. He glanced at Serena—who looked no happier—then hastily turned back to Annie. "I did bring her to the festivities."

Annie tipped her chin up. "Then I mustn't keep you any longer."

"But you were crowned queen," he replied. "The mayor was most determined that the king escort the queen."

Annie saw red. She waved expansively. "Heavens, Mr. O'Toole! Don't put yourself out on my account. I don't need an escort, certainly not an obligated one. Besides,

Rosaleen is my guest. I shan't be alone. Especially since your friend Mr. Dooley can't seem to pry himself away from her side. Go on. We wouldn't want duty to get in the way of your pleasures, odd though they might be.''

Patrick's lips thinned, and his frown deepened. He again peered at Serena. He turned back to Annie. He swallowed, hard enough that his Adam's apple bobbed.

''Very well,'' he said, and walked away. But before he took more than a couple of steps, Serena huffed audibly, tossed her flaxen hair over her shoulder, and stomped off, leaving Patrick to watch her vanish into the crowd.

Annie couldn't stifle a chuckle. Served them both right!

She returned to the bench and sat next to Rosaleen. ''So, how do you like Woodbury's May Day celebration?''

'' 'Tis fine,'' Rosaleen answered.

''A fair pleasure, I'll say,'' Eamon added.

A shadow fell on Annie's lap. It belonged to Patrick, who stood before her, an odd light in his eyes. ''Mind if I join you?'' he asked.

She gave him a frosty look. ''I thought you were otherwise engaged, Mr. O'Toole.''

He gestured toward Serena. ''Seems I exhausted her patience.''

''Too bad,'' Annie answered insincerely. ''You may join us. If the others don't object, that is.''

Rosaleen smiled. ''Welcome.''

Eamon pointed at the grassy ground in front of the bench. ''Sure and you can join me, boyo! At the ladies' feet, o' course.''

Patrick arched an eyebrow and donned a crooked smile. ''At Her Majesty's feet, you mean.''

Eamon nodded. ''Aye, at your queen's feet.''

''Faith,'' said Rosaleen, a twinkle in her jade-green eyes, ''and do ye know the meaning of the Maypole dance?''

32   GINNY REYES

Annie shook her head. "Aside from it being part of every spring, no."

" 'Tis a good story, that," Eamon said, winking.

"Oh?" Patrick asked.

Rosaleen laughed, sending a ripple of expectation through Annie. That laugh carried more than its fair share of suggestion. Annie felt poised on the brink of learning a forbidden secret.

Rosaleen leaned forward. "A good story, indeed. An old one, too. Remember when ye asked about the Great Earth Mother and her Horned Consort, Annie?"

"Of course."

"Well . . . in the days before Patrick—'twould be the saint, ye know—and his faith came to Eire, everyone honored the Triple Goddess—Maiden, Mother, and Crone. 'Tis from the Mother all things come, even mankind. But to give birth, she needs the God, her Consort. We celebrate their joining at Bealtaine."

Annie blushed to the roots of her hair. "You mean, May Day was once a . . ." She couldn't put words to the improper image that crossed her mind.

But Rosaleen could, and did, that sensual gleam sparkling in her eyes. "Aye, Annie. Bealtaine celebrates fertility, conception, the ripeness to come. And the Maypole is but a representation of the Consort's . . . contribution to the process."

Annie twisted her fingers. She bit her lips.

A choked sound came from just beyond her feet. She peered at Patrick and found his cheeks as red as hers felt. She couldn't think of a thing to say after what Rosaleen had revealed. Not even to change the embarrassing topic.

"And," Eamon tossed in, "the dancers weave together the ribbons. White for the White Moon Goddess, and red for the Horned God. The dancers stand in for the deities."

"The dance," Rosaleen continued, "represents their

A FAERIE TALE   33

coming together, the joining of the Lord and the Lady, the union of man and—''

''Yes, well,'' Annie burst in, ''I understand. But just now, I'm feeling ravished—''

''*O-ho!*'' whooped Eamon. ''*Ravished*, eh, Annie, lass?''

Annie wished to die. ''No, no! I meant famished! *Famished*. I'm hungry. Anyone else ready to eat?''

Rosaleen chortled.

Annie's temples throbbed.

Eamon slapped his thigh, laughing heartily.

Patrick did nothing, said nothing, apparently as mortified as she. ''Well?'' Annie asked again. ''Food anyone?''

She could think of nothing more prosaic than eating, and she'd had to come up with something to dispel the graphic pictures Rosaleen's words had conjured. Patrick's expression told her she wasn't the only one affected.

To think she had always viewed the Maypole dance as a mostly childish enjoyment! Why, the very idea of Patrick representing the Consort to her Queen as they cavorted around that . . . that upraised male *symbol* was simply outrageous, scandalous.

Patrick scrambled up. ''I could do with a bite to eat.'' He grasped her elbow, then turned to Rosaleen and Eamon, who still wore wicked smirks. ''Will you join us?''

The humor in Rosaleen's clear green eyes turned to a speculative gleam. ''Mayhap in a wee while.''

Eamon turned to her. ''If 'twouldn't vex you, Rosaleen, I'd be liking to keep you company.''

Rosaleen smiled. '' 'Twill be fine.''

''Go on,'' urged Eamon, ''we'll be along soon enough.''

Patrick led Annie in the direction of the food stands at the far end of the square.

Finding herself alone with Eamon, Rosaleen studied the man, again feeling the niggle of recognition she had experienced when they met. ''Faith, and I've never met ye

34 GINNY REYES

before, Eamon Dooley, but there's something about ye . . .''

"Aye, Rosaleen, that there is. I feel it, too."

Studying his red-gold hair, his dark green eyes, the sharpness of his features, the silver buckle on his black leather boots, Rosaleen smiled when she realized what she'd missed before. "Why, you're one o' the gentry, ye are!"

His eyes widened momentarily, then a matching smile brightened his face. "Sure and you are one, too! I'm a leprechaun by trade. What brings a lovely young faerie this far from *Tyeer na N-og?*"

"Patrick O'Toole wished at a well. King Midhir sent me to help."

"A well sprite are you, then?"

"Aye." Rosaleen frowned, remembering her ignominious arrival. "I need more practice or I'll never earn me magic wand."

Eamon studied her a bit. "You've trouble casting spells, have you?"

"Not a'tall," she hurried to clarify. "Some simply go awry at the very last."

Eamon winced. "I know what you mean. I've come to bring fair Annie luck, but . . . me luck's not always good. I've a pot o' gold to earn meself."

His words gave her an idea. "What if we worked together, Eamon? Seems we could each use a wee bit o' help."

"Nay. Leprechauns always work alone."

Biting her lip, Rosaleen nodded. "Very well, then, I'll be off. Annie will be waiting for me, and I've Patrick to be looking after."

Eamon nodded. "Aye, I must be seeing to Annie's luck meself."

"Farewell, then."

"Mm-hmmm."

Rosaleen went in the direction Patrick and Annie had

A FAERIE TALE

gone. Eamon stayed behind, taking a seat on the vacant bench. 'Twould have been nice if he'd been willing to help, she thought. Then she squared her shoulders.

She didn't need help. King Midhir had sent her to keep Patrick O'Toole from making the greatest mistake of his life. She had to prove she could do it; she had to prove herself fit to wield a magic wand. Rosaleen Flynn would make sure her faerie godchild married the right woman. Even if he'd been heading in the wrong direction of late.

'Twas Bealtaine. A splendid time to cast a magic spell.

A few hours later, after gathering what she needed for a love charm, Rosaleen wandered to the outskirts of town, past a clearing, and to a stand of willows, ashes, and oaks. Although a water sprite herself, the spirits of the trees called to her, welcoming her, offering their protection, sharing their power.

The sun had dipped below the edge of the earth, and the silver quarter moon had begun her voyage across the vast canopy of night. For her magic, Rosaleen chose a spot just beyond the shadow of the trees.

She had bought candles at the general store—actually, *Annie* would be the one buying the candles sometime in the future. The attendant at the store had identified Rosaleen as ''Annie's guest'' and added the cost of her purchases to the Brennan household account. Which was just as well, since she didn't have a cent, not for the candles or the scarlet scrap of satin she had felt would strengthen her spell. Not even for a box of matches to light the candles.

Quickly, hoping to complete her ritual before anyone strolled by, Rosaleen spread the glossy red fabric over a patch of moonlight-silvered grass. She set the two candles at opposite ends, then heaped a handful of honeysuckle petals between the tapers.

Finally, using her index finger, Rosaleen drew a magic circle around herself, enclosing the items she had laid out within its confines. Raising her arms, she lifted her face

36 GINNY REYES

to receive the power of the Great Moon Goddess. Slowly, carefully, she began to turn, bit by tiny bit faster with each revolution. A ripple of excitement—that surge of energy she felt whenever she performed magic—tripped down her spine, then spread through her body, making her tingle from head to toe. Softly she began to chant.

> *"In this night and in this hour*
> *I call upon the Ancient Power*
> *O Goddess Bride and Consort Bright,*
> *I ask thee now to bring your Light!*
> *For this young man must need to see*
> *Who his right love is to be."*

Kneeling, Rosaleen struck a match, then applied the flame to the wicks. When both caught fire, she blew out the match and took the tapers, one in each hand. Lifting the flames toward the moon, the source of her powers, she brought them together, the separate blazes melding into one. Rich as the symbolism was, so Rosaleen concentrated on Patrick and his need for the right mate.

> *"Bring him the one who will love him true,*
> *The one who'll join him and he'll ne'er rue,*
> *The one whose emotions, passions, and fire*
> *Will match just precisely his heart's desire."*

Carefully she placed the candles back on the satin square, and quickly, so they wouldn't wobble and tip, she laid her hands on the honeysuckle petals.

> *"Like the sweetness hidden here within*
> *Beckons the bees whether far or near,*
> *So shall the sweetness of the one he'll win*
> *Draw him to her who'll e'er be his dear."*

A FAERIE TALE

With the candles still glowing, she whispered, "So mote it be."

As quickly as she had prepared for her spell, Rosaleen brought it to an end. She folded a linen handkerchief Annie had lent her around the honeysuckle petals, taking care not to miss any. Then she blew out the candles and, when the wicks cooled sufficiently, she rolled them up in the scarlet fabric. Everything went back into the box the lady at the store had given her.

From the direction of town, she heard the sound of a band tuning up. Dance music! She smiled. Perhaps her spell had already begun to work. There were few things more romantic and magical than a dance in the moonlight. In the springtime. At Bealtaine.

After eating a light supper in strained silence, Annie was ready to pull her hair out. Or Patrick's. It had grown glaringly obvious the man would rather be anywhere but at her side. He couldn't even muster polite conversation.

She wished someone else, *anyone*—yes, even Serena Keller—had been crowned Queen of the May. Then Annie would have been spared the effort to maintain a semblance of cheer. Why was Patrick always so . . . so serious? Why did he so rarely smile?

Especially since smiles did wonders for his strong, masculine features. Annie stole a glance at her silent companion. Her very handsome, silent companion.

Patrick was quite possibly the finest-looking man she had ever seen. His dark brown hair waved over his forehead in a surprisingly careless fashion, while everything else about him spoke of precision and meticulous grooming. His clean-shaven skin revealed strong features, his broad cheekbones framing warm amber eyes that often made her think of heat. Like now, as he stared at her.

Annie blushed. "Is . . . is something wrong?" she asked.

One of his rare smiles softened the line of his well-defined lips. "I can't help recalling the look on your face when you said you felt 'ravished' earlier today."

Annie gasped. "O—oh, how simply *awful* of you! No gentleman would remind a lady of a lapse like that!"

"Perhaps," he conceded, a surprisingly mischievous twist to his grin. "But remember, there is always a man somewhere inside the gentleman, and no man worth the name would forget that moment."

Just then the band in the gazebo struck up a tune. Annie breathed a prayer of thanksgiving. "How lovely! A waltz. If you'll excuse me, Mr. O'Toole—"

"Patrick, Annie. It's Patrick."

"Yes, Patrick. If you'll excuse me, I'll go watch the dancers—"

"Faith, and I finally find ye, Annie!" exclaimed Rosaleen as she approached, cutting off Annie's escape.

"Where were you?" she asked her new friend, resigned to her fate. "Patrick and I have been here at the square since we left you and Eamon earlier this afternoon. Mayor Keller insisted we preside over the games and contests. He wanted us to give out the awards."

Rosaleen wouldn't meet Annie's questioning gaze. "I . . . I went exploring a bit."

"Exploring?" Rosaleen's odd response surprised her.

"Where's Eamon?" Patrick asked.

Rosaleen shrugged. "I couldn't say. Haven't seen the man in a while."

That overly breezy tone didn't ring true. Annie frowned. "Did he just leave you there? All alone? How rude!"

"Nay, Annie. 'Twasn't like that a'tall. We agreed we both had . . . matters to attend to."

"But I thought he was so interested in you—"

"By gum and by golly, here you all are!"

And there *he* was. Annie turned and gave Eamon a terse nod.

A FAERIE TALE

"So, Annie, lass," he said. "Ready to try your luck again at the dancing tonight?"

The thought horrified her. "After Rosaleen's tale about the Maypole? Not in a million years."

Rosaleen *tsk-tsk*ed. "You don't know what ye might be missing, Annie."

"Oh, yes, I do, Rosaleen Flynn. I can do without another story of your Ancient Ones and their cavorting!" Annie felt her cheeks heat up again. "Besides, no one has asked me to dance."

Eamon chuckled. "Why, lass, 'tis not a problem. We have us a fine fellow right here." He slapped Patrick square in the back.

Patrick coughed, shaking his head vigorously.

"Oh, no, you don't, Mr. Dooley," Annie said. "Not after you and Rosaleen made all that fuss about the Goddess and her Consort and the King and Queen of the May. I'll never dance with Patrick O'Toole again!"

Annie turned and was about to leave when something soft and sweet-smelling cascaded over her face. "What's this?"

"Flower petals," answered Rosaleen.

"Where did they come from? My crown?" Reaching up, Annie found the wreath in place, the blossoms intact.

Rosaleen waved gracefully, vaguely, an innocent smile on her lips. "I couldn't be after saying, not for sure."

That innocence struck Annie as suspicious.

"Harrumph!" At Eamon's forceful sound, Annie glanced his way. A frown pleated his forehead as he glowered at Rosaleen. How strange! Earlier today he had done nothing but bow and smile and flatter her new friend. Now he looked murderous!

Rosaleen sniffed and tipped her chin up.

Eamon's scowl deepened. Then he turned to Patrick and, frowning, began batting at the banker's shoulders. Patrick swatted back.

"You daren't let that challenge go unanswered, boyo!"

40   GINNY REYES

"What challenge would that be?"

"Why, the lass has sworn she'll ne'er dance with you again. 'Twould seem you'd want to rise to the task."

Patrick looked queasy. Annie remembered his stiff movements as they circled the Maypole. He had seemed out of place, awkward even. He clearly didn't enjoy dancing, and wasn't very good at it. In fact, he had seemed to lack experience, displaying no mastery of the simplest of steps. Could it be . . . could he possibly not know *how* to dance?

He began inching away. "I have done all the dancing I am going to do. If you will excuse me, I'll head home—"

"Ladies and gentlemen!" boomed Mayor Keller from not ten feet away. "Our king and queen will lead off tonight's entertainment with a waltz. Prepare to join them, if you please."

Had Patrick's expression not resembled that of a hunted buck, Annie might have laughed at the passion in his muttered expletive. He turned to Mayor Keller with a hopeful smile. "It is getting late, sir, and I've much work waiting for me at home."

The mayor shook his head. "Won't hear of it. It's time for dancing, and the king and queen always start it up."

"But I thought we did that around the Maypole."

"That was this afternoon," the mayor replied. "This is now. Come on, come on. The ladies are anxious to show off their dresses."

Looking like stock on its way to the butchery, Patrick quit fighting. Annie followed, surprised by the sympathy welling in her. When they reached the asphalt street around the square, the glow from two gaslamps revealed the grimness in her king's eyes.

"It won't be so bad," she murmured, lifting her arms. "Follow my lead."

For a moment, his jaws worked, then he gave a sharp nod and slipped one hand around her waist. With the

A FAERIE TALE 41

other, he clasped her fingers. A current ran through Annie, making her tremble and meet his gaze again.

Patrick's eyes widened, and she knew he had felt her reaction. The palm at her back pressed her closer. Anticipation simmered inside her.

The music began.

Sweet notes filled the cool night air, swirling around them. Discreetly Annie counted the beat, leading Patrick in the three-quarter-timed step-step-close pattern of the waltz. At first, he moved stiffly, and Annie swore a stretched-taut canvas would have taken to the task with more grace. But then something happened. As if by magic, he seemed to learn what dancing was all about. He began to sway with the notes, taking over the lead.

Annie looked up and found him studying her in apparent bemusement. "What's wrong?" she asked. "Are you surprised to discover you can enjoy a waltz?"

"Something like that." With a smile, he pulled her closer still, sweeping them in a wide turn.

For a man who always held himself in tight control, Patrick suddenly seemed to acquire an ease that lent fluidity to his powerful frame. Annie found herself breathless, excited, feeling more feminine than she ever had before.

As they glided to the music, she noticed a honeysuckle petal on the lapel of Patrick's suit coat. Strange. There were no flowers in his ivy crown. She remembered the shower of blossoms she'd recently experienced. And she remembered Eamon's strange attack on Patrick's shoulders.

Patrick twirled her in time to the ebb and flow of the music, and Annie looked to the spot where they had stood just minutes before. Rosaleen and Eamon remained there, watching them dance, indulgent grins on their faces. Annie narrowed her gaze, remembering Rosaleen's excessive innocence.

Could the Irish girl have had something to do with the

42 GINNY REYES

flowers? Could the petals be responsible for Patrick's sudden dancing talent?

"Oh, how silly," she chided herself. As if a drifting of blossoms had the sort of magic that could turn a grim man into a charming dance companion. "What nonsense!"

"You said?" asked Patrick, lowering his head.

He came so close that Annie felt the warmth of his skin against her lips. If she were to take a deep breath, she could kiss that cheek where a sandpapery trace of stubble showed. Her lips tingled at the thought.

A very masculine scent teased her nostrils, and Annie drew in a deeper measure. Not only did Patrick look wonderful, he smelled wonderful, too. His fragrance consisted of a blend of bay rum, citrus, and . . . man, she supposed. Annie wasn't quite certain, since she had never been this close to a man, but she had to assume the deeper, pleasing note could only come from Patrick himself.

She sniffed again, surprised to find so much to like about Patrick O'Toole. The hand at her back held her firmly, and Annie found herself being swung into another spiraling turn. "Looks like dancing isn't as bad as you feared."

"Not bad at all," he answered, his amber eyes capturing her attention. The music began to slow, and Patrick shortened their steps accordingly. As the waltz faded into the night, Annie realized they barely swayed in time to the vanishing sound. In fact, she thought, mesmerized by the heat in his gaze, their dance had turned into an embrace.

She found she couldn't look away. The music, the night, the man had woven a spell around her, and all she could do was wait. . . .

She knew what she waited for. Something she had never expected. Something she anticipated with everything female in her.

"Annie," he whispered, then brought his lips to hers.

A FAERIE TALE

43

She tasted sweetness in his gossamer touch. Her eyes fluttered shut. When he rubbed his mouth against hers, her every sense came alive. She sighed, wishing he would press closer still, imprint his kiss on her lips.

He did, molding his mouth to hers. Annie trembled at the surge of feelings his caress evoked. He held her closer to his warmth. He kissed her again, this time tracing the contours of her lips with his tongue, then the seam between.

Gently he wooed them apart, and Annie yielded to the pressure. She had never known anything to move her so, to awaken such a need inside her, a hunger for closeness, for touching, for Patrick's kiss.

When his tongue touched hers, Annie started, but the gentleness of his caress eased her surprise. She accepted his seeking. Tentatively she responded with her own exploration. A tremor shook him then. Annie went to pull away, afraid she had done something wrong, but Patrick wouldn't let her go. She surrendered to the pleasure of his touch, the excitement of his lips against hers.

His mouth was soft but firm. Warm but gentle. Persuasive but tender. His arms held her tight, cradled against his powerful frame. Annie felt delicate, feminine, cherished.

The world seemed to shrink to only the two of them. And Patrick's kiss. Annie wished they could stay like this forever and ever and ever. . . .

Suddenly talons bit the arm Annie had curled around his neck. "Patrick O'Toole!" shrieked Serena Keller. "How dare you!"

Annie felt lost as he tore his mouth from hers. His arms abandoned her. His strong body reclaimed the support it had offered. His voice came out in a gravely croak. "Serena!"

"Yes, Patrick. Serena. What do you have to say for yourself?"

Annie prayed for the earth to open up and swallow her

whole. She had never been so embarrassed in her entire life. Peering to see who else had witnessed the scandalous embrace, she sighed with relief when she saw the three of them stood alone on the dark side of the Emory home. How had they gotten there?

She remembered the swirling twirls of their dance. Somehow that waltz had taken a turn for the intimate—and Serena had found them, lips clinging, Annie's arms around Patrick as tight as a fat lady's corset. "Oh, dear."

"I'll say!" spit Serena. "Go on, Miss Brennan! Go wrap yourself around another man. I'm sure you can find one willing to pick up where this one left off. Patrick O'Toole is taken."

Loath to be cowed by Serena's superior attitude, Annie tipped her chin up. "I don't see you wearing a wedding ring, *Miss* Keller."

Serena made a growling sound, but Annie stepped away before the other woman could formulate a retort. As she put distance between herself and the fiasco, she heard the mayor's daughter demand an answer from Annie's erstwhile dance partner.

"You didn't answer, Patrick. What were you thinking?"

Looking over her shoulder, Annie saw Patrick shake his head. "Nothing much," he muttered.

"Don't tell me nothing much, sir! You've spent months courting me, and now I find you with that Brennan girl. What *were* you doing?"

Despite her embarrassment, Annie waited for his response. As she watched, a smile curved his mouth, the mouth that only minutes earlier had thrilled her own. It quirked up higher on one side, in a very masculine way. Turning slightly, Patrick looked straight at her. Holding her gaze, he ran the tip of his tongue around his lips. Annie froze.

What had come over Patrick O'Toole? Where had the

A FAERIE TALE

serious, dull banker gone? Where did this . . . rogue come from?

Then the rogue chuckled. Unrepentant. "Why, Serena, it's May magic, of course. Didn't you crown me king of the May? Well, the King claimed a kiss from his queen."

Four

Eamon watched Patrick twirl his charge in time to the lilting notes of the waltz. So far, his luck seemed to be holding out. Annie was in the arms of the man meant for her. No mishaps appeared in the offing. Since matters were proceeding so splendidly, Eamon turned his attention to more personal interests.

"I see your toes a-tapping," he said to Rosaleen.

She nodded, turning her seductive smile on him. A ripple of the oddest energy surged through Eamon.

"Aye," she said, her voice a throaty caress. "The music is inviting indeed."

"Might I have the pleasure, then?"

Her smile grew warmer, her green eyes promising . . . he didn't quite know what. But whatever Rosaleen's smile promised, Eamon knew he wanted it. He feared the lovely water faerie had enchanted him.

As he took Rosaleen's outstretched hand, the warmth in her fingers rushed right through him. He didn't know what was happening to him, but he liked it. Perhaps too much.

When he held out his arms, she walked right into them, her slender body light as a feather in his clasp. Meeting her gaze, Eamon led them into the waltz. The music

A FAERIE TALE 47

flowed through him, and in true leprechaun fashion he let it transport him. As long as the band played, he would revel in the pleasure of the dance.

Glancing down at his partner, he smiled. "Enjoying yourself?"

"Mm-hmmm . . ."

Rosaleen's soft nod caused her silver-gold hair to caress his cheek. Soft as the glow of the moon, silky as seduction itself, its scent caught his attention, inspiring him to repeat the action again.

She smelled like the world after a spring rain. Fresh and sweet, a hint of herbs and flowers underscored her fragrance. Almost without conscious effort, he drew her closer and spun them into yet another swirl.

"You're a fair dancer, ye are!"

"Many thanks, *cailin*. You're a dream to partner yourself."

"Faith, and you're a flatterer!"

"Nay. Eamon Dooley always speaks the truth."

Rosaleen's laughter flowed over him like a waterfall over rocks in its path. A bewildering tremor shook him. "I don't know what you're doing to me, *cailin*, but I like it. I like *you*, Rosaleen Flynn."

He pulled back to see what effect his confession had on her, and was amazed and pleased when her cheeks donned the shade of budding roses. For a moment, she met his gaze, and Eamon again experienced the thunderbolt of sensation he had felt when he first met her. Her lips curved into her seductive smile. "You're a fine one, Eamon Dooley."

Caught by the magic in a pair of jade-green eyes, Eamon spun Rosaleen in dizzying spirals, over and over, until she laughed with delight. Glancing around, he noticed they had come close to a large oak, and he followed his urge for privacy.

Never breaking the rhythm of the waltz, he led them behind the tree. Its springtime gown of green shielded

48 GINNY REYES

them from the light of the moon, giving him the sensation of solitude, just the two of them and the music. Nothing and no one else in the world.

"Ah, *cailin* . . ." He obeyed the foreign yearning that had led him this far. He lowered his lips to hers.

For a moment, she seemed to freeze in place, then, with a shimmer of her lithe body against his, she came closer and pressed her mouth to his.

Eamon hesitated. This was the first time he had kissed a woman. Romance didn't exist in *Tyeer na N-og*, so he had no prior experience, but a sudden instinct drove him to explore the mouth Rosaleen offered up to him. He parted his lips over hers and tasted her mouth.

She murmured a husky sound, full of the yearning he felt. He ran his tongue across the line where her lips met. She trembled, then opened for him. Again, Eamon paused, but a rushing inside his head, a pulsing throb in his veins, led him to proceed, to dip inside the sweet cavern she invited him to explore.

With one taste, Eamon wondered why faeries didn't bother with kissing. A man could become addicted to such sensations. Ripples of pleasure ran through him as he met her tongue, felt the velvet rasp of its caress. He shuddered and pulled her flush against him, no room between them for even a breath.

Rosaleen tasted sweet, fresh, yet the touch of her tongue against his, on his lips, made him hot. Eamon had never known such heat could exist, but he was burning, his entire body taut, ready. To his amazement, an exceptional feeling of fullness, of urgency settled in a private and, up until now, rudimentary body part.

As he delved into Rosaleen's mouth again, he heard himself groan at the wave of pleasure that flooded through him. *More*, his senses begged. *More, much, much more*, his body demanded. Allowing his hands to roam her slender back, Eamon explored the narrowness of her waist, the gentle curve of her hips. Tentatively, he let his hands

A FAERIE TALE

cover her buttocks, loving the way her flesh filled them. He pressed her closer to that hot, swollen part.

He groaned again and rubbed himself against her, harder this time. As he did, Eamon discovered he fit perfectly against her, into a valley that seemed carved just for him. To his surprise and elation, Rosaleen mimicked his motion, rubbing herself against him. Instead of finding relief, however, his urge grew greater, driving him to press against her again and again.

So this was what drove mortals to madness! Eamon gave in to his body's demand and ran his hands up Rosaleen's sides, reaching the gentle curve of her breasts. It was her turn to moan. But she didn't push him away or pull back. Eamon continued his exploration, never breaking the spectacular kiss.

He cupped both breasts in his hands and relished the warm weight of that feminine flesh. The tips turned hard against his palms, and he rubbed against them, pleased by Rosaleen's sharp intake of breath.

". . . that wasn't part of our plan! It only made matters worse. I found them *kissing* in the dark. That won't help at all, Father."

At the sound of the peevish female voice, Eamon tore his mouth from Rosaleen's. The last thing he wanted was for strangers to intrude on the magic they had found all alone. Then he realized the voice sounded familiar.

Wearing a puzzled look, Rosaleen pulled back. "What—"

"Hush." He pressed her face to his shoulder. "Someone's walking by."

She nuzzled in, seemingly content to stay in his arms. Eamon felt a rush of pride, of masculine pleasure. But an irritated male voice brought him back to the unfolding events.

"I'm glad you remember I'm your father, Serena," Woodbury's esteemed mayor said. "I make the decisions, since I have more experience in these matters."

GINNY REYES

As the pompous man spoke, Eamon felt tiny tremors run through Rosaleen. Again her sweetness stole over him, threatening to rob him of his common sense, but his sixth sense urged him to pay attention to the conversation between the Kellers. He smoothed a hand down Rosaleen's back, keeping his ears attuned to the interlopers as he caressed her.

"Your experience recommends that you encourage kisses between Patrick and Annie?" Serena asked.

"I don't want to hear more of your impertinence, young lady! Of course I have no interest in a tawdry liaison between them, but I do intend to continue being pleasant to Annie Brennan. I don't want her to grow suspicious of me."

"But, Father, Annie only thinks of art and her dreadful paintings. She'll never notice anything."

"She will certainly notice once her funds disappear. I want her to remember my pleasantness, my admiration—"

"You mean your fawning over her and her wealth. I think that sort of behavior will make her more aware of your interest in her assets."

"Serena, again I must remind you that I'm your father. I make the decisions. You just need to follow my directions. Concentrate on learning from Patrick all you can about the workings of the bank. I will see to the rest."

"But, Father, you should have seen how he was kissing her. He has *never* kissed me like that, and we're supposed to be getting married."

"Ahhh . . . so jealousy is behind your contrariness."

"Of course not! How could you say something so silly, so absolutely ludicrous? I could *never* be jealous of that . . . that foolish, childish *artiste*. Besides, Patrick *will* marry me."

The mayor chuckled nastily. "You know, Serena, I don't care whether Patrick O'Toole marries you or not. I care about your help in gaining access to the Brennan

A FAERIE TALE 51

fortune. As far as I'm concerned, Patrick can romance whomever he pleases.''

''Ooooh! How can you say that, Father? Do you want me humiliated before the whole town? Why, everyone is already asking why Patrick hasn't proposed.''

''That will be enough, I say! It doesn't matter what Patrick O'Toole does. He can kiss and marry whomever he wants. You just get the information we need. Nothing else matters.''

''Patrick O'Toole's kisses matter to *me*!''

''Don't you let them matter more than business.'' The mayor's voice took on a menacing tone.

''Oh, fine!'' Serena hastened to say. ''I'll take care of your *business* for you, but I'll take care of *my* business, too. And Patrick is my business.''

As the Keller duo's voices faded, Eamon released Rosaleen. A glance at her beautiful face revealed her concern. ''Aye, *cailin.* 'Tisn't good for your godchild, but then, 'tisn't any better for me charge. Although the dancing and the kissing were naught but pleasure, I'm afraid I must be seeing to this matter.''

Rosaleen stood tall. He couldn't help the bolt of admiration that shot through him at the sight of such loveliness. And pride. ''Very well, Eamon,'' she said. ''I must see what I can do for Patrick meself. As ye said, he is me godchild.''

Eamon frowned. ''Now, Rosaleen, *ma vourneen,* I didn't miss the flower petals you tossed over them earlier tonight. And you have admitted that your magic often goes awry. I do believe you'd do best staying out o' this altogether.''

''How dare ye say such a thing, Eamon Dooley? 'Twas me magic that got them dancing. 'Twas me magic that got them kissing, too. I don't believe that went awry, and you can't believe it, either.''

''Sure and you didn't hear anything, then! If your spell

52 GINNY REYES

had worked, Serena wouldn't have chanced upon them. The spell *did* go awry.''

"Only in the teeniest wee way!" Her lips clamped shut, leaving only a hint of curve visible. What a pity! he thought. Those lips in their natural state were so sweet and sensual. Then she crossed her arms over her lovely breasts. Her frown deepened.

"So where was your blasted luck whilst that horrible Serena went bungling where she wasn't wanted?" she asked. "Hmmm?"

Stifling the urge to wiggle in discomfort, Eamon waved the question aside. "Why . . . I haven't begun to put me luck to use yet. So do me—and your godchild—a favor, *cailin*, let me take care o' this. I don't need your interfere—er . . . *help*, you know. Leprechauns always work alone.''

She arched a graceful eyebrow. "You may have worked alone before, but King Midhir sent me to see to Patrick's future, and I intend to do just that.''

"And how do you intend to do it, Rosaleen Flynn? By botching spell after charm? You've even said your magic often fails.''

"Just as *you* yourself said your luck isn't always the best. I can't leave Patrick's future to a luckless leprechaun.''

Eamon winced. Her assessment was unfortunately on target . . . at least, on target for a number of times. But he didn't need a flighty faerie—no matter how well he liked her kisses and sweet body—meddling where his future, and that of Annie Brennan, was concerned. "I'm warning you, Rosaleen. Annie's future is too important for a spell to go wrong.''

"Don't ye mean Patrick's future is too important to entrust to bad luck?''

"Nay, 'tisn't bad luck I have. Sometimes me luck just isn't as good as at others.''

"Fine, Eamon! *You* can bring your luck to Annie—

good or bad—and I'll look after Patrick meself. I can work magic just as well as any other faerie, and I mean to prove it, I do.''

''Fine, Rosaleen, see to your godchild all you want. But don't go casting more fey spells on Annie Brennan. Her future can't depend on whether your magic will or won't work. I must study the matter, consider the options, then bring her the luck she needs exactly when she needs it. And I don't need your meddling a'tall!''

''I'll have ye know I don't meddle!''

''I'll be the judge o' that, *ma vourneen*!''

''Poor Annie! Wee lass doesn't know how luckless her future looks, what with all your 'studying' and 'considering' and all that. You're likely to study and consider right up to the time the Kellers make off with her fortune.''

''And you're likely to turn poor Patrick into a frog, casting your impulsive spells.''

''I'll have ye know I have never turned anyone into a frog!''

''Yet!''

''Enough, Eamon Dooley!'' She turned and stalked away. Before she got too far, however, Eamon heard her ''Harrumph!'' As he watched the lithe flow of her body, she muttered, ''And ye thought ye liked those kisses o' his!''

Eamon smiled. She hadn't had to say a word. He knew she'd liked their kisses just as much as he.

After Rosaleen left, Eamon breathed a sigh of relief. She had the most disturbing ability to throw his thinking askew. He couldn't quite focus on anything with her around. Matters were such that he *had* to think clearly at all times.

Annie's fortune had been targeted by a pair of thieving spalpeens. No wonder she had wished for a leprechaun. She clearly needed her three lucky wishes to preserve her livelihood. Eamon had no illusions regarding Annie's ability to earn a living for herself.

No, his charge was too impulsive, too impractical, too fey to think of basic necessities. She seemed consumed by her artistic urges—strange though they certainly seemed. 'Twas fortunate her da had left her well off enough that she wouldn't be forced to earn her way through life—*if* she didn't squander her money on her notions and the Kellers didn't succeed with theirs.

Eamon remembered the bizarre creation she'd come up with that morning. Fresh mud looked more attractive, he thought. Still, that faith in her own abilities endeared her to him, regardless how pathetic those abilities truly were.

Her spontaneity had its appeal, too. Why, the moment she realized that Rosaleen needed help, Annie hadn't hesitated. She had taken the drenched faerie under her wing. If he wasn't much mistaken, the pretty green frock Rosaleen wore belonged to Annie. She had even invited Rosaleen to stay with her as long as the faerie remained in Woodbury.

True, Rosaleen's presence in town would make his mission that much more difficult, but Annie's gesture had been sincere. She truly liked helping, as her offer demonstrated. Why, when the crooked mayor crowned her Queen of the May, he mentioned Annie's generous nature. One couldn't help but like the lass.

Even if her generosity ensured Rosaleen Flynn's presence in the middle of things, distracting him from his efforts. He feared frequent encounters would remind him of the kisses they had shared, making him want more of them—more of *her*.

He also had to worry about her very fallible magic. Since he already had to cope with his own changeable luck, he didn't need Rosaleen's half-baked spells to complicate matters. He could do that by himself very well indeed.

Ultimately he didn't think he could do much about Rosaleen. He couldn't force her to leave. Especially if she had been sent by King Midhir himself. Eamon would have to work around her. And keep his hands—not to mention his mouth and other body parts—to himself.

First order of business would be to find Patrick and warn him of the Kellers' designs on Annie's money. As he set off toward the town square, Eamon heard footsteps on the street behind him, a cheerful whistle underscoring the pace. Turning around, he realized the stroller was none other than Patrick O'Toole.

He grinned. "Patrick, me lad! And would you be wanting to let me in on what's put you in such a fine mood?"

Bemusement crept over his face. "A gentleman doesn't tell, Eamon."

" 'Twas one o' the ladies put that gleam in your eye, then."

Patrick shrugged. "Seems that way. But . . ."

Eamon waited. When Patrick didn't continue, he prodded, "Go on. You can't just leave a man hanging like that."

Patrick chuckled. "She's the damnedest female I ever met! I can't believe she'd get me this—"

"Oho! 'Tis wee Annie, then. The dancing must have been special."

"Dancing, nothing," Patrick muttered. "I said I wouldn't discuss private matters about a lady. I meant it."

Eamon waved expansively. "Foine, foine, me lad. Then perhaps we should talk about your work. How goes it at the bank?"

Patrick's eyes suddenly widened. "Just the same as I left it yesterday . . ."

Eamon suspected Patrick had shocked himself by enjoying his free day. He seemed the sort of man who took life most seriously, worked diligently, keeping an eye on detail. *His* kind of man.

"You don't often leave your work, do you?"

56 GINNY REYES

Patrick shook his head. "Can't remember the last time I did."

"And much less to celebrate Bealtaine, eh?"

"Never before."

"So what was different this morning?" Eamon figured it would be advisable to lead up to the unpleasant information he had to impart in this oblique manner.

"Serena pestered me until I agreed to bring her to the celebration." Distaste twisted his mouth. "And just look at the fine mess I made of things!"

"Fine mess?"

"Indeed. I got myself crowned king to Annie Brennan's queen, I reenacted some ancient lascivious rite with her, then I wound up the evening dancing and kissing her—"

Eamon whooped. "So that's what's got you all a-whistling! You've been stealing kisses from wee Annie, then."

To Eamon's amazement, Patrick's cheeks reddened. "I said I wouldn't discuss it."

"Foine, foine!" Eamon could afford to be generous now that he'd obtained evidence of Patrick's interest in Annie. He could proceed with the more serious matters regarding his charge. Aye, he was going to bring Annie excellent luck. "Well, you haven't done anything odious, me lad. You just stole a kiss from a pretty lass. We're all likely to err likewise, if I do say so meself."

Patrick eyed him shrewdly. Suddenly, Eamon felt like hiding behind the forsythia bush at the side of the house they'd just passed. "Well, now, as a banker—"

But Patrick wouldn't be put off. "I thought I saw you dancing with Rosaleen."

To his horror, Eamon felt his cheeks blaze. He had *never* blushed before today. "Well, and o' course, me lad. 'Twouldn't have been gentlemanly to leave her there while everyone else went dancing."

Patrick's dark eyes narrowed with suspicion. "I see.

You danced with Rosaleen because it was the proper thing to do. Not because she caught your eye or anything of the sort.''

''No, no!'' Eamon shook his head violently. ''I'm beyond all that. I . . . just felt sorry for the *cailin*, with her toe a-tapping and all.''

''Mm-hmm.'' Patrick's murmur was as trustworthy as a boy on April Fools' Day. He went on, to Eamon's chagrin. ''Then the besotted look on your face when you met her was misleading. You find Rosaleen ugly, don't you?''

''Ugly! Why she's the fairest lass I've ever . . .'' Eamon allowed his words to trail off. Patrick had him fair and square. ''Aye, she's a beauty, she is. But I've more important matters to attend to than gazing on a fair *cailin*.''

''Business matters?''

''You could say that.''

''Of what sort?''

''Ah . . . well . . .'tis difficult to explain.''

Patrick again donned that suspicious expression. ''Why don't you give it a try?''

Eamon scrambled through the yarns he might spin, but discarded them all as too fantastical. Although kissing Annie had thrown Patrick off-kilter, the man was no fool. Eamon chose to stay close to the truth. ''Well, you see, me lad, I'm an old friend o' Annie Brennan's da. Before he died, he asked that I keep an eye on her. Like an uncle, you know?''

The skepticism rolling off Patrick threatened to flatten Eamon. He had to turn the man's attention away from himself and to the matter at hand.

The Kellers. And their schemes. 'Twouldn't be easy. ''He didn't want anyone to take advantage o' his lass.''

''I don't think that's likely to happen. I handle her financial matters. No one takes advantage of me.''

''Wouldn't be too sure o' that, boyo.''

58 GINNY REYES

Those dark eyes narrowed once again. "Explain yourself."

"What would you say if I told you I overheard a plan to rob your bank? To steal Annie's fortune?"

Patrick's big hand shot out and grabbed the lapels of Eamon's favorite green suit coat. The strapping banker lifted him off his feet. "I'd say you'd better start talking before I take you to the police."

Doom was at hand, and Eamon didn't like the looks of it. "Put me down, you lunkard! How'd you want me to speak when you have me a-dangling like this?"

With a mighty shake, Patrick let Eamon fall to his feet. Shaken, he dusted himself off and met those fiery dark eyes. "Well, me lad, 'tis like this . . ."

Five

As he listened to Eamon's outlandish tale of intrigue, starring Woodbury's mayor and his daughter, Patrick couldn't deny the apprehension that slithered through him.

What if, against all odds, Eamon was correct? What if the Kellers *were* plotting to steal from the Woodbury Fiduciary Bank? What if Serena's assiduous interest in him was only a pretense to gain access to the funds held by the bank?

Despite his sudden concern, Patrick couldn't force himself to acknowledge the possibility. "Really, Eamon. I think you have had too much mead. Mayor Keller is a fine, upstanding citizen, and Serena . . . well, Serena and I are about to become betrothed. I certainly trust her."

"Methinks, boyo, that you'd better not trust so much, and keep your eyes and ears wide open. I heard them talking, I did. Serena was mad as a raging bull because her da crowned wee Annie as your queen. She didn't want your sympathies engaged elsewhere. She wants you docile and hers."

Patrick waved away Eamon's words. "You must have misunderstood. I have known the mayor and his daughter since they moved here four years ago."

Eamon's eyebrows flew toward his hairline. "Only four

years in town and the man's the mayor? He does work fast, don't you think?''

''I think he's a decent sort. Everyone recognized his merits early on. That is why he was elected.''

''Or it could all be part of a well-executed plan. You must consider that possibility, too.''

''Tell you what. Since you were such a good friend of Annie's father, why don't *you* keep an eye on the dastardly Kellers? I will keep my eyes on my responsibilities at the bank and my future with Serena.''

''I think you're making a splendiferous mistake, me lad. But I'll help you. I'll keep an eye on those scheming thieves. Annie's a lucky lass indeed. Eamon Dooley is on her side.''

Patrick couldn't help but roll his eyes. He didn't think Eamon would do much good policing Annie's interests, but as long as pursuit of imagined pilfering kept the Irishman out of his way, Patrick would go along with just about anything Eamon proposed.

And seeing how dangerous contact with Annie could be, Patrick would gladly hand the responsibility of looking after her to anyone who wanted it. It would be best for him to concentrate on work and his upcoming marriage to Serena Keller.

No more kisses in the dark for him. At least, no more of *Annie's* kisses.

After spending the night on Patrick O'Toole's parlor sofa—not the most comfortable place to sleep, if he did say so himself—Eamon awoke with the sun filtering in through a mullioned stained-glass window. As he basked in the colors of springtime warmth, he considered Patrick's easy offer of hospitality, even after Eamon had revealed what he'd heard the Kellers discuss.

The people of Woodbury seemed warm and welcoming. First Annie offered shelter and clothing to Rosaleen, then Patrick willingly housed a man who voiced serious accusations against his intended. Interesting.

Stretching, Eamon rose. He had to find Annie. After observing his charge for the better part of yesterday, he had discovered her tendency to be flighty, overly impulsive, and not at all prone to giving due consideration to self-preservation. He wouldn't be able to simply warn her about the Kellers. With her fey nature, she would never believe a word he said. His only recourse was to remain at her side.

He hoped his good luck held out for as long as she needed it, too. Not only did he want to earn his very own pot o' gold, but also he didn't want anything untoward to happen to his charge. Especially since she had wishes coming, and he wanted her to make the best possible use of the luck they would bring her.

Hearing footsteps on the stairs, Eamon straightened his rumpled shirt and trousers. "Top o' the mornin' to ye, Patrick!"

"Morning."

Eamon lifted an eyebrow. "Don't fancy mornings?"

Patrick grunted, then walked straight through the parlor and down a hall. Eamon followed his host to the ample kitchen. In silence, Patrick went to a wall-hung oak cabinet and brought out a package labeled "Arbuckle's." From another similar cupboard he withdrew a square wooden box with an iron attachment on top from which a curved crank handle jutted out.

Eamon pointed at the contraption. "And what's that you're after using?"

"Coffee mill."

"Ah . . . can't say I care for the brew. Have you any good Irish tea?"

Patrick shot him a challenging look. "Can't take the strong stuff?"

"Nay, nay. Just don't like the bitter taste. But I guess you haven't a spot o' tea. Too bad. I'll do as you yourself, then."

62 GINNY REYES

Patrick nodded, then turned back to the mill. Moments later, he reached into the cupboard where he'd found the machine, took out a large coffeepot, and filled it with water. After adding the beans he'd ground, he placed the kettle on the large black stove at the back of the room.

Eamon observed his host's economic gestures and noticed the pleasing organization of the kitchen and its utensils. A man after his own heart. Eamon smiled. "Nice kitchen you have here."

Patrick sent him another odd look. Then he shrugged. "As kitchens go."

"Fair talkative you are this morn!"

"If you don't like the silence, you could always go—"

"Nay, nay!" He was right where he needed to be to carry out his duty. "I'm surprised, but I find meself looking forward to that cup o' coffee you're making."

He stifled a shudder, regretting the wee lie. But since he relished wandering the streets of Woodbury to wait for a more propitious time to seek Annie even less than the cup of coffee, it was for the best. He didn't, however, think Patrick wanted to hear that.

Or perhaps he would. "Where do you think I'd be finding wee Annie today?"

Patrick spun away from the table where he'd been slicing a large golden loaf of bread, a wary expression on his strong features. "How should I know?"

"Oh . . . I don't know. P'r'aps you've seen her on other spring days. Do you think she'll be painting again?"

Patrick grimaced. "So you know she fancies herself an artist."

Eamon chuckled. "Aye. But, you know, lad, I have me doubts about her talent."

Placing thick slabs of bread on two plates, Patrick snorted. "I don't. I'm certain she has none. Have you seen her 'art'?"

A FAERIE TALE

Wincing, Eamon took the offered plate. Patrick then went to the stove, poured two inky cups of coffee, gave one to Eamon, and sat, gesturing for his guest to follow suit across from him.

"Aye," Eamon said, sitting. "Yesterday's masterpiece was . . . odd at best."

"More than likely hideous."

" 'Tis true, but I like the wee lass. I wouldn't want to hurt her feelings."

Patrick frowned, his eyes lighting with earnest intent. "Annie must learn the truth," the young banker said. "She's *not* an artist. She doesn't have a scrap of talent. In spite of that, she wants to establish a . . . I guess a heaven for artists. She plans to fill the place with other talentless idealists who will tell her how marvelous her messes are. With the money she inherited from her father, no less. The money Michael Brennan intended to keep his daughter in comfortable circumstances."

Eamon rubbed two bread crumbs between his thumb and forefinger. "Seems you don't much value a dream."

"True. One especially can't place value on Annie's artistic nonsense. If I let her have her way, she would run through that fortune in no time at all."

Eamon studied Patrick. "Whose fortune is it, me lad?"

"Why, hers, of course. But I am the executor of Michael Brennan's will. And an officer of the bank. It is my responsibility to advise her on the best way to manage those funds."

"Advise, you say. Not decide."

A white rim appeared around Patrick's compressed lips. The skin over his cheekbones ruddied. "True again. But you can't mean you agree with her! I *cannot* go along with her crazy notions. Not and do my job adequately. I pride myself on the work I do."

"Hmmm . . . a lot of buts you've offered. And pride, you said. P'r'aps 'tis your pride getting in the way here.

P'r'aps that's why you're so obstinate about Annie's dream.''

Eamon's host stood, straightening to his considerable height. ''You offend me, sir. I do not invest myself personally in such matters. I just know that idealistic dreamers come to no good end. Since I'm responsible for the disposition of Michael's will, I cannot endorse the whims of his fanciful daughter. She can only achieve disaster if she follows that dream.''

Eamon rose as well. ''If you'll forgive me, Patrick, 'twas never my intention to offend. I think I'll be after going for a walk. Don't know when I'll be back—*if* you're still willing to let me stay here.''

''Sure, sure.'' Sitting again, Patrick spread a thick coat of butter on his bread. ''I'll leave the door open for you, and you can help yourself to anything you might want to eat. I need to spend some time at the bank.''

Eamon grimaced, but didn't comment on Patrick's plans for the day. ''Thank you kindly.''

Patrick munched in silence, swallowed, then swigged the black-as-sin coffee. ''Welcome,'' he said, then bit off another third of his bread.

Since he had nothing more to say for the moment, Eamon took his leave. As he strolled down Main Street, it occurred to him that whereas Patrick seemed to need ample quantities of solid sustenance, others might need equal amounts of spiritual nourishment. He believed Annie Brennan belonged to the latter group.

''Aye, and me luck holds!'' he exclaimed when he saw his charge exit a large white frame house down the street. He called out a greeting.

''Good morning, Eamon,'' she replied, smiling. Apparently she'd decided to drop the hint of frost she had addressed him with last night before the dance.

''And where might a fair lass be off to on such a splendid morn?'' Although *he* knew perfectly well, since he'd spied on her the day before during her odd, blindfolded artistic ritual, *she* didn't know he knew.

As he expected, she blushed, making each freckle on her cheeks stand out like a sprinkle of spice. "Oh, I thought I'd try to capture the essence of the day. You see—" she tipped up her chin and showed him the canvas in her right hand—"I'm an artist."

One had to admire her determination and courage. "And where do you plan to do that?"

"Would you like to see?"

Her offer surprised him. "Would you mind if I watched?"

Never breaking her purposeful stride, Annie studied him briefly. "No one has ever watched me work, but I suppose there must always be a first time for everything."

Mischief tweaked a smile on his mouth. "Since your offer is so gracious, how can I refuse?"

Her cheeks pinked again. "I didn't mean to sound so—"

"Ah, don't you fret now. I was only funning with you. I know what you meant, Annie, lass."

She nodded, but fell silent. They went through town— all there was of it—and soon came to a rolling field on the outskirts. In the distance, about a mile or so away, Eamon noticed a familiar stand of trees. If he wasn't much mistaken, a wee faerie mound lay not five feet away from the shade they cast. 'Twas where he had been when Annie wished for a leprechaun the day before.

After a bit, Eamon gave in to his desire for additional information. "Tell me, Annie, have you studied the arts long?"

She slanted him an odd glance, but didn't slow her march. "Not formally, no. But I have books filled with pictures of masterpieces from all over the world, and I've been to Philadelphia's Museum of Fine and Industrial Art."

"So your art is the instinctive sort."

A sudden smile brightened her wholesome, pretty face. "Why, that's a lovely way of putting it, Eamon. Thank you. Mind if I use it from now on?"

As long as you don't tell Patrick where you got it! "I'd be honored."

With another cheery smile, she sped up her pace, clearly anxious to reach her destination. Eamon wondered what she had planned for today's artistic endeavor. But he didn't ask. He'd see for himself soon enough.

With a lot of fussing, adjusting, and staring at the trees with one eye closed, Annie finally nodded in satisfaction. "There!"

Eamon couldn't help comparing her fluttering gestures with Patrick's economy of movement. And these two were meant to be soul mates? Only if they didn't murder each other first! "Are you ready, then?" he asked.

Annie popped open the brown leather satchel she had brought with her. "Almost. First I must prepare my palette."

Curiosity sent him closer to her side. He observed as she opened tube after tube of paint, then dabbed globs of color on the oval dishlike item, seemingly at random. Noticing the wide range in shades, Eamon asked, "What exactly are you aiming to paint today?"

"For three days now I've tried to capture the essence of spring." She tipped her chin at the trees. "I think those oaks and ashes and willows are the purest embodiment of the season."

Eamon again studied the assortment of shades she had squeezed from her tubes. "Tell me, Annie, lass, where does the purple come in? The red? The pink?"

Donning the look of a schoolmistress, Annie expounded. "You see, these aren't for the trees as they really are. I plan to use these colors for shading . . . highlighting . . . giving depth and layers of feeling to the painting."

"Layers o' feeling?"

A FAERIE TALE

She nodded. "It's like this. You've seen paintings before, haven't you?"

"O' course."

"Well, in my opinion, any artist can paint exactly what she sees before her. And that's too . . . ordinary, to my way of thinking. I try to . . ."

"You try to . . . ?"

Taking a deep breath, she squared her shoulders. "I try to paint what I *feel*."

"What you . . . feel."

"Precisely." Suddenly Annie whirled around to face him. She set her paint-covered dish on the grass and wiped her fingers on a streaked scrap of cloth she withdrew from the leather case. She took his hands in hers.

"Oh, Eamon," she said, her voice rough with emotion. "I have so much inside, so much that I feel when I look at those trees, the daffodils, the field all covered with new grass. Those are the feelings I want to paint."

Eamon scratched his chin. "I hear what you're saying, but I've never seen anything like that."

A smile broke through the intensity on her features. "That's it! It hasn't been done before, but it's what I want to do. I have to paint the emotions inside me, all this . . . this . . . oh, I don't know what to call it." She seemed to grow impatient with her failure to find the right words. "I just *feel* so much. And I *have* to let it out, share it with . . . someone. Sometimes I fear I'll explode if I keep the emotions inside."

"What emotions are you speaking of?"

"Oh, you know, joy, sadness, excitement, grief, that thrumming anticipation that comes with spring, the happiness of summer, the melancholy of autumn, the loneliness of winter. Then there's the warmth of friendship, the icy cold of loss, the fullness of love . . ." Her voice shook, and she turned her back on him. "I've especially missed that since my parents died."

Eamon felt a sharp pang at the sadness in Annie's

voice. Aye, the wee lass needed someone to love. Someone to love her. P'r'aps more than to earn his pot o' gold, than to protect her funds or help her achieve her dream, this was why he had come. To bring some luck to Annie, and help her meet that soul-deep need for love by the one man meant only for her. In some unlikely way, p'r'aps he was her treasure after all—the very unlikely Patrick O'Toole.

A shuddering sigh shook her, and she squared her shoulders again. "Oh, Eamon, I'm sorry. I didn't mean to go on like that. You wanted to watch me paint."

"So you'll be painting those feelings o' yours."

"I'll be trying."

"And how will you go about it?"

She shrugged. "I'm not sure I have it figured out yet. But I will. If my wishes come true, I'll soon have company in my efforts."

Eamon's ears perked up at that. "Oh? What wishes?"

Wringing her hands, Annie faced him. Her eyes narrowed, and she studied his face. He felt the urge to squirm, her scrutiny made him so uncomfortable, but something told him this discomfort was one he'd best bear.

"Can you keep a secret?" she finally asked.

Eamon puffed out his chest. "Sure and I can."

Clearly nervous, she walked to the grassy rise leading up to the faerie mound. "Will you sit with me awhile?"

He joined her, crossed his legs, and took a seat.

"You see, my father left me some money when he died. And the house, of course. But it's not big enough. The house, I mean."

She glanced at him expectantly, but he had no idea what she wanted from him. He nodded and maintained an interested expression. She went on.

"I wish to share the feelings inside me, and I've always done so in my art. But it's a lonely life, the artist's life. I want to establish a . . . community for artists, where we

A FAERIE TALE

can come together to express ourselves in our chosen fashion.''

Her eyes grew dreamy. ''The Artist's Haven has to be larger than my home. You understand. I mean . . . I need room for the artists to work—space for studios, rooms for instruments, large windows for light. I figure that once the Haven is ready, the artists *will* come. I'll advertise, and they will come from everywhere, wanting a spot in a place like that. A place where they can fulfill their dreams.''

''Do you mean something like a rooming house?''

Annie frowned. ''Yes, but not just a place to live. Artists will come to paint, to write, to compose, to play lovely music, to sing, perhaps even to dance. And they won't have to worry about such details as rent and food and supplies.''

''You mean you will *give* these artists o' yours all this for . . . nothing?''

Her chin tipped up again. ''Not for nothing. I'd have their company, their support, their opinions, their teaching. That's a lot, Eamon.'' A haunted look darkened her pretty blue eyes. ''Believe me.''

No wonder Patrick thinks her fey! She is fair daft. ''Don't you think, Annie, lass, it would make more sense to have them pay for the privilege of coming to your Haven?''

''But if they had to pay, why would they bother to come?''

''Oh, I don't know, methinks an artist would appreciate the presence of others like him . . . or her. And if everyone worked to sell their art, paid a bit for their keep, why then . . . you wouldn't have to spend all your da's money on others.''

Bleakness darkened her features. ''Tell me, Eamon, what good is that money doing me in the bank? What do I have to show for it?''

She had him there. ''I don't know,'' he said, ''but it seems a mite unfair if you must pay for all the others.

P'r'aps there is a way for you to have your Artist's Haven without bankrupting yourself.''

Sighing, Annie stood and retrieved the wooden slab dotted with blobs of paint. She picked up a brush, then eyed the blank canvas before her. Moments later, she gazed at the trees. "Eamon," she said, "would you be so kind to sit over there, at the foot of that huge oak?"

"What's that, lass?"

"I'd like to have you in this painting. Your green suit will surely add to the feeling of spring."

Skeptical but willing, Eamon did as asked. "Here?"

"Mm-hmmm . . ." She scarcely spared him a glance as she daubed her brush with paint. Puckering her lips, she narrowed her eyes. Then she began to apply color to cloth.

For a while she worked in silence. Then, "Do you really think there might be a way to establish the Haven without taking too large a sum from the bank?"

Uh-oh! He had to tread carefully. "Sure and you must examine all the possibilities in great detail. There are always different ways to achieve the very same goal."

"Hmmmm. . . ."

Eamon thought over all he knew about Miss Annie Brennan. Above all, two facts stood out. She had wished for a leprechaun, and she got him. Then she wished to share her feelings, and he supposed 'twas up to him to find a way to help her do so. But how?

He would have to study the situation. But in the meantime, mischief got the best of him. "You know, Annie, lass, I'm known for being lucky."

The vague, dreamy look on her face disappeared with his words. "Lucky?"

"Aye! That I am. Luck seems to follow me. P'r'aps I can help you reach your dream."

"Would you really?" she asked, excitement in her voice, her eyes.

"I would."

A puzzled expression filled Annie's features then. "But

A FAERIE TALE

why? We're practically strangers. Why would you want to bother helping? Sharing your luck?''

Eamon nearly told her the truth. But he couldn't reveal what he was. So he chose to say what he could. ''Why, Annie, lass, don't you know? I have all the luck in the world. 'Tis the luck o' the Irish I bring you!''

Eamon's words hung between them for the rest of the morning. Annie painted while Eamon sat and posed. When she finally permitted him to stand, she refused to let him view the results of her work. With pleasant farewells, they parted. As he went back to Patrick's house, Eamon wondered how she really felt about his offer.

Hours later, after she retired, Annie lay wide awake in bed, listening to the downstairs clock sound out the hour. Twelve bass counts filled the loneliness of the night.

The mere possibility of having someone help her with the Haven was enough to steal her sleep. Yes, she could use a bit of luck. Especially after the dance—and that embrace—she and Patrick had shared.

Even in the dark, in the privacy of her room, Annie's cheeks heated at the memory. Her body again knew the sweet heaviness it had felt when he plied her mouth with hot caresses. Business dealings with Patrick had never been easy. Now, after what had happened, dealing with him would likely become nigh unto impossible.

Annie feared that achieving her dream and putting an end to her loneliness would indeed require all the luck o' the Irish.

Six

As Wednesday morning approached, Annie seemed unable to forget her conversation with Eamon. Lucky, he had said. *"All the luck o' the Irish."* Precisely what she suspected it would take to persuade Patrick O'Toole to release her money.

Could Eamon be as lucky as he said?

Could *she* be so lucky as to have stumbled on the luck she needed?

"Oh, dear." She sounded like her da. Next thing she knew, she would be seeing faeries everywhere.

If only she were so lucky!

Knowing that fear and nerves would only hurt her cause, and after hours of dreaming and wishing, Annie decided to take Eamon at face value. She would believe in his brand of luck, especially since it seemed she couldn't take a step away from home without the man tagging along in her wake. After he offered his luck, she grew so accustomed to his presence while she painted that she stopped incorporating him into her pictures and let him observe her as she worked.

Not that his presence—on canvas or off—did much to improve her artistic efforts. Her paintings still lacked . . . something. Something wasn't right with them.

A FAERIE TALE

Despite Eamon's constant company, Annie wondered why her loneliness, that emptiness she felt, refused to abate. It didn't make sense. She wasn't alone. Eamon was *always* there. When he wasn't, Rosaleen was. So why did she still feel that lack? Why did her inner yearning never end?

If truth be told, Annie spent much of her time pursuing her artistic dream and often missed seeing Rosaleen. At dinner time, however, the Irish girl did join her, and they spent the evening hours discussing all sorts of topics. Still, Annie didn't see her friend much during the day. On occasion, she found herself wondering where Rosaleen went during that time, what she did while Annie painted, but she didn't think it proper to inquire. If Rosaleen wanted Annie to know, she would surely tell.

While Eamon's presence did nothing to relieve her loneliness, it did serve to make her more determined to produce appreciably worthwhile art. He seemed so intent on her efforts, so observant of even her slightest move, that she felt compelled to produce something to justify his interest.

But her art continued to lack something, and Annie continued to feel lonely . . . empty. That inner void remained, and she didn't know how to fill it. A crucial part of her seemed to be missing.

Two days crawled by in this frustrating manner, and when Wednesday finally dawned, together with its gray and misty weather, it brought Annie bushels of anxiety over the upcoming meeting with her banker.

Her erstwhile dance partner.

The only man she had ever kissed.

Although she tried to forget the dance and kiss, she would probably have more luck seeing faeries than forgetting the effect of Patrick O'Toole's advances. She wasn't even sure she wanted to forget moments so exciting, so intimate, so enervating.

But she did have business to transact. With him.

As she rose, Annie wondered why today couldn't have been one of those glorious, southern Pennsylvania May mornings—brilliant with sunlight, the clear blue sky arching over lush, grassy hills, and the sweet scent of just-opened blossoms borne on a mild breeze. A morning when her spirits soared, just from the beauty of the day.

"And a lovely morning to ye, Annie!" chirped Rosaleen from the door to the bedroom.

Annie grinned wryly. "It could be cheerier, don't you think?"

With a wave, Rosaleen dropped onto the rumpled bed. "*I* think the morning will be what ye make it. And ye don't need sunshine to make it a lovely one."

With a noncommittal "Hmmm . . ." Annie began pawing through the garments in her oak wardrobe. She didn't want to wear anything too frilly, too bright, too whimsical, but unfortunately she didn't own many garments one might describe as sedate.

"Will you help me?" she asked her guest, undecided between a rose-colored dress and a lavender walking suit.

"Help ye do what?"

"Choose what I should wear to my appointment with Patrick O'Toole. At the bank."

Glancing at the two outfits Annie held out, Rosaleen shook her head, then came to stand at her side in front of the large piece of furniture. With a critical eye, she scanned the contents. "Why don't ye wear a plain white shirtwaist and a skirt? You'll feel comfortable, not fancied-up, but you'll look nice and neat."

"I guess. . . ." What Rosaleen said sounded sensible, but Annie wasn't convinced. "That sounds so . . . boring and drab."

"Business *is* boring, lass. Think o' Patrick. What does *he* wear?"

Annie grimaced. "Plain black suits, plain white shirts, plain black ties. I suppose he also wears plain black socks and plain black shoes, but I've never bothered to look."

A FAERIE TALE   75

"My point exactly! Ye don't want him to notice your clothes. Ye want his attention on your words. Right?"

For a moment, Annie couldn't respond—even though she knew what she should answer. She had liked it when Patrick paid her so much attention that a kiss came about, and she couldn't be certain she wanted to lose that sort of attention. Not that she should invite it or anything. He was practically engaged. Almost as good as married. To Serena Keller, no less.

Besides, today's meeting was about the Haven. Not about stolen kisses, regardless how spectacular they might be.

Still, if Patrick was about to marry the mayor's unpleasant daughter, then ... why *had* he kissed Annie? What had the kiss meant?

Oh, how silly of her! The kiss hadn't meant a thing. It had surely come about as a result of Rosaleen's wild stories of fertility rituals, the excitement of May Day, the magic of a waltz. It hadn't mattered at all.

Still, she couldn't help but wish it had.

"Bah!" As if she could waste time on kisses! She had more important matters to attend to.

"Ah . . . I want his attention on the Haven, of course," she finally answered. But Rosaleen's sensual grin and twinkling eyes revealed that Annie's pause hadn't gone unnoticed. "Really! I want him to listen to me. To hear my plans, and agree they can work. I *need* him to understand how important the Haven is."

"Mm-hmm. . . ."

"Why, of course, Rosaleen! I need to persuade Patrick to see things my way. Until I turn twenty-five, he has the final say in how I can use my very own da's money. And I intend to use it to make a success of the Artist's Haven. I *will* surround myself with others who, like me, must pursue their art."

Rosaleen's knowing look told Annie she had protested too much; she hadn't convinced anyone her thoughts of

Patrick O'Toole pertained to her inheritance.

Well, perhaps they didn't *all* pertain to business, but she would make sure from now on they did. No exceptions allowed. "Business, Rosaleen," she said. "That's what Patrick O'Toole is to me. A business matter."

As Annie left the house, Rosaleen chuckled at her friend's determined efforts to disguise what hopefully was a strong personal interest in Patrick. If 'twere so, Rosaleen's goal would be that much simpler to attain. But just to make certain things went as they should, she would cast a spell.

Knowing Annie had errands to run before the eleven o'clock appointment, Rosaleen set off to find Patrick. Preferably alone. About the only time and place she could imagine doing so was on his way to work—since she couldn't very well march into the bank and proclaim, "I have a spell to cast on ye, Mr. O'Toole."

As she approached Patrick's house—which Annie had identified—Rosaleen saw Patrick and Eamon come outside. She frowned. She hadn't counted on the leprechaun's presence. She hoped he would mind his own business, leaving her to mind hers.

As if in response to her wishes, the two shook hands and called out farewells. Eamon set off toward the outskirts of town while Patrick picked his purposeful path to the bank. Mentally scrambling, Rosaleen tried to come up with an effective spell to cast on her godchild—one that wouldn't violate any rules of respect, of course.

Although King Midhir had sent her to help Patrick find his true love, Rosaleen couldn't cast a spell that might hamper a person's freedom in choosing his mate. That would be manipulative at best and calamitous at worst—not to mention forbidden to a faerie. The most she could do was invoke a charm to draw love to her godchild. Especially since that had been his original wish at the magic well.

But Patrick's pace remained brisk, and she doubted a man so focused on business could be diverted long enough to explain the intricacies of magic, faeries, spells, charms, and love. Giving him a love amulet would have to suffice.

So where in this tiny town would she find a decent amulet?

As she looked around, she noticed a hint of red among the blades of grass at the edge of the street. What could it be?

"Aha!" she exclaimed upon discovering a smooth red rock. "Faith, and 'twill make the perfect love amulet."

Quickly calling on the powers of the Great Mother Goddess, Rosaleen charged the rock. In a soft murmur, she intoned,

> *Stone of fiery passion's height,*
> *Sealed by you in strength and might,*
> *Released again only by my will,*
> *Your power spent to work this love spell.*

Passion and love. The two gifts her godchild most desperately needed. The very gifts she had been sent to ensure he received.

Now the rock was charged, the spell was cast. Rosaleen only had to get Patrick to accept and keep the rock, since the amulet had to be in his possession for the magic to work.

"Patrick!" she called out.

The man up ahead came to a stop and turned. "Good morning, Rosaleen," he said, a distinct lack of enthusiasm in his voice.

Uh-oh. "Expecting a busy day at work, are ye?"

Patrick frowned. "No more so than usual. Was there something you needed?"

"Nay, not really. I was . . . just on me way to town when I saw ye up ahead. Might I join ye?"

His right hand dove into his waistcoat pocket and pulled out a silver fob watch. He checked the time. "If you don't mind hurrying. I'm already running late this morning."

Rosaleen walked faster and, catching up, continued at the quickened pace. Now what? How on earth could she get this pragmatic banker to take an amulet?

It occurred to her that, like Annie, he might feel himself in need of luck. "Have ye many important transactions to negotiate today?"

"I don't know that I'll have *important* negotiations to handle, but I do have to keep your friend, Annie Brennan, from doing something fairly foolish."

Rosaleen pretended ignorance. "Annie? Foolish? Nay, I cannot believe it o' her!"

Patrick made a sound very close to a snort. "Then you must not know her well. She's flighty, impractical, impulsive, illogical, and absurdly certain she's meant to be an artist."

"And a fair dancer, too, no?"

To Rosaleen's amazement—and satisfaction—Patrick's cheeks reddened. "What does dancing have to do with her inability to make business decisions?" he asked.

"Nothing a'tall, but I thought ye were enumerating her better qualities!"

Her godchild groaned. Out loud. Rosaleen winced. He hadn't even noticed she'd been funning with him. Ah, well. She had to remember the matter at hand. *In* her hand, to be precise. "So," she said, "ye expect Annie to give ye trouble, do ye?"

"Doesn't she always?"

Innocence again seemed appropriate. "I wouldn't know."

"Well, I do! Aside from all those other 'qualities,' as you called them, she's stubborn as a mule. The woman absolutely refuses to listen to reason."

A FAERIE TALE

79

"You've had no luck persuading her to your way o' thinking, have ye?"

"None whatsoever."

Rosaleen smiled wider. "Then perhaps today is your lucky day!"

A wary look sped her way. "How so?"

She opened her hand. "I have here me best magic charm." When he rolled his eyes, Rosaleen almost groaned herself, but proceeded with her mission. "I'd be happy to lend it to ye, since 'tis for such a good cause. And even if ye don't believe in charms, why, what harm can a pretty stone do?"

He blinked.

She smiled.

He blinked again, then allowed himself a lopsided smile. "None, I guess."

Success! "Ye see? 'Tis no problem a'tall. Here, hold it in your hand when things get . . . troublesome."

"Can't hurt, as you said."

"Aye, can't hurt, and who knows? A touch o' magic never hurt a man."

Sparing a scant glance at the red rock, and with his cheeks burning to a match, Patrick took the love charm and slipped it into his trousers pocket. "You must excuse me," he said, "but I really must be going. I'm late for work."

"O' course, and ye must. Farewell, then."

He acknowledged her with the briefest nod as he hurried through the gleaming glass-and-brass doors of the Woodbury Fiduciary Bank and disappeared in the cavernous depths. Rosaleen smiled broadly, satisfied with her efforts.

"Now all I need do is find a good spot to observe the results o' me magic," she murmured, following her godchild into his place of business.

To Rosaleen's consternation, however, not more than a moment later Serena Keller put in an appearance at the

80 GINNY REYES

hallowed halls of finance. In her high-pitched voice she demanded to see Patrick.

A sick feeling hit her middle, and Rosaleen couldn't stifle an exclamation of dismay. Serena wasn't supposed to be there. 'Twas Annie who was to meet with Patrick. She frowned. Her magic wasn't about to go awry now, was it?

Moments later, Serena disappeared into what Rosaleen imagined was Patrick's office. The muffled whir of business as usual reigned in the large, marble-lined chamber. Although everything gave the appearance of normalcy, Rosaleen's middle continued to tighten. Something didn't feel right.

Then, as if to justify her unease, she caught sight of the one person who would more than do so. In a totally ludicrous attempt at surreptitious movement, Eamon Dooley darted inside the bank. Six towering marble pillars ranged down the room—three on each side—and the man dashed from column to column, seeking to hide behind each one.

His odd behavior caught more than one alert eye.

Rosaleen smiled, feeling somewhat better. Mayhap his ridiculous conduct would get him thrown out of the building. Mayhap a wise clerk would suspect skullduggery. Mayhap Eamon would get himself arrested.

Her smile widened as she elaborated on her wishful thoughts. Then she heard a hiss. She glanced around, but saw no one who might have called her.

"Psst!" she heard again. Still, after looking in all directions, she found only bank employees intent on their work.

"Rosaleen! Sure and are you deaf, *cailin*?"

She groaned. Apparently Eamon's furtive actions hadn't yet got him tossed out on his ear. "What do ye want?"

"Shhhh!" he responded. "Not so loudly. We don't want anyone to know we're here, now, do we?"

"Eamon Dooley! Faith, and that's the most ridiculous

A FAERIE TALE   81

thing I've ever heard. The way you're after skulking, everyone's seen ye. I'm only amazed ye haven't been arrested.''

''Nay, *cailin*, I'm a fair hand at *feth-faidha*. I can change me form, make meself invisible, I can.''

''O' course, and ye can't. I see ye perfectly well. Especially in that green suit.''

Auburn brows came crashing over the bridge of his straight nose. ''And what's wrong with me foine suit?''

''Nothing, o' course. *If* ye want to fade into a forest glen!''

With a careless wave, he dismissed her words. ''Bah! No one knows I'm here but you. And I'm suspecting you're only here to get in me way again.''

That piqued her temper. ''How dare you? I'm here to see to me godchild's welfare.''

''Like you saw to his welfare at the May Day dancing?''

Rosaleen narrowed her gaze. ''I got him to dance with Annie, didn't I?''

Giving up all pretense of stealth, Eamon stalked toward Rosaleen, and stopped directly before her. ''Aye, you did, *cailin*,'' he said, wagging his finger at her. ''But your spell fell apart, and that Serena woman appeared.''

Rosaleen glided up to her full height, coming nose to nose with the handsome but meddlesome leprechaun. ''Ye can't blame a faerie for everything that goes wrong,'' she said in her defense. ''I can't influence Serena's choices, and you know it, too. Besides, who's to say Serena didn't come upon them due to *your* luck gone bad?''

Eamon's frown deepened. ''*I'm* to say so. And I'm here to bring wee Annie a spot o' luck today.''

Rosaleen sniffed. ''Bad luck, I'm sure. Why don't ye leave before she comes? I've taken care o' everything already.''

At that, he glared. ''Aye, and you would like that. I'm not leaving her to your spells gone wrong! The lass needs something to go right for her. Eamon Dooley is here to make sure it does.''

Why was he so obstinate? ''Don't ye go interfering now!''

''You interfered first,'' he countered. ''You were here before I was.''

Rosaleen didn't give an inch. ''I wasn't interfering. King Midhir sent me to Patrick.''

His chin rose pugnaciously. ''And Annie wished for me!''

Rosaleen couldn't refute fact. ''Oh, fine. Stay, then.''

Satisfaction filled his face. '' 'Twill be fine indeed.''

Both sat on overstuffed leather chairs in the very center of the chamber, Eamon's efforts at invisibility abandoned. Rosaleen tried ignoring him, but it wasn't easy. She had to admit he was a fine-looking man. His reddish gold hair waved back off a high forehead, and she remembered the way it felt when she ran her fingers through it as they kissed.

Thoughts of that kiss reminded her of the sensual fullness of his bottom lip, its soft, firm pressure against her mouth, the heat his touch had sparked. She had never known anything like those moments in Eamon's arms.

A part of her longed to find her way back into the clasp of those strong, lean arms. She would never forget how his whip-lean body had felt against hers—insistent and hot, as intimate parts nestled in a perfect fit. He'd seemed determined to fuse them into one.

She glanced at him and caught his deep green eyes studying her. Her cheeks grew hot.

His eyes opened wider. A cocky grin tilted his mouth, and she realized the fiend had guessed precisely what she'd been thinking. Remembering.

He crossed his arms across his chest, puckered his lips, and began whistling the waltz they had danced to. Kissed to. ''Hush!'' she begged.

He winked, but kept on whistling. As Rosaleen wished

A FAERIE TALE   83

she could turn him into a vile form of vermin, Annie entered the bank. A horrified glance at the large brass clock on the wall told her it was precisely five minutes before eleven. Five minutes before Annie's scheduled appointment with Patrick. Five short minutes before doom.

Serena Keller was with her godchild.

The feeling in Rosaleen's middle grew more ominous by the second, but there was nothing she could do—except hope Annie didn't see her. Or Eamon. They had no explanation for their presence at the bank.

But Rosaleen needn't have worried.

Oblivious to the world around her, Annie approached Patrick's secretary. "Good morning, Mr. Pearson."

"Good morning, Miss Brennan."

Although the man had never said anything to verify her suspicion, Annie knew he disliked her. In all likelihood, he wouldn't cooperate with her unless she forced him to do so. "May I please go in? I have a scheduled appointment with Mr. O'Toole for eleven o'clock."

Mr. Pearson smirked, his jowls jiggling. "He's busy at present."

Plunking the gallon of turpentine she had just picked up at the general store on the secretary's desk, Annie took a deep breath, hoping to settle her nerves. If only this meeting didn't matter so much. But it did. "Please let him know I'm here. As I said, I have an appointment."

"I'm afraid I can't interfere, Miss Brennan."

Afraid, nothing! The bulldoggy face fairly beamed with glee. Annie's impatience took hold. With a glance at the clock on the far wall, she saw it was exactly eleven o'clock. After another look at Patrick's secretary, Annie groaned. The beast was enjoying her discomfort as much as his canine cousins would a tasty bone.

Her nerves stretched to their limit, it took little to make her temper rise. Mr. Pearson did. Measurably.

His delight grew. Equally.

The silence in the bank roared. Audibly.

84 GINNY REYES

Still, Patrick's office remained closed. Annie's foot resumed tapping. The blood in her head rushed, its beat deafening in her temples.

Then a voice seeped out from behind the door. "But I don't *want* to wait!"

Such petulance was unmistakable. Serena was impinging on Annie's time. Her temper bubbled hotter, and she strained to hear more.

Patrick's response followed, too muffled to make out.

"No!" cried Serena. "Not a moment longer. It's now or never."

At Mr. Pearson's snigger, Annie realized she wasn't the only eavesdropper. His hound's eyes fixed firmly on the heavy oak door, the secretary drooled snoopiness.

But all they heard was a reasonable-sounding rumble.

In what Annie identified as a clumsy attempt at nonchalance, Patrick's guard dog scooted his chair closer to the office door. It screeched against the marble floor, sounding much like a mortally wounded pooch.

To her amusement, Mr. Pearson flushed, shot guilty looks all around, then fidgeted when he realized he'd fooled no one. He picked up a stack of papers and pretended to read the sheet on top.

At that moment, Serena's voice shrilled out again. "Now, Patrick! Now, now, now!"

"Fine," countered the banker, his voice louder than before. "Will you marry me?"

Annie's jaw dropped.

Mr. Pearson fell off his chair. Papers flew everywhere.

Across the room, someone gasped.

A woman cried out, "Oh, no!"

A man spit, "Damn!"

Annie relived the heat of Patrick's mouth, the velvet of his tongue, the passionate clasp of his arms. How could he? After kissing her like that not four days ago!

Especially when he was supposed to be meeting with *her*!

Annie saw red. The red of anger. The red of shame. The red of hurt.

Through the haze, she made out the door before her. Grabbing her glass jug of turpentine, Anne turned the brass doorknob, she turned it, wishing she held Serena Keller's slender throat in her hand. With every ounce of her strength, Annie threw open the door. "Patrick O'Toole, how *dare* you!"

Serena spun around. "Wha—"

"Annie!" Patrick exclaimed, collapsing into his chair.

"Yes, it's Annie, *Mr.* O'Toole! The Annie who had an appointment with you at eleven o'clock. The same Annie you have kept waiting while you dallied with this arrogant brat. The very same Annie you called your queen on Saturday night. The one you danced with and kissed—"

A chorus of "Oooohs" rang out behind her, pulling Annie up short.

The fascination of the listeners was so avid, Annie could nearly touch it. Fully aware she had gone too far, knowing she should never have insulted Serena or reproached Patrick for a kiss she had oh-so-willingly yielded to, but unable to keep the anger from rushing out, Annie raised her hand and slammed it on Patrick's vast mahogany desk, forgetting she held the bottle of paint thinner.

It shattered. Her hand stung where slivers of glass pierced her skin.

The pungent stench of turpentine assailed her nostrils. Oily, resiny liquid splattered onto her fingers, and Annie looked down to assess the damage she had wrought.

"Oh, dear!" To her dismay, the smelly paint thinner oozed all over Patrick's gleaming desk, then cascaded onto the intricate oak parquet floor. Shards of glass glittered on the desktop, the floor, her hands.

At her side, Serena's frown melted into a superior smirk.

86   GINNY REYES

"Yes, Patrick," said the blonde in an arrogant voice, "how dare you choose me, when you can have the elegant, proper, and decorous Annie Brennan for your wi— er, queen?"

Seven

"Congratulate me, Father. He is absolutely, positively mine!"

Matthias Keller looked up from the paper he was reading, narrowed his eyes, then asked, "What does *that* mean?"

Sinking into the worn leather armchair in front of her father's desk, Serena removed her white kid gloves, a finger at a time. "Why, Father, dear, it means your daughter is *finally* engaged to be married. To Patrick O'Toole."

"That's nice, but what about the money?"

Exasperated by her father's single-mindedness, Serena pouted. "You don't care about me, do you?"

With a grimace akin to those caused by biting sour pickles, the mayor answered, "Of course I do." He dropped the document, and leaned forward, a piercing light in his pale blue eyes. "And that is why I must know about the money. I'm looking out for your interests."

With a gesture matching his, Serena narrowed her gray eyes. "I don't think so. You're looking to line your pockets. Otherwise, you would congratulate me for my accomplishment."

The mayor made a scoffing sound. "I hadn't realized you were quite so desperate to marry."

"I said nothing about desperation or marriage." Allowing a mental image of her intended to form, Serena again smiled. "It's Patrick I want."

Matthias stood and began to pace. "Don't forget the money he manages, daughter." Spinning to face her again, he jabbed a finger in her direction. "*That* is the reason behind your interest in the man."

"Speak for yourself, Father. *You* may only want Patrick's access to the Brennan fortune, among the many accounts at the bank, but *I* want the man. The money . . . it will come in handy, I'm sure."

"Enough of this nonsense! As you said, you have the man. Very well. Now where is the information I need?"

Serena pouted again. She didn't want to discuss her father's plans. She wanted to plan her wedding. Especially since she had nothing to report. "It's taking time to get Patrick to discuss his work. Perhaps now that we are engaged, he'll open up more."

Matthias sent her a shrewd look. "I imagine that is up to you."

She frowned. "What do you mean?"

"Don't pretend." His voice turned nasty. "Ignorance and stupidity do not become you. As you well know, women have ways of learning whatever they wish from a man, especially one who fancies himself in love."

Although her father had been leading up to this for months, Serena registered a measure of distaste. "But, Father—"

"But nothing! Romance the details out of the man. I don't care how. Seduce the fool. He should be happy to bed you sooner than later."

"But, Father . . ." she wailed. "I love—"

Matthias raised a hand to halt her complaint. "Not another word about love. You cannot afford to get sloppy and emotional. We're close, Serena, very close to achieving our goal. If you should happen to snag yourself a husband while you're at it, then fine."

A FAERIE TALE

89

"But—"

"*Enough!*" Matthias roared in a most mayoral tone. "And I do indeed mean it. You know what you must do. Now do it!"

Clamping her jaw against further argument, Serena stood. Since she truly wanted Patrick, she would accede to her father's demands—so long as they didn't endanger her future as Mrs. Patrick O'Toole. After all, access to the funds at the bank should come easier to a lawfully wedded spouse. "Very well," she said between gritted teeth. "I'll see what I can do."

"You will do what you're told."

Although it had never happened before, Serena thought a threat colored her father's words. Words that by leaving she made sure were his last.

For the moment—since despite her wishes, she knew they wouldn't be his last regarding Patrick O'Toole and the Brennan fortune.

Wadding up another stack of ruined papers, Patrick found himself cursing Annie Brennan again. Why had she happened to him? Why had he been saddled with the confounded woman?

"Lovely lass, our *cailin*," offered Eamon from the other side of the desk where he, too, worked on the devastation.

"Who?" Patrick asked, not paying much attention to his new friend's patter.

"Annie Brennan, o' course."

"Annie?" he asked in amazement. "She's a disaster on legs!"

Cramming more sodden papers into the waste receptacle, Eamon chuckled, then murmured, "Mighty fine pair o' them, too."

Eamon's assessment of Annie's legs didn't sit well. Patrick narrowed his gaze. "When did you go looking at Miss Brennan's legs?"

Eamon laughed. "I didn't go a-looking. She displayed them while prancing and waltzing with you the other night."

Visions of ankles and calves danced in Patrick's head. If what little he had glimpsed looked so fine, how much finer mightn't the still-hidden lengths be? "Mmmmm. . . ."

"Glad you're in agreement, boyo!"

Niggling discomfort lodged in the more scrupulous corner of Patrick's mind. "I didn't say a word. I never discuss young ladies' attributes with other men."

Eamon *tsk-tsk*ed. "Then with whom do you discuss them? The ladies themselves? I don't believe so."

The thought of telling Annie how attractive he found her legs brought on such additional, enticing images that Patrick forgot about eliminating the evidence of her chaotic visit. That young lady possessed more for a man to explore, admire, and appreciate than just a pair of splendid legs . . .

Eamon's chiding voice cut into Patrick's enticing vision. "Patrick, me lad! Will you watch what you're doing? We don't want to clean up more than we already have."

Patrick blinked, the tempting images fleeing like thieves at dawn. With a glance, he realized he had dripped turpentine on the seat of his chair. "Confound Annie Brennan!" It was, after all, her fault he couldn't keep his thoughts off her. "Confound her legs, too! If you have nothing better to talk about than that calamitous female, then you'd do well to leave me to my business."

Eamon laughed. "Patrick, me lad, you're distracted all on your very own. But me guess is that when a man has more than one lady vying for him, well, it can't be too easy to choose."

Patrick blushed, remembering Annie's protestations. He winced, knowing himself the subject of the town's latest scandal. "I've already chosen. I'm a man betrothed. Prac-

A FAERIE TALE

91

tically married. To Serena Keller, a fine young lady, and a beautiful one, too.''

Snorting, Eamon threw another pile of debris into the waste can. ''If you like them sour and thieving.''

Patrick called on his considerable dignity. ''Watch yourself, Mr. Dooley. You're speaking ill of my fiancée.''

From the corner of his eye, Patrick caught Eamon's grimace. The Irishman muttered something, and except for it being too ludicrous to consider, he thought Eamon said, ''Not for long.''

He chose to ignore the comment. ''I'll have to persuade Mr. Millthorpe to assign the Brennan account to another bank officer. I can't be bothered with this''—he waved at the mess—''sort of disaster again.''

The turpentine had ruined everything he'd had on top of the desk. His pen-and-ink stand, his brass nameplate, the stacks of documents Stan Pearson had brought in for his signature earlier that morning. Even ledgers awaiting his review were irreparably damaged.

Patrick didn't know if the desktop itself could be restored to its previous gloss. It displayed the effect of the paint thinner. The turpentine had eaten away varnish, polish, and oil wherever it landed. Naked blotches of wood now alternated with patches of gleaming mahogany.

And the floor . . . well, at least he and Eamon had done a decent job of sopping up the puddles of resiny stuff. It, too, had been victimized by Annie Brennan's flightiness.

Still, every time he thought of the embarrassing event, he couldn't help remembering the hurt darkening her big, sapphire eyes, the anger reddening her cheeks, the accusations pouring from rosy lips.

Lips he had tasted—and he couldn't deny it had been a distinct pleasure to kiss Annie. A pure delight to savor her sweet mouth.

He remembered how she had sighed and parted her lips for him. How her arms had slid around his neck, holding him closer to her. How her lush curves had pressed into his body, searing her imprint in his memory.

Why . . . if he thought about it long enough, he could still feel the seductive fullness of her breasts against his chest, the arousing length of her legs against his, the yielding curve of her abdomen against his—

"Take a breath, boyo! You're panting like a bellows. What *are* you thinking?"

Horrified, Patrick sucked in air. He ran a shaking hand down his face, only too aware he had been caught indulging in forbidden fantasies. "Danger, Eamon. That woman is nothing but ambulatory peril. And I had better make sure she stays as far from me as possible."

Or I might just take her in my arms again, lose myself in the magic of Annie Brennan's sweet kiss.

"Well, boyo, I warned you the other night, I did."

Patrick blinked. "Wha—say that again."

Eamon sighed. "Pay attention, lad, 'tis a matter o' grave importance. I said I agreed with you. Serena Keller is fair dangerous. I tried to warn you the other night, but you wouldn't listen. The mayor and his daughter are after wee Annie's wealth."

Patrick blew out a frustrated breath. "Are you back to that again?"

"What did you think I meant?"

Annie. Annie, Annie, always Annie. "Er . . . I thought we were discussing the danger of doing business with such an impractical dreamer as An—Miss Brennan. A crazy, impulsive, excitable, irritating, infuriating—"

"You've done some thinking about the lass, then."

"Of course I have. And I'm determined to pass the responsibility for her fortune to some other unsuspecting fool. I have a career to guard, a future to ensure. I *won't* let another dreamer wreak havoc with the security of that future. Never again. I will not risk ruin for a crazy notion or an elusive ideal."

Eamon's intrigued scrutiny told Patrick how vehement he had sounded. By now familiar with his companion's mile-wide curious streak, however, Patrick went on before Eamon began digging at information Patrick preferred to keep private.

"Yes, Eamon, I have more important matters to see to than Annie Brennan's harebrained schemes. I'd rather let another banker argue against housing an army of derelict artists, feeding them, and encouraging their futile efforts—not to mention her own. A splendid future awaits me."

Eamon murmured noncommittally. Patrick took the sound as encouragement to return to his cleaning efforts. For a time, the two men worked to return the office to some semblance of order, banishing the evidence of Annie's visit.

Now, if he could banish the memory of their dance, their kiss . . . "Damn!"

"Something wrong, Patrick?" asked Eamon.

Patrick gave up on his cleaning efforts. "It's clear I won't get a lick of work done today. This office stinks, and I can't concentrate. I won't be able to keep track of even the simplest addition this afternoon."

"Methinks, boyo, that you're after needing a rest."

Patrick frowned. "I had a fine night of sleep, thank you very much."

Eamon shook his head in obvious disgust. "Sure and I didn't mean a nap! I meant an afternoon o' leisure."

"An afternoon of . . . leisure?" Patrick asked, running the word through his thoughts as if seeking its meaning.

"A foreign concept, that?"

Patrick straightened his spine. "I'm not given to sloth."

"Nor to levity, boyo! I didn't tell you to become a layabout. I just think an afternoon away from work would do you wonders. Especially after such an . . . eventful morn."

Patrick considered Eamon's suggestion. For about a minute. Bewilderment set in. "But . . . what would I *do*?"

"Do?" his companion asked, the expression on his features displaying disbelief. "Why, you wouldn't do anything, lad! You could watch a bird fly, look for castles in the clouds, listen to the song o' the wind.''

''Huh?''

Eamon rolled his eyes and sighed. ''You could always pack a picnic.''

Patrick remained unconvinced. ''Where would I go?''

Eamon's emerald eyes twinkled mischievously. Something about that sudden flicker of knowledge, that gleam of purpose, sent unease winging through Patrick. He braced himself.

But Eamon only said, ''There are places around this wee town where a man can go for a bit of peace. Why, even I, a stranger, know such a place. Would you like directions?''

With a final look around, Patrick acknowledged there was little more to be accomplished until his desktop dried, until the floor was again safe to navigate, until the leather in his chair didn't exude turpentine when pressed. And he could never concentrate in the main lobby of the bank. There was too much activity, too many distractions there.

Your biggest distraction is the memory of a forbidden kiss, a wicked corner of his mind taunted.

Patrick knew when he was beat. ''I can't think of anything better than to waste the remainder of my day watching birds, clouds, and listening to the wind.''

''Don't be forgetting the food, me lad.''

As he buttoned his suit coat, Patrick gave Eamon a wry look. ''Won't forget a thing,'' he said, fearing his words might prove only too true.

''I can't believe I marched in there and said all that,'' Annie moaned for the hundredth time later that afternoon. She scrubbed Fergus O'Shea's shaggy head in response to his sympathetic *mrreowww.*

Although she also made a commiserating sound, Rosaleen couldn't believe her friend had done so, either.

A FAERIE TALE

There wasn't much she could say. Even if Annie's interest in Patrick gave her reason to smile.

"A whole jug of turpentine," Annie continued in the same vein. "I have so little left, and it will take a week for the new order to come in to the store."

"How about watercolors?"

Annie shrugged. "They hardly count. The colors are so . . . washed-out. I prefer the vivid shades of oil paints."

Again, Rosaleen had nothing to offer. She had seen Annie's "art."

But Annie didn't wait for a response. "You *do* agree that I have ruined what chances I had of persuading Patrick to approve the money I need for the Artist's Haven, don't you?"

Pinned by Annie's bright blue gaze, Rosaleen had to answer. "I fear 'tis so."

A morose expression spread over her friend's face. Annie flung herself back onto the bed. Poor Fergus leapt for his life with a yowl as she narrowly missed landing on him. "I knew it! I just knew it. Now what am I going to do?"

You could always put away your supplies and give Serena a run for the husband, Rosaleen thought, but decided 'twas the wrong time to encourage such actions. Even though she felt the strongest urge to do so. "Ah . . . er . . . perhaps you should paint a new picture."

"To what purpose?" asked Annie, despondence in her usually cheery voice. "It looks as if my dream's come to death by turpentine."

"P'r'aps the Haven's no longer possible, but ye can always paint for the love o' painting."

"I suppose."

Rosaleen thought and thought some more. It shouldn't be so hard. She only wanted to bring Annie and Patrick together again, and the greatest bone of contention between them was Annie's determination to become an artist. If she could only bring them together again as they were at the May Day celebration . . . like two passionately attracted adults.

But Annie lay sprawled across her bed, and the last she saw of her godchild, he'd been ankle deep in Annie's turpentine. If she tried long and hard enough, Rosaleen could probably persuade Annie to go somewhere to paint. Then she would only have to lead Patrick to the same spot. After that, she might cast a wee spell and let nature take its seductive course.

She didn't know if she could pull it off, but deemed the effort worth a try. That meddlesome Eamon Dooley had best keep his unlucky self out of the picture this time. In her opinion, his unfortunate presence at the bank had caused today's dismal results.

She put her plan into action. "Aye, Annie, methinks ye ought to paint your sorrows away. One's talents are there to help one over the disappointing times, ye know."

Annie sat up slowly, weighing Rosaleen's suggestion. "I suppose . . . put that way . . ."

Encouraged, Rosaleen prodded her friend. "Show some enthusiasm, lass! 'Tis art you'll be plying."

Annie went to the window and peered out. *Uh-oh.* Rosaleen had forgotten the day's dreary weather. Mentally scrambling, she hit on an idea. "Fancy that! 'Tisn't a bright and happy day, either. Ye can draw on the dismal weather and your gloomy thoughts for today's masterpiece."

Annie shot her a skeptical look, and Rosaleen feared she might have gone a mite far. But before giving her a chance to come up with another idea, Annie said, "I may as well take you up on your suggestion. I won't even mind the rain, should it come back. I feel like a spring shower myself, all sad and weepy."

Rosaleen nearly groaned. Such feelings didn't bode well for a romantic interlude, but what was a faerie to do? She had to take advantage of every opportunity. "That's the spirit, then. Here's a fresh canvas. And don't be forgetting the paint satchel.''

With more determination than verve, Annie left the room. Rosaleen followed, just as determined. But where Annie's goal lay on a field at the outskirts of Woodbury, Rosaleen's objective was a certain young banker, presumably at work in the middle of town. The two friends went their separate ways.

To her surprise, Rosaleen found her godchild walking down Main Street, awkwardly holding a napkin-covered basket. ''Well, well, well,'' she said. ''Fancy meeting ye here, Patrick O'Toole. Are ye finished working early this fine day?''

He scowled. ''What fine day? It's overcast, and it rained earlier. Besides, I have more work than ever. It's your friend's fault I'm wandering the town like a fool. No one could work in that office after Annie Brennan finished with it.''

Uh-oh! Patrick obviously hadn't found humor in the silly scene he and the two young ladies had played out. ''Why *are* ye wandering the town, basket in hand, then?''

To her amazement, he blushed. For such a tightly disciplined man, Rosaleen found it promising indeed that Patrick's feelings could overrun his considerable control.

''Eamon insisted I go on a picnic.'' A startled expression appeared on his face. ''I can't believe I considered the possibility. Even worse, I can't believe I'm here, with a basket of food, having this conversation. The man's got the most uncanny powers of persuasion.''

For a moment, all Rosaleen could think of was the persuasive power of Eamon Dooley's lips. Aye, her godchild had a point. Eamon was indeed endowed with uncanny powers—magical powers.

At that, she frowned. If Patrick was doing something so distinctly out of character, was Eamon Dooley up to his interfering, unlucky tricks again? Had Eamon let loose yet another bolt of misfortune to ruin her latest bit o' magic? Rosaleen certainly hoped not. She wouldn't stand for another opportunity lost through his meddling. "Where are you planning to picnic?"

"On some field Eamon suggested. He described some trees about a half mile east of town."

Rosaleen caught her bottom lip between her teeth. That sounded very much like the spot Annie described as her latest favorite scene. Coincidence or . . . Eamon?

Rosaleen had to take advantage of the opportunity, regardless. Once her godchild was headed toward the encounter with his future, she would deal with Eamon. "Aye! Sounds like a fair place to go. Are ye planning on company?"

Patrick shook his head.

Rosaleen allowed a slow smile to curve her lips, imagining precisely how nature *might* take its course. Good. And she didn't have to worry about Serena this time. All she had to do was make sure her godchild made it to Annie's painting spot. For that to happen, she had to keep Eamon out of the picture.

After the dancing and kissing at the May Day celebration, Rosaleen knew just how to engage the leprechaun's interest. It was, however, an idea fraught with danger to her peace of mind. Perhaps her sanity even.

Still, one had to take certain risks in order to achieve one's goals. She strengthened her resolve. " 'Tis a fine prospect for a lazy afternoon, Patrick. Enjoy your own company, then. Oh, and I nearly forgot. Have ye seen Eamon?"

"We parted at my house. I'm sure if you're looking for him, he'll be most happy to see you. He seemed smitten with you the other night."

He didn't allow feeling smitten to spill over into minding his own business this morning, now, did he? "Faith, and I'm sure 'twas merely the magic o' Bealtaine ye saw."

A FAERIE TALE 99

Patrick chuckled. "If the dancing was part of the magic, maybe."

Rosaleen's cheeks warmed. Did Patrick really have to remind her of that moment of weakness? Right before she intended to capitalize on it? " 'Twas just so, I'm sure. I must be off now. I have much to do this afternoon."

Knowing Patrick's gaze followed her after her abrupt farewell, Rosaleen went to find a certain troublesome leprechaun.

Shaking his head, Patrick grinned and watched Annie's Irish guest walk away from his side. Funny how that lady's undeniably stunning looks and seductive femininity did nothing to him. The thought had occurred to him more than once since meeting her.

It was nearly as unfathomable as his lack of response toward his future wife. But damn if Annie Brennan didn't make his blood sing! Patrick couldn't understand that bewildering response, either.

Feeling more foolish than before, he resumed his leisurely stroll. He had to catch himself every few paces, since his natural tendencies had him speeding up, urging him to reach his destination as soon as possible, as efficiently as he could. Meandering felt strange, and Patrick didn't know if he was doing it right.

"Why, darling!" he heard Serena call out as he walked past Town Hall. "Why aren't you at the office?"

When his fiancée slipped a hand into the curve of his elbow, Patrick switched the awkward picnic basket from his right to his left hand. "I found it impossible to work there. After this morning, you understand."

For a moment, Serena remained silent. With a glance, he noticed a line of white rimming her lips. Clearly his intended had not appreciated Annie revealing that Serena's future husband had kissed *her* only days before proposing.

"Yes," she said. "A most *interesting* experience. As I have always thought her, Annie Brennan behaved like a

100 GINNY REYES

common tart. I don't know a single lady who would bellow such intimate details in a public place.''

Something turned Patrick's gut when Serena called Annie common and a tart. Something remarkably similar to guilt. "I doubt her offense at my unforgivable actions labels Miss Brennan as harshly as you do.''

Serena slapped his forearm. "Don't tell me you're taking that cheap little beast's side—''

"Enough, Serena. Annie Brennan's no cheap little beast. If you must berate someone, berate me. I took advantage of a weak moment, if you must know.''

Serena turned her piercing gaze on him. Then, smiling sweetly, she said, "See? That's one of the things I love most about you. You are such a fine, decent gentleman. You'll even assume someone else's blame. But you don't have to, darling, not with me. *I* know who's to blame!''

Growing more uncomfortable by the minute, Patrick sped up his pace. "I don't wish to continue discussing this affair. It's been embarrassment enough. I would much rather discuss our upcoming wedding, since you badgered me so strenuously into proposing.''

"Ooooh, Patrick! I'd just *adore* discussing our wedding.''

Sighing in relief, Patrick smiled briefly. "I'm off to a picnic. Would you care to join me"—he tried sweet talk on for size—"dear?''

Cooing again, Serena agreed. To the sound of his fiancée's patter, he led them out of town.

To the spot by the trees.

For a private, romantic interlude.

Eight

Why hadn't she thought of this before? Annie wondered as she gazed out over the rolling fields from her perch high in the canopy of the lush maple. It would seem she'd been looking at this painting from the wrong angle altogether. As it turned out, the trees should never have been the subject of her composition. The fields with their rich green pelt were what actually inspired the feeling of newborn spring.

Viewing the land from above ... why, it was a truly inspired concept! A splendid scene lay before her, despite the smoky sky, the hazy moisture in the air, the lack of sparkle from the sun.

Securing the stretched canvas on her lap, Annie began applying oils to her palette. The excitement of inspiration again filled her, and she was determined to bring it to life with brush and paints.

Once her supplies were ready, and after double-checking the meager amount of turpentine she had left, she peered between two branches and studied her subject anew. Indeed. The simple beauty of the Pennsylvania countryside, unmarred by road or town, looked practically perfect from where she sat.

With a happy sigh, she dabbed her brush into a glob of chartreuse.

For a while, Annie hummed as she worked on her painting, holding disturbing thoughts at bay. But eventually she could no longer escape the memories of what had happened. The waltz with Patrick had been bad enough—well, not the waltz itself, or even the kiss. Serena's sudden arrival had been mortifying. This many days later, Annie still felt shame at the thought.

Then, this morning's fiasco. She shuddered to think she had charged into Patrick's office and reproached him for the stolen kiss. With Serena present. And the office door wide open.

By now, not a soul in Woodbury had missed hearing every last detail of her scandalous conduct. On both occasions.

Although everyone considered her eccentric, Annie knew she would be seen from now on as a hussy at best. She'd been caught kissing another woman's beau.

Why couldn't she keep a better hold on her temper? Her wild impulses? Why did she *always* yield to the urgings of her heart?

They only seemed to get her into worse trouble each time. One thing became clear earlier today. Patrick O'Toole would never dance with *her* again. She wouldn't run the risk of receiving another of his dazzling kisses.

Although that should relieve her, it served only to disappoint her. Surely she was the most foolish woman alive.

But being foolish didn't mean she had to compound her problems. She intended to ask the management of the Woodbury Fiduciary Bank to assign her financial matters to another officer. Nothing on earth would force her to face Patrick O'Toole again.

Starting today, she would run in the opposite direction when she saw him coming. Especially since he was likely to approach with Serena hanging onto his arm, bearing a remarkable resemblance to a limpet.

"Yes, sir." Mind made up, Annie achieved a measure of peace about the morning's disaster. The sense of ease

A FAERIE TALE 103

following her decision gave her the freedom to spend long minutes engrossed in her work, not even sparing her future former banker a thought.

A while later, however, approaching voices disturbed her concentration. Someone was coming toward the stand of trees from the direction of the road. Annie wiped her brush clean, then glanced down at the intruders.

"Oh, no!" Heading for her maple were none other than Patrick O'Toole and his newly affianced intended. They were the last two people Annie wanted to face, especially since she had just decided to avoid them forever.

Now they were there, heads drawn close, presumably exchanging endearments. Annie felt sick.

She hurried to assure herself that the pang she had just felt merely signaled hunger. She harbored no tender feelings toward Mr. O'Toole. He could murmur whatever he wanted into whomever's ear was close.

To Annie's horror, Serena pointed at her tree. "There!" the woman exclaimed. "The perfect spot for our picnic."

Picnic. Annie groaned in dismay. That meant they might linger for hours. She would be forced to spend those very same hours in the tree. She couldn't think of a worse way to waste her afternoon than watching lovebirds eat and woo, bill and coo.

Why had she followed her stupid impulse to climb the tree for a better view?

"Are you hungry?" Patrick asked Serena as he spread a red tablecloth at the foot of the tree.

She gave him a simpering smile. "Not really, darling, but don't worry about me. Go ahead and eat. I'll be happy to serve you."

Don't worry about me, darling, mocked Annie in silence from her perch. *I'll be happy to drool all over you.*

Moments later, the aggravating blonde handed her companion a platter with slices of ham, a chicken leg, a mountain of potato salad, and a fragrant dill pickle. "Go ahead," she repeated, "enjoy your meal."

Patrick's thanks were muffled by the proximity of a mouthful of salad to his lips.

Annie's legs began to cramp. An itch developed in the middle of her back. She concentrated on remaining immobile.

After a long silence, during which Patrick demolished the contents of the plate, a slice of pie and some cookies from the basket, Serena put away the soiled tableware.

"I'm so excited, darling!" she chirped when she lowered the lid of the basket. "I can't wait to consult with Mrs. Dawson on the pattern for my bridal gown."

A frown bloomed on Patrick's forehead. "I hope you won't choose something too . . . fussy."

Serena patted his knee and laughed. "Don't be silly, darling. I'm not the fussy sort. Fussy is for foolish girls like Annie—"

"I'm glad you're not planning on fussy," he jumped in, just as Annie's temper began to simmer. "Do you think we can try for small and intimate?"

Now it was Serena who frowned. "You can't mean you don't want me to have a nice wedding."

Patrick sighed. "I suppose you'll want attendants and a party afterward."

"Why, of course! Every woman dreams of a wonderful celebration. I'm just like the others."

Patrick arched an eyebrow.

Annie stifled a snicker. Serena was *not* like most women. She was snide, arrogant, unpleasant, selfish—

"And afterwards . . ." murmured Serena in a syrupy voice, laying her hand low on Patrick's middle. "How many . . ." Her voice dropped a notch, and Annie had to strain to catch what she said. ". . . babies do you want?"

Annie's eyes popped wide open. *Oh, dear!* She didn't want to hear any more. But when Patrick flushed, her curiosity got the better of her.

"Ah . . . well . . . I hadn't thought that far in advance." Discomfort blazed from his stiff shoulders, his clamped

A FAERIE TALE 105

lips, the twitching muscle low in his cheek. He inched away from Serena. "Let's stick with the wedding right now."

Serena followed, practically sprawling across his front. "Let's not," she whispered. "Let's do something more"—she dropped a kiss on his sealed mouth and brought her hand to his belt—"interesting."

Patrick turned redder. A sheen broke out on his brow. He clasped her wrist and pried her fingers off the silver buckle. "Serena! You don't know what you're doing!"

Serena answered with another, more lingering kiss and a throaty chuckle. "But you'll show me, right?" Her hand covered the bulky placket of his black trousers.

Patrick jerked upright and replaced the roaming hand back in Serena's lap. Her jaw flapped open and shut, reminding Annie of a just-caught carp.

She gulped, squirming. Watching Serena kiss Patrick with such familiarity didn't sit well. In fact, if it weren't such a ridiculous notion, she might think she was . . . jealous.

Surely it was nothing more than ordinary, decent discomfort at being privy to an intimate tryst.

"Patrick . . ." wailed Serena, clearly displeased with the results of her attempted seduction. "We're getting married. Why won't you let me . . . ?"

Serena dropped her other hand into Patrick's lap, and he shackled it, too. "Stop!" he ordered. "It's best to wait until after the wedding for this."

"But why?" cried Serena. "We're getting married anyway."

"Someone might see."

She twisted in his clasp. "There's no one here but us."

Annie covered her mouth to avoid revealing her presence.

Serena wriggled again, this time obviously seeking to get closer to him. Patrick fought just as hard to hold her at bay. "This . . . it's not proper!"

106 GINNY REYES

"Who cares?"

"Why . . . everyone cares."

"But who's to know?"

Annie could have told Serena she hadn't a chance of winning the argument, if by nothing more than reading Patrick's ominous frown.

"I would know," he said with dignity. "And I'd much rather wait until *after* the wedding."

Serena screwed up her face and tears appeared in her eyes. "You don't want me."

Patrick seemed to freeze, then he looked at his intended as if she were a stranger. "Nooo . . ." he said, "that's not . . . it. I just think . . . it's best if we wait."

His words had no appreciable effect. Serena sobbed louder and covered her face with her hands. "You don't lo-o-ove me!"

Patrick shook his head in apparent exasperation. "Serena, for heaven's sake! I asked you to marry me this morning. What more proof do you want?"

Annie knew, she just *knew* what Serena was about to do. But she had no way to warn Patrick. Besides, he *had* asked the wailing banshee to marry him, after all. He deserved everything he got.

Artfully Serena peeked out from behind one hand and dropped the other onto Patrick's groin. "*This!*"

Patrick leapt up like a scalded cat.

With another shriek, Serena fell back onto the grass.

Startled, Annie lurched sideways, dropping her palette. It landed on Serena's white lawn dress, leaving streaks of viridian, chartreuse, ivy, and burnt sienna across the woman's chest.

"Oh, dear!" she cried, then watched her canvas fall to Patrick's feet.

Serena's wails increased in volume. Patrick knelt to offer assistance, but stared up into the tree, rage twisting his ruddied features.

Faced with such a powerful glare, Annie scooted back

to escape behind a large, leafy branch, but lost her footing. Before she could prevent it, she felt herself fall . . . right into Patrick's outstretched arms.

The impact knocked him onto his rear, and he issued a loud "Oooph!"

Serena scrambled to her feet, still screaming. "Look what you've done *this* time, Annie Brennan!" She tried dabbing at the smears of paint on her bodice but made the mess worse. "You've ruined my dress! And our picnic. Why must you follow me everywhere I go?"

Oblivious to the unfairness of her accusation, Serena stamped her white-booted foot, then turned and stormed off, yelling imprecations at Annie.

Annie scarcely heard the insults since her attention was squarely on the man she had leveled. The man whose face lay not two inches away from her own. The very large, warm, sturdy man whose body cradled hers.

Annie tried. She really tried to tear her gaze away from Patrick's, but something about the darkness of his eyes, the intense way he stared at her, rendered her helpless. She stared back, just as stunned by this response as to that crazy May Day waltz.

If she didn't know better, she would have sworn flames flared in his eyes. Their heat seeped into her, and she realized how intimately she was pressed against him.

Her breasts were flattened on his chest, and her abdomen nestled against his. Her legs twined with his, one knee intimately nudging the juncture of his thighs. At that spot she could feel a tightening, a muscular reaction to their nearness. She jerked her knee away, but ended up groin to groin with Patrick. Moments later, she felt a prodding, an insistent movement that told her his reaction matched hers.

As time stood still, that prodding became a rigid, insistent demand, a hot brand on her flesh, despite their clothes. Instinctively she pressed closer to his fire.

He groaned.

She caught her breath, fearing what she felt—in both of them.

She placed her hands on his shoulders to push away from the danger he posed, since her body obviously didn't know any better, or so she told herself. But when he held her in place, her fingers ran greedily over the width of those shoulders, down his arms, over his chest, around his neck.

Her instincts again told her what was about to happen, but although she held the power to stop it, she realized she didn't want to. She acknowledged that ever since Saturday she'd been yearning for another of Patrick O'Toole's kisses.

One was only seconds away.

She sighed and parted her lips. Patrick muttered her name, then brought his lips against hers, tight, hot, nothing tentative in the pressure and scope of this kiss. His tongue swept deep into her mouth, retracing territory he'd explored before.

Annie responded, curling her tongue around his, pressing closer to him. As the kiss went on and on, she became aware of muted sounds, moans and gasps, and was shocked to realize they came from her.

Patrick's hands ran up and down her back, rounding over her hips, clasping her buttocks as he pressed that hard ridge against her yielding flesh. The kiss went on, as did her own exploration of whatever her hands reached.

His body was hard, muscular, and gave off the most intoxicating heat. Annie knew she wanted more of it, more of his enervating caresses, his addictive kisses, Patrick's dark, delicious taste. She stroked his tongue with hers, sucking gently, as his hands shook against her flesh. Those hands left her derriere, climbed up her sides, and cupped the curves of her breasts. She should have refused him the intimacy, but something inside her made her move to give him better access instead.

When he palmed her, Annie was lost. She didn't want

the moment to end. She didn't want Patrick to stop touching her, exploring her body, revealing the pleasure he found in her by the insistence of his touch, the ragged breaths he took, the bucking of his hips against hers, as if seeking to bind them as one.

It was the most exhilarating madness, the most tormenting need Annie had ever known. And all because of Patrick O'Toole.

Through the haze of sweet aching, Annie grew aware of intrusive sounds. Voices!

Someone was coming . . . *two* someones . . . and she lay wantonly draped over the front of an engaged man! Mouth to mouth. Breasts to chest. Groin to irrefutable, visible evidence of what they were doing.

She began slapping at Patrick's demanding hands, those wicked fingers intent on kneading the fullness of her breasts, exploring her cresting nipples. In alarm, but with unbelievable reluctance, she tore her lips from his.

"Stop! Someone's coming."

Patrick blinked owlishly. He rasped a couple of breaths. His hands stopped their motions, but stayed where they were, his hips frozen tight against her.

"Let me go!" she demanded.

Patrick blinked some more, but remained motionless.

"Didn't you hear me?" she asked. "Someone's coming! Let go of me."

"You're—" he said in a croak. Then he cleared his throat and tried again. "*You're* laying on top of me. *You'll* have to get up."

Annie realized he was right. *She'd* had control of their intimate position, but she'd been unwilling to break the contact. With alacrity, and more embarrassment than she remembered ever feeling, she leapt off him, turning away to survey the state of her clothes.

"Oh, dear!" Where his large hands had clasped her breasts, wrinkles had formed on the starched white cotton fabric. The hem of her shirtwaist hung out over her skirt.

Any intelligent observer would know what had caused her disheveled appearance.

A draft cooled the flesh of the upper rear of her right thigh. Turning to find the cause, Annie realized that Patrick must have lifted her skirt in his exploration, since her petticoat and serge skirt were caught in her garter, exposing the better part of her leg.

Whirling around, she yanked and pulled to straighten her garments, and noticed her lips felt hot, puffy, throbbing. Running her tongue over them, she tasted Patrick and sighed. They *were* puffy, obviously from pressing in sensual hunger against his mouth and teeth. "Oh, dear!" she cried again, then pressed her palms against her scalding cheeks.

The voices came closer, and she accepted she couldn't hide the evidence of that passionate interlude. A passionate interlude with Patrick O'Toole. And how was *he* faring at the moment?

When she glanced his way, she groaned again. Woodbury was about to experience a scandal the likes of which it had never known before.

Patrick's brown eyes still glittered with sensual fire. His cheeks still bore stains of red, as did his lips. His jaws were clamped tight, a muscle jumping under his ruddied skin as he obviously fought to bring his body under control.

But it didn't look as if his will would win out any time soon, since his arousal stood proud, distending his black trousers in an unmistakable fashion. Mr. O'Toole, it seemed, remained as rigid as when his mouth had devoured hers, his hands had explored her, his flesh had sought a home in her. No living, breathing person could miss that prominent bulge.

Just as Annie thought matters couldn't get any worse, she recognized the intruders.

"Faith, and there ye are, Annie!"

"Patrick, me lad! How did your picnic go?"

As if a piercing pin had deflated him, Patrick collapsed onto the crumpled tablecloth, drawing his legs against his chest. He dropped his forehead to his knees. "Hello, Eamon, Rosaleen," he muttered, his words muffled by his position.

Annie refused to turn, so she continued to stare at the inopportune duo over a shoulder. Her neck began to cramp. She had to get out of there, but she wasn't going to give her new friends any more to comment on than that she and Patrick had been found under a tree, alone.

"Well, and how did the painting go?" asked Rosaleen.

"Aye, lass," added Eamon. "Will you be showing us today's work?"

Glancing around, Annie found the object of her salvation, albeit a momentary salvation at that. After today, she suspected she was doomed for eternity. Intimate embraces with another woman's future groom would certainly do that.

She bent and picked up her canvas. "Here's today's . . ."

Her voice trailed off as she glanced down at the object that hid her appearance. This piece of art looked even worse than many of her other efforts, as it had fallen face-down on the ground. Bits of grass clung to the smeared oils, which hadn't fared well in the fall. To add insult to injury, a trail of ants marched across the center of the mess, aiming straight for her hand.

She had to make a choice in the next few seconds. She could either wait until the insects covered her hand or she could drop the canvas, revealing her crumpled garments.

Her hatred of insects won out.

After the canvas thudded back to the ground, the silence grew deep, telling. Eamon's eyes widened. Rosaleen frowned. Annie stood uncovered, the untucked ends of her blouse and the wrinkles over her breasts revealing more than they should have.

She stood frozen as time crept by. Then, unable to bear

GINNY REYES

another second's scrutiny, she dashed off without another word.

Three pairs of eyes followed her escape.

A foul eruption from Patrick's lips pierced the silence.

Four green eyes turned on him.

He ran after her.

Irish eyes watched, underlined with satisfied smiles.

Nine

Damn, damn, damn, damn! Each step he took caused another curse to ring out in Patrick's mind.

How could matters have gotten so far out of hand? What had happened between the fight against Serena for his puny virtue, and the venture with Annie Brennan in delighting the flesh?

He felt betrayed. By his thoughts, his desires, his libido . . . even his own flesh had betrayed him.

He had trouble accepting his flaccid state when his future wife tried to seduce him. Especially when compared to his startling deployment the moment Annie landed on his lap.

A tremor of residual arousal shook him, and he cursed yet again. What kind of power did that woman hold over him?

He couldn't even say he liked her, especially since she dragged chaos and havoc around with her. Patrick preferred order, discipline, control. Annie hadn't a clue what any of those concepts meant.

Still, he couldn't deny her courage. She soared toward her dreams despite the judgment of those around her. Everyone knew she couldn't paint, draw, or sketch well enough to save her soul. But she'd set her sights on an artistic future, and by damn, she went at it with all she had. Patrick was man enough to admit he didn't know if he could stay as true to his resolve were his goals as out of reach as hers obviously were.

Annie possessed the most cheerful nature of anyone he'd ever met. Aside from the moments of embarrassment she seemed to tumble into with predictable regularity, he'd never seen her out of sorts or grumpy. He supposed that with a name like Annie a sour disposition was likely impossible.

"Damn!" Now his thought patterns were following similar paths of illogic as hers seemed to do. What difference could a person's name make on their inner nature?

Serena presented a case in point. She didn't inspire serenity, nor was serenity a particularly characteristic state with her. She would be anything but serene after this afternoon's fiasco—even *before* she learned how much worse matters grew after she left. He wondered how long it would take Eamon and Rosaleen to spread the word about catching him in a compromising position with, of all women, Annie Brennan.

He continued castigating himself all the way home. When he ran up the steps, he realized it would best serve his purpose to make amends with Serena—even though he'd done nothing wrong. At least he'd done nothing wrong until she'd abandoned him to Annie's seductive mercies.

Despite Patrick's better judgment, a smile tilted his lips. Amazing the effect she had on him! And damned if it hadn't felt better than heaven on earth.

As he pulled out a fresh change of clothes from his armoire, Patrick's libido relived the more pertinent parts of that momentary lapse of sanity. Annie had come alive in his hands. Her response had served only to further inflame his senses. Loving Annie had felt as if he'd held dynamite in his arms, and he feared he'd never experience that same madness with any other woman, regardless how many he might "sample" in the years to come.

Catching a glimpse of himself in the washstand mirror, he came to a grinding halt. Reflected in the glass stood a stranger.

His eyelids had narrowed, his cheeks flushed. His nostrils flared with each breath he took, and his lips bore a foreign, sensual smile. Even worse, he'd begun to harden again, just by thinking of Annie.

At that moment, Patrick fully understood how dangerous his train of thought truly was. He couldn't afford to let sexual attraction come between him and his carefully plotted future. Physical desire came dangerously close to the romantic love that led his mother to marry passionate idealist Sean O'Toole. That idealism led Patrick's father to fight for his political dream, a dream that eventually took his life just when his wife and unborn son needed him most.

Patrick would never permit a fickle emotion to interfere with what he knew would be best for his future, his family. He'd worked too hard and too long to achieve what he had. Marrying the mayor's daughter would provide him with the social position he wanted, the position denied him and his mother because they were Irish. It would be the final jewel in his crown of achievements.

No matter what havoc Annie's sensuality played with his fickle flesh.

After pouring water into the washbasin, Patrick splashed his heated cheeks, hoping to cool the ardor still plaguing him. He had to plan what he would say to Serena, choose his words, have complete control of his thoughts and deeds. He couldn't afford to offend her, to make her regret accepting his proposal.

He'd probably have to make some kind of physical advance, too, just to prove he did indeed want her. And damned if the prospect held no excitement for him. Or his flesh. That condition didn't bode well for his efforts. Or their marriage.

How did a man force himself to respond to the woman he *should* respond to? To the woman who left him as cold as a dead fish?

In his frustration, Patrick kicked out, forgetting he'd doffed his shoes. The sharp crack of bare toes against the bedroom wall reminded him plenty fast. A virulent stream of curses burst from his mouth.

As he hopped around on one foot, clutching his possibly broken toes, an imperious knock came at his front door. Glancing at his drawers—the only thing between him and indecency—he cursed again. When would this hellish day end?

With little regard for his throbbing toes, Patrick pulled on the clean trousers and shirt he'd taken from the armoire. As he limped down the stairs, he buttoned the pants, but arrived at the door before starting on the shirt. He twisted and yanked the doorknob, all semblance of welcome long gone, and growled, "Yes?"

To his horror and dismay, Serena stood on the front porch, thunderclouds in her expression.

"Fine way to greet me," she said. "May I come in?"

A hop and a hobble brought him a few inches back. The door came with him. "Please do."

Serena marched in. Her jaw set in fighting form, she drew off immaculate white kid gloves. She'd also changed from the frock Annie's paints had ruined.

Silent moments went by. "What do you have to say for yourself?" she finally asked.

He leaned against the doorjamb to take the weight off his smashed toes. "Pathetically little, if you must know."

Serena's sandy brows drew close. She hadn't liked his response. Even though he had known the gossips would rush right to her, he couldn't help but be impressed by their astounding speed. He was in deeper trouble than he'd feared. "I mean—"

A FAERIE TALE 117

"No, sir," she said, stomping right up to him. "You will hear me out. I demand to know how you intend to prevent another recurrence of today's abominable circumstances."

Patrick flushed to the roots of his hair. She had every right to her anger. She probably had the right to draw and quarter him, too, but by asking instead of automatically condemning him, she seemed willing to give him another chance. Although he should have felt humbled by her magnanimity, a rebellious corner of his mind didn't want to swear off Annie's kisses for the rest of his natural life.

What a quandary. Engaged to one, wanting the other.

The silence grew more unpleasant. At Serena's raised eyebrow, he shook his head, closed the door with more force than he'd intended, and hobbled to the sofa. Collapsing and trying to think of an adequate response, he delayed indecently longer.

"I hope you agree this nonsense with Annie Brennan must end," she offered, clearly irked by his unwillingness to commit to a course of action.

He nodded, but the rebel in him kept his tongue tied in knots.

"You cannot permit her to follow us everywhere we go," Serena continued in his silence. "Especially since she seems prone to offering testimonials of your advances in the presence of one and all."

"Good heavens, no!" he cried in horror, imagining what Annie might reveal should she reproach him for today's interlude.

The gleam in Serena's gray eyes let him know he'd played right into her wishes. "Well, then, sir," she said with a nasty twist to her lips, "what are you prepared to do to keep the hussy from accosting you at the altar the day we are wed?"

Visions of Annie as a virginal sacrifice on a pagan altar rushed into Patrick's mind. On the heels of those images, he realized they had to have earned him at least a decade in Purgatory, so detailed were they in their lusty sensuality. Annie . . . on an altar. . . .

Reason followed, however, bringing memories of his earliest childhood, of times when he and his mother went to sleep, their bellies groaning for lack of food. Those were supplanted by one where other boys in school recounted tales of adventures with their fathers . . . and Patrick had none to tell. Over that picture, his mother's worn, lined face materialized, wistful, sad, as she had appeared even after years of marriage to Guenther Mertz. Her heart had always belonged to Sean O'Toole, in spite of the pain, loneliness, and poverty his idealism had condemned her to.

Surely insanity was imminent, as evidenced by the rapid-fire parade of disturbing visions, memories, and images that worked on his every emotion. "No! I swear I will *never* again touch or kiss Annie Brennan for as long . . . as . . . I . . ."

Only then did he realize his mistake. From the way Serena's jaw gaped, it became clear she hadn't yet heard how far he'd transgressed.

Her gray eyes narrowed. "You won't *touch* or *kiss* Annie Brennan *again*?"

Patrick's mutinous side suggested he now knew what a fire-breathing dragon looked like. The dragon continued. "Just how much *touching* and *kissing* have you done with Annie Brennan?"

"Ah . . . er . . . well, not *that* much really."

Serena's eyes glittered in their narrow slits. "More than with me, I'll wager."

Could a man's scalp scorch off from embarrassment? "Well, actually . . ."

"I knew it!" she exclaimed. "You didn't want me earlier today because you're already getting what you want from that little tramp. How could you, Patrick? And you haven't even demanded discretion from your tart!"

Patrick bolted up. Pain shot through his leg. He howled.

But he couldn't let her speak of Annie that way. "She's not a tart," he spit through gritted teeth.

"Well, if she's so blastedly wonderful to *touch* and *kiss* that you feel the need to defend her, then why don't you just marry her?" Serena's lips twisted sardonically, as if she already knew the answer to her shrewd question.

His worst fears were rapidly coming true. "Because I want to marry *you*!"

"I'll have you know, sir, I won't tolerate adulterous scandals."

"I swear it will *never* come to that."

Serena granted him a superior smile, slapping the kid gloves against the palm of a hand. "*If* we marry. Of course, *I'll* make sure of that."

Her words sounded offensively like a threat. "How do you presume to do that?" Patrick asked.

His future wife assumed a loathsome expression. "Since you're so quick to defend the object of your dalliance, I presume you wouldn't want her reputation sullied as it would be, should I make known what a loose sort she is."

Patrick's stomach turned. "Surely you wouldn't go to such extremes."

Serena chuckled—without humor. "Don't do anything to make me, darling. That is, if you still intend to marry me."

"I . . . why—"

For a moment, Patrick couldn't reassure Serena of his intentions. He turned away, needing to think, but his gaze fell on a tatted lace runner topping the walnut sideboard. His mother had made it, saying as she gave it to him that she hoped his future wife would like it.

Thoughts of his mother *always* brought him back to reality. "Of course I'm going through with our marriage."

"Name the date, darling."

120 GINNY REYES

Patrick recognized the challenge. He didn't rise to it. "Shouldn't you?"

Triumph glowed in Serena's predatory smile. "Thank you, Patrick. I'll be happy to. I believe we should marry no later than mid-June. With your . . . *appetites* as great as they appear to be, it seems prudent to marry immediately. Mid-June will give me just enough time to prepare a wedding."

And none to let you wriggle out of my grasp, her glare seemed to add.

"So . . . soon," he said.

"Oh, no, darling. It won't be a moment too soon." She approached. Running a finger down his chest between the unbuttoned sides of his shirt, she paused when she met the waistband of his trousers. "I, for one, can't wait."

Patrick gulped and stepped back. "Ah . . . er . . . neither can . . . I."

"That's more like it, darling," she purred. Standing on her toes, she lifted her lips to his. He dutifully kissed them, regretting the lack of fire in the caress.

When he pulled away, she gave him an odd look, then began donning her gloves. "I'll have Mr. Robertson run an announcement of our engagement and upcoming nuptials in the *Woodbury Daily Sentinel*. Tomorrow."

"So . . . soon," he found himself repeating as his stomach churned one more time.

"Of course," she said. Then she went to the door. "Don't forget, Patrick, stay away from your floozy. Otherwise . . ."

The closing door cut off the end of his future wife's threat.

Patrick's gut again turned, sickening him. He had to avoid doing anything that might harm Annie again.

A short while after Serena left, Patrick could no longer control his temper. Why on earth was he so ready to take on the responsibility of keeping Annie Brennan safe? After all, she brought her problems upon herself.

And him.

If she hadn't flaunted those slender ankles and curvy calves while prancing around the Maypole, he might never have noticed how womanly she was. *You mean you wouldn't have noticed her generous breasts, her small waist, and round hips if it hadn't been for her feet?* asked his suddenly anarchistic conscience.

Yes, he would have, but if she hadn't been so willing to teach him to waltz, he would never have fallen under the spell of the moon, the music, and all those womanly attributes.

You really think you could have walked away without sampling those delightful lips? continued that traitorous side of him.

"I certainly would have," he stated, determined to bring the mental insurrection back under control. But it seemed that for once his will lacked the power to bring his baser side to heel.

And if Annie hadn't gone out of her way to tempt you while in your lap today, the voice in his head taunted, *you would have helped her stand and left her completely alone?*

"Oh, hell." Even in his delusional state he couldn't accuse Annie of deliberately arousing him. She might have avoided falling from the tree, she might even have managed to skip landing on him, but he had to admit she'd done nothing overt to cause his body to respond so impressively.

"Fine," he muttered, pacing the parlor despite his limp. "She didn't purposely seduce me. But this morning's spectacle at the bank was her fault, and it led directly to this afternoon's . . . troubles."

To Serena's threats.

Annie simply had to stop following him. And Serena. If not for the sake of his sanity, then for her very own sake.

And it was up to him to inform her of that.

She was in the tree before you got there, piped in the devil in his head. "Damn, damn, damn!"

He saw no other way around the situation. He had to persuade Annie to stay out of his life. For both their sakes.

Now that he'd made up his mind, he saw no point in postponing the unpleasant deed, so he grabbed a light jacket against the chill in the evening air, and set off toward the Brennan home.

When he remembered Annie had a houseguest, he hoped Rosaleen would make herself scarce. The conversation he and Miss Brennan were about to have was not one he wished to have overheard.

As he marched—as well as he could with bruised toes—toward his nemesis, he couldn't help blaming Annie for even the afternoon's sensual interlude. She had no right being so attractive and such a thorough distraction.

Had *he* done anything to turn her into a constant upheaval in his careful, disciplined existence? Of course not. She had stormed his office displaying more passion than a legion of women should manage to muster all on her very own.

He remembered the flush on her freckled cheeks, the fire blazing in her sapphire eyes, the way her lips had caressed—yes, dammit, caressed—each word she'd spit at him, and no man could ever forget the quivering of her breasts with each gulping breath she'd taken.

She'd been magnificent.

Vibrantly alive.

Mesmerizing.

Naturally, when she'd made her inopportune landing on a very susceptible part of his anatomy, that part had instinctively responded to those spectacular womanly attributes.

And she had never said, "No."

It was *indeed her fault!* he thought. *From the very start of this ridiculous series of calamities. Now she had better put an end to it.*

He stormed up the front steps of the Brennan house and, with every ounce of his irritation adding vehemence to his strength, pounded the solid mahogany door.

Light shone dimly through the front windows, suggesting she was perhaps in the rear of the home. Most likely she had been eating. Too bad. He'd been too angry, too distracted by her antics to swallow even the slightest bite. And it took an enormous upheaval to steal his appetite.

The upheaval opened the door. "Patrick!"

He froze. He'd never expected to find her garbed in little more than a cobweb. The light from the hallway behind her rendered the already sheer fabric of her nightdress virtually superfluous. Hills and valleys, light and shadow, revealed the most intimate details of her form. How dare the maddening woman open the door dressed like that?

"Won't you . . . come in?" she had the gall to ask, moving back.

Fool that he was, he followed. But he did have a reason for his visit. He didn't think it prudent to put their conversation off till tomorrow. And theirs wasn't the sort of thing one discussed on the front porch where interested neighbors could lean out a window and listen. Besides, he was firm in his resolve.

He would never touch this woman again.

No, sir.

Never.

"Why on earth would you open the door dressed like that?" he bellowed, his question condemning, but not nearly as much as his common sense condemned his undisciplined tongue.

"Dressed like . . . what?" she asked, stepping back.

Never taking his gaze from her, Patrick's eyes widened more with her every motion. He blinked. Whatever she'd done had made the fabric cling to her breasts, the dark circles in their middles visible through the flower-sprigged veil of cloth. "Like . . . like . . ."

She threw nervous hands up in frustration. "Patrick O'Toole, if you must know, you look ridiculous muttering incoherently. As you can see, I'm ready for bed. Even you would agree that today has not been a good day. I'm tired, and if you have nothing else to say, you had better go and leave me alone."

The phenomenal effect of her breathing on his libido began once again. It only served to make him angrier. "Of course I have better things to do than stand here! In fact, I came out of the goodness of my heart. I came to offer you valuable advice."

"Bah! I've heard all I want of your advice. You say one more word about high-yield accounts, and I vow I'll . . . I'll . . . oh, *spit*! I don't know *what* I'll do, but I promise, it won't be something you'll like."

"Of that I'm sure. But this has nothing to do with your money. This has to do with something more valuable than dollars and cents. I came to warn you of the harm you're doing to your reputation."

"My reputation! Pray tell, what am *I* doing to harm my reputation? What's been done to sully it was done by you."

"Me! I'm guilty of nothing but being the poor fool whose life you've decided to ruin!"

"How so, Mr. O'Toole?"

"By flaunting yourself before me every chance you get. By tempting me with your curves with every breath you take. By following me—me and my future wife—everywhere we go. By disturbing every last moment of my waking life. By making Serena so jealous she's threatening to break our engagement. By kissing every word you utter, and making me wish it were me you kissed—"

"Patrick!"

A FAERIE TALE

"Oh, damn!"

He pulled her into his arms. Their mouths came together in a fiery explosion. Neither seemed able to taste enough, to kiss enough. Patrick cupped her face in his hands, tipping it this way and that, giving himself better access.

Annie clung to his arms, her fingers digging into his flesh. But it didn't seem to be in defense, since deep in her throat she again made those exciting sounds that stoked his desire ever higher. It seemed the lady was struck with the same sensual hunger he was.

Without breaking away from her mouth, he curled an arm under her knees and picked her up close to his chest. His toes protested, but the rest of him sang. He ran his tongue over her teeth, then nipped her bottom lip. She rewarded him with another of her seductive moans.

Tearing his lips from hers, he scanned the parlor and spotted a sofa not too far away. He kissed her again, and kept his gaze on his goal. When he reached the piece of furniture, he sat, cradling Annie in his lap.

The position had much merit. It gave him access to the breasts that had riveted his gaze from the moment she'd opened the door. But a row of buttons stood in his way. With much fumbling, he eventually undid them all, never stopping the intoxicating caresses until her warm flesh filled his palms.

Annie cried out.

He froze.

"Don't stop!" she demanded.

He laughed and ran questing fingers over the full, firm flesh. Her nipples peaked, and with his thumbs he rubbed the turgid buds. They tightened even more.

Annie whimpered and arched her back.

He dropped his lips over one crest, and incredible sweetness filled his mouth. It was his turn to moan.

In pleasure.

Delight.

Need.

As he suckled, his hand roamed over her hip, cupping a firm buttock, then running the length of her thigh. He was on fire for this woman! He'd never known hunger like this before.

"Annie," he murmured against her breast.

"Mmmmm . . ."

He inched the length of her nightdress up that leg, needing to touch her skin, to feel that satiny expanse with nothing between them. At that incriminating moment, the front door smacked open against the wall. A gasp followed the bang.

Patrick dragged his unwilling mouth from Annie's flesh and pushed her flimsy garment down her leg. His eyes, however, refused to focus just yet.

But his ears heard.

"Faith, and it seems we've come at a horrid time," said Rosaleen.

"Aye, *cailin*," concurred Eamon mournfully. " 'Tis twice now we've interrupted something they don't look like they'd be wanting us to interrupt."

Ten

"Faith, and you're the most unlucky fellow I've ever known," Rosaleen said as she dragged Eamon back out to the porch. Patrick and Annie needed a few discreet moments to put themselves back to order.

Eamon shot her a glare. "Why, Rosaleen Flynn, I'm not in the least unlucky. Your spells are just the worst I've ever known."

Rosaleen forced a laugh. "If 'tweren't for your interference with each blasted one, those two would likely be at the altar by now."

"You're a daft one, you are. You can't cast a simple love charm and have it work, yet you're perfectly happy to blame a man for your mistakes."

"Mistakes!" How dare he? "Everything goes fine until *you* show up. I'll have ye know, Eamon Dooley, I haven't yet made a mistake save agreeing to dance with ye on Bealtaine!" The moment she finished spitting out her words, she realized she'd made a second mistake. She'd brought up a matter that should have been laid to rest.

Eamon's eyes sparkled with unholy glee. "Hmmm... seems you're recalling plenty o' that *mistake*. And mightn't it be less a mistake than a moment to remember?"

Rosaleen's cheeks heated up. "Absolutely not! Why, 'tis a foolish faerie who would forget there is no romantic love in *Tyeer na N-og*."

A broad grin and a wink sped her way. "Ah, *cailin*, there you have it! We aren't in *Tyeer na N-og* just now. And we *can* have all the loving we would be lacking back home right here. You seemed to like me kisses the other night, you did."

"Why, 'tis preposterous . . . I didn't . . . you're sadly mistaken, Eamon—"

"We shall see, won't we, now?" he asked, taking her in his arms.

Rosaleen felt a charge everywhere their bodies touched, and when his lips dropped to hers, desire filled her once again.

For a leprechaun who'd presumably never kissed before Bealtaine night, Eamon knew just how to kiss a faerie till she felt she'd melt from his touch. His lips rubbed hers, making her want more. His tongue tasted her as if she were the finest of delicacies. His teeth nipped and tugged, entreating the most startling responses from her.

Rosaleen mimicked his actions, tasting his wine-dark flavor, testing the rough velvet of his tongue, teasing the heated silk of his lips. She murmured in pleasure, and his hands seemed to take the sound as an invitation to roam. They meandered down her back, cupped her rear, slid up her sides, and homed in on her breasts.

The shocking sensation of his touch pleased her more than it should have. She knew she should rebuff him, that this sort of contact could only bring heartache once she returned to *Tyeer na N-og*, but in truth, she wanted more of the magic simmering between them, the intoxicating passion Eamon Dooley sparked in a body that felt foreign the moment he touched it.

"You're the loveliest female, you know," he whispered as his lips followed the line of her neck. He dipped his tongue into the hollow of her throat, and another shock

A FAERIE TALE 129

raced through her. Private parts of her body felt swollen, ripe, needy. Instinctively she knew Eamon would soothe that need, satisfy it, satisfy *her*.

Emboldened by his hunger, Rosaleen began an exploration of her own. Although Eamon was nowhere near as large and strapping as Patrick, she discovered he hid an abundance of lean muscle beneath his garb. His shoulders were solid, his arms hard. As she pulled back to give him better access to her breasts, Rosaleen let her hands rove his chest, reach his abdomen.

In response to her efforts, he groaned. "Don't you dare stop now, *cailin*!"

The play of his fingers on the tips of her breasts left Rosaleen breathless. His demand registered, but her inexperience made her hesitate. "Wha—what would ye like me to do?"

"Anything, *ma vourneen*, anything your heart desires."

When he rubbed his thumbs against her nipples, Rosaleen cried out, and decided if it felt this good to her, it might also feel good to him. She followed his example, and was immediately rewarded.

"Aye, *cailin*, that's it!"

To her surprise, he bent her back over his arm, and brought his mouth to her fabric-covered breast. She felt the heat of his breath, the dampness of his mouth through the cotton of her bodice. And wanted more. And less. Less clothing in their way.

He must have read her mind, since he began to fumble with the buttons at her throat. His lips followed the path his fingers blazed, and she gasped and whimpered at each new sensation. His moist tongue felt more wicked on her virgin flesh than anything she'd ever known. She couldn't wait until he reached his goal: her naked breast.

At that precise moment, heavy footsteps set the floor of the porch beneath her feet to shaking. Rosaleen cried, "Oh, no!" and tried to close her bodice once more.

Eamon's mouth got in her way.

Patrick's laugh rang out into the night. "So . . . you're no more willing to be interrupted than I, are you, Eamon?"

The man laving her flesh suddenly pulled away, and Rosaleen emitted another whimper. Moments later, however, she snapped into action and buttoned her dress all the way up.

With a glance, she saw Eamon run a shaky hand down his flushed face. "Wha—what might you be wanting *now*, Patrick?" he asked. "Couldn't you see I was occupied?"

"Mm-hmmm . . . as I was when *you* barged in on me."

"Shall we call it even, then, boyo?" he asked, peering at Rosaleen. "We can both get back to what we were doing."

"No!" cried Rosaleen, pushing him away as he reached for her. " 'Tis well past time to go. And don't be coming back this way. We'll not be needing the likes o' ye two around here. Aren't I right, Annie?"

Silence reigned for a moment. Then, in a weak voice, Annie said, "Ri-right." She coughed discreetly. "You heard my friend, Patrick O'Toole. Leave. Go back to your fiancée, and don't bother me again. Come, Rosaleen. It's time to retire."

The slamming door cut off the men's protestations.

Rosaleen pushed a hank of loose hair off her forehead. "Oh, aye. 'Tis best to lock the door against the likes o' them. One never knows when they'll be back a-kissing and a-touching one, making one feel things one oughtn't to feel."

"Indeed." Annie sighed. "Are you hungry? I've plenty of stew—"

"Nay. I couldn't swallow a morsel right now. Breaking me fast in the morn will be soon enough, it will."

"I know what you mean," answered Annie, turning the key to extinguish the gaslamp in the hallway. "Patrick's touch does the most amazing things to my middle. I lose every bit of my appetite when he . . ."

A FAERIE TALE

131

Rosaleen glanced at her friend when her words trailed off. A bemused smile curved Annie's lips.

"Your appetite, ye say ye lose," Rosaleen murmured, considering the words. "I wonder if 'tis hunger ye lose or 'tisn't one kind o' hunger that overtakes the other."

Annie spun around and met Rosaleen's gaze. Her response glowed in her blue eyes with a hint of fear.

On the walk home, Patrick refused to let Eamon's chatter get the better of him. He would *not* discuss what had happened in Annie Brennan's parlor. Not with Eamon, not with anyone. Not even with his own, traitorous mind.

Matters had grown disastrously worse when he'd tried to make them better. He should have known. *Nothing* about Annie Brennan came easy.

Except maybe looking at her.

And kissing her.

Falling under her unnaturally powerful spell. "Damn!"

"You said, me lad?"

"Nothing," he muttered, glaring at his companion. He would, he vowed, keep his mouth shut from here on in.

To his distinct irritation, Eamon began to whistle a sprightly jig. The lilting sound had his nerves on edge mere seconds into the tune. But Patrick feared if he demanded the man stop his chafing racket, he would only open himself up to more questions than he wanted to answer.

He didn't want to answer any.

He had no answers.

Only questions.

What was it about Annie Brennan that incited him to madness? She was no practiced seductress, no raving beauty. True, she was easy on the eyes, as he'd already admitted, and her figure inspired a man to the most erotic and detailed of fantasies, but if truth were told, Serena was far more beautiful than Annie.

Still, there was something about Annie . . . something

elusive . . . magical. And that magic had ensnared him more times than he cared to admit.

Since he'd finally decided to be honest about his response to her, he acknowledged her crazy notions inspired more sympathy than scorn, even though he had tried to steel himself against it. Scorn should have prevailed. She *was* crazy, after all. And she was making him crazier than he'd ever thought possible.

Crazy with wanting her.

There! He'd finally admitted *that*, too. Whereas he could dredge up no physical desire for his lovely future wife, madness boiled through his veins, inciting him to the most sensual of caresses, whenever Annie came within reach. And when he *had* to let her go, to set that sweet, ripe body away from his hungry one, it seemed the most difficult action to take.

Worse yet, he suspected he wasn't going to get over this ridiculous craving anytime soon. Certainly not until *after* satisfying his every last want, his every last need, his every last fantasy. Quite possibly hers, too.

Even then, if kissing and touching her alone could be this addictive, this consuming, what was to say that fully possessing the little sprite would be any less so?

At that, Patrick knew fear.

Would he *ever* get enough of Annie Brennan? Would he *ever* be free of the hunger raging inside him? Would he *ever* be free to walk away from her?

Would he ever want to?

He suddenly noticed his shaking hands. Whether they shook from unfulfilled sexual hunger or fear, he didn't know. He did, however, know one thing. He could no longer entertain thoughts of marrying another woman while he felt this way about Annie. He couldn't do that to Serena, to Annie, to himself.

He had to cast off Annie's enchantment before he could continue to court the mayor's daughter. He had to recover from Annie before he could wed Serena. Even if it took

A FAERIE TALE

the better part of his life, as he feared it might.

Taking his watch out with unsteady fingers, Patrick saw it was only half past eight. Certainly too late to go calling for purely social reasons, but not too late to right a wrong.

Less than happy at the prospect, he squared his shoulders. "Why don't you go on home without me, Eamon? I have an important matter to attend to. I shouldn't be more than an hour or so."

He refused to meet Eamon's gaze, but was glad his Irish friend didn't voice the queries he read on his face. "Make yourself at home," he added. "Help yourself to whatever you'd like in the kitchen."

Eamon snorted. "Ah, boyo, I'm afraid what I'm hungering for cannot be found in your kitchen. I'm after thinking to make it an early night."

Patrick nodded. "I know *exactly* what you mean."

"I'll say you do, lad! We're in the same fix."

They parted ways, and Patrick went past his house and down a short side street toward Mayor Keller's home. Noting the bright lights in the parlor, he swallowed hard. He girded himself for combat—as he suspected Serena would make a battle of it—and knocked on the black-painted door.

He heard the sounds of a heated argument. Clearly the adversaries hadn't heard his knock. He tried again, harder this time.

The voices suddenly fell silent. Great, Patrick thought, he'd certainly chosen a good time to come give his fiancée the worst of bad news.

When the door opened, the mayor met him, nose to nose. "Patrick!" the portly man boomed out in surprise.

Patrick ran a finger around the collar of his shirt. "Yes, sir, it's me. I . . . I need a moment with Serena. In private, you understand."

The mayor's pale eyes took on a speculative gleam. "Why, certainly, son. My little girl says you plan to marry right away. Welcome to the family!"

The man's effusiveness made Patrick want to run. Especially since there wasn't going to be a wedding between him and Serena. At least, not anytime soon. He had no idea what to say.

Serena came to his rescue. "Darling! What a lovely surprise."

Patrick found no way to avoid the pink lips that landed on his for a resounding, sucking buss. To his horror, he felt nothing but disgust.

He must have masked it well, since Serena didn't seem to notice. She closed the door behind him, then, slipping her hand into the crook of his elbow, led him into the parlor. "Come sit with me on the settee."

Patrick went, feeling much like a canary calling on a cat. He perched on the edge of the seat. "I . . ."

His voice trailed off when he realized the mayor still stood at the mouth of the hallway, staring at them. How could he say what he had to say with her father present? How could he ask the mayor to leave his own parlor?

He muttered a curse under his breath.

Serena understood. Turning to her father, she said, "If you please, Patrick did want to speak with me alone."

The mayor harrumphed, but disappeared down the darkened maw. Although relieved they no longer had a witness, Patrick felt no better about what he had come to say. He sighed. There was no better way to say it than to just . . . say it.

"I've done a lot of thinking since you left my house this afternoon," he began.

"Splendid!"

The smile Serena beamed on him turned his stomach almost as badly as her threats against Annie. "I'm afraid you won't think so once I'm done talking."

"Oh?"

He stood. Running his finger around his collar again, he began pacing in front of the settee. When he bumped his knee against a fussy, carved walnut table covered with porcelain miniatures of shepherds and shepherdesses, he muttered yet another curse. He despised that sort of thing.

But bric-a-brac didn't matter at present. He had something much more important to address. Like their engagement. "You see, Serena, I've come to the conclusion that you were correct in some of your observations. I—I *have* found myself in various incriminating positions with Annie Brennan of late."

Serena nodded, a magnanimous smile on her lips. Patrick remembered their recent kiss, and its memory gave him the courage to forge ahead. "These occurrences haven't all been her fault. You see, I find her . . . irresistible."

Serena's cheeks turned puce. "Why . . . how dare you speak to me like that?"

He gulped. "Because I'm trying—desperately, you understand—to be honest with you. You deserve my honesty, if not my faithfulness."

"As your intended bride, I deserve and *demand* both."

"That's just it," he said, glad she had brought the matter to a head. "I can't in all fairness proceed with this engagement, much less marry you, while I feel this way about another woman."

Serena's jaw gaped.

Seeing his words had struck the woman speechless, Patrick hammered on. There was nothing else to do but finish. "I must break our agreement—"

"No!" she shrieked, rage making her nostrils flare unattractively. "I will not stand for the humiliation. You can't be serious! You couldn't possibly prefer that . . . that cheap tramp to me."

It dawned on Patrick that although difficult, what he was in the process of doing might be a very good thing. Until today, he'd never been privy to Serena's foul temper and ugly nature. He might have to thank Annie for her interference. She could very well have saved him from a fate worse than death or even Hades itself!

"Actually," he said, a strange calm overtaking him, "after the scenes you have subjected me to today, Annie's ineptitude, awkwardness, and cheerful nature offer far greater appeal than your venom does."

Again Serena's jaw flopped open.

He reached across and, with his index finger, closed her mouth. "That slack-jawed look is almost as unappealing as your shrewish nature, Serena. If you wish to find yourself a man—and keep him—I would urge you to sweeten both."

The clatter of metal hitting metal rang out from the rear of the house. Patrick suspected her father had heard every word they'd spoken, and hadn't particularly liked any. At the sound, Serena's anger seemed to drain from her features as fast as the heightened color left her cheeks. Her gray eyes widened, and he could have staked his reputation on it, so certain was he that fear replaced what other emotion she might have felt.

"Of course, Patrick," she rushed to say. "I'll do it. Of course I'll be sweeter. You'll see. I'll do anything you say. Only . . . give me the chance. Please."

Serena Keller pleading?

She wasn't finished just yet. "Don't be angry, darling. I . . . allowed my feelings for you to make me jealous of a woman I shouldn't give the time of day to. I won't do that again. And I certainly won't speak ill of Miss Brennan in the future. I should never have voiced my complaints."

Backtracking, even? Patrick couldn't give his ears credence for what he heard.

"You'll see," she repeated. "I promise I'll never allow jealousy to mar our time together again. And I'll improve my temper. I can do it. I know I can. Give me the chance to prove it."

Patrick found it difficult to keep his own jaw from gaping. What had caused this radical change? He honestly didn't think it had anything to do with undying love.

A FAERIE TALE

Then Serena darted a glance toward the hallway. The one her father had taken when he left the parlor at her request. Patrick followed her gaze, but saw nothing there to give birth to her awe-inspiring transformation. When he looked back at her, she lifted trembling fingers to her heart.

It couldn't be. Fear? Again?

With nothing further to add to the conversation, Patrick remained silent, his gaze firmly fixed on Serena's face. And, yes. From where he stood, she certainly looked like a woman in the grip of formidable fright.

The only explanation he could think of for her response seemed too ludicrous by half. Her father? The Honorable Mayor of Woodbury?

She couldn't be afraid of him. Everyone found the man harmless, albeit pompous and self-important. But as Patrick watched Serena virtually quake in dread, he realized it was no longer his business to make matters right for her. Not that he wished her ill—after all, he had wronged her by his unfaithfulness, and that was bad enough. Still, he didn't have to fix her life for her. He had his own disrupted one to worry about.

Time had come to put an end to this awkward episode. "I'm sorry about the embarrassment you expect to feel. Still, it's best to end the engagement now. It would be wrong of me to prolong the situation. It is certainly unfair to you."

"No, Patrick," she said, shaking her head, her eyes growing wilder with each word. "You don't want to do this."

This seemed a fine time to leave. "If you'll excuse me—I won't ask your forgiveness, as my behavior is unforgivable—I must go home now."

"Oh, no!" she cried. "Please, don't go. Not yet. Wait . . ."

He turned a deaf ear to her plea, scared she might persuade him to stay, to postpone the end of this untenable situation. He couldn't do that. He knew it would be best, even for Serena, to make a clean break right now. "I'll let myself out."

Closing the door behind him, he took a deep breath of fresh, spring night air. It was sweet and cleansing and pure. He might have made a number of mistakes in recent days, but at least he'd had the sense to avoid making this greater one. He'd narrowly avoided marrying Serena Keller.

"So, Serena," said Matthias Keller, "he's completely and totally ours, hmmm?"

Serena didn't like the meanness in her father's beady eyes. From where she stood, they looked like an angry pig's. Panic skidded up her spine. Somehow she had to placate him. "Perhaps not totally. But you'll see, Papa," she offered, choosing the childish title in the hope of avoiding his spleen. "I'll get him back. I *always* get what I want, you know. And I want Patrick O'Toole."

He laughed maliciously. "He doesn't want you."

Her father's words sliced through her, perhaps more painfully than even Patrick's rejection. But she couldn't let him see how much they affected her. He'd only take advantage of her weakness. Again.

She stood taller, pride in her carriage. "He has been momentarily blinded by that tart's attentions. You'll see. He'll come back. He knows what's best for him." She thumbed her chest. "And that's me."

The mayor gave another nasty chuckle. "I certainly hope *you* know what's best for you."

Again Serena heard the threat in her father's voice. Although he'd been known to speak hurtful words, he'd only threatened her once before. The time when they'd discussed the information he wanted regarding Annie's wealth. "You have made yourself perfectly clear, Father. I will get the information for you. You will have Annie Brennan's money yet. I promise."

A FAERIE TALE

139

After today Serena longed to hurt the young woman who had caused her such pain. In that moment, she vowed to win back the man she loved, and at the same time hand her father the means by which to appropriate the Brennan funds.

"It will be my pleasure, indeed."

Eleven

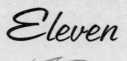

Thursday dawned bright and clear. Patrick stretched, thinking through all the things he had to do. Starting with the repairs to his office.

He couldn't believe what a foul day yesterday had turned out to be. Still, on his walk home from the Kellers, a strange sense of peace had filled him. Breaking off an engagement he'd thought he wanted only hours earlier had been difficult, but in retrospect, the only honorable course to take. Patrick prided himself on being an honorable man.

The urgency he had felt during the last few months was gone. He hadn't realized the strain his courtship of Serena had posed. Today, however, he felt free.

Freedom felt good indeed.

He smiled sheepishly. He couldn't deny appreciating the freedom he'd regained last night, especially since Annie Brennan's beautiful sapphire eyes materialized before him with stunning regularity.

Anticipation began to thrum in him. He would make a point to see her today. He had to let her know he no longer had a commitment to Serena Keller. He now had every right to see Annie, to hold her, kiss her, and enjoy whatever else might happen between them.

A FAERIE TALE

141

He leapt out of bed, a cheery whistle on his lips, and raced through his morning ablutions, ready to tackle the challenges sure to greet him at the bank.

Thoughts of his destroyed office brought back memories of Annie's anger yesterday morning. Patrick couldn't help the satisfaction that rushed through him. She really hadn't liked Serena's hold on him, had she? It seemed she reciprocated his attraction to her. A most promising state of affairs. One upon which he would certainly capitalize.

Today.

Remembering the yearly Woodbury Community Church Benefit Supper scheduled for Saturday night, he decided the event offered a splendid opportunity to escort the new object of his interest. Attending such a function with Annie Brennan on his arm would make an unmistakable impression.

Annie on his arm . . . *in* his arms . . . a tempting prospect indeed.

Annie's nerves felt as taut as fresh canvas stretched on its frame, as they had ever since Patrick came by on Thursday after work and announced he no longer had a fiancée.

Although his words had made her heart pick up its beat, Annie had thought it prudent to display no overt interest in the banker's sudden announcement. Especially since on Wednesday he had been every bit the affianced man.

But when he asked her to accompany him to the Woodbury Community Church's Benefit Supper, she hadn't had the internal fortitude to turn him down—even though her instincts warned her against getting more involved with the wickedly attractive but miserably conventional man.

Annie would have to be on her best behavior—not to mention maintain extraordinary control of her tongue—the entire evening. Her spontaneous nature would need serious bridling, and she wasn't sure how long she could maintain that much restraint.

In the end, she based her decision on want. She *wanted* Patrick to escort her. She wanted to see if the intoxicating effect he had on her would continue, especially now that he was no longer forbidden fruit. She also wanted to attend a social event on the arm of the most handsome man in town.

The man who, to her dismay, made her heart speed, her flesh tingle, and her mind conjure sinful images with the greatest of ease. No matter how much she thought about it, she couldn't for the life of her figure out why. Patrick O'Toole—serious, methodical, predictable—seemed the least likely man to capture her interest. But he had.

His magical touch and spellbinding kisses had stolen what little common sense she had ever possessed.

So tonight, in preparation for the social, she donned her prettiest spring dress, a royal blue silk trimmed with black velvet piping around its modest sweetheart neckline. The party gown accented her finest features—her blue eyes and abundant black hair. Annie knew she looked her best.

A knock came at her bedroom door. "Come in," she called, knowing Rosaleen had worked feverishly, trying to make a suitable garment ready in only two days.

When Rosaleen entered, Annie's breath caught momentarily. "Dear me! You'll put the rest of us to shame."

Rosaleen twisted her fingers together. "Oh, fie, Annie. Don't tease me so. How do I look?"

It never ceased to amaze her that Rosaleen had no concept of her own spectacular looks. In brilliant emerald satin, she looked elegant, quintessentially feminine, womanly in every way. Her sleek figure had just enough of the curves and valleys men looked for, and she moved with a natural sensuality that always garnered masculine attention. Annie remembered Eamon's besotted expression each time the Irish gent laid eyes on fair Rosaleen.

She chuckled. "I feel great sympathy for poor Eamon."

"Faith, and what do ye mean?"

A FAERIE TALE

"Why, the poor man's eyes will surely pop out the moment he sees you. After what I saw on that porch Wednesday evening, you'll have your hands full fighting his off!"

Rosaleen's cheeks turned rosy again. "You really think he'll like this?"

Annie laughed out loud. "Just look at yourself in that mirror."

Rosaleen approached the glass hesitantly. After a prolonged scrutiny, however, that slow, sensual smile of hers appeared. "I do look fairly fine."

A powerful pounding on the front door kept Annie from answering. Instead, she said, "Come with me. Let the men tell you how wonderful you look."

But as she opened the door to let in their escorts, Patrick's gaze turned to her. The light in his dark amber eyes grew hot, and a flush rose up her exposed chest and the length of her neck all the way to the roots of her hair.

A rogue's grin appeared on his lips, and she blushed even more, remembering the tug of that mouth on her flesh. He came to her side and caressed her heated cheek with a knuckle. "That color suits you."

"Th-thank you. Everyone says blue becomes me. My eyes, you know."

He chuckled. "I meant the blush."

"Oh!"

Never taking his gaze away, he clasped her elbow, rubbing her bare skin with a long finger. "Do you have a wrap? It's turned chilly outside."

Annie broke away to go for the requested garment, and only then noticed the scene playing out between their friends. Eamon did indeed look thunderstruck, but the fascination in Rosaleen's green eyes amused Annie most. It matched that of her admirer.

The evening felt ripe with splendid promise.

Moments later, the two couples left the Brennan house, Patrick's left hand covering Annie's fingers where they

144 GINNY REYES

lay on his right arm. She had never felt so special, so feminine, so admired.

As the foursome approached Town Hall, where the festivities were always held since they attracted every resident Woodbury counted, Eamon broke the companionable silence. ''Have I told you the story o' Seamus, the leprechaun?''

Annie glanced at him, puzzled by his sudden question. She hadn't known him long enough to have heard many of his tales. At her side, Patrick chuckled. Looking at him, she understood. ''So,'' she said, ''he likes to chat.''

Patrick lowered his lips to her ear, kissed it, then said, ''Incessantly.''

Excitement shimmered through her. She forgot what they'd whispered about, forgot they weren't alone, forgot where they were headed. She only knew the wonder of being a woman clearly admired by the man at her side. Could this really be happening to her? Could Patrick O'Toole, calm, methodical banker, really be attracted to her? To whimsical, artistic Annie Brennan? The most unlikely woman for him?

Patrick's thumb slipped between his arm and her palm to rub secret circles on her sensitive skin. At her gasp, he winked.

Her eyes widened. The rat! He knew what effect he had on her. Well, she thought, he hadn't seemed unaffected by her up to now, so . . . two could play that game.

Remembering his hunger for her those two earlier times, she pressed closer to his side, letting her breast rub against his arm. With a glance, she noticed his startled blink. As she smiled, pleased with her results, another of those shimmers of pleasure tore through her.

From a distance, or so she thought, she heard Eamon speak. ''. . . Aye, Annie. Methinks the story o' old Seamus is a good one for you to know.''

To her amazement, she realized Eamon hadn't stopped

A FAERIE TALE

talking, although she'd missed every word he'd said. "Ah
... er ... how would that be?"

Eamon cleared his throat. "Well, lass, 'tis no secret you
have a pile o' gold in Patrick's care, nay?"

"Papa's money."

"Indeed."

Annie shrugged. "I've never paid much attention to it,
except for asking Patrick for some when I need it—and
hearing his 'No' more often than I like."

Smiling mischievously, she saw Patrick frown.
"Well!" he exclaimed, straightening into what she considered his "bankerly" stance. "It *is* my responsibility to
execute your father's will to the best of my ability—"

"Oh, stop!" He hadn't realized she'd only been teasing. She sighed. "Not tonight. I don't want to hear you
say one word about how foolish you think my Artist's
Haven dreams are."

Patrick cleared his throat. Although he refused to meet
her gaze, he muttered, "Agreed."

"Go on," she said to Eamon.

"Aye, wee Annie. You have a fortune, and I suspect
there's some who'd be too happy to help you spend it."

"Patrick?" she asked, enjoying his moment of discomfort.

The affronted banker blustered. "Botheration, woman—"

"O' course and not Patrick!" Eamon exclaimed. "He's
the sensible sort, you know. My kind o' man."

Annie laughed. She hadn't meant her question seriously, after all. "Sensible, orderly, methodical, predictable—"

"Stop!" Patrick cut in. "You make me sound ancient!"

Annie bit her bottom lip to halt another peal of laughter.
"If that's how you feel ..."

"Anyway," Eamon cut in, clearly determined to tell
his tale, "Seamus had a large pot o' gold. You know

about a leprechaun's luck, don't you, lass?''

"I heard plenty of Irish tales at my da's knee. He never tired of them. I know all about leprechauns.''

Eamon's right eyebrow rose, giving him a devilish appearance. "Hmm . . . all about them, you say. Well, and I'd be betting you don't know this tale, you don't. So I'm going to tell it. You know, don't you, that if a mortal catches a leprechaun he can keep the pot o' gold?''

At Annie's nod, Eamon continued. "One day, Old Seamus Ban sat before a fire with a Cluricaune and some Fir Darrig friends—other faeries, them. And he recounted the only time one o' the Big Folk, as faeries sometimes call mortals, managed to lay hands on him.

"One fine morn, when Seamus was but a lad, he headed toward a nearby stream to work for a spell under an oak. There he sat, all alone as he thought, pounding nails into a fine black boot. Leprechauns are cobblers, you know.''

Annie nodded.

"Well, lass, suddenly one o' the Big Folk pounced on him. And wouldn't you think old Seamus would be afraid?''

Annie murmured her assent.

He chortled. "But nay! For you see, faeries think Big Folk are just plain stupid!''

At that, Annie gave him a skeptical look. Eamon threw his arms up defensively. " 'Tis naught but what *some* faeries think!''

"Go on,'' she said, wondering where this would lead.

"Aye, then. Old Seamus painted his captor as a giant man, three times his own height, and with powerful arms. Poor Seamus couldn't get away. The greedy poacher, for 'twas what he was, demanded Seamus's pot o' gold and threatened to drown the lad if he refused. Seamus had little choice, so he led the man on a merry dance, over a bridge and to a nearby quarry. In the end, Seamus took the man to a certain flat stone and said 'twas there he kept

A FAERIE TALE 147

his gold. So the man tugged and dug and pulled, but couldn't move the stone.''

For a moment, Eamon fell silent. His eyes held a faraway gleam, wistful, poignant. Annie thought surely he missed his home.

With a deep breath, however, he picked up the thread of his tale. ''Giving up, the brute said he would go for pick and shovel. When Seamus asked what he ought to do now that he'd helped all he could, the man sent the leprechaun on his way. Seamus walked a wee while down the road, but stayed close enough to spy. Before long, with a piece o' flint, the poacher cut a cross in the rock. Then he left for his tools.''

By now Annie's curiosity had been well and fully piqued. ''What happened next? Did the man get Seamus's pot of gold?''

Eamon chuckled. ''O' course, and he didn't get the treasure. Seamus made sure he got naught but trouble instead. Sure as soon as the man left, Seamus cut a cross into all the stones in that quarry!''

Patrick smiled.

Rosaleen murmured her appreciation.

Annie laughed. ''Another tale of a leprechaun and his tricks. I hadn't heard that particular one before, but Da told me others like it.''

By the light of the gaslamp, Annie saw Eamon don an earnest look. '' 'Twasn't just a story, Annie, lass. Seamus had wit and some smarts, he did. He knew that sometimes one needs to out-trick a trickster. Something tells me you might need to do that someday soon.''

That brought her up short. ''Me? But . . . why?''

Beneath Annie's fingers, Patrick's arm tensed. Glancing his way, she saw him shake his head. She turned back toward Eamon and read resolve in his sharp nod.

''Annie, lass, you can't go through life thinking only o' pictures and paints. There's evil and cheats everywhere.

148   GINNY REYES

You must take care o' what's yours, plan for your future, think your plans through with care.''

Annie frowned. "But . . . that's what Patrick's for!"

Clearly her comment shocked the man at her side. "What?" he asked.

"Well, yes. You're good at all those boring things. And you're in charge of Da's will—"

"I'm not 'in charge,' I'm the executor of the will. Those are two different things. We've been over this—"

"Ad nauseam," she inserted. "And I don't think it's pleasant conversation for a party. We can discuss this again the next time I go to your office . . ."

She let her words die off. *Oooops!* Patrick's annoyed look had changed to a glare. She shouldn't have said that. She'd spoken her mind without thinking through the effect her words might have. Again. *Oh, dear!*

Could Eamon and Patrick possibly be right about her spontaneous tendencies? Surely not. She was a woman, instinctive, open, unaffected. They were just men—methodical, logical, slightly dull.

Patrick's kisses were anything but boring, she thought, blushing. True. Not *everything* about the man could be considered dull, flat, lifeless . . .

Still, his refusal to heed her wishes about her own money remained an irritating reality. Despite all the times they'd discussed her inheritance, Annie couldn't say just why he refused to approve her request for the funds to open the Artist's Haven. She began to wonder what he might be keeping from her. After all, he had to have a reason for turning her down. She didn't really think "because it's inadvisable" sounded like a very good one anymore.

Not after hearing Eamon's story.

She cast a glance Patrick's way, but saw nothing besides his usual "banker" look: serious, focused, unyielding.

A FAERIE TALE   149

Why? Why did he continue to refuse her the means to fulfill her dream?

Sudden mistrust clouded her earlier excitement. Could Patrick have ulterior motives? Could he be the kind of cheat in Eamon's warning?

Surely not her straightlaced banker. Not Woodbury's most upright citizen. Not the man she seemed unable to resist.

Oh, dear. Annie realized this matter required careful consideration. To be honest, she didn't have much experience thinking things through. Not logically or meticulously. She'd always been better at acting, reacting, following her impulses. This time, though, she didn't think her instincts could be trusted. Not when it came to Patrick O'Toole.

His effect on her natural urges was too often devastating.

Realizing they'd stood outside Town Hall now for a while, she untangled her hand from Patrick's clasp and turned toward the open doors. The hum of voices inside grew louder the closer she came. Over the sound, she heard Patrick call her name.

"Come on," she said, "we're late. If we stay outside any longer, we might miss the food."

The others followed her lead, Patrick clearly not pleased by her efforts to elude him. But Annie knew she wouldn't do *any* clear thinking if he laid even one of those wicked, talented fingers anywhere on her.

She had to uncover the motivation behind his unreasonable refusals. It was her own money he continued to deny her.

A hideous possibility stole her breath, paralyzing her. Did he have designs on her money? Might he have decided to gain control of her inheritance by romancing it from her? Had that decision led him to break off his engagement to Serena? Had he invited her, Annie of the careless tongue and unguarded actions, to this evening's affair to launch his campaign?

With a gulp, she followed her companions—who had walked straight past her as she entertained her misgivings—to the long tables laden with food. Although they tried to draw her into the conversation, Annie found she couldn't speak around the fear in her throat. Her suspicions made her sick. Even after she served herself a slice of ham and a spoonful of potatoes, she didn't think she could swallow a bite.

Unable to further delay the unavoidable, she made a dash for a chair across the table from Patrick instead of taking the one at his side, as he obviously expected her to do.

That drew almost as many stares as their arrival had.

Everyone in town knew of the disaster at the bank. They also knew Patrick had ended his engagement the same day it started. So when he entered Town Hall in the company of the woman who figured prominently in the scandal, all eyes had turned on them.

Where they had stayed all this time.

Annie tapped a toe in frustration.

At the repeated sound, Rosaleen looked up from a dish of strawberries and cream. "Aren't ye hungry, Annie?"

"No."

Rosaleen's green eyes narrowed. "There's something wrong."

"Yes."

"Won't ye tell me?"

"Look around."

Rosaleen did as asked. "I see. You're the evening's entertainment, ye are."

"Mm-hmm."

"Are ye ready to go, then? We can, ye know."

She knew Rosaleen made her offer out of sympathy. But Annie wouldn't make her friend leave just because she had again blundered her impulsive way into a sticky situation. "No."

"Did ye expect any different?"

Annie sighed. "Not really. But it's not just them. Eamon's story . . . well, it has me worried."

"Fie, Annie! Don't ye give it a minute's thought. 'Tis but an old tale."

"But you must admit he had a point. There could very well be someone out there who wants to cheat me out of what's mine."

"Hmmm . . . ye haven't seemed too interested in the money up to now. Not since I met ye. At least, not for more than that Haven o' yours."

"Have you seen my Haven yet?"

"What Haven?"

"Precisely! I *have* no Haven. Do you know why?"

"Well, ye said Patrick opposes the idea because ye might lose all ye put into it. A bad investment, ye said he thought it."

"Hasn't it occurred to you that his opposition is a mite . . . vehement for a mere banker?"

Rosaleen's wave and smile discounted Annie's concern. " 'Tis obvious the man is more than a banker to ye, and you're more than a client to him."

Misery filled Annie's middle. "But just what *am* I to him? The key to a bank account? He's not rich, you know."

"I'm appalled to hear ye say that! Sure and ye can't mean what ye just said."

Misery made her wail, "How can I know?"

"Faith, and the man broke his engagement! No sooner than done with that task, he came running to tell ye. His actions—*and kisses*—suggest he's sweet on ye."

Annie stared at her twined fingers. "Or my money."

"Oh, Annie, I shouldn't think so. Give him a chance."

"I'm scared, Rosaleen." Annie gnawed on a thumb-

152 GINNY REYES

nail, then voiced her greatest fear. "I don't want him to think me a fool yet again."

"I know you're scared. Men are a frightening lot." Rosaleen cast a heavy-lidded glance at the two seated across from them. "Ah, lass. Just look at me. Eamon Dooley scares me more than a banshee's wail!"

"Bah! A blind man can see Eamon's crazy for you."

"One could say the same about Patrick O'Toole and you."

Annie wished she dared believe her friend's words, but now that doubts had crept into her mind, she couldn't shake them off. Not until she knew more about Patrick's motives, about the man himself.

"Perhaps," she said, sorry to have brought up the unpleasant topic during a festive event. "Look, there's no point in being gloomy tonight. I can't do a thing about it now, so let's smile and have a good time."

Rosaleen seemed relieved by her words. Annie didn't know if she could carry it off, but she would try her best to pretend.

An hour and a half later, however, after dodging Patrick repeatedly, she approached the punch table, still mulling over her troublesome thoughts. She had reached no conclusions, had no more answers than when she confided in Rosaleen.

Her back to the table, she scanned the crowd, but saw no sign of the ever assiduous Mr. O'Toole. He hadn't been easy to evade.

"Why the dismal expression, my dear?" the Reverend Birmingham asked as he approached. "Aren't you having a good time?"

"Oh, I don't have the melancholies," she lied, pasting her cheeriest smile on her face. "I'm taking a breather. I've talked myself dry."

"Might I serve you a cup of lemonade punch?"

"How kind of you, Reverend!"

"A pleasure, my dear."

A FAERIE TALE 153

With a murmur of thanks, she took the cup he offered. After a single sip, however, she stifled a grimace. Someone with a sweet tooth had gone too far with the sugar. Determined to put on a good face for the kind man at her side, she forced herself to take another taste.

"Did you lose your escort?" he asked.

Annie's cheeks warmed. "I . . . er . . . needed a moment to myself."

The reverend's doe-brown eyes filled with concern. "Mr. O'Toole hasn't made a nuisance of himself, has he?"

A nuisance? "No . . ." A problem? Definitely. "Not really," she said. "Although he seems to take escorting a lady a bit seriously."

"Oh, that boy's been like that ever since I've known him."

"Since he came to work in Woodbury?"

The reverend shook his shiny head. "No, no, dear. I've known his family longer than that. I met them while I pastored a small congregation south of Lancaster. He's always been too serious for his own good. It's splendid to see him with you."

Annie lifted a brow but, choosing discretion over curiosity, took another sip of the awful lemonade. A lemon slice nudged her lip, the rind's tang bitter despite the excessive sweetness. She put down the cup, unable to stomach another drop.

The Reverend Birmingham's attention seemed to turn inward, toward the past. "Yes, he had a nice family. His poor mother went through a lot, as I heard her tell, raising him on her own in a foreign land."

Annie's curiosity became engaged for the second time that evening. "I didn't know."

"He doesn't say much about it, but Maggie related some of the hardships they endured when he was young. The boy's father died before he was born, you see."

Her own pain upon losing her father brought a surge

of sympathy for Patrick. It seemed far worse never to have known a father's love than to lose it after years of joy. "How sad."

"Indeed. Still, he grew into a good man, if somewhat dull."

Annie shrugged. "*If* that's really what it is."

"What do you mean by that?"

Annie bit her bottom lip, wondering if it wouldn't help to unburden herself to a man of the cloth. "I know you're not a priest, but do you hold to the same rules of silence for private matters?"

A smile brightened his round face. "What do you think?"

"Well, after all you've confided about Patrick . . ."

The Reverend Birmingham chuckled. "No, dear. What I told you were plain facts many people know about your young man."

"He is *not* my young man."

With a wink, the reverend countered, "That's not how I hear it! But that's not the point, is it? Have no fear. Whatever you say dies with me."

Annie sighed in relief. "It suddenly occurred to me that perhaps the reason Patrick is so obstinate about releasing funds from my account—he's the executor of my da's will, you know—is that he has . . . designs on those funds."

The Reverend Birmingham's sparse eyebrows darted up toward his naked scalp. "Designs? Surely you don't mean—"

"Yes, I do," she said, cutting off the very words Rosaleen had voiced only a short while ago. "Why else would he spend months arguing with me, making me feel like a fool, then suddenly start kissing and—"

"Oho!"

She waved impatiently. "No, no! Listen to me, please. Why would Patrick treat me like a bothersome pest ever since my father died—while courting Serena Keller—then

... *poof*! He breaks off their engagement only hours after proposing. The very next day, he comes calling on me, trying very hard to charm me.''

"I'd say the boy got some sense knocked into him," answered the reverend.

Annie smiled. "Thank you for the compliment, but I don't think that's it at all. Don't you think he might have realized that since someday I'll get control of my trust, it would be to his advantage to romance his way back to it? Maybe even—the louse!—marry me for Da's money?''

A plethora of curses shot up from the vicinity of Annie's ankles. The punch table began to rock. The curses mushroomed to a roar. One end of the table rose sharply. The punch bowl teetered, then slid down the upsurging side. As the table jerked the rest of the way up, the massive glass vessel flew toward Annie and the Reverend Birmingham.

They ducked, dropping out of the heavy container's trajectory. Sticky-sweet beverage doused them. Then the bowl crashed into a wall, showering the area with dangerous glitter.

As Annie wiped her eyes, she saw the good pastor pick slices of lemon from his well-padded middle. One errant yellow wheel slithered down the man's pate toward his nose.

The expletives never faltered.

Patrick stormed out from behind the table. "How dare you accuse me of such foul behavior?" he bellowed. "I have spent months fighting this . . . spell you've cast on me! I'd sooner swim to Ireland than marry your money. You're driving me crazy! You, Annie Brennan. Just you!"

Twelve

Marching home, wrapped in what dignity she had left, Annie gave serious thought to moving from Woodbury. Not only did everyone always know her least indiscretion the moment she made it, but each time she and that miserable Patrick O'Toole tangled, not a soul missed hearing every mortifying detail.

She was sick of being the town's favorite scandal.

Poor Reverend Birmingham. He had only been trying to help, but all he got for his effort was a ruined suit and a spoilt evening.

Why had Patrick hidden under the punch table? Annie didn't know a soul—not even herself—who would think of doing that.

Who would have thought the controlled, dignified, and oftentimes dull banker possessed such a magnificent temper?

Annie heard footsteps behind her. With a startled sound, she spun around. When she realized Patrick had nearly caught up with her, she turned, tipped her chin, and picked up her pace.

"Annie!"

Why couldn't he just let her crawl home and die in peace? "What do you want?" she asked without slowing.

A FAERIE TALE 157

Two heartbeats later he reached her side and, grasping her elbow, pulled her to a standstill. "I brought you to this latest calamity and I will see you home."

"Oh, I see. It's still—as always—a matter of your blasted pride."

"No, dammit!" he spit out. "You made some accusations back there and you won't even let me defend myself."

"Why should I? Your actions come across loud and clear."

He raked back the brown waves tumbling over his forehead. "Yes. I believe they do." He began ticking off his fingers. "I have done my damnedest to protect your inheritance—your livelihood—from your most far-fetched notions. I have turned my life upside down to avoid dragging you into scandal. I broke off an engagement I sought for months so that I could in good conscience explore this . . . passion between us. After all that, you can still accuse me of ulterior motives?"

Annie refused to meet his gaze, as she knew what she'd find there. "All I know, Patrick, is that *nothing* ever works when you're involved."

"I could say the same about you."

"You have. Frequently."

"Is that it?" he asked, clearly bewildered and exasperated. "Are you trying to get back at me for hurting your artistic sensibilities?"

"I'm *trying* to get back home." She resumed her trek. "If you don't mind, I'm dripping and sticky, uncomfortable and tired."

"Don't forget bullheaded and ornery and confounding, too."

"Lovely." What on earth had she found to admire in the man? "Thank you for your praise, sir. Your efforts to improve the situation are impressive. You must persuade lots of folks by insulting them regularly."

He made an odd grinding sound.

Fine. She didn't have to talk anymore, either. She was mad. Disappointed. Frightened by the attraction between them. Scared he might indeed be feigning his interest in her. She had no energy or desire for polite chitchat, and since he obviously wasn't listening to her ...

When they reached her house, she didn't break stride but kept right on going up the porch steps and to the door. Unlocking it, she slipped inside and tried to shut him out, but he was too quick for her. Sticking the toe of his polished black shoe between the door and its frame, he forced his way in.

Slamming the door when he showed no intention of leaving, she asked, "Why won't you leave me alone?"

"I want to talk to you."

"But *I* don't want to talk to *you*. I have nothing more to say."

Following her to the parlor, he took her hand when she headed for the sofa. He made her face him, then, pulling her closer, placed her hand on his chest. "There's always this," he murmured.

Beneath her fingers, his heart beat faster. He curved his hands around her waist. Her heart picked up its beat.

The intimacy in their position, the knowledge that just touching affected them both so much, made Annie tremble. Although she'd never had a beau before, she had danced with other young men, but none had made her knees weak, her head spin, her body burn like wildfire.

Patrick O'Toole did.

Although her head screamed warnings, reminding her of the threat to her trust fund, her heart continued pounding its song for Patrick. Annie knew it would be wisest to send him home, but the words stuck in her throat.

Patrick gathered her right up against his warm firm body, and Annie stiffened, but not from fear or distaste. She wanted their closeness, to feel his arms tight around her, his lips hungry at her mouth, even while the questions roared through her head. No, her hesitation sprang from her inexperience, her lack of knowledge as to how to proceed. For she knew they would indeed proceed unless she told him to go.

"Are you fighting me?" Patrick whispered. "I won't hurt you. I just feel . . . so much when I'm with you. I know you feel it, too."

Annie lifted her gaze to his. The flames she had often seen there glowed darkly, beckoning her, luring her closer with their heat. She had tasted Patrick's passion before, and she feared she'd grown addicted already.

"Should I leave?" he asked.

"N-not yet."

"May I . . . ?"

"What?"

"This. . . ."

With exquisite gentleness, Patrick molded his mouth to hers. The first touch of his lips brought a rush of fire searing through her. The heat stunned her, as did her sudden hunger.

Maddeningly, he kept the kiss chaste—almost, since before too long, his gentle nipping along the line of her lips gave her more of what she wanted. Her breath caught for a second, then she sighed, opening her mouth to his. Patrick's arms tightened, bringing her flush up to every hard line, every tough ridge of his body.

The tip of his tongue entered her mouth, painting bonfires wherever it touched. Annie trembled, and each tremor brought her into new contact with the heat raging in Patrick, the heat he willingly and masterfully shared with her.

When his teeth closed over her bottom lip, Annie felt her body's response in every private crevice and mound. He laved her captive flesh with his tongue, making her head reel in response. With another stroke, he made fireworks burst behind her closed eyelids, then releasing her lip slowly, he allowed his teeth to rake softly across it as it slipped from his grasp.

Annie's breasts responded, growing heavy, the nipples tightening. She gasped at the sensation, and felt his tongue follow her indrawn breath farther into her mouth. His caress deepened, became intimate, shocking. A husky sound broke deep in her throat.

As usual, Patrick remained in control.

Annie grew frustrated, knowing she'd felt wildness in him before. She wanted to feel it again, not knowing why he fought so hard to contain it. She began to return his kiss, making long, repeated glides over his tongue.

Everything urged her closer to him, begging her to fuse them as one. Bringing her arms around his neck, she pressed her aching breasts against his chest. The pressure momentarily soothed her need, but soon she wanted—needed—more. She deepened her kiss, tasting his rich flavor.

And she went up in flames.

Wanting to scorch him with her, she caught his bottom lip with her teeth, as he had done to her.

He moaned.

She sucked gently, hungrily.

He trembled.

When she lapped at him with her tongue, his arms turned to hot steel around her, his tongue shooting deep into her mouth as if his very life depended on the essence of her desire.

As he drank of her, Patrick's shaking hands roved her back, shaped her waist, fitted themselves to her buttocks. He lifted her that way, pressing the hard ridge low on his abdomen into her yielding, fabric-shrouded center. Annie groaned, consigning the cloth to perdition, wanting more of the recklessness she felt thrumming through him.

His fingers sank deeper into her flesh, and he ground himself against her once more. Annie mimicked the motion of his hips, loving the guttural noise she wrenched from him.

A FAERIE TALE

Another searing sweep of his tongue. Another flex of his hips. Another sound from his chest.

Annie felt herself melting, her most private core softening. Then his hands left her bottom, running up her ribs to cup her breasts. She whimpered, rubbing—*hard*—against his hands. She wanted to feel his mouth on her again, like that other night, when his wet heat had covered the aching crests.

Patrick seemed to interpret her need without words, for his hands slipped to her back, and he began undoing the silk-covered buttons down her spine. Not once did his mouth abandon hers, though, his tongue seeking, stealing her secrets. Then she felt a coolness at her back.

His hands went to her shoulders. Awkward in his urgency, he struggled to lower the dress. He fought the fullness of the sleeves, tried to drag them down her arms. A sound of frustration rumbled in his chest, but he never left her lips.

Annie reached up, hungry for his touch, and pushed his hands away. In two swift strokes, she dislodged the bodice, and it pooled at her waist. He took over, dragging his fingers across the low edge of her chemise, pulling at the satin ties that held it closed. Seconds later, her breasts felt first the chill of the night, then the burn of Patrick's hands.

She wanted Patrick to satisfy the ache in her flesh. When he tore his mouth from hers, she knew what would come next. She arched her back, met his mouth on its way down. When his lips closed on an aching nub, she hissed, "Yessss . . ."

Patrick heard Annie's welcome, and the last of his restraint broke. Her scent of jasmine and woman filled his senses, just as the flavor of that taut nipple flew straight to his head. He suckled, he nipped, he drew her breast deeper in his mouth, again exhilarated by her passion, her response, her heat. With a soft kiss to the tip he'd just loved, he turned to the other and resumed his feasting.

Annie's back bowed higher as she sought more contact with his mouth.

Without releasing her, he slipped an arm beneath her knees. He brought her up against his chest, and her arms curled around his neck. "Upstairs?" he asked.

"Mm-hmmm . . ."

Cradling his precious cargo to his heart, he studied her pretty face as he took the stairs with care. Annie's eyes resembled pools of healing waters, deep, mysterious, but somehow familiar and refreshing. The freckles over the bridge of her nose and across the curve of her cheeks lent her an innocent sweetness that her fiery passion belied. And yet Patrick knew the artlessness was real, just as real as the hunger and fire burning in her. The flush on her cheekbones gave evidence of her passion.

With a downward glance, he caught sight of the abundant, creamy flesh he had paid homage to only moments ago. Everything about Annie was generous, even her dimensions—not fat, just lush and satisfying for a man. A hungry man, one whose attention grew riveted to the tightened, pebbled flesh of her nipples. Velvet soft. Sweet. He dropped a kiss on one hard crest.

"H-here," she said.

He turned into the room she indicated, and immediately identified it as hers. Jasmine and Annie bloomed there, perfuming the air. Patrick gave himself up to passion, to need, to Annie's intoxicating allure.

Setting her on her feet by the bed, he cupped her face. Their gazes met. He read her desire in the depths of her eyes, the reddened flesh of her lips, the proud tilt of her breasts. He took a rough breath and asked, "Are you sure?"

"More sure than I've ever been."

"And your suspicions—"

"Hush," she whispered, covering his mouth with her fingers. She pressed her naked breasts against him, stealing his breath. "I'm sure."

A FAERIE TALE 163

Patrick trembled, knowing that in seconds she would again catch fire in his arms, under his hands, his mouth, his body. He wasn't overly experienced, but in that experience he had never known a woman to come alive at his touch as Annie did.

She humbled him. Burned him. Scared him.

"Sweetheart . . ." At that moment, he realized how much she had come to mean to him, not just as a sensual woman but as the most intriguing female he had ever known. The only one to incite him to madness, to tear through his reserve, to destroy his plans for his life.

She replaced them with magic and passion. "Annie . . ."

"Kiss me. Again."

This kiss was different from their earlier ones. It had purpose. She gave, he took, then gave back to her again.

He'd dreamed of claiming her mouth like this, he'd longed for it, hungered for it, and now she gave him the right. Lifting her arms around his neck, she made him forget the differences between them, bringing him only thoughts of pleasure, need, desire.

Soon, it wasn't enough to kiss her and feel her soft flesh through his clothes. He wanted more—*everything* she had to give. He pulled his lips from hers and turned her around.

"Patrick?"

"Shhh . . . your dress, it's in my way."

"Mm-hmmm . . ."

In his rush, he tore off a blue-satin ribbon at her waist and cursed his clumsiness. She giggled. The sound brought an ache to his heart, making him hunger still more. Finally he finished the task, then dragged the masses of feminine froth down her legs.

Which were as appealing as he once imagined, especially covered in cobwebs of midnight lace. Satin garters cinched her thighs, and Patrick swore his heart would leap from his chest at the sight. His wildest fantasies had failed to conjure a picture so erotic, so intimate, so his.

He studied the vision of femininity before him. Round pale breasts crowned in deep rose, creamy skin blushed with a hint of pink, black curls hiding dark treasures, legs so curvy and delightful a man could spend hours adoring them.

His body refused to let him wait so long. He rubbed a knuckle against a garter, then hooked his finger through it. His lips blazed a trail of kisses as the lacy stocking dropped without its support. He nibbled, licked, and tasted every inch he uncovered, knowing he'd return at some other less urgent time to retrace his discovery.

When he reached her ankle, Annie placed a hand on his head, a hand that trembled. He glanced up and saw eyes slitted to a burning blue, lips damp, the tip of her tongue at the corner of a small, seductive smile.

His fingers shook as he removed her other stocking, but despite his urgency, the raging hunger of his flesh, he took the time to kiss this leg, too. When only her feet remained covered, Patrick lifted them one by one, and removed the satin dance shoes and the last of the cobwebbed silk.

She stood proudly, surprisingly at ease with her nakedness, even though no other man had gazed at the feast before him. Then she smiled, and with purpose took hold of his tie. She pulled him up, whispering, ''I think you're wearing too much.''

His eyes popped open, and his breath snagged in his chest. Annie had said that? Looked at him with such bold intent? *His* Annie?

She slid his tie free of his collar. A bundle of surprises, his Annie. The woman whose fingers deftly unfastened his shirt buttons in a flash. When those gifted digits reached for his belt, however, he covered them with his hands. ''I'd better take over from here, or I can't promise much.''

Her quizzical look made him chuckle.

''You'll learn.''

"I hope so."

This time he laughed and dragged his belt from his trousers. He undid the buttons and dragged the pants down his legs. For the moment—and for the sake of his lasting power—he kept his drawers on.

Smiling in delight, he scooped the warm, silky woman into his arms, then laid her on the bed. Against white cotton eyelet, Annie's skin gleamed like cream, her hair shone like midnight, her eyes sparkled like sapphires. And her lips . . . ah, her lips parted and offered him another taste of heaven.

Leaning on an arm, he came down at her side. He filled his free hand with a breast. His mouth cherished hers. Together they stoked the flames of passion hotter than before.

Soft hands raced across his shoulders, soft fingers tangled in his chest hair, soft thumbs rubbed his nipples. And he tasted Annie, sweet, passionate Annie. Who would soon be completely his.

Leaving her mouth, he kissed a path to her breast, again drinking in her jasmine scent. As he drew a ring of kisses around the plump white mound, Annie's legs scissored, and she made a delicious gasping sound. When he lapped at the tight rosy nipple, she crossed one leg over the other, and the gasp roughened to a moan. When he finally drew the velvet crest deep into his mouth, the moan became a cry of need, and her belly quivered.

He covered that satin skin with his hand, then slowly, inch by excruciating inch, he went lower, until his fingers met crisp curls. Again she surprised him. Instead of stiffening, as he'd expected, she parted her thighs, an invitation he hastily accepted. With infinite care, he delved through the hair until he reached intimate flesh.

Annie was damp and hot; she felt so good against his hand that Patrick had the urge to rip off his drawers and sink all the way to ecstasy. But he couldn't. Not yet. He had to take his time, as this would be her first.

He buried his fingers in the heat between her thighs. Annie cried in surprise, but didn't clamp her legs shut. Her response led him further. His hand curled into her, his fingers deepening his caress.

Annie's body bowed, and she called out in pleasure, the sharp sound mellowing into another deep, raspy gasp. He dragged his hand across her flesh, caressing, pressing into her hidden silk.

She cried out once more.

He repeated his motion, just to hear her moan for him.

And he knew he couldn't take much more. Standing, he ripped off his drawers and came down upon her. She tipped up her hips, seeking more of him.

Patrick nudged her legs apart, and she gave him room. Slowly he probed her entrance and began to join them as one. Her murmurs were sounds of pleasure, so he proceeded with the same care. Shivers ran through her the deeper he went. He clenched his teeth to keep from plunging all the way in.

Sweat beaded on Patrick's forehead from the effort of his restraint. Annie's slick flesh felt better than he'd dreamed, and his body, primed and desperate, clamored for swift release. But his habitual control again came to his aid.

He pushed in again, shuddered again, hungered again. Soon, however, he reached a barrier. He paused, bit his lower lip to keep from driving through, and groaned.

"Why—why'd you . . . stop?" she asked.

"Your body stopped me. Does it hurt?"

"It's *enormous*, and I can't believe you got it all in there, but it doesn't hurt."

Patrick dropped his forehead to hers and chuckled grimly. "Only you, Annie, would say something like that at a time like this. I'm glad you're impressed, but I'm barely in. What comes next may—probably will—hurt you."

"You mean . . . there's more?"

A FAERIE TALE   167

He gave thanks for the eagerness in her voice. "Oh, sweetheart, there's more, lots more, but I'm afraid this time won't feel so good to you."

"I don't know, Patrick, everything you did felt great— *feels* great!"

He laughed again, glad for the reprieve. At least he wouldn't rip through her like a raging bull now, and perhaps he'd manage to slow down enough to comfort her in her pain. "You're so sweet . . ."

He kissed her, and let his hips resume a gentle rocking. Then, taking a deep breath, he pushed through. She gasped. Bucked. Shoved at his shoulders. Cried into his mouth.

Patrick held himself still, thinking of bank accounts, the combination to the vault, the chaotic state of his office. But nothing took his attention from her hold on his flesh. When she fell back onto the bed, he felt the drag of her depths against him, and moved forward again, following her. Slowly he pulled out then returned. Through sheer willpower, he kept his movements slow and deliberate, and was soon rewarded by one of her gasps of desire.

Perhaps . . . he could bring her pleasure after all. Rising onto an elbow, he slipped a hand through wet folds and found the jewel sheltered there. In counterpoint to the movement of his hips, he slowly circled then skimmed the nub, watching Annie's eyes close, feeling the pleasure sweep through her as she raised her hips against his. More and more he sought her response, and soon she cried with each breath she drew, each touch he gave.

Her slick embrace heightened his need, but he braced himself against the urge to climb toward the approaching peak. Hunger raged through him, demanding release.

Then tremors rippled inside her, and he deepened the pressure of his caress, the depth of his penetration. Once . . . twice . . .

Surprise rang out in the rough sound that burst from her throat. Pleasure roared through her bowed body and shone in her flushed skin. Patrick felt her completion in the hot helpless convulsions of her inner flesh.

That slick clenching drew at him, and he responded by driving deeper into her. Her knees clasped his sides, and she murmured his name. He pushed as deep as he could go, then took her mouth in a kiss equally deep. He moved faster, harder, losing control.

His breath failed him, and he ripped his mouth from hers. With each thrust of his hips, she called his name in a rough voice, the sound another intimate caress. She clung to him, moved with him, returned the pleasure she had received.

Abruptly Patrick locked his hips against hers. He bucked, lifted his head, then closed his eyes and shuddered violently, repeatedly. Ecstasy ripped through him.

His senses swirled, and her name broke from his lips.

It took him a while to recover enough to push away and examine his partner. He feared his loss of control might have hurt her, frightened her—worse, disgusted her. But when he looked at Annie, he noticed first her smug smile. Then he dared glance at her eyes and found knowledge there. A woman's knowledge.

His Annie. Tenderly he kissed her puffy lips, then slowly withdrew. Her cry of dismay flowed over his mouth, and he whispered, ''I'm not going anywhere. I'm just too heavy—''

''You're not,'' she shot in response.

''It's better for you this way,'' he murmured, glad she wanted him near. He curled her into his side, cradling her head on his shoulder. Silky black hair cascaded over his skin.

He couldn't believe he noticed. He was shocked he could even think. The pleasure he'd found in Annie's body should have scorched what coherent thought he might once have been capable of. But he seemed to have impressive powers of recovery. He suspected he'd soon hunger for her again.

A FAERIE TALE   169

He'd take it slower next time. She would undoubtedly be sore. Yes, he'd give her precisely that. Long slow loving, tender and sweet, for his Annie.

With that in mind, he surrendered to oblivion.

Patrick's breath deepened in slumber. Annie couldn't imagine sleeping right then. Not when her body still felt ghostlike shimmers of pleasure shooting through it, the slight soreness between her legs reminding her how it had felt to be stretched by him, claimed by him, loved by him.

"Magic," she whispered. The man had given her magic.

Despite her lack of experience, she knew she'd done the same for him. That sort of knowledge seemed instinctive, the kind a woman gained when she satisfied her man.

She'd seen Patrick's eyes close as his body tautened above hers. She'd seen the skin of his face pull harshly over drawn features. She'd felt the convulsive spasms of his hips, the hidden pulsing of his flesh, the heat of his release.

She'd heard the desperate way he called her name, as if she were the only person alive, the only one who mattered, the only one for him.

Again she smiled, remembering the pleasure. He'd taken her straight to heaven.

Her blood began to simmer. Private areas quickened. Her smile turned wicked, and her eyes closed. She wondered how soon they could go there again.

"Sure and they should have closed the window," muttered Eamon as he led Rosaleen from Annie's porch.

Her cheeks blazing from the sounds they had heard coming from Annie's room, Rosaleen shot him a glare. "I doubt they spared the window a thought."

Eamon shrugged. " 'Tis true. But what if the Reverend Birmingham had come to look after wee Annie?"

"Aye, but he didn't." Embarrassed, she was. She also feared Eamon's unlucky proximity to the lovers might have an unfortunate impact on the excellent results of her latest magical spell.

"I think we should . . . go for a walk," she said, giving him her most inviting smile. "Until the light in her room goes out, ye know." She took off with a swish of her hips, heading toward the outskirts of town.

With a glance over her shoulder, she checked Eamon's reaction. His eyes followed each tilt of her behind, and if he didn't watch himself, he'd likely trip over his tongue.

Then she saw him shake his head and follow in her wake. She chuckled, pleased with her effect on the poor man.

"Won't you be waiting for me?"

"Catch up—if ye can!"

Sooner than she'd expected, he grabbed her hand and matched her steps. By the light of the full moon, Rosaleen noted the speculative stare her companion gave her. "And what might ye be thinking, Eamon Dooley?"

"Hmmm . . ."

"What kind of answer is that?"

"That of a man who is thinking a bit."

Rosaleen gave him a slow wink. "How rare o' ye."

He blinked. "Hush, *cailin*. 'Tis just I've had an idea."

"Novel," she retorted.

"Sometimes you talk too much, but you're so lovely a man is willing to forgive you much."

"Thank ye kindly. And will ye be sharing that thought ye had?"

They'd come out of town in the direction of Annie's painting spot. When Rosaleen realized how close they were, she decided to continue to the stand of trees, dispatch Eamon shortly, and cast another spell on the lovers in Annie's bed.

She walked a bit farther and wondered why Eamon wouldn't answer. "Well?" she asked, giving him another slow smile.

His eyes twinkled. "I have something to show you."

A FAERIE TALE

''Really?'' She made sure she sounded interested, just not too much. 'Twas best to keep him on his toes.

''Really.''

''What would that be?''

''Would you be wanting to see my . . . *shillelagh*?''

''What would I be wanting with your walking stick?''

Deviltry danced in emerald eyes. A naughty grin tweaked his lips.

Rosaleen groaned. She'd been had. By a consummate trickster.

'' 'Twasn't me oaken staff I meant. Although tonight the one bears a stiff resemblance to t'other!''

Thirteen

Rosaleen blinked. Mayhap her flirtation had worked a wee bit *too* well! Although she truly liked Eamon, and his interest flattered and thrilled her, she had other matters to see to. Like Patrick's future. Her magic had gotten her godchild right where she wanted him, but as an added measure of assurance, she really should cast another spell.

First, though, she needed to come up with a distraction—and quick! A reason to send Eamon away so she could get back to business. Which wouldn't be easy, since she'd just used her sensual wiles to lure him along behind her.

She didn't want him to lose interest in her altogether, however, as she reciprocated that interest. She just wasn't ready for what he proposed. "Faith, and I'm flattered, Eamon. Only, I think we ought to know each other better. Ye see, I've never been kissed before, or felt what I feel when ye kiss me . . ."

Rosaleen thought he preened at that. *Good, good.* "I think ye can understand me wanting to wait awhile, then." She lifted her hand and caressed his cheek.

Red spread over his face. "Oh, aye, *cailin,* I understand. I've never felt like this"—he gestured to the front of his trousers where she saw an impressive bulge—''before, either.''

Rosaleen stared. She couldn't help herself. What he displayed struck her as daunting indeed.

Before she could come up with a response, he added, ''Don't make me wait too long. I'm learning a man could fair *die* from this condition.''

She gulped. ''I-I'll be thinking on it.'' How could she not? That would create a problem, too. She had to concentrate on her mission. ''But first I must see to Patrick's future.''

Eamon gave a careless wave. ''Don't you be giving it a care. Eamon Dooley has everything under control.''

She narrowed her gaze. ''How could ye even say that after the disaster ye made o' tonight's Benefit Supper!''

''They're together in bed now, aren't they?''

Rosaleen gaped. ''You're taking credit for it?''

A bullish expression spread on his face. ''I am that.''

Crossing her arms under her breasts, she tapped a toe. ''Who gave Patrick the fine idea of crawling under a table to eavesdrop on Annie and the good reverend?''

Eamon smacked his fists on his lean hips. ''Well, I didn't tell him to go roaring and throwing tables and pouring buckets o' lemonade on the man! Patrick did that all on his very own.''

Rosaleen lifted a skeptical eyebrow. '' 'Twould seem to me your *un*lucky presence at the supper caused the trouble in the first place.''

''What do you have to say about him following wee Annie home?'' he asked with a triumphant smile. ''I'll say I brought me lass good luck. Patrick followed her, and 'twould seem he did his explaining.'' Taking hold of his lapels, he rocked back on his boot heels. ''How about the mattress dance they're doing? You can't say I brought her bad luck there. She didn't sound angry a'tall. You heard her call his name all husky and happy.''

Rosaleen's cheeks heated. Would she make those same

174 GINNY REYES

sounds if she and Eamon were to do the same . . . mattress dance? The possibility intrigued her. She took a speculative survey of the man before her.

Hmmm. . . .

Then she remembered the bulge. Just how would *that* figure in? Sure and 'twouldn't fit . . . would it? She shivered, partly in fear—but only partly.

'Twouldn't happen tonight, but she didn't think she'd go back to *Tyeer na N-og* without exploring all the human possibilities!

Then she pulled the reins on her thoughts. She had to concentrate on her task. *Fie on your foolishness, Rosaleen!* She had to think of Patrick—Patrick and her magic and the wand to be earned. " 'Twas me love charm that brought about their loving.''

From out of the corner of his mouth, he blew a lock of hair off his forehead. "Sure and you're the most stubborn o' women! If you weren't lovelier than life, why I'd . . . I'd . . .''

Although the compliment went straight to her head, Rosaleen chose to ignore it, and waited for him to continue. Then waited some more. Finally, when he made it obvious he couldn't go on, she realized she'd won the argument. She smiled. "Can't come up with a fitting torture, eh?''

He snorted. "I don't want to torture you. I told you what I want with you, but you said you need more time.''

Rosaleen bit her bottom lip. One of these days she'd learn to think before she spoke. "Go on with ye, Eamon. Leave a lass alone to her thoughts. Go wait for Patrick to return home.''

"Aye, 'tis more than obvious you're a fractious one tonight.''

Rosaleen bit down on her tongue to keep from spitting out a retort, since it was in her best interests—and Patrick's—for Eamon to be gone. "Go,'' she urged. "I don't want to argue any more with a luckless leprechaun.''

A FAERIE TALE

Gesturing in frustration, Eamon countered, "You're the one who doesn't know how to cast a decent working spell! Why, I'd wager that silly charm o' yours caused the lemonade disaster."

"O' course, and it didn't!"

"It surely did! Your magic *always* goes awry."

Rosaleen's temper heated at his unfair accusation. "You've frightful bad luck, ye do, and 'tis your luck that caused tonight's trouble. Go to bed and keep that cursed luck far from me godchild!"

" 'Twas your spell gone bad."

" 'Twas your bad luck."

With a final glare, he said, "Foine, foine. I'll leave. Soon enough, you'll see whose magic works best."

She gave him a superior smile. "Aye, Eamon, soon enough *you'll* see."

"Will you be all right if I leave—"

"O' course, and I'll be fine."

His chin jutted out pugnaciously. "I don't like leaving you—"

"I asked ye to go, and I'm after telling ye I'll be fine. I didn't get to live four hundred years and not learn a thing or two."

"Oh, you're ancient, you are, lass," he scoffed. "Come back when you get to be *six* hundred and you've found a wee dram o' sense, like some of us older faeriefolk have!"

"Eamon Dooley, if I have to ask ye to leave me alone one more time, I'll never give another thought to your blasted *shillelagh*!"

His jaw dropped. He blinked. Finally he burst into peals of glee. "Aha! So you *do* think about me cudgel, then!"

Rosaleen near died. How could she have said that? "I'm after warning ye! Me answer's going to be a loud no—"

Eamon clapped a hand over her mouth. "Hush! Don't say no. You don't really mean it."

GINNY REYES

When she shook her head to shake off his hold, he raised his hands in surrender and took a few steps back. "I'm leaving, I'm leaving, but remember, one day I won't." He turned and walked down the field toward the road. He turned his head then and tossed over his shoulder, " 'Twill be *our* turn soon enough."

'Tis what I'm a-fearing, she thought, then reminded herself she'd succeeded in sending him away. She stifled the tweak of disappointment she suddenly—suprisingly—felt.

"Patrick," she muttered as she watched Eamon jog down the road. "Patrick, Patrick, Patrick." She had to concentrate on her godchild and the spell she planned to cast, one that would reinforce the successes she'd already obtained. But . . . what exactly should she do? She had already sprinkled Patrick with charmed petals—even Annie caught some, too, that time—and she had given him a love amulet.

Rosaleen thought and thought, then smiled. "A love potion!"

A field like this one might yield the ingredients she needed. Now, if she could just remember what other faeries had told her about love potions. Which herbs worked and which ones didn't? O' course, and she would also need a proper spell to chant while she made the brew.

To her dismay, however, she found naught she could use. Plain clover didn't have magical qualities as far as she knew, and neither did stray blades of grass.

Gazing up at the moon, she lifted her arms and called down the power of the Goddess to help her with her mission, one she simply *had* to perform well.

As Rosaleen made her way back to Annie's house, hoping the lovers had finished . . . mattress dancing, the moon darted in and out of cloud clusters, alternately bathing her in its gleam and shrouding her in shadow. Rosaleen kept a keen eye out for any herb or wildflower that might prove beneficial in a potion, but she began to get discouraged the longer she walked. Nothing. She could see nothing that would work.

Then, when she least expected it, she found precisely what she had been looking for.

About ten feet from the side of the road, at the base of what was once a farmhouse but had become a pile of rubble, a pair of leafy stems danced in the mild breeze. A beam of silver flowed straight from the moon and surrounded the unpretentious plants with sparkling light.

Approaching, she examined the bits of green. From the hairy stems and leaves emanated a noxious stench, and when Rosaleen touched the tip of a finger to the plant, she felt the stickiness characteristic of henbane. She'd often heard of henbane's strong aphrodisiac powers, and she knew the Goddess had led her straight to the plants. She gave thanks for the Lady's help.

Now she could prepare the potion and persuade Patrick to drink it. With a wicked smile, she remembered henbane supposedly made a man "delectable" to a woman. That sounded just like what she wanted to achieve.

With enormous care, and after thanking the plants for their contribution to her mission, Rosaleen broke off a number of leaves and wrapped them in the white linen handkerchief in her pocket. Humming a pleasant ditty, she hurried back to Annie's house.

When she arrived, however, a surprise awaited her— snoring—on the Brennan front porch. "What are ye doing here, Eamon Dooley? Didn't I send ye to Patrick's house?"

Eamon blinked repeatedly, then stood and yawned. "Wha—what d'you want?"

"I want to know why you're here again. Do ye want your foul luck to spoil everything now?"

Eamon's lingering sleepiness fled. "Hah! I came to bring me wee lassie luck. As I left you on that field, I turned around for a last look and had the pleasure o' watching you lift your arms to the Goddess. I heard you ask for help with your spell. I wasn't inclined to let you ruin the results o' me lucky presence at the supper tonight.''

Rosaleen gave him a smug smile. ''I'll have ye know I didn't cast a single spell.'' *Yet.* ''And 'twould indeed be for the best if ye went on home. I'm frightful tired and will be retiring as soon as I'm inside.''

''O' course, and you're after sending me home! Who's to say what you'll *really* be doing once I leave? I can't abandon Annie to the mercies o' your worthless spells.''

Rosaleen sputtered indignantly. ''Why . . . who . . . how dare ye say that? Annie is my *friend*! I would *never* do her harm.''

Eamon made a conciliatory motion with his head. ''Foine, foine, *cailin*, no need to get so fractious. But remember when you cast that flower-petal spell on Patrick? 'Twas wee Annie who suffered embarrassment when Serena found them kissing.''

Rosaleen jabbed a finger at his chest. '' 'Twas after ye interfered that Serena showed up.''

Eamon grabbed the pointing digit. ''I didn't 'interfere,' as you say. I was there at your side all along.''

She tugged at her captured hand. '' 'Tis the same.''

He refused to let go. ''How so?''

Rosaleen felt the heat of his grasp. ''Ah . . .''

Eamon drew her to him. ''As I'm here with you now.''

Before she could demand her release, he slipped his free hand to the small of her back and pulled her into his embrace. When their bodies touched, Rosaleen shivered from the pleasure of being held so close.

''Ah, *cailin*,'' he murmured in a tender voice, then placed the hand he held around his neck. He tucked a stray wisp of her hair behind her ear.

Their gazes met. He ran a finger down her cheek. She trembled again. He smiled as his mouth came toward hers. Rosaleen parted her lips in expectation.

Then he kissed her, and as had happened before, the

effect of the caress caught her by surprise. Rocking from side to side, his lips felt firm and warm against hers. The tip of his tongue took careful tastes of her, first at one corner of her mouth, then the other. Eamon's kiss felt as comforting as the warmth of a hearth, as exciting as its leaping flames.

Rosaleen also remembered flames in his earlier kiss and wanted more of the passion he had sent rushing through her before. Her tongue met his. The dance began in earnest. At first the internal music of desire led them in a slow, deliberate step. Lush, leisurely glides delved and explored, gave and took in equal measure.

Then Eamon pulled his mouth away and drew a ragged breath. *"Cailin,"* he whispered again, and returned to feasting on her lips. In place of the languorous dance came a hunger that stunned her with its power, its intensity. It echoed in her.

She returned his kiss, running her hands over his shoulders and onto his chest. She opened his shirt, burrowed fingers inside the fabric to touch the man. Still the kiss continued, delicious, enervating, the strength of his desire against her belly tantalizing.

Before long, his hands cupped her breasts, caressing, molding the mounds to his palms. She loved the flood of sensation she felt in that flesh, the tingling at the tips, the relief his hands delivered. But it didn't last long, for the need returned, in greater waves each time.

Hunger pooled in Rosaleen's middle, spreading to the swollen dampness between her legs. She pressed her thighs together, trying to ease the feeling, but it didn't help. When Eamon's thumbs rubbed her nipples, she wondered if his touch would perhaps have the same effect in that throbbing private spot just outside her womb.

Then he released her breasts. He caressed her sides, clasped her waist and brought her hard up against him again. She rubbed her breasts against the muscles of his chest and moaned at the pleasure.

His hands continued roving, this time slipping over her bottom, palming, squeezing the fullness there. The need in her middle grew demanding.

"More, Eamon," she murmured when he drew back for a breath of air. She ran her fingers down the ridges of muscle on either side of his spine, and when she reached his bottom, she explored the hard contours there. He felt quite different from her.

But he responded just as she did. Emitting a guttural sound of pleasure, he captured her lips again. Kissing her deeply, ravenously, he rubbed the ridge at the base of his abdomen against the spot atop her thighs that wept with need.

He felt hot, solid, large.

Suddenly Rosaleen remembered the size of the protuberance he'd pointed out at the field. Tentatively she rubbed against him one more time. He groaned in response, but she learned what she wanted to know.

That . . . *thing* was big! While she loved the sensual hunger, the delicious taste of Eamon, the way his hands felt as they touched her, Rosaleen felt great respect for the weapon in his trousers. She couldn't imagine how it could be used the way she understood it was meant to be used.

In her.

She loved the kissing and the holding and the touching. She loved the burning inside, and suspected soothing that burn might feel wonderful, too. But that final consummation frightened her. Her fear served to douse the hunger that only seconds earlier had threatened to devour her.

She dragged her hands from Eamon's rear end. Reluctantly, to be sure, since she liked the tight muscular angles. But he had again rubbed his pelvis against her, and he felt bigger than before. She had to put an end to this before they went too far to stop.

Dragging her lips from his wasn't easy. She loved the way he kissed. Loved how his lips felt on hers, how he

A FAERIE TALE

tasted. But she was scared. "Eamon, stop!"

For a second time, he blinked. "Wha—what do you want?"

"I want ye to stop!"

"Now?"

"Aye! Right now."

He groaned, no pleasure in this sound. "You want to kill me, you do."

"O' course, and I don't. But I—I'm not ready."

He dropped his forehead to hers. A shudder ripped through him. "You're not ready . . . yet."

He hadn't asked, but she replied, "Not yet."

"Will you ever be?"

As he hadn't moved away, she could still feel that hard length nestled up against a very sensitive, vulnerable place. "I don't know."

Eamon took a slow step back, still holding her shoulders. In a flat voice, he said, "You . . . don't know."

In the interest of honesty, however, she softened the blow by admitting, "I hope I will be. I like your kisses and how ye touch me. I love how ye hold me so tight. And I love how ye show ye like me, too. But this is new to me, and . . . I'm scared."

His eyebrows shot up to his hairline, and he took his hands away. "Of me?"

"Not really. I'm afraid of what ye want to do . . . what I *think* I want to do."

He chuckled. "At least you 'think' you want to do it, too."

"Don't ye be making fun o' me, Eamon Dooley!"

"I wasn't!"

"Ye laughed at me."

"I laughed at *me*. I'm dying for wanting you, lass, and all you can say is that you 'think' you want me, too."

All of a sudden, suspicion filled her. "Where did ye learn so much? Ye say you're a leprechaun, and ye dress like one, too, but ye know an awful lot about this romancing and loving.''

He laughed harder. ''All I know is what I've learned at your side! Every time I see you, Rosaleen, all I want is to hold you and kiss you and . . . well, *you* know.''

''Aye, I know. But I'm not—''

''Ready. I know.'' He brought the edges of his shirt together and buttoned it back up. ''You're right. 'Tis best if I leave.''

Rosaleen breathed easier. ''Good night, then.''

With a shrug and a tug to his coat, he said, ''Good night, *cailin*. Dream of me.''

She chuckled, then gave him a saucy wink. ''Mayhap.''

With a ''Hummph!'' he ran down the porch steps and continued at a snappy pace. Without turning, he called back, ''Soon!''

She laughed again as she let herself inside. Leaning back against the closed front door, she listened to her heart thumping against her ribs. He made her mad, he made her laugh, he made her burn. But he also soothed her fire.

If you asked her, she was falling in love. Her a faerie, too.

What would happen once she and Eamon returned to *Tyeer na N-og*? Romantic love didn't exist there. Nor sensual love, either. Both were growing in her. For Eamon.

Love. Desire. Mortal, human passion. For another faerie. 'Twould doubtless lead to a very human broken heart.

She did right sending him home.

Besides, she had a potion to brew.

In the kitchen, she found Annie's white-speckled blue-enamel teakettle at its spot on the cookstove. Rosaleen hadn't yet approached the black iron monster, but since Annie always kept a small fire going under one of the back burners, Rosaleen called on her courage. Setting the

A FAERIE TALE

kettle at the correct spot, she leaned against the sink to wait for the water to boil.

While the romance between Patrick and Annie seemed to be headed in the right direction—for once—she now had to ponder the wisdom of assuming mortal form. Yes, like other well faeries, she had occasionally longed for a human form. She had also longed to learn about the sensual nature of that form.

Shortly after attaining her mortal shape, she learned that her looks indeed gave her great power. Recalling the May Day festivities, she thought of the butcher's reaction to her, and that of the young man who had driven his bicycle into the postmistress. She giggled.

She had also learned she could affect a man's behavior by the way she moved, the way she touched him. Eamon, for one. But she hadn't thought a man would affect her as much.

There was power in one's body.

The power of woman over man.

Of man over woman.

Nibbling on a fingernail, Rosaleen considered her feelings for Eamon. Despite his proclivity toward bad luck, she liked him and admired his commitment to helping Annie. Then, too, she longed for his loving. After all, Annie hadn't sounded offended or, worse, hurt, when she and Patrick had been, as Eamon said, doing their mattress dance. It couldn't be so bad . . . could it?

Perhaps men—mortal men—weren't quite as large as Eamon seemed. She flushed, remembering precisely how she had determined Eamon's largeness.

To her relief, the kettle let out a piercing shriek. She removed the lid and dropped the henbane leaves into the bubbling water. She set the pot back on the burner, certain the leaves needed to simmer a bit.

To her dismay, however, she heard a masculine rumble upstairs. Patrick was still there.

In a way, that was good. She could probably give him

the potion tonight rather than wait. On the other hand, being *here* while he was up *there* felt a tad embarrassing, as if she had invaded their privacy. It was bad enough hearing what she and Eamon had heard.

Then Annie chuckled. A series of thumps followed the laughter. A rustling followed more laughter, this time low and intimate.

Total silence came next.

It went on and on.

Finally bedsprings squeaked, and her cheeks blazed hot as the steam from her brew. They couldn't possibly be . . . *doing* it again. Not with her in the kitchen, where she could hear every last little sound.

Perhaps she should have stayed longer at the field. She could have charged the leaves, cast a spell on them.

"So," Patrick said from the kitchen doorway, startling her, "you're our prowler!"

When she turned, Rosaleen again flushed various shades of heat. *Her godson hadn't donned his shirt!* She turned her back on him and stirred the potion. "I'm no prowler, Patrick O'Toole, and you'd do well to thank me."

"Thank you?"

"Aye! I've made a wee something for ye."

Puzzlement appeared on his face. "You. Made something. For me."

"Aye!" She held out a cup full of potion. "Drink up."

"What is it?" asked Annie, suddenly appearing at his side.

Rosaleen cast her friend a glance and saw that she at least wore a discreet robe. She gave them a broad wink and a knowing smile. "Since he has been . . . *busy* tonight, I made Patrick a special tonic. 'Tis known to restore a man's strength and stamina. Might do him good."

Annie and Patrick exchanged intimate smiles. Smiles full of knowledge, secrets. Private smiles.

Rosaleen felt her heart quicken. She knew the secrets

A FAERIE TALE

of Eamon's kisses, his caresses, how his body felt against hers. She understood.

But she had a mission to accomplish and a wand to earn. "Go on, Patrick. Drink it all."

Without taking his gaze from Annie, he reached for the cup. "Ouch!" he yelled. "It's hot."

"And how else would ye be making a tea?"

Ignoring her indignant response, he took Annie's hand and led her toward the parlor. Moments later, Rosaleen heard the murmur of private conversation.

To make sure no one else consumed the potion, she emptied the kettle of leaves and remaining liquid, then filled it back up with plain hot water from the reservoir at the side of the stove. She set the pot in the enameled sink and left it to soak till morn. She would wash it out then.

Yawning, she turned off the kitchen gaslamp and went to bid the lovers good night. "Enjoy your tea, Patrick."

"Mmmm . . ." he responded, wrinkling his nose at the stench, taking a sip, making a face.

She turned to her friend. "Good night, Annie."

"Sweet dreams, Rosaleen."

Of Eamon. And her. Together. "They will be that."

She ran up the stairs.

Undressing quickly, she took a moment to examine the human body she had recently acquired. It was attractive. Eamon's avid interest had convinced her of that. It responded to touch far more than her faerie form ever had.

Rosaleen smiled. Well, if she had to learn to live with a broken heart sometime in the future, at least Eamon seemed determined to make it worth her while. As she studied her firm breasts, her flat belly, and long legs, she admitted that soon, as he had said, they would indeed not stop.

With that exciting thought in mind, she crept into her bed. But as sleep overtook her, she heard Annie call out. "Rosaleen! Come here. Quick!"

Donning a robe but dispensing with slippers, she ran to Annie's room. "Faith, and what's wrong?"

"Look!" her friend cried, pointing at Patrick, who lay sprawled across her bed.

Rosaleen frowned. She saw nothing to cause Annie's alarm. "Should I be surprised to find him in your bed? Eamon and I heard ye from the open window a while ago."

"You did?" asked Annie in horror. "Oh, dear!"

Rosaleen waved carelessly. "Don't be fretting so, Annie. 'Tis fine with me. Eamon, too."

"Oh. But look! Patrick's just . . . lying there! I can't wake him up."

Rosaleen frowned. "Ye can't wake him up?"

"No. We stayed downstairs while he finished that horrid stuff you gave him. He kissed me and decided to tuck me in, then go home. But we came up and kissed some more and . . . then he just . . . fell. Like that. I can't wake him up."

At least the potion seemed to have worked fine. From what Annie said, Patrick had been delectable enough to keep her kissing him instead of saying farewell.

But such sound sleep? 'Twas surely strange. From what she remembered, Eamon hadn't been anywhere near sleep when they'd kissed earlier tonight and she had found him delectable enough.

Approaching the bed, Rosaleen poked a rousing finger at Patrick's arm. "Hmm . . ."

He remained as still as a statue, albeit a fallen one.

Then Annie turned on her, suspicion in her eyes, a frown wrinkling her forehead. "Just what was *in* that tea you gave him?"

Rosaleen's eyes widened in fear. Oh, no. Was this one of those times when her magic went awry?

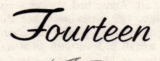

Fourteen

Annie and Rosaleen had tried to kill him.

As Patrick recuperated in bed the next day from the women's attempt at murder, a stream of visitors flowed through his room. There was nary a sign of the thwarted homicidal lunatics, however. Certainly there was none of the woman who had addled his brain with sweet loving, then conspired with her friend to do away with him.

All to get her hands on her inheritance and fritter it away on the most noodle-headed notion Patrick had ever heard.

That did it, though. He would indeed divest himself of all responsibility for the Brennan trust when he returned to work. He valued his life a hell of a lot more than someone else's savings account. Even one as large as Annie's.

He hoped to never set eyes on the little fraud again.

He still had trouble accepting that Annie had gone as far as to give him her innocence and seduce him for the money to fund that crazy Haven of hers. What sort of woman would do such a thing?

The kind that went by a foul epithet of a name, a name he refused to apply to Annie until she forced him to do so. Even though she had treated him shabbily, he hated thinking of her in those terms. He had thought she felt for him what he felt for her.

He made his mistake when he let himself trust what he thought he saw in her eyes. He had begun to think maybe, just maybe, there might be something to all that dreamy love stuff after all. Annie had always seemed sincere, if somewhat flighty. Her artlessness, her candor, and her eternal optimism had been part of her charm.

He'd begun to fall in love with what turned out to be nothing more than an illusion. It was hard to accept how much that stung.

It hurt to learn he'd fallen for a lie and a pretty face, that he had been taken for a fool by sparkling blue eyes and innocent freckles over velvet-soft skin.

The sweetest mouth on earth.

The hottest passion in creation.

The sort of loving a man fantasized about, a loving too spectacular to really expect to experience.

Oh, yes, he'd been a fool. A fool led by the lure of passion. The promise of . . . love.

Patrick set his jaw against the roiling in his stomach. He was sure what he felt didn't come only from the poison he had consumed. Thoughts of how Annie misused him had the power to sicken him.

At any rate, he had learned his lesson well. He would never make the same mistake. He would never again waver from his carefully considered, logically plotted, sensible approach to life. Certainly not when it came to personal matters.

As he had suspected all along, dreams of love and happily ever after only brought pain and loss. After all, he saw his mother suffer both.

Now Patrick himself knew the pain of loving.

Now he also knew loss.

He had lost hope—a hope he never knew he harbored. The hope Annie Brennan's dishonesty killed.

•   •   •

A short while later, Serena showed up. With an upward tilt of her aristocratic profile, she bestowed a superior smile on Patrick. "I couldn't believe my ears! But then, who would have thought Annie Brennan would go so far as to poison you? On the other hand, Patrick, I did warn you against the little tart's—"

"Serena," he growled, hating to hear his worst feelings voiced by his former fiancée, "I warned you against calling Annie names. I meant it then and I mean it still."

Her lips tightened to a white-edged line. "If you insist. Anyway, I couldn't just let you lay here and suffer. That's why I made you a kettle of chicken soup. It's mild enough for convalescence but should restore your strength."

Remembering Rosaleen's strength-restoring tea, Patrick shuddered. "If you'll set the pot in the kitchen, Eamon will put it away. I thank you for your concern."

For a moment, Serena looked startled. "Of course I'm concerned, darling!" Then she blinked repeatedly. "Why . . . I haven't stopped caring for you, even though you threw me over for that—for another woman."

Why did life have to get so complicated? All Patrick ever wanted was a normal stable life and a normal stable wife with whom to build a normal stable family. None of his efforts so far had produced normalcy, much less got him any closer to that secure, stable future he so wanted.

He sighed. "I haven't changed my mind about our engagement. I can't plan a future with you. At least, not at this time. Should I reach a different decision, you'll be the first to know. Until then, this matter is not open for discussion."

Her eyes shot darts of rage when she again compressed her lips. Clearly Serena wasn't used to being thwarted, but Patrick's head felt so muddled at the moment that the last thing he wanted was to be pushed into promising anything to any woman. Certainly not before he came to a better understanding of his feelings for Annie.

His stomach churned again.

Serena gave him another coy smile. Patrick felt nothing but distaste. He kept his counsel, however.

"What you need," she said in a compelling voice, "is a woman who is interested in *you*." She prattled on, unaware of his displeasure. With a pat to her coiled yellow hair, she gave him the full impact of her gray-eyed attention. "One who will look after your needs and who cares about your interests. Why, you spend so much time at the bank, working endless hours, it's clearly very important to you."

Patrick smiled weakly, wondering what she was getting at, but said nothing. He had nothing *to* say. It was best to hear her out.

Serena approached the bed. "I've always been fascinated by what happens at the bank. All the details you oversee so that people's money can grow safely." She perched on the edge of the mattress. "That seems so noble to me."

"Noble?" Banking was one of the most uninspired of enterprises. What was Serena up to?

She again donned an unnaturally coy smile. "Do you think ... perhaps ... you could teach me about your work? In the interest of greater knowledge and understanding, of course."

Patrick wondered if the poison Annie and Rosaleen had given him could cause hallucinations, perhaps make a man hear things that made no sense. "What did you just say?"

Feigned surprise broke out on Serena's face. "That's it! I'd like to become your apprentice. I want to learn *everything* there is to know about money—er ... banking. *Everyone* knows you're Woodbury's expert on that."

Narrowing his gaze, Patrick studied the woman whose hip suddenly nestled against his. Serena was up to something. Ingenuousness was not one of her stronger traits. Whatever she wanted, it had to do with money. The bank's money. Her slip of the tongue hadn't gone unnot-

A FAERIE TALE

iced. He wasn't that much a fool. Or that sick.

"I couldn't answer," he said. "Such matters aren't up to me. You would have to take it up with the board of directors of the bank. I suggest you do that if you are serious about entering the world of finance."

Gauging her reaction to his suggestion, he noticed the grimace she tried to suppress. Sudden love of the banking profession had *not* inspired Serena's suggestion, and Patrick doubted she simply wanted to resume their aborted engagement. An interest in banking had never been one of his requirements for a life mate, and she knew it.

"I believe I'll do just that, darling. I'll let you know how it turns out."

"Oh, I'm sure the bank will notify me of their decision soon enough." He hoped their response came as a resounding *no*. "I hate to sound inhospitable, so please excuse my poor manners. I must ask you to leave. I'm afraid I'm about to fall asleep. Fatigue, you understand."

He endured Serena's simpering and sympathy for the following interminable minutes. She hovered over him, fluffing his pillows, cooing wishes for a swift recovery, driving him nearly out of his mind.

How could he ever have entertained the notion of marrying this woman? He couldn't tolerate even a half hour in her company, never mind the prospect of a long married life!

"Now you take care of yourself, darling," she admonished. "And if you need anything, *anything* at all—"

"Yes, yes. I know. I'll send for you if the need arises."

With a satisfied smirk, Serena swept from the room.

Collapsing against the pillows at his back, Patrick closed his eyes. He still felt the effect of whatever those crazy women had tricked him into drinking, and his thoughts spun madly in his head. Nausea threatened.

Why had Annie tried to kill him? Did she hate him that much? And why did Serena want to learn about the bank? Did she really want him that much?

192   GINNY REYES

Patrick didn't know what to think. He just knew he hated to think of Annie's betrayal.

As Annie approached the front door in response to a knock, she heard the unmistakable voice of Woodbury's mayor. "Now you just let me do all the talking," he boomed.

What kind of talking had he come for? He couldn't seriously believe what she'd heard was rumored all over town, could he? No one in their right mind would believe Annie had tried to kill Patrick. Not after they attended the Benefit Supper together, and especially after what happened later—

Stop! she scolded herself. She couldn't think of that right then. Not while the mayor stood outside her door. "Come in," she said.

As she ushered in her guest, she noticed the man's companion. His daughter followed behind his considerable bulk. Annie forced herself to smile despite her annoyance. "You, too, Serena. Please come in."

Leading father and daughter to the parlor sofa, Annie tried but failed to come up with a possible reason for their visit. She sat across the room in the rocker where her mother had soothed her to sleep as a child.

"Harrumph!" With his usual pomp, Mayor Keller swiped his sweat-beaded forehead with a white handkerchief. "I'm sure you're wondering why we are here."

"I must admit I am."

"Well, little girl, it's like this. We hear you need a large structure for that Artist's Refuge—"

"Haven," she hastened to correct. "The Artist's Haven."

The mayor waved a hammy hand. "Yes, that." Stuffing the handkerchief into his coat pocket, the portly man settled back into the sofa. "As I was saying, you need a large building to make that Haven place possible. And as

A FAERIE TALE

I hear tell, you won't have any money until you turn twenty-five—''

"That's not exactly so," Annie cut in, not wanting him to think her destitute. "I receive a monthly stipend, as stated in my father's will. The problem is in the amount of the stipend. It isn't enough to purchase the property I need."

"That's it!" the mayor exclaimed. "So, since you can't buy the place you need right now, I—"

"Ahem!" Serena dabbed her lips on a lacy hanky.

Her father shot her a quelling glare. "Well, yes, I meant *we* decided to help you. You know, little girl, I always look out for the best interests of everyone in Woodbury."

If he called her "little girl" one more time, Annie swore she would kick his shins like a little girl in the heat of a tantrum. Intrigued by his words, however, she controlled her inappropriate urge. "Go on," she said.

"We have a proposition for you. We think we can help you achieve your Asylum while helping ourselves as well."

"Haven," she corrected.

The mayor looked peeved. "Er . . . Haven."

"And that would be . . . ?"

"You see, little girl—"

"Annie, if you please," she said through clenched teeth.

The mayor blinked. "Of course. You see, *Annie*, when we came to Woodbury, we thought we wanted a house as large as the one in Philadelphia. Truth is, we don't. We're rattling around the place on Windy Lane, just the two of us. All the while, here you are, looking for just such a house."

The idea taking form in Annie's mind held a certain appeal. The Kellers' large home boasted spacious rooms, wide windows, and a generous porch where one could set up numerous easels at the same time. But Patrick would never release the money. "I'm afraid I can't buy your home, Mr. Mayor—"

"Hold it, little gi—Annie. Who said anything about buying?"

"Please explain. I don't understand what you mean."

"It's like this. If you are willing to rent for the next seven years, I'm willing to wait to be paid—once you come into your trust fund, you understand. At that time you can pay the fair value of the house, plus a percent in interest I would charge for those years you took to pay in full."

Annie felt she should know what he was talking about, but truth was, she had no idea what half of it meant.

"Percent . . . interest . . . I don't understand a lot of this. I'm sorry, Mayor Keller. I know very little about business."

The mayor leaned over and patted her knee with a meaty hand. "That's what I'm here for!" he bellowed.

Annie winced. Woodbury's mayor had the deepest, loudest voice she had ever heard. "How so?"

He rubbed his bulbous belly. "I'll explain. You've said you want to open your Institution . . . er . . . Haven right away. I own a house that's too big for us but ideal for you. We can rent you our house. Are you with me so far?"

Annie nodded, wrinkling her brow in concentration.

"Good, good!" He patted her knee once more.

She squirmed.

He drew out his handkerchief and again mopped his florid face. "Very well, Annie, we agree that seven years' rent will not cover the price of the house, right?"

Annie had no idea, but she bobbed her head agreeably.

The mayor then stood and paced the parlor, narrowly avoiding the newly arrived Fergus O'Shea. The floorboards squeaked and shook under his bulk, and the cat dogged the man's every move. "Since you take possession of your funds at twenty-five, you won't need Pickle-Face Patrick—''

''Father!'' Serena cried in outrage. ''Patrick has a *very* nice face. You shouldn't speak like that of him.''

Annie agreed but bit her tongue before blurting her opinion.

Her father gave Serena another scathing scowl, and she subsided. As if nothing had happened, the man continued. ''What I meant to say was that you won't need *anyone's* approval then to use the money your father left you. That's when you would pay me for the house.''

Annie nibbled at her bottom lip. ''What about that fair value and interest stuff? You still haven't explained what it all means.''

''*Tsk-tsk,*'' the mayor chided. ''The impatience of youth! I was getting to that, little girl—er, Annie. When you turn twenty-five, we have the bank assess the value of the house and you can pay me what they determine it is worth—plus the interest we agree upon now.''

''But what does interest mean?''

''Oh, it's just a formality. It's a little extra we agree you will pay me because I kindly loaned you the use of my house for all those years. Banks do it when they lend their customers money. They consider it the cost of borrowing money. With me, it will be the cost of borrowing my house, since while you use it, I won't have the house or the bulk of my money. And since you can't pay right now. . . .''

Annie stood up, suddenly understanding. ''A fee.''

''Exactly! It's not so difficult, is it?''

She smiled. ''Not when you take the time to explain it. Thank you, Mr. Mayor. You've been most kind to take so much of your valuable time to help me. Tell me, how much would this interest be?''

''Oh, the usual,'' he said, placing a hand on Serena's shoulder, making her flinch.

Annie nearly laughed out loud. The man didn't seem

to know his own strength. She shook her head. "What do you mean by 'the usual'?"

"Banks do it all the time, as I said." He patted Serena's shoulder, then gave it a paternal squeeze. This time she whimpered, and Annie felt sorry for her. Fergus emitted a throaty growl, puffing up like a furred balloon.

The mayor continued. "I'd say twenty-five percent—just like your age of majority—would do just fine."

For all of about a second, Annie considered the Kellers' offer. There really wasn't much to think about. She could open her Artist's Haven if she agreed! She would never have to pester Patrick for money again. He would never again fight to protect her money, to make sure she didn't squander or lose it, and maybe then, with the trust fund no longer an issue between them, they could pursue more personal matters. Her smile turned private, wicked.

"Harrumph!"

Clearly the mayor wanted her attention back on the matter at hand. *Oh, dear!* How mortifying to be caught thinking of Patrick and . . . *that.* At least the Kellers couldn't know exactly what she'd been thinking. Her cheeks heated, regardless. "Er . . . I think that will be fine. How soon could I have the house?"

The mayor pounced on her hand and pumped it vigorously. "Excellent decision, my dear! Excellent." He turned to his daughter. "What do you say, Serena? A fortnight?"

"Two weeks?" his daughter cried out in horror. "You want me packed and ready to move in that short a time?"

Her father narrowed his gaze. "You assured me you were in complete accordance with me on this matter, did you not?"

Annie frowned. How odd. It sounded as if Mayor Keller was threatening his daughter. Surely not. She had to be mistaken. More than likely, his deep loud voice made his reminder come out harsher than intended.

Her attention fixed on her fingers, Serena said, "Yes,

A FAERIE TALE

Father. I guess a fortnight will be . . . fine.''

Turning back to Annie, the mayor said, ''Easily resolved. You can have the house in two weeks. I won't ask you to pay rent until the first of July.''

A thrill ran up and down Annie's spine. Her dreams were finally coming true! Her dream of an Artist's Haven, as well as her very private, never before shared dream of a man to love.

Unsure of what to do next, she asked, ''Ah . . . should we . . . shake hands . . . sign papers? What is customary?''

''Shake first, of course, my dear. We'll shake on our agreement.'' Putting actions to his words, the mayor once again abused Annie's right hand. ''Then I'll bring you papers that clearly spell out our agreement. For protection, you understand. You always want to get business agreements in writing. For the future. That way no one can change their mind . . . or pull a fast one on you.''

''I would never think that of you! Why, you've been kindness itself.''

The mayor smiled, ran his tongue around his lips, then smacked them together. ''That's me, my dear. A pillar of the community and kindness itself.'' But his cheer suddenly crumpled, and he hollered, ''Hell and damnation!'' He hopped in circles, shaking a leg. ''I'm under attack!''

To Annie's horror, Fergus's lethal jaws clung to the mayor's meaty leg, and he showed no sign of letting go.

''Fergus O'Shea, you naughty thing!'' she cried, catching the tom despite the mayor's ludicrous ballet. ''Let go right now. I have some nice catnip in the kitchen for you.''

With a final yank, she set the mayor free of her pet. She kept a firm grip on the spoilt beast.

As Mayor Keller put himself to rights, Annie smiled, trying to smooth the awkward moment. She had, after all, plenty to smile about. She now had one person on her side, and an influential one, at that. The kind mayor of Woodbury was going to help her make her dreams come true.

198   GINNY REYES

Farewells were brief, understandably. As Mayor Keller limped away, Serena at his side, Annie let Fergus loose and leaned on the door frame. Today had turned out very lucky indeed. She hadn't needed a leprechaun after all.

"I tell you, Patrick," Eamon said, "I heard them with me own two ears! They want wee Annie's money."

Patrick frowned, still reluctant to believe ill of the Kellers. "I hesitate to do anything extraordinary, but as I told you, Serena is up to something. I don't know what, so I won't argue anymore. I will take precautions, though. I can't let them get away with theft."

Eamon rubbed his hands in glee. "Sure and I can help! You know I have the luck o' the Irish. We'll take care o' them Keller spalpeens!"

"Be careful, Eamon. You can't accuse them of theft since nothing has been stolen." Patrick feared his friend might get carried away by his enthusiasm. "We must watch them, study their actions, plan what to do if they make a move."

" 'Tis the very thing. Careful planning and thoughtful study will do it."

Patrick raised a warning finger. "But you mustn't let Annie know what we suspect. She's so unpredictable one can never know what she's likely to do."

Eamon nodded solemnly.

Patrick had a sudden vision of disaster. "She might confront them with our suspicions!"

Green eyes widened in horror. "By the Goddess, we can't be having that! O' course, and we can't tell the wee lass. Who knows what she might do?"

"You know, I'm glad you decided to stay in Woodbury awhile. I can certainly use help in this matter."

Grasping his lapels, the Irishman rocked back on his heels. "Aye, Eamon Dooley's luck will see us through this."

Patrick chuckled. "If you insist, but I think careful ob-

A FAERIE TALE 199

servation and vigilant protection will go a lot farther to make sure nothing happens to Annie.''

With another grin full of glee, Eamon rubbed his hands together. ''Sure and you're right. You'll make sure nothing happens to the wee—''

A knock at the door cut off Eamon's chortling. He trotted from the room, shaking his head. ''I don't know what we'll be doing with another kettle o' stew.''

Moments later, Patrick heard polite conversation. It sounded as if his visitor was of the female gender, as most had been. Making certain the blanket ensured decency, Patrick prepared for more fussing.

Light footsteps ascended the stairs. Sharp heels clicked down the hallway. A vision in blue and white striped muslin appeared in the doorway.

Patrick's heart slammed in his chest. His temples throbbed. Another part of him came awake, reminding him of what he should forget. ''What are *you* doing here?'' he roared.

''Oh, Patrick,'' exclaimed his would-be murderess, ignoring his question and his ire. ''I have the best news. I won't have to bother you about the Artist's Haven again! Mayor Keller has taken care of all my problems for me.''

''No!'' he bellowed, finally accepting what Eamon had been saying. ''He couldn't have . . . *you* wouldn't have . . . what on earth have you done *now*?''

A pained expression marred her pretty face. ''Well, if you're going to be like that,'' she said in a mutinous voice, ''I just won't tell you after all.'' She crossed her arms and jutted out her chin.

As she glared belligerently, Patrick collapsed onto the mountain of pillows. He felt as though someone's fist had plowed through his gut. His head spun. Nausea clawed up and down his throat at the thought of Mayor Keller ''solving'' Annie's money problems.

She *still* meant to kill him.

Fifteen

Patrick accepted that Annie, the woman he'd been falling in love with, was out to kill him, even though it did seem a bit extreme. He also accepted that the Mayor of Woodbury was out to steal her blind. But he couldn't, in good conscience, let it happen, no matter how things stood between him and Annie, and he couldn't tell her his suspicions.

He had to protect Annie, even though she obviously didn't want protection. At least not *his*.

Tamping down his mixed-up feelings, Patrick asked, "How is the good mayor helping you?"

At that, she uncrossed her arms and smiled. "Why, you won't believe how kind he has been!"

Oh, yes I would! "Exactly *how* kind, Annie?"

She clasped her hands between her breasts and smiled rapturously. "He's going to rent me his house for the Haven until I turn twenty-five. I'll pay him in full then— when I no longer need *your* signature to use *my* father's money."

He frowned. "When I said exactly, I meant details. How much rent is he charging? How much will he want for the house in seven years? Will he charge a fee to let you do this? Will you get the agreement in writing?"

A FAERIE TALE

"Goodness, Patrick!" she exclaimed, her expression smug. "We took care of those details. I'm not stupid, you know."

She wasn't stupid, but he suspected she was in over her head. "I never said that. I'm just looking out for your interests."

"Don't give it another thought. The Artist's Haven is no longer your problem. The mayor and I will take care of it."

Patrick ground his teeth. "Just answer my questions."

Her eyes took on a mutinous light. "You asked so many, I might forget one or ten." Then she threw her hands up in surrender. "Very well, I'll try. *If* I remember them all. In seven years, he will have the bank assess the house. I agreed to pay what they say. He will charge interest—as the bank would if I borrowed money from them—and I'll pay that in seven years, too."

She paused, as if to remember what else he had asked. "Oh, yes. We will, of course, have a written agreement. One should *always* get business matters in writing. That way no one can change their mind later or try to pull a fast one."

Despite her satisfied smile, Patrick noticed she hadn't mentioned a crucial detail. "What about the interest, Annie?"

"I already *told* you. Weren't you listening? I will pay him interest."

Patrick narrowed his gaze. "I *was* listening, and you never said how much interest he is charging."

"Oh, the usual," she offered with a breezy wave. "Twenty-five percent."

"Twenty-five percent?" He leapt out of bed and marched right up to her. "Are you mad, woman? That's not the usual, it's outright thievery!"

Annie's eyes flew to his drawers. Her cheeks turned red. "Ah . . . er . . ."

He smiled. She had seen much more, and it seemed she

remembered plenty. Good. He didn't care to be forgettable. Certainly not as easily as she dismissed his concern for her. "Larceny, Annie. He is swindling you out of your money. Tell me you haven't signed anything yet. Please."

She blinked, met his gaze, and pushed out her chin. "How dare you accuse Mayor Keller? Why, the bank charges interest, and you wouldn't accuse the bank of larceny, would you?"

Patrick paced the room. "Of course, the bank charges interest, but never one fourth of the loan amount! That's usury, extortion, outright burglary!"

Every word he said heightened the anger in her eyes. "You're just mad because I'm making my dream come true," she said, "and you won't have a say in it. You hate to give up control. I *was* right. All you want is Da's money."

"Annie," he growled, "if you say that again, I . . . I . . . Oh, hell! I don't know *what* I'll do. Rest assured of one thing. I want nothing from the Brennan trust. All I want is yo—"

He cut off his words before they landed him in worse trouble. Nothing, not anger, not her lack of business knowledge, not even the crooked Kellers, would make him confess how much he cared for a woman who had tried to kill him. One who was still trying to do him mortal harm. If she didn't succeed, she undoubtedly would drive him stark, raving mad.

He had to be careful. He had to think things through, control his feelings, work through this problem logically, or he would end up like his mother, reacting emotionally, making matters worse.

He would end up with a broken heart, just as she had.

"Let me put it another way," he offered in a conciliatory tone. "I must do the right thing—as an officer of the bank, not to mention as executor of your father's will. The sole purpose of the trust fund is to provide for you, and I must make sure it continues to do so. I must protect

A FAERIE TALE

what is yours. That is what an executor does.''

Her glare told Patrick she hadn't bought a word.

''If that's the case,'' she said, ''then I suppose I need a new executor.''

Patrick's temper flared again. ''It won't be that easy. Your father trusted me, and I will fight anyone who questions my motives. I only want the best for you, you little fool!''

''Oh—oh—ooooh!'' she gasped. ''How dare you? I thought you liked me! If that is how you see me, then I have nothing further to say. Good day, sir!'' She blew out of his room like a summer thundershower.

''Damn!'' He took trousers from the wardrobe. Perfect example why indulging his feelings was a stupid thing to do. ''Wait, Annie!'' He stuffed his right leg in the pants. ''I didn't mean it that way!'' Then the left. ''Wait—''

The front door slammed as he buttoned the waistband. ''Oh, hell!''

He had made a mess of things. He had chased Annie away, probably straight into the crooked mayor's hands. What was he going to do about this latest complication?

What was he going to do about Annie?

No sooner had Annie vanished up the stairs, than Rosaleen turned in triumph to Eamon. ''There, now! You can't say 'twas your luck that brought *this* about!''

He buffed his fingernails on his lapel. ''Can't say I poisoned the fellow, either!''

Rosaleen tried on a disdainful glare, hoping to control the heat that rushed up her cheeks. ''I didn't poison Patrick! 'Twas an aphrodisiac I gave him!''

Eamon had the audacity to laugh. ''What good is an aphrodisiac that puts the man to sleep? Sure and you're a dangerous one, *cailin*! Just what did you give the poor lad?''

Rosaleen smiled. ''A wee bit o' henbane. *Every* faerie

204 GINNY REYES

knows 'tis a powerful herb to make a woman want a man.''

Eamon's laughter stopped. His eyebrows disappeared under a shock of red hair. ''You gave him *henbane*? To drink?''

Rosaleen nodded.

He smacked a palm on his forehead. '' 'Tis true, then. You're the most inept faerie *Tyeer na N-og* has ever known! Rosaleen Flynn, henbane's a poison. It kills animals and men, you know. 'Tis only thanks to me lucky self the lad's alive!''

Rosaleen frowned. ''But everyone knows it makes a man delectable to the ladies.''

''Aye, *cailin*, that it does. But 'tisn't by drinking the stuff, 'tis by using a wee bit in a conjuring bag or sachet. The lad was right. You near killed him.''

Rosaleen went ice cold. She hadn't meant her godson any harm. ''Will I ever earn me wand?''

''How can you be thinking o' the wand at a time like this?'' Eamon asked. ''You could have done murder!''

Just then, a woman's heels *tap-tapp*ed down the stairs. Annie flew by, her face red with rage. Without so much as a ''good-bye,'' she opened the front door, then slammed it shut behind her.

''I suppose you'll blame me magic for her leaving, too.'' Rosaleen fought back tears. ''I only want the wand to do more and better magic.''

''Since I did naught to cause Annie to leave like that,'' Eamon countered, ''and something made her do it . . . besides, 'tisn't a wand that will fix your magic. Your magic comes from you, and methinks you're just not magical a'tall!''

''O' course and I'm magical! I come from the *Tuatha De Danann*, just like every other faerie does.'' She squared her shoulders with pride and studied him through narrowed eyes. ''Tell me this. Did you go home when I told you to leave? Or did you turn around and stay the night on the porch?''

When his cheeks colored, Rosaleen had her answer. "Aha!" she crowed, jabbing him in the chest. "I should have known. 'Twasn't me magic that went wrong, after all, 'twas your bad luck that ruined everything. You just had to bring it back when I had everything going right, did you not?''

He grabbed her finger, but remembering the other night, Rosaleen yanked it back. He then met her nose to nose. "Tell me, *cailin*, how would you have brought the lad home without me? You couldn't even wake him up!''

Rosaleen waggled *her* finger at him. "Patrick should have stayed in Annie's own bed. By now they could have been married. Instead, everyone in town is after accusing Annie and me o' poisoning him.''

"Hah! Goddess knows what you two would have fed him next! He might be good and dead now if I hadn't been there. *I* saved the lad's life.''

Heavy shoes clattered down the stairs. Moments later, Patrick stalked by, saying, "Make yourselves at home. I have a murderous madwoman to find!''

He slammed the door on his way out.

Rosaleen frowned. "A murderous madwoman?''

"See? 'Tis as I said.''

She gnawed on a thumbnail. "But I didn't mean to hurt him. And I didn't mean to cause trouble between them.'' She shuddered. "Faith, and I've really done it this time.'' She collapsed on a wine-colored brocade settee and drew another shaky breath. Twin teardrops fell from her eyes.

Eamon watched misery fill Rosaleen's beautiful face. 'Twas true, she hadn't meant to harm Patrick. "There, there, *cailin*,'' he said, sitting by her, wrapping an arm around her. "No need to weep. What matters is that you *didn't* do in the lad.''

"Oh, Eamon,'' she cried into his shoulder.

He wrapped his other arm around her and pulled her

onto his lap. Rocking her, he made soothing sounds, hoping to ease her anguish. The sweet herbal fragrance he had come to associate with her tickled his senses, and he breathed in again. He noticed the pulse at her temple, the skin so clear and fine its delicacy stunned him.

He dropped tiny kisses wherever his lips landed. Aye, he was glad Annie wished for a leprechaun that day at the burgh on the field. If for naught else, then for the privilege of meeting Rosaleen Flynn, for the newfound joy in their sensual attraction, for the strong feelings he had come to have for a certain inept faerie.

The dainty curve of her ear caught his attention. He kissed the edge, then followed it to the fleshy lobe. With a featherlike flick of his tongue he tasted the velvety softness. She trembled in response.

He repeated the caress, and she quivered again. Her sobs stopped.

Wanting more, Eamon darted his tongue into a hollow behind her ear and was rewarded with a silky sigh of pleasure. Remembering earlier explorations, he caught her earlobe between his teeth and nipped.

A moan escaped her lips.

His friend below the waist woke up.

Since she hadn't rebuffed his touch thus far, Eamon traced Rosaleen's cheekbone with slow kisses. She angled her face to follow his mouth, prolonging the contact. Finally he approached her lips—her tears had stopped and the only hitch in her breath came when he touched her skin with the tip of his tongue.

He tasted the corner of her mouth, and she smiled. Although he hadn't solved her problems, he had distracted her. There was much to be said for distraction.

With a firmer touch, he covered her lips, only to have her part them. Sure and she was responsive! Eamon joined their tongues in a passionate duel. Both won, if the faster pace of their breathing, the more deliberate pressure of the kiss measured anything a'tall. Before he realized his

A FAERIE TALE 207

intention, Eamon brought his hands to her breasts.

"Oh . . ." she breathed into his mouth.

"Mmmm . . ." he answered.

Cupping her flesh, Eamon felt the tips bead against his palms. He had never wanted anything so much as to see those mounds without the barrier of her clothes.

Moving her a fraction away, he began to unfasten the buttons down her soft, rose-colored bodice. When he looked up to make sure she didn't object to his exploration, he found her gaze on his hands, a sensual smile on her lips.

There was no resisting that smile.

Eamon kissed Rosaleen again as he dispatched the buttons. When he parted the sides of the garment, he found yet another fabric shield. This one was lighter, however, nearly transparent, frosted with lace, and had only a simple ribbon tying it closed. Pulling on the pink satin, Eamon unveiled a fragrant valley between plump, velvet hills.

With trembling fingers, Eamon lowered her garment and caught his first glimpse of Rosaleen's breasts. He gazed in awe. Soft and full, her flesh was pale, faintly veined, and crowned by dark plum buds that beckoned his mouth. He didn't resist.

Tenderness overwhelmed him when his lips touched one tight bit of flesh. He rubbed his lips over the pebbled surface, then darted his tongue out for a taste.

Rosaleen's back arched, and a keening sound broke from her throat. Her breasts rose to his hungry mouth.

Eamon took one nipple in his mouth, suckled it, swirled his tongue around the sensitive tip, and wrought whimpers, sighs, and tremors from Rosaleen.

The fellow in his pants stood to his full height.

Rosaleen squirmed, grinding her buttocks against Eamon's risen flesh. He hissed, his hips bucking in response.

"Fair's fair," she whispered. "And ye offered to show me that *shillelagh* before."

"Are you ready, then?" he asked, nipping at one of the plum-velvet crests.

"Ah, yes . . ."

With awkward haste, he placed her on the settee and divested himself of his shirt before she could change her mind. Rosaleen watched, her eyes wide and bold in their admiration. Suddenly she laughed. "Faith, and I don't know why you're after fussing with the shirt when your staff is in your pants!"

"I'm getting there, lass!" He unfastened his waistband. "Besides, you're still half-dressed."

"I can take care o' that."

For a moment, he grew serious. "You realize we'll be in the mortal realm for just a wee bit of time. We'll be going back to *Tyeer na N-og*, and then what? Will you regret this? Are you sure 'tis what you want?"

Rosy color swept up her breasts, her neck, and across her face. "I want *you*, Eamon. Even if I'm not sure why." She frowned. "You're a fair tease, contrary, and have the worst luck, but I feel drawn to you. So much, I can't fight it anymore."

She reached out and placed her hand on his abdomen. Eamon's gut tightened. She smiled. "See? That's what I feel when you touch me. And I know there's more." The flush in her cheeks deepened. "I asked Annie if 'twere awful, that more. She smiled a splendid smile. Although she wouldn't give details, she did say 'twas the best thing in life, what she and Patrick shared."

"And you want that with me?" he asked, scarcely believing his luck.

"Aye, Eamon, I do. Only with *you*."

The intensity in Rosaleen's green gaze stole his breath. He felt taller than mountains, mightier than bears. For that look, Eamon would gladly slay dragons. For Rosaleen's desire he was willing to challenge fate. The fate that had deemed them citizens of *Tyeer na N-og*, a place where love between man and woman didn't exist.

He shucked his pants, then got rid of his socks and shoes as well. When he turned back to the woman on the settee, a stab of need made his head spin.

Against the plum-colored settee, she was a vision in cream, darkest rose, and silver-gold hair. The curling fringe between her legs tugged at Eamon's curiosity; he would learn her every secret.

With enormous care, he came down on her, fitting their bodies, one to the other. Everywhere they touched, heat sizzled, skin tingled, hunger nipped. He brought his mouth back to her breasts while his hand sought treasures he had still to uncover.

He explored the silken skin of her belly, thrilled by the muscles undulating beneath his touch. Leaning to one side—nearly falling off the damnable settee—he made room for his hand to proceed lower still. He ran his fingers through the tangled hair and went further to hot, damp folds of responsive flesh.

Rosaleen's hips rose against his hand. Eamon parted the delicate layers, loving the sleek feel of her, the smoothness of her private parts. His finger found a tiny opening, and with care he began exploring. Deeper he went, stunned to feel her inner clasp.

By the Goddess, if this was the spot he suspected it was, his stiff, throbbing flesh would soon enter Paradise.

The throbbing increased. His hunger became a ravening beast, urging him to join their bodies. Reluctantly withdrawing his hand, he again levered himself over Rosaleen. She moved, accommodating him. Eamon parted her thighs.

With great care, he brought the raging part of him to the opening he'd found. Pausing, he sought her gaze, and finding it, read the invitation there.

Rosaleen's breath caught in her throat when she met Eamon's gaze. His thick shaft nudged her most private part. For a moment, she felt fear. Then she remembered the feel of his finger caressing her, bringing her pleasure.

Realizing he had stopped, she read the question in his green eyes. She wanted more of the delicious sensations he had brought her. More, the more Annie had spoken of. The more he was ready to give her.

She nodded, and wrapped her arms around him.

His hips pressed closer, and that hot, blunt part of him began to part her flesh. She felt herself stretch, as she knew she had to, given the size of his staff.

Deeper Eamon went.

Deeper Rosaleen felt him, and he began to fill a void she hadn't known existed until that very moment. The fullness grew to a stinging pressure, as if he'd never stop until they melded into one.

Then his hips jerked hard. She felt a stab of shock, a piercing. Dull discomfort followed, but his body covering hers felt wonderful, intimate. As did that foreign presence in her womb. She felt possessive . . . as if now he was somehow hers.

Eamon pulled back, and a ripple of awareness ran through her. She tightened her inner grasp, unwilling to let him go.

He uttered a ragged groan and returned to her depths. Sensation again flooded her, higher this time.

He withdrew. Plunged back. The flood rose each time.

His pace grew faster, wilder. Her sensations stronger, richer.

Deeper and deeper Eamon dove, again and again and again, each time making her feel he touched her heart, her soul. Her hips met his thrusts, and she read raw pleasure on his face. It echoed what she felt where they were joined as one.

She wrapped her arms around him, needing him closer, but it wasn't enough. She curled her legs around his thighs, pulling him deeper, feeling only scant relief. She needed more of him. All he had to give.

All he seemed intent on giving her.

Each push of his body shot liquid fire through her,

stealing her breath. She gasped. Cries broke in her throat. She clung to Eamon, moved with him, felt each pulse he sent through her. His fire seared deeper and deeper in her.

Suddenly feral pleasure struck her. She yielded to the ecstasy, flying higher, higher toward Paradise. At the pinnacle she cried his name in a burst of flames.

A mindless moment later, as the frenzy eased, Eamon's hips crashed hard against hers. His fingers bit her flesh. His body stiffened atop her, inside her. He dropped his head back, his features drawing into a fierce expression of the ecstasy she'd just known. Her name burst from his lips, the sound rough, elemental.

Holding him close, she felt shudders rack him, at first crash upon crash, one after the other, then slowing, finally growing random. Still she held him tight, enjoying the weight of his body, the heat of her man.

He was her man. Just as she had become his woman. Rosaleen smiled. All the wonders of *Tyeer na N-og* couldn't touch that mortal truth.

In proprietary luxury, she ran a hand over Eamon's flank, then closed her eyes and remembered.

Sixteen

Magic had happened.

That was the first thought that crossed Rosaleen's mind when she woke up a while later, her legs tangled with Eamon's, his hand holding her breast. The soreness between her legs reminded her how high he had sent her soaring.

Their loving was the single most magical thing she had ever experienced. And her a faerie, too.

Strange. She'd had to come to the mortal realm to discover magic. A magic that hadn't failed partway through.

A magic she hoped they would repeat as often as possible.

She smiled, remembering the piercing pleasure of Eamon's possession. They would have to do this again soon.

Running a hand down his chest, she chuckled as his stomach clenched the lower she went.

"You're playing with danger, *cailin*," he growled.

"Nay, not danger." She dropped a kiss on his smiling lips. "Pleasure."

"Mmmm. . . ."

At his murmur of assent, his flesh quickened against her thigh. She let her fingers creep closer still.

"You know the consequences of your actions now,"

A FAERIE TALE

he said in a teasing voice. "Are you ready to pay up?"

"With interest," she whispered in his ear, then ran her tongue around the rim as he had done to her. Her fingers reached their goal. She wrapped her hand around his shaft and relished the hot hard feel of him.

"Methinks," he said, covering her hand with his, "we would do better in a bed. More room, you know."

She nipped his earlobe. He shuddered, and his hips bucked. Pressing against him, she murmured, "Lead the way."

Without warning, he rolled off the settee, then swung her up in his arms. Rosaleen laughed, squealing as he nuzzled her neck with a stubbling chin. "Just you wait till I get you on that bed, *cailin*. I'm going to—"

"I can't," she said, cutting off his teasing. "I don't want to wait, Eamon. I want you again. *Now!*"

Seconds later, they entered a bedroom, and he placed her on a large bed. Rosaleen ran her hands over the navy-and-black-pieced quilt covering. It felt cool against her heated flesh. She hadn't expected passion to come so swiftly, bite so sharply, especially not so soon after having scaled its highest peaks.

Suddenly she realized Eamon hadn't joined her on the bed. She glanced up and saw him staring at her, a reverent look in his green eyes. "What is it?"

"Sure and I've never seen a lovelier sight."

'Twas true. Eamon couldn't believe his luck—again. The most beautiful female alive had just said she wanted him, after having shared herself with him a short time ago.

He studied her pale curves, her smooth shoulders, her ripe breasts with their dark nipples, her slender waist, her silk-covered mound. His flesh tightened, remembering, but he tamped down the urgency. Her rounded hips tapered to long, sleek legs, legs that had grasped and held him deep inside her, as if she would never let him go.

By the Goddess, and he had felt all-powerful in her clasp—in her arms, the grip of her legs, the hold of her depths. He needed to touch her, to kiss her again.

As he lay at her side, he said, "I love you, Rosaleen."

What? Where had that come from? Eamon caught his breath. He couldn't believe he had said that. But it was true. He did. "I truly love you, *cailin*."

Her potent smile appeared again. A knowing light brightened her jade-colored eyes. "Aye, Eamon Dooley, 'tis best ye do, for I love ye, as well."

A rough tremor shook him, and he took her in his arms. Bringing her close, he pressed her head into his shoulder, her breasts against his chest, her hips against his. "You're mine now," he added, as it was his only thought.

"As you are mine, too," she answered, wriggling her luscious body closer to his.

He kissed her. At first the kiss was tender, as if with its gentleness he could show her the depth of his feelings. Too soon, however, his hunger demanded different expression, and the kiss grew erotic, imitating the union to come.

Rosaleen's hands grew bold. When she held him again, he groaned his pleasure, giving himself up to her exploration. "Beware, *cailin*, 'tis a ravenous beast you hold."

"Just what I was after hoping to find." The teasing note left her voice. "I feel empty without you," she whispered.

He sucked in a breath at her admission. "We cannot be having that, then." He pressed her back on the bed and, finding his way between her thighs, he made them one again.

Patrick grew frantic. He had left the house nearly an hour ago, and had yet to find any trace of Annie. He had, of course, checked with Mayor Keller first. He hadn't wanted to arrive too late to prevent disaster. But in the Keller parlor he found a pale, teary-eyed Serena on the sofa, a handkerchief at her nose.

The mayor's face had been redder than usual, his protruding forehead damp. Father and daughter had clearly been in the midst of another argument, and Patrick had only stayed long enough to ask after Annie.

"You needn't trouble yourself about the girl," the mayor had boomed out. "I'm going to help with her Asylum—"

"Haven," Patrick had bit out, disliking what the mayor's slip of the tongue implied. Annie had a flighty nature, but she certainly didn't need institutionalizing.

The mayor had responded, "You, too?" Then he had shaken his head. "Never mind that. I'll be helping her from now on, and you needn't chase her down. She's probably buying stuff for her project."

Patrick had gone to the General Store, but hadn't found her there. She hadn't been home, or anywhere else in town, for that matter. Finally it occurred to him to run out to the scene of his fated picnic. As he approached, he caught a glimpse of blue-and-white cotton in the canopy of the maple she had occupied that day.

The closer he came, the better he heard her string of curses. Here and there, she voiced his name—not in dulcet tones, either.

It seemed Annie Brennan spared no love for him, even though he suddenly found it necessary to win her love. It scared him to think he loved the irritating, infuriating, bewildering, bedeviling, would-be artiste of Woodbury, Pennsylvania.

He'd be damned if Matthias Keller and his foultempered, spoilt brat would get away with stealing from the woman Patrick O'Toole loved.

Even if she hated him.

"Annie," he called from about six feet away, "could we talk?"

"I don't want to talk. Not with you."

"I know." She wouldn't give an inch, nor would she make things easy for him, but he wanted the best for her. The best when it came to her money, and the best when

216   GINNY REYES

it came to her future. And he now knew *he* was the best for her. He just had to prove it to her. "Will you come down if I promise not to argue?"

"Hah! You never speak to me without arguing."

"I bet I can this time."

"Can't."

"We didn't argue in your bed."

"Oooooh!" she wailed. "You *are* a cad, Patrick O'Toole."

"A mighty happy one, then. You were purring, too."

"See? You don't want to talk. You want to mortify me."

"If that's what it takes to get you down from that tree . . ." *And back into my arms*, he added, tucking the thought in his heart.

"I'm staying right here. You'd do well to return to the cave you escaped from."

"Cave?"

"Yes. Ill-tempered bears live in caves, I'm told."

He ground his teeth. He was on the verge of ill temper again, even though he couldn't afford it. "Annie, please. We must talk. Like adults."

"I am an adult. You're the child here. When I try to use my own money, you get all huffy and mad. You can't stand for someone to take away your toys, can you?"

There she went again, doing everything in her power to make him mad. But not this time; Patrick wasn't going to let her do it. "Annie, I don't want your money. I can earn enough for me and mine."

"What do you mean, yours? I thought you dumped Serena." Silence reigned for a minute. "Were you hiding someone somewhere while you did what you did in my bed?"

Patrick chuckled. "Can't call it by its name, can you?"

Silence ruled again.

Hmmm . . . interesting. "Can't you say we made love?"

A FAERIE TALE

217

A bird tweeted as it flew away. Patrick peered between the leafy branches and caught a glimpse of a fire-red cheek. He smiled. "Do you honestly think me that dishonest?"

Not a sound. Good grief, she was stubborn.

"Annie Brennan, you know damn well I ended my engagement to Serena *before* I invited you to the Benefit Supper. Do you think I would take you to bed, share your beautiful body, if I were tangled with another woman?"

When she still refused to respond, Patrick sighed. "You leave me no other alternative." Swinging a leg over the lowest branch of the maple, he scrambled up to where she sat.

Grasping her chin, he made her face him. "Look at me."

To his amazement, she did. "Look at me and tell me you believe I played you false."

Her eyelids shielded her magnificent sapphire eyes.

"You know me better than that," he said. "I wouldn't do a thing to hurt you. You must believe me."

She caught her bottom lip between her teeth. Suddenly the urge to taste that lip grew into a demand, but Patrick knew it would doom him forever in her eyes. And he was playing for forever. He exerted his considerable control.

"Please look at me again." She did. "I only want to protect you. And I *know* Mayor Keller and Serena want your money. They don't care a fig about your dreams."

Pain appeared in her eyes. "And you do?"

He smiled wryly. "To my surprise, yes. I don't particularly enjoy your misery. I would much rather you smiled as you did the other night."

She colored again and averted her gaze. "If you mention that one more time, I will shove you out of this tree."

He had pushed as far as he should. "Fine. I won't mention that night again—after I tell you I'll *always* treasure the most splendid experience of my life."

She gasped.

He continued. "But we have another matter to discuss. A more urgent one at the moment."

"Do you really think Mayor Keller is trying to swindle me? That is what you said."

"I may have been too blunt, but I know he's up to something rotten. Twenty-five percent interest is not normal. It is as unethical, dishonest, greedy, and practically illegal as he can get. He wants your money, that much I know."

"But why would he help me?"

"That's what I'm getting at. He is *not* helping you. Has he told you yet what he wants in rent?"

She nodded and whispered a sum that came dangerously close to her monthly stipend.

"Sweetheart," Patrick said in what he hoped sounded like a concerned, loving tone, "you can't afford to pay that. You won't have enough left to eat if you do."

"There are more important things than food, Patrick."

Like you, he thought, and bit his tongue to keep from saying it. "I know that. And so do you. If you think about it, you'll understand why I'm so upset. This crazy scheme of his will hurt you just as surely as it would hurt you to fall from up here."

"But I don't know what to do . . ."

"You could try listening to me."

She bit her lip again, but refused to meet his gaze. Clearly Eamon's crazy tale had placed doubts about his motives in her mind. She didn't trust him. At that moment, Patrick vowed to win her trust even if it was the last thing he did while drawing breath.

"You're afraid," he said. She nodded. He went on. "I have a suggestion. Since you can't trust the Kellers—"

At her skeptical look, he stopped and glared. "You *can't* and you know it, even if you won't let yourself trust me. Anyway, why don't you take the papers they want you to sign to an attorney? One *you* choose. If he determines they are legal and protect your interests, I promise

A FAERIE TALE 219

to keep my mouth shut when it comes to the Kellers. Furthermore, I promise to help you with your Haven in any way I can.''

The sapphires met his gaze. "You . . . really mean that?''

The hope in her expression tugged at his heartstrings. He was in trouble when it came to this woman. "I promise, sweetheart.''

"Don't call me that!''

"Reminds you too much of the other night—''

"You promised, you skunk!''

He raised his hands in surrender. "I know, I know. I apologize for the lapse,'' he said, making clear he felt no regret whatsoever. "Well? Will you do it?''

She grew serious. "Why not?'' she countered. "I have nothing to lose but time.''

"Do you know an attorney?''

"Not personally, but some of Da's business acquaintances in Harrisburg offered their help after he passed on. I'm sure one of them could recommend a reputable one.''

"Sounds like an excellent idea. You can use the bank's telephone to call.''

Annie nodded. "They both have those newfangled contraptions at their offices in town. A call would move matters faster than a letter would.''

For the first time in his life, Patrick felt the need for instant action. He was glad they lived in a progressive area of the country where telephones had been available for years. As far as he was concerned, the sooner he proved how crooked the Kellers were—and that Annie could trust him in every respect—the better it would be. "An excellent observation. We may make a businesswoman of you yet.''

"I just want to be an artist, if you please.''

As her chin rose, he gave it a kiss. *That* caught her attention. He saw emotions war in her expression, and he felt a rush of satisfaction. He would give her time to figure things out. Since she refused to discuss intimate matters, he would make sure her memories stayed fresh.

He would let their lovemaking fight his battle for him. For the moment.

Soon, Annie Brennan, he thought. *Soon you'll be mine.*

Later, after again experiencing more magic than he had known in *Tyeer na N-og*, Eamon remembered why he'd come to the mortal realm in the first place. "Ah, *cailin*, what a distraction you are. The best sort, of course, but a distraction nonetheless."

"I can say the same about you."

He chuckled. "I suppose you could, that. But I have serious matters to see to. I cannot be spending all my time in bed with you—no matter how much I would rather that than worry over the Kellers and their next dastardly deed."

Covering her beautiful breasts with the navy-and-black quilt, Rosaleen sat up. "And I have Patrick's future to ensure. You're the distraction here—an accomplished seducer, I would say."

Eamon couldn't help smiling with pride. "Seeing you're my first experience seducing, I'll thank you for the praise."

Rosaleen rolled her clear green eyes. "Still and all, I must be seeing to Patrick." Still clutching the quilt, she tried to stand. Eamon remained ensconced in his portion.

She tugged.

He grinned.

In the end she gave up, dropped the quilt, and went to the bedroom door. Eamon admired every lithe, feminine glide of her legs, the sleek curves of waist and hip, the sway of rounded buttocks.

"If you're so concerned about your charge," she said, opening the door, "I would suggest you dress and go mind your magical business."

"And leave you to yours, eh?"

A FAERIE TALE   221

"Precisely."

He watched her leave, catching a tempting glimpse of a swaying breast from the side. Rosaleen was the best thing that had ever happened to him. And truth be told, Eamon had no idea what he would do when he had to return to *Tyeer na N-og*. He wasn't sure he could give her up—not without losing the greater part of himself in the doing.

But she was right. He had important matters to see to.

Downstairs Rosaleen greeted him with a shocked gasp. "Eamon!" she cried. "Why, you're . . . naked!"

"Aye."

Eamon noted her refusal to look his way, and the bloom of roses on her cheeks. "Don't just stand there!" she cried. "Patrick could come back any minute now. Get dressed."

He crossed his arms over his chest. "You didn't seem interested in my getting dressed a wee while ago. In fact, your hands were mighty happy to go a-wandering over me—"

"Eamon Dooley! Mind your mouth."

"Aye, *cailin*, seems we both did fine at that, too."

She glared. "That was then, and this is now."

Eamon grew serious. "Regrets, *cailin*?"

She sobered immediately. For a long moment, she stared at her twisting fingers. Then she met his gaze. "None. But 'tis time to do what I came to do."

"Agreed." He fell silent as he dressed. Although the concept felt foreign to him, a thought occurred to him. "Do you think . . . would you care to . . . well, we seem to be working for the same end, and 'twould seem more practical and efficient . . . that is—"

"Aye, Eamon, methinks we ought to work together," she said, putting him out of his misery. "In fact, I suggested it from the start, I did."

His cheeks warmed. "Aye, but now that we have . . ."

"Have what?" She arched an eyebrow.

He scowled. "I don't care to argue with you anymore. Nor do I wish to try and best you. I think 'twould be in everyone's interest if you and I worked our magic together, for the good of all, you know."

"Faith, and 'twould seem you're suggesting cooperation."

"Don't you laugh at me, woman!"

"I hear no laughter."

"Ah, but there's chuckles and then there's the deeper, silent sort of laugh. 'Tis sure I am that you're laughing at me that way."

"Mayhap a bit." She cupped his jaw in her hand. "But methinks you've earned it, with your stubbornness and your interfering ways. Not to mention your bad luck."

Eamon frowned. "Nay, 'tisn't me luck that's bad, 'ist your fey spells that go awry."

"And we're at it again," she said. "Can't we stop the arguing? What really matters here, more than me wand and even your pot o' gold, is that Patrick and Annie find happiness. We want to make sure Annie's money is safe, and that Patrick's heart is in her safekeeping."

Eamon looked at Rosaleen with admiration. "As it should be," he said. "Aye, that matters more than me pot o' gold. So we're agreed. From now on, we're partners."

"Partners," she echoed, giving him a smile filled with tenderness and . . . more. The love she had confessed. Eamon's heart filled with emotion. If only . . .

But no. There was no time for empty wishes.

Seventeen

A week later, Patrick escorted Annie to the law offices of Bergmann, Keiser, & Buntz in Harrisburg. With his hooked, pugnacious nose and meager stature, Mr. Buntz reminded Annie of a bantam cock.

Lacing her fingers to hide their trembling, she waited as the lawyer studied the documents Mayor Keller had presented for her signature. She hadn't shown them to Patrick, knowing he would object regardless of what they said. She had, however, accepted his offer to escort her to Harrisburg, sorely needing the bolstering effect of his presence.

And resenting how much his company had come to mean.

As the moment stretched and grew more ominous, Annie caught her bottom lip between her teeth. What if Patrick was right? What if the Kellers *were* up to something foul? What would she do next?

She had no answers, so she stared at the attorney, noting each time he wrinkled his hawkish nose at what he read. His occasional frowns didn't give her much hope for his verdict.

Blast Patrick O'Toole! He was probably right about the

Kellers. As he seemed to be about practically anything and everything at all, to her dismay.

As she suspected he'd planned from the very start, she hadn't forgotten a minute of that night in her bed. Why, the very thought of the man conjured scandalous images at the most inappropriate moments. She would never forget how Patrick had looked, naked and aroused, just before—

"Ahem!" Mr. Buntz's cough caught Annie's wandering attention and brought it back to the matter at hand. Nothing, however, could dispel the heat in her cheeks.

Tugging reading spectacles down his beak, Mr. Buntz eyed Annie. "Young lady, I am *very* glad you brought these papers to me. I would hate to think Michael Brennan's child could lose everything he left her when I can prevent it."

"Oh, dear," she murmured. "So it *is* true . . ."

"I don't know what you are referring to, my dear, but if you sign these, you will lose the greater portion of your trust fund. Something I am sure you don't want."

Annie fought tears. "I want to open my Artist's Haven."

The lawyer's marblelike eyes narrowed. "What's this about a Haven?"

In broad verbal strokes, Annie painted a picture of her dream. Mr. Buntz listened, gnawing on the temple of his spectacles. When she was done, he remained silent for long moments. Then with another wrinkle of his impressive nose, he said, "I don't know that it would be the same thing, but I have heard tell the Chautauqua Foundation has some artistic endeavor in Mount Gretna. I don't believe Woodbury is too far from there."

"No . . ."

"Perhaps you can visit their establishment, gather ideas. We could then consider options for your . . . Haven, you said?"

She nodded. For a moment, she couldn't find the words

A FAERIE TALE

to speak. Mr. Buntz hadn't discounted her dreams. And he had offered to help.

The attorney tapped blunt fingers on his desktop. "I'll tell you what. If you do as I say, I'll be happy to meet with you after you have gathered details. We can evaluate your findings, discuss the best way to proceed. What do you think, Mr. O'Toole?"

For a moment, Patrick seemed taken aback. "To be honest, it hadn't occurred to me to investigate this matter, and for that, I apologize, Annie—Miss Brennan."

Annie gaped. This was a radical change. She narrowed her gaze. When the idea came from her, it was a bad one; but when Mr. Buntz did the proposing, it suddenly turned good. Hmm. . . .

Mr. O'Toole would hear how his client felt about that, and she would make sure he never made that mistake again.

Later.

"I like your suggestion," she said. "Very much. And if I can count on Mr. O'Toole's cooperation from now on"—she glared at the banker in question—"we will notify you when we complete our investigation."

"Excellent, my dear!" Mr. Buntz stood. "Just don't sign *anything* without first checking with Mr. O'Toole. Especially *not* what these swindling Kellers present to you."

Annie nodded. "I understand. And if, as you said, you are willing to help, then perhaps I don't need their house after all."

At her side, Patrick muttered, "You don't need anything the Kellers have to offer."

"Yes," she answered, "I'm beginning to see that now. But sometimes it's difficult to tell who is on one's side."

"Not if one uses a drop of common sense," he countered.

Annie's dander rose. "Are you implying I don't?"

"I'm not implying anything. *I* am stating fact."

226 GINNY REYES

"Don't you insult me, Patrick O'Toole!"

"And you haven't insulted me? When all I wanted was to protect you?"

"Ahem!" Mr. Buntz's cough reminded Annie they weren't alone.

An amused, indulgent expression softened the attorney's sharp features. Speculation gleamed in his bright black eyes. "It is gratifying to see Michael's daughter has a sensible champion looking out for her interests."

Annie shook her head. "It's not at all like—"

"Thank you, sir," cut in Patrick. "I take my responsibility to Annie most seriously. I will not let anything or anyone hurt her. Not if I can prevent it."

Mr. Buntz chuckled. "She is a lucky lady, indeed."

"That's what I try to tell her," Patrick said, "but she refuses to listen to anything I say."

The lawyer's laughter increased. "Perhaps the problem lies not in what you say, but in who does the saying. Advice is difficult to accept from those who matter most to us."

Annie gasped. Patrick's dark eyes met hers. An intimate smile curved his lips. She remembered a night full of other smiles, and flushed at the memories.

He chuckled. "You don't say. . . ."

Oh, dear! She had revealed too much, and she feared Patrick would capitalize on his newfound knowledge.

She also *hoped* he would.

Annie and Patrick exchanged not a word on the way back to Woodbury. A stifling presence shared the buggy with them—invisible but nearly palpable. Although Annie felt relieved that disaster had been averted, she didn't like knowing Patrick had been right about the Kellers.

Could he also be right about her Artist's Haven? Was it a crazy idea? If so, what did she have to look forward to?

Tears stung Annie's eyes. She had no one on earth to

A FAERIE TALE 227

call her own. Now it seemed she might also have nothing to live for. Her future seemed bleak indeed.

A pile of money in the bank didn't suggest any palatable possibilities for that empty stretch of life. What would her future bring?

When the horse came to a halt, Annie realized they'd arrived at her home. Patrick leapt out and came to her side of the vehicle.

"Thank you for coming with me," she murmured, exiting the conveyance.

He took her hand and tucked it into the crook of his arm. "I wasn't about to abandon you then, and I'm not about to do so in the future, either."

Her heart skipped a beat. Then she remembered how seriously he took his business. This was still about the Brennan fortune. The other night had been an aberration, or perhaps worse, a way to sway her into letting him maintain control of the account. Her heart called her crazy for thinking so, but Annie no longer felt sure about anything. Time would have to tell.

She would give Patrick time to show his true colors. "Now that Mr. Buntz is helping me," she said, taking her hand from his clasp, "you needn't worry about my trust fund. I won't squander it, I assure you."

He shot her an odd look. "Who said anything about you squandering your fund?"

"You have. Many times." Was he becoming forgetful now? "I see no reason for your continued concern—or interest. Mr. Buntz seems sensible enough even for you. I think you can trust him to keep me from endangering your responsibility to the bank—"

He whirled around, grasping her shoulders in his big hands. His eyes appeared nearly black. "Listen to me, Annie Brennan. Aside from not wanting to see you lack for anything, I couldn't care less what you do with that money. True, I take my work seriously, but I don't take

228 GINNY REYES

the money itself that seriously. The security money provides is what matters.''

When her gaze turned skeptical, he stuck his jaw out, and his stance grew stiffer. ''It's *you* I refuse to abandon. I don't want anything to happen to you. I don't want anyone to hurt you, and I know the Kellers will if you let them. I . . . care about you.''

Again, Annie's heart seemed to hop around in her chest. ''You . . . care about me.''

''Yes, I care about you. In fact, I lo—''

''There you are, boyo!'' Eamon strode out onto the front porch followed by a rosy-cheeked Rosaleen. ''We were a-wondering when you'd return.''

''And what you learned in Harrisburg,'' added Rosaleen.

Annie looked at her friend and smiled. Not only were the Irish girl's cheeks reddened, but also her lips were puffy, and her eyes sparkled. Her usually neat coil of silver-blond hair had come loose, and wayward strands framed her face.

''Hmm . . . are you sure you did any wondering while we were gone?'' Annie asked, mischief in her voice. ''It looks as if you might have been busy . . . with each other.''

The color on Rosaleen's face deepened, and Eamon preened. ''Aye, lass,'' he said, ''with me Rosaleen around, why, 'tis difficult to think but o' her!''

''Eamon!'' chided Rosaleen.

Patrick laughed. ''So, I was right.''

''How so?'' asked Eamon.

Patrick winked. ''Rosaleen doesn't tickle your fancy.''

Rosaleen scowled at Eamon. Eamon glowered at Patrick. Patrick laughed louder still.

A twinge of envy struck Annie. Lucky they who had found each other. At least the matter of a trust fund didn't lay between them.

''Ah, yes, but what did the big-city lawyer have to

A FAERIE TALE 229

say?" asked Eamon, obviously seeking a change of topic.

"Suddenly curious, are you?" teased Patrick.

"Oh, stop," said Annie, sympathizing with the mortified Rosaleen. "Let's go inside. We can sit in the parlor and discuss what we should do next."

Once they were all seated, the details of the visit to Mr. Buntz's office were relayed to Eamon and Rosaleen.

"Sure and I told you, I did," Eamon said, his auburn brows meeting in a frown.

Patrick nodded. "I owe you an apology for doubting you. Won't question your opinion again."

Eamon nodded. "Aye, but that isn't important now. What shall we do?"

"I don't think there's anything to *do*," said Patrick, "but we should keep a watch on the Kellers."

"I can watch the mayor," said Eamon. "You'd do well, boyo, to keep a close eye on matters at the bank."

A muscle worked in Patrick's cheek. "I plan to do that."

"Faith, and I can watch that nasty Serena, I can," offered Rosaleen.

"Better you than me," said Annie. "If I come too close, I might do. something I'd regret!"

Patrick and Eamon exchanged horrified looks. "Yes!" Patrick said. "Leave Serena to Rosaleen. We know how well you do regrettable things."

Annie scowled. "If you're referring to the turpentine, that was an accident. I didn't mean—"

"You never do," cut in Patrick. "But somehow things just . . . happen when you're around."

"Not only bad things," said Eamon with a wicked grin. "I'm after remembering a Bealtaine dance, and a night in wee Annie's bed—"

"Eamon!" scolded Rosaleen. "You're embarrassing the lass."

The reminder of that night made Annie wonder if it had

230 GINNY REYES

been as real for Patrick as for her. He'd said it had, but she couldn't shake the lingering worry.

"We weren't discussing that now," she said, hoping to turn the conversation back to its original topic. "We were talking about the Kellers. Besides, Patrick's engagement to Serena certainly qualifies as a regrettable action."

Patrick rose, looking decidedly uncomfortable. "There's nothing further to discuss. The Kellers are crooks. Sooner or later they will slip up and get caught. I intend to make sure their actions don't affect Annie." He gave her a dizzying smile reminiscent of those they had shared that special night.

Did it mean—

Silly! she scolded herself. She couldn't afford to think of such things. She had to protect herself—from the Kellers and from a broken heart.

She stood. "Since there's nothing more to talk about, then I'd better get some things accomplished. I won't have an accurate picture of my needs for Mr. Buntz if I don't make plans."

Patrick went to the door. "I have work at the office."

"I've a thieving mayor to go after," said Eamon.

Rosaleen made a face. "And I've a spoilt brat to follow."

After brief farewells, they dispersed. Annie went upstairs and plopped down on her bed. Her head spun, and a great pressure grew in her chest, suspiciously close to her heart.

She had to face the truth. No matter how she tried to deny it or escape it, she had fallen in love with Patrick O'Toole. Perhaps stranger things had happened in history, but this one seemed odd enough to her.

An artist in love with a straitlaced banker.

Yes, she was, and afraid to trust him. By all indications, Patrick was honorable and trustworthy, but he certainly appeared intent on protecting Annie.

Or Annie's funds.

A FAERIE TALE 231

She wondered if that intensity came from the caring he'd expressed, or if it came from some overgrown sense of duty to his work. Everyone knew Patrick took everything relating to the bank most seriously. The state of her trust fund would certainly reflect on the banker charged with its care.

She had always been aware of Patrick's determination to keep matters in control. He did whatever he could to make sure things went his way, even to the point of withholding her own money. Now he'd set himself up as Annie's chief protector.

She had never noticed the extent of his need to control. She wondered where it came from and wondered if that need to control his business affairs had extended to her. She *was*, in a way, a business matter.

Was his apparent personal interest just part of that need to control? Was that why he disdained her artistic nature, because it defied control?

What did he mean, he cared for her? Did he have deep feelings for her? Or was caring just another word for control?

Annie didn't know, and she had no idea how to go about learning if it was or not. The only thing she knew was that time would eventually reveal Patrick's intentions toward her.

But she had never been known for her patience, and she felt the strongest urge to know *now*.

Did Patrick O'Toole really and truly care for her? If he didn't now, could he later come to care for her as much as she cared for him?

Fiddlesticks! What was all this caring nonsense about, anyway? She should call it by its rightful name. Could Patrick O'Toole ever love her, Annie Brennan, as much as she loved him?

Across town, on her way to her father's office, Serena Keller fought the depression that had come upon her since

232 GINNY REYES

the night of the Benefit Supper. Evidently Patrick had meant it when he'd said he wouldn't marry her.

It was clear Annie Brennan had got farther with her feminine wiles than Serena ever had. To her chagrin, she remembered her unsuccessful efforts to seduce her fiancé during that disastrous picnic not so long ago. Every time she remembered Annie's unexpected appearance, she felt like screaming.

Knowing Annie saw her touch Patrick intimately—not to mention Patrick's efforts to evade her touch—made Serena angrier still.

She couldn't bear the humiliation Annie's unfathomable effect on Patrick had caused her. After all, he had never kissed *her*, his intended, as Serena found him kissing Annie on May Day night. It burned to think he would let Annie touch him when he had refused Serena the right to do so.

The more Serena thought of all the wrongs she had suffered because of Annie Brennan, the more determined she became to exact vengeance on her rival.

"Rival. Pah!" They weren't rivals for anything. Patrick had made his choice. He wanted Annie.

But Serena wanted him. Or she had. Now she wanted revenge. She wanted to get back at the two who had disgraced her before the entire town, the two who had denied her what she wanted, for the first time in her life.

Her mind made up, Serena opened the door to her father's office without knocking. The sight that met her eyes stunned her. A tall, well-dressed man stood not two inches away from Woodbury's mayor, a knife in his left hand. His right hand held the mayor's fine black silk tie.

"I warned you, Matthias," the stranger said in a deep voice, "that money was mine. I only offered you a loan. I expected you to pay me back. I want it *now*."

Neither man noticed her arrival. Frightened but curious, Serena closed the office door behind her.

A FAERIE TALE 233

A bead of sweat slithered from her father's brow to his round red nose. The mayor said, "I need time, Stephenson. If I had a way to come up with that large a sum, I wouldn't have had to borrow from you. I will pay you, but I need more time."

The man's grip on her father's tie never lessened. A shaft of sunlight entered the window behind the desk and caught the edge of the knife, making it wink wickedly. Serena gulped. The man holding that knife meant business.

"How much time?" asked Stephenson.

Desperation shone in her father's pale blue eyes. "I don't know. I can get the money, I just don't know when."

Like a cat would a mouse, Stephenson shook his prey. "Not good enough. Give me a date and stick to it."

Matthias Keller's nostrils flared. He paled, then turned puce. "Ah . . . er . . . July. Yes, July! Surely by then I'll have the money."

Stephenson shook the mayor again, then let go. Serena's father fell into his chair.

"Not good enough," said Stephenson, studying the play of light on the blade's edge. Then he looked at Matthias again. "But I feel fanciful today—and I would much rather have my money than your corpse. Midsummer Day. You had better have the money then, or else . . ."

The mayor gulped. "I'll do the best I can."

"No. You will have the money then."

"Or else?" asked Serena, remembering a time when her father said the same to her. Now she understood his vehemence that night.

Both men started.

"What are you doing here?" asked her father.

"Who the hell are you?" asked Stephenson.

"Mr. Stephenson," Serena said, extending her hand. He took it, and the strangest pang of energy flew through her flesh. "I'm Serena, the mayor's daughter."

Ice-blue eyes bored holes in her. "Pleasure," he said, not a hint of the emotion on his face or in his voice.

"Serena!" her father cried. "You haven't answered. What are you doing here?"

"Meeting your . . . associate," she said, never looking away from those strange eyes. "I believe you were discussing a loan?"

Mr. Stephenson's gaze didn't falter either. "Yes."

"Well, Father, isn't this a propitious occasion? I came to tell you I'm prepared to help with your Brennan project, after all. Any way I can."

Hope sparked in her father's eyes. "At last you see reason," he said.

"Yes, Father, at last I see . . . a reason." She turned back to Mr. Stephenson, and noticed the scar running from the corner of his right eye to his jaw. It did nothing to mar the man's dangerous appeal. Serena shivered deliciously.

The man's lips quirked in a semblance of a smile. "An interesting development . . ." he murmured, the smile not reaching his ice-blue eyes.

Serena smiled as excitement, fear, she didn't know which, shimmered through her. "Interesting indeed."

Eighteen

Early the next morning, Annie responded to a knock at her front door. To her amazement, Mayor Keller and Serena stood on the porch, smiling perhaps *too* broadly. What did they want with her now?

Donning a smile of her own, Annie gestured for them to come inside. "To what do I owe your visit?"

"Well, my dear," boomed the mayor, "I gave you that rental contract some days ago. Since I didn't hear back from you, I thought it would be wise to see if you had signed it."

Oh, dear! Of course she hadn't signed it. She had no intention of doing so, but she also had no idea how to handle this development. Where was Patrick O'Toole when she needed him most?

At the bank, of course. Where else?

"Ah . . . well, you see . . ." she started weakly, then cleared her throat and tried again. "I've been terribly occupied with plans for the Haven and haven't had time to read all those pages."

Annie groaned inwardly. Surely she could have come up with something more sensible than that. She sounded like the world's greatest fool, a matter she saw didn't escape the mayor's notice.

236   GINNY REYES

"Annie, dear," he said, wrapping a heavy arm around her shoulders. She scooted out of his reach.

He continued as if nothing had happened. "You cannot open the Haven if we don't sign the documents, you understand. All your planning will be wasted if you don't have a place to house your establishment."

Flustered, Annie decided to continue with the flighty artist impression. "I understand," she said, "and I promise to read everything. Soon, too. I just haven't done it yet."

Serena's cynical sniff caught Annie's attention. "I do realize," the mayor's daughter said in a superior tone, "not everyone is gifted with business acumen, but we can't promise to hold our offer open indefinitely. We must resolve this matter posthaste."

Annie's temper threatened to run away with her, but she bit down hard and counted to ten. "I understand, Serena. Really, I do. I promise to read the contract immediately."

"And sign it," inserted the mayor.

"I will take care of it."

Serena chuckled nastily. "Sometime between art projects and Patrick, I presume."

"My personal business is none of your concern. Or does losing come so hard for you?"

Red circles blotched the fair woman's cheeks. "Losing? When have I ever lost, Annie Brennan?"

Annie gave her a pointed look. "It seems you're no longer betrothed. I would say you lost a fiancé."

Irritation made Serena grimace, but then a greedy gleam blossomed in her eyes. "Let's just say I have recently found a more . . . appealing prospect than a small-town banker."

"Serena!" barked the mayor.

"Oh, hush, Father," she said. "You can keep Patrick O'Toole, Annie, insipid and dispassionate as he is."

Annie's eyes nearly popped out. *Dispassionate?* Not

A FAERIE TALE

the Patrick she knew! But it was in her best interest to keep that knowledge to herself.

"I'm glad you found a new suitor," she said in a conciliatory tone.

But Serena was in no mood for conciliation. "Yes, Annie, a provincial like you must take what you can get. Those of us with more sophistication have choices, and I recently decided to explore one of my choices."

"Serena!" bellowed the mayor. "We didn't come to discuss this with Miss Brennan. We came because we have an unsigned contract outstanding—for a substantial sum of money."

"Ah, yes," murmured Serena. "The money. There is that. Really, Annie, it is most inconsiderate of you to keep us dangling like this. You simply must stop behaving like a crackpot artist. Do sign those papers."

The crackpot artist comment nearly made Annie explode. "As I said, Serena, Mr. Mayor, I'll see to it soon. Now, if you will excuse me, I have a previous engagement."

"With your paints, I presume," murmured Serena.

"A painter must paint," Annie answered, knowing she sounded more eccentric than ever. Then she remembered. *They* were crooks—far worse than artistic or flighty, as she had so often been called.

Squaring her shoulders, she led them to the door. "I *will* take care of the documents."

The mayor's piggy eyes narrowed. "See that you do, young lady."

A cold shiver ran through Annie at the threatening note in his voice. She had actually considered going into business with this man? What had she been thinking of?

"Good day, Mr. Mayor, Serena."

The moment Annie closed the door, Serena turned to her father. "It shouldn't be too difficult. After all, everyone thinks she's missing a few parts up here." She tapped her temple.

"It shouldn't prove difficult to spread word around that she has gone beyond eccentric," said the mayor, going down the steps, "but how do you intend to get past Patrick now?"

Serena shrugged. Aside from making sure he got what he deserved for his role in her humiliation, Patrick had slipped from his previously significant position in her concern. "I just will. And we'll have the documents giving us access to Annie's money. You can pay Mr. Stephenson, and then I can . . ."

Serena's voice trailed off as she allowed her imagination to conjure possible scenarios starring the deliciously dangerous Mr. Stephenson. "What is his first name, Father?"

The mayor gave his daughter a blank stare. "Whose?"

Serena responded with a toss of the head. "Mr. Stephenson, of course."

"Oh." Her father fell silent. "I don't know. Never had need for it."

"I guess it's up to me to find out."

"Don't go fooling with that man, Serena. He's dangerous."

"*Mm-hmm* . . . and I suddenly find myself hungry for a touch of danger."

"You could get hurt."

She arched a skeptical brow. "You're suddenly worried about my feelings?"

"Not your feelings. Your life."

She chuckled. "I'm not the one who owes him a great deal of money. I just happen to like the way he looks."

"Serena . . ."

"Oh, stop with your threats. You need me. You can't get the money to save your hide without me, and you know it. I will take care of Mr. Stephenson for you. With pleasure."

"Don't make any mistakes. You know what's at stake."

A FAERIE TALE   239

"Yes, you," she said, but her mind was back on the mysterious Mr. Stephenson. This time she would succeed. She now saw the error in her earlier ways. Patrick wasn't the man for her. She needed a stronger man, one with an exciting edge, like Mr. Stephenson.

This time Annie Brennan wouldn't figure into the picture.

"All you need to do, Father, is get Annie to sign the rental agreement. I'll copy her signature, and get it past Patrick. In the meantime, make sure everyone in town hears how batty Annie has become."

"Perhaps their romance can play in our favor."

Serena considered the possibility. "You may be onto something there. Let folks know how love has made her even more flighty than usual. Tell everyone how forgetful she is, how she can't remember what she says and does. Like signing contracts for a great deal of money."

"Will you be able to copy her signature well enough?"

"I daresay."

"This isn't a game, Serena. You saw Stephenson."

"Oh, yes," she purred, "I certainly saw the man."

The mayor made an exasperated sound. "Pay attention, daughter, or we will both end up at the bottom of the mighty Susquehanna on Midsummer Day!"

"Speak for yourself, Father. I intend to spend that day with my new beau."

"The money, Serena, first the money."

"Very well, Father, first the money. I promised to help, and I will." A wicked smile curved her lips. "Just imagine how angry Patrick will be when he realizes how much money Annie has signed over to us. He won't be kissing her for a while! Of course, I'll help you get the money. It will be a pleasure to sour Annie Brennan's days as she soured mine."

When Patrick appeared at Annie's front door two evenings later, she found herself agreeing to the twilight stroll he proposed. She hadn't seen him in days, and she'd begun to fear he had lost all interest in her after she agreed to consult with him—and accept his recommendations—on matters regarding the Haven.

Then he showed up at her door, looking ever so handsome in his dark suit and white shirt, his hair waving back from his forehead. She couldn't have refused him, even if she had wanted to.

And so, when the sun began to set over Woodbury that June night, Annie held Patrick's arm as they crossed the town, chatting.

Although the weather was not foremost in her mind, Annie didn't know how to turn the conversation toward more intimate matters without seeming overly forward. She had no idea how to go about learning if a man loved her. She was sick to death of discussing the effect of the mild temperatures on the corn crop. As they approached the bank, she asked, "How are matters at work?"

Patrick shot her a disbelieving look. "I thought you hated discussing business."

"I find I hate the state of the weather even more."

Patrick stiffened. "There is no pleasing you."

I wouldn't say that, she thought, remembering how well his caresses pleased her. But she didn't dare voice such a bold thought. She tried another tack. "Have the Kellers done anything suspicious?"

Patrick made a face. "Suspicious? Nowadays everything they do seems suspicious, but I can't say they have done anything larcenous." His gaze turned piercing. "You haven't signed anything, have you?"

Annie shook her head. "But they came to my house the other day to urge me to do so."

"And did you?"

"Of course not! Didn't Eamon give you my message?"

"Yes, he did. But I wondered if you would eventually cave in. After all, that Haven has been the most important thing in your life for quite a while now."

A FAERIE TALE   241

Until you, Annie thought, but kept it to herself, as well. "I said I wouldn't do anything foolish, and I haven't."

"That's good." He fell silent, and they continued their walk.

Annie's discomfort grew with their silence. Just as she was about to explode, she noticed a flicker of light at the side of the bank building. "Look!" she cried, pointing. "What is that?"

"What is what?" Patrick asked.

"That light. Near the bank's rear door."

"I don't see any light." Patrick tried to resume walking. Annie balked. "Are you sure you saw—"

"What?" she asked, glaring. "You're going to accuse me of imagining things?"

"Well. . . ."

Annie yanked her hand back and, as she did with its mate, slammed it fisted on her hip. "I saw something! If you insist on being offensive, I shall see myself home."

"I wasn't being offensive, Annie. I was just wondering if you just thought you"—he shrugged—"saw something. It happens to people all the time."

"Does it happen to you?"

"Ah . . . er . . . well, no."

"Again, if you must be offensive, I'll see myself home—"

"There!" he cried. "I see it now. Someone's at the back door of the bank. Run and get Officer Riley. It looks like someone is trying to break in!"

As fast as her skirts allowed, Annie took off with only a wistful glance toward Patrick. He would surely be in the thick of the fun, while she went to summon the police. But if he was right, and someone *was* breaking into the bank, why, then she might help catch the thieves.

Oh, my! How exciting. A bank robbery in sleepy old Woodbury. Nothing like this had happened before. And Annie Brennan was taking part in the excitement.

242 GINNY REYES

She wondered how Patrick would handle the robber. Would he face danger?

Hiking up her skirts, she ran faster, fearing for Patrick's safety. It was up to her to protect the man she loved from the crooks. She would bring him help.

As soon as Patrick was sure Annie had gone to fetch Riley, he turned to the matter at hand. Robbers. Breaking into *his* bank. Not if he could help it.

Approaching the rear of the red-brick building, his heart pounded faster. How many of them would he have to confront? Were they armed? And just how was he going to keep them from making off with the money in the vault?

That last made him pause. Perhaps he ought to wait until Annie returned with Riley. But no. Then he would have to worry about *her* as well as the bank funds.

As he considered his options, he heard a familiar voice. Serena? Serena Keller was breaking into the bank?

Squinting in an effort to see through the moonless dark, Patrick caught sight of a familiar, bulky figure. As he watched, the mayor of Woodbury squatted before the door and began working at the lock. A third figure hovered in the shadows, but Patrick wasn't able to identify the man.

Realizing he couldn't take on all three perpetrators, Patrick chose to remain hidden and wait for Riley to appear. In the meantime, he watched the events unfold before him.

While the mayor worked doggedly at the door, it became obvious that his daughter was not particularly interested in Matthias Keller's criminal efforts. Instead, she returned to the other man's side time and again, and Patrick, having once been the recipient of her attentions, realized that Serena had found a new object for her affection.

Patrick wondered who the man was, since he didn't recognize the tall figure shrouded in shadow. To his amazement, he realized he didn't harbor the slightest regret over his ended engagement to the mayor's daughter. Certainly not after learning what a dishonest sort she was.

As he studied the tableau, well aware of the passage of time, he wondered when Riley and Annie would arrive, if they would even get there before the mayor made it into the bank. At the very least, before the three took off with the loot.

As if conjured by his thoughts, Riley huffed and puffed to a halt by his side. "What's this Miss Brennan says about a break-in?"

Patrick pointed toward the mayor. "Matthias Keller's trying to get inside."

"Why that . . . So she *was* right."

He gave Officer Riley a disgusted look. "Annie? Of course, she was. Did you think I sent her on a joke?"

"No, no, no, no. It's just . . . well, everyone's been saying she's . . . sappier than usual these days."

"Annie?" Patrick asked, stunned.

Riley shuffled his feet. "Well, yes. They say she's crazy as a loon in . . . love."

"Annie Brennan?" He hadn't noticed the change, and Patrick was sure he would have.

"Yes! They say after you took her to the Benefit Supper, she's battier'n before. She forgets what she says, does things and doesn't remember she's done 'em."

Patrick frowned. "That doesn't sound right. Yes, she can be flighty at times, but I can't say she's crazy. Who is saying these things?"

Riley shrugged. "I dunno. Everyone, I guess."

Something wasn't right here. Annie's behavior had been more reasonable than usual of late. "Where is she, anyway?"

The policeman shook his head. "Didn't say where she was going. She just took off."

That didn't sound like the woman Patrick knew. He'd expected her to return with Riley, not wanting to miss a thing. As he debated whether he should leave the crooks

244 GINNY REYES

to the officer and go after Annie, he heard the mayor exclaim in triumph. He had broken the lock. A possible explanation for various seemingly unrelated things occurred to him. "I wonder . . . could the gossip and the mayor's actions tonight be connected?"

"Yes, well, Mr. O'Toole," said the policeman, "we can talk about this some other time, but right now it's late, and a man is walking into the bank. I have to catch him afore he cleans out the vault."

"I'll help," said Patrick, sudden anger burning in him. Anger at the Kellers' audacity in breaking into his bank, and anger at the ugly rumors he suspected they'd been spreading.

As Patrick followed Riley through the open door, taking advantage of Serena and her beau's continued embrace, he didn't see Annie return.

Heading toward the rear of the bank, Annie kept looking for Patrick, but saw no sign of him. Which was just as well in her opinion, since he would most likely have sent her home like an errant schoolchild. Annie was not about to miss the capture of the first robber in Woodbury's history.

After fetching the officer, she had gone to find Eamon, thinking Patrick and Riley would need reinforcements. But she hadn't found the Irishman at the O'Toole home, and unwilling to miss the excitement, she had hurried back to the bank.

As she approached the door where she had first spotted the light, Annie noticed two figures in the darkened space between the bank and Woodbury's general store. A man and a woman were caught in what appeared to be a most passionate embrace. If she wasn't mistaken, the woman was none other than Serena Keller. What on earth was she doing behind the bank, kissing some stranger, while the bank was being robbed?

Suddenly everything fell into place. "Of course!"

Annie's money wasn't enough for the greedy Kellers.

They wanted everything in the bank. The man with her must be their accomplice! But why were they kissing at the scene of the crime? Where were Patrick and Officer Riley? How did they intend to catch Serena and her crooked lover if they weren't anywhere near the action?

"Well, it looks as if they left it all up to me," she said and, squaring her shoulders, started toward the couple.

A few steps later, her toe bumped something hard, and Annie bit her tongue to keep from crying out in pain. Bending to see what nearly felled her, she found a thick board, caked with dirt, but solid enough and heavy enough to offer protection.

Hefting her weapon, she resumed her advance. When she came close enough to hear the couple's ragged breathing, their broken murmurs, she frowned. Now what? How was she supposed to capture the two of them? All by herself, no less.

Then she noticed the open door to the bank and the dim light burning inside. Someone had broken in.

Of course! The mayor must be inside.

Tiptoeing toward the building, Annie lifted the board high above her head, ready to use it should the need arise. But before she knew what was happening, it was snatched away, and a deep voice murmured, "I'll take that."

Shocked, Annie looked up into a nearly colorless pair of eyes. The tall stranger who had seconds earlier been kissing Serena now held Annie's weapon and studied her, malevolence in his icy stare. "Who are you?" he asked.

"She's nobody," answered Serena. "Just a convenient heiress."

The man set one end of the board on the ground at his side, then leaned on it, never taking his ghostly gaze from Annie. "The one your father swore he'd get the money from?"

Annie stiffened with indignation. "I'll have you know I'm not some gullible, small-town fool—"

Serena laughed. "Of course you are, Annie. That's why

246 GINNY REYES

Father is in the bank right now making sure all the lovely money your father left you ends up in our hands—not yours.''

''He won't get away with it,'' Annie said. ''I got Officer Riley.''

Serena laughed louder. ''That fool wouldn't know what to do with the pistol he carries. He'll probably end up shooting himself in the foot.''

A shot rang out inside the bank building. A cry of pain followed.

When Serena's accomplice glanced toward the open door, Annie saw her opportunity. She kicked the board out from under him and as he tried to regain his balance, she grabbed the slab of wood and ran inside the bank.

A shadowed form came at her and Annie raised the board high in the air. With all her strength, she brought it down on the man's head.

''Oooooff!'' she heard in a familiar voice.

Uh-oh. If her worst fears were right, she had just felled—

''Patrick, me lad!'' exclaimed Eamon from the doorway. ''What is he doing on the ground? And why are you staring at him like that, Annie, lass?''

''Where have you been?'' she asked. ''The mayor is cleaning out the bank, Officer Riley is who knows where, a gun just went off, Serena and some strange, scary man are kissing outside, and . . . and I'm afraid I just killed Patrick!'' She knelt to inspect the damage done to Patrick's head.

''Faith, Eamon Dooley, and don't ye have just the worst luck of all!'' exclaimed Rosaleen as she stepped over Patrick.

''Nay, *cailin*. The lad was like this when I got here. I had naught to do with it.''

Rosaleen shook her head, clearly doubting everything he said. She turned to Annie. ''Serena and some man are outside, you say?''

A FAERIE TALE   247

Annie stopped rubbing the goose egg growing on Patrick's forehead. "Why, yes," she said. "And he took the board from me. Then, when we heard the shot, I got it back. I came inside, but I couldn't see well, and when someone ran toward me, I thought it was the mayor, and I . . ."

"Aye, Annie, lass, you certainly did, didn't you?"

"He has a huge bump on his head," she said, scared. "Do you think I . . . killed him?"

Eamon shrugged, then knelt and checked for Patrick's pulse. True, she had slammed him with the board, but she didn't think she had done so *that* hard. Surely not hard enough to kill a man. The man she loved.

"I couldn't have killed him," she said, her throat tightening, eyes stinging. "Could I?"

"Nay, lass, he's not dead. But his disposition won't be pleasant for a day or two."

Annie tipped up her chin. "Then I shall nurse him back to health to make up for my mistake."

"Aren't you forgetting something?" asked Rosaleen.

"The mayor!" cried Annie.

"The mayor!" cried Eamon.

"Won't be going nowhere," said Officer Riley as he entered the room, puffing out his chest. "I just got me Woodbury Prison's first prisoner. Shot 'im right through the foot, too."

"Aren't you forgetting someone else?" asked Rosaleen.

Annie met her friend's gaze. "Serena!"

Rosaleen nodded. "There was no one outside when Eamon and I arrived."

"Are you sure?" asked Annie.

"Sure and we're sure," answered Eamon.

"They must have got away," Annie murmured. Then she turned to Officer Riley. "Follow them! They were part of the scheme. You must catch them, too."

Officer Riley scratched his head. "Don't know, Miss

248   GINNY REYES

Annie. All's I saw when I got here was the mayor at the lock and two people kissing in the alley. I can't go arresting folks for kissing, now can I?''

Annie stomped her foot. "But Serena *told* me they came to rob the bank.''

"Miss Keller *told* you she came to rob the bank?'' the officer asked.

"Well, not exactly. She said her father was in here helping himself to my money.''

"Did anyone else hear her say that?''

"Sure. The man she was with.''

"And where is he, Miss Annie?''

Running to the door, Annie looked one way, then the other. There was no one in sight. Of course. By now, they would find no trace of Serena or her companion. Although crooked and petty, Serena Keller wasn't stupid. She wouldn't stay around Woodbury long enough to be arrested.

And the man she'd been with ... Annie shivered. Those eyes. "They're gone, and I'm sure we'll never see them again.''

A pathetic moan burst from the man on the ground. Annie returned to his side. "Oh, Patrick! Are you all right?''

Horror rounded his eyes. "Get away from me, you madwoman! This is the second time you tried to kill me. I won't let you near enough to succeed!''

Annie's throat tightened. A vice gripped her heart. Tears spilled from her eyes. What was she going to do?

Patrick believed she had tried to kill him. He wanted nothing to do with her. She wanted nothing to do but love him.

Nineteen

"Annie . . . oh, yes, *Annie* . . . ANNIE!" Gasping, his body shaking from the effort to hold back, Patrick relished Annie's methods of nursing a man to health. "Where did you learn to do that?"

Smiling wickedly, she lowered her lips to his and, with deft fingers, repeated her stunning touch on his aroused flesh. "You taught me, and I'm a quick learner."

She ran her fingers lower, lightly caressing the sack beneath his erection. He strained upward. When she rubbed a thumb across the tip, he moaned, arching his back off the bed.

"I'll say you learn quickly." Trapping her hand against his belly, he rolled over, pinning her to the bed.

"Do you believe me?" she asked, her eyes earnest.

"What? That you weren't trying to kill me?"

She gasped when he licked a tight nipple. "Yessss . . ."

"After you've spent ages now torturing me with your fingers and mouth? Of course you're trying to kill me, woman! But not with a wooden board."

Her gaze turned sultry. "Then why don't you go ahead and put us both out of our misery?"

With a tilt of his hips, he entered her partway. "Like that?"

"More . . ."

He gave her more.

"More, Patrick, more . . . I want *all* of you!"

Since it was what he wanted, too, he gave it to her. With joy and passion and, yes, love. He loved Annie, and he used his body to demonstrate how he felt about her, how much he wanted to please her, to make her his.

They climbed the heights of passion, and at the peak, reason vanished. Reality burst into shards of joy. They spun though eternity on spirals of pleasure, and finally came back to earth in each other's arms.

Long, slow touches. Warm, gentle kisses. A lingering closeness felt too intimate to sever, and Patrick wondered how life had existed before Annie, how it could continue without her. He refused to consider the possibility. "I love you, you know."

She caught her breath but remained silent.

"I do," he repeated. "I don't know why or how or even when it happened, but I do know I love you. And I want you with me forever. Will you marry me?"

"You . . . really mean that? After everything?"

"I wouldn't ask otherwise."

"You asked Serena."

"That was different."

Shrewdness burned in her stare. "How so?"

Patrick reached down and cupped Annie's chin. Caressing her silky skin, he read questions and doubts in her blue gaze. He saw fear in her face. Kissing the tip of her nose, he tightened his other arm around her. "Because I didn't love her, and I *do* love you."

A slow smile brought wonder to her features. "You *do* mean it!"

He kissed her forehead, her eyelids, her lips. "I love you. It surprises me how much, and how spontaneously, naturally it happened. At first you simply irritated me, then one day I saw you . . . differently. Now when I look at you, my heart feels full enough to burst, I feel like

A FAERIE TALE

laughing, like picking you up and spinning you around. I want to rush you to the nearest bed and make love to you again and again and again.''

She winked. ''Hmmm . . . can't say I object.''

He laughed. ''No, a little while ago you weren't objecting at all!'' Running a hand down her side, he smoothed the satin warmth of her skin, the ripe curve of her hip, the full softness of her buttock. She pressed tighter against him, and Patrick's body responded again.

''So?'' he asked.

Mischief danced in her eyes. ''So what?''

''Will you?''

''Will I what?''

''Annie . . .''

She laughed a new, throaty laugh. ''Don't threaten me, Patrick O'Toole. I wouldn't be here draped over you without a stitch on if I weren't about to say yes.''

''So you'll marry me.''

''Of course.''

''Why?''

''What do you mean, why?''

''Annie . . .''

She rose to her knees, a vision in rose and cream draped in black velvet. Her hair parted over her full breasts, the pink nipples enticing him in a way he couldn't ignore. Patrick reached out and caressed one of the budded crests.

''I love you, Patrick,'' she whispered, her voice breaking as his touch grew insistent. ''I love you more than I can say. But I can show you. Again.''

She came down to him, her tender, wicked lips demonstrating her desire, her need, her love.

Annie was his.

Desperation bit hard as Rosaleen looked at the man atop her. Eamon's eyes glittered with passion, his features etched by his tautened skin. His biceps bulged as he held himself still, studying her as if to memorize every detail.

252   GINNY REYES

Reaching up, she outlined his russet eyebrows, his straight nose, his lips.

Those lips . . . they were truly magical, more magical than anything she had ever known in *Tyeer na N-og*. He used them to bring her more pleasure and joy than she had ever imagined existed. "Kiss me again," she whispered, running her fingers through his hair.

" 'Twill be my pleasure, *cailin*."

"Nay, mine. All mine." When he touched her, she sighed, opening for his searing kiss.

Long, hot lashes of his tongue ravaged her mouth, and Rosaleen couldn't stifle the whimpers at the back of her throat. Clasping his shoulders, she dragged him down on her, enjoying his hot weight against her flesh. She wanted him. Needed him.

Loved him.

Her fevered hands ran over his back, cupped his tight buttocks. She curled her legs around his. All of him, she wanted all of him, and not just for now. She returned his kiss, nipping his lips, sucking his tongue, seeking the hidden corners of his mouth.

Still hungry for more, she undulated against him, pressing her hips to the hard flesh nudging her center. She wanted him *now*. Digging her fingers into his hips, she angled hers to bring him to where she wanted him most. "Please, Eamon, I need you."

"Ah, *cailin* . . ." He plunged deep. Urgency blazed through her, making demands on her, pushing her to demand more from him.

She bucked. He thrust. She arched. He delved. Swift and wild, their joining was a rough affirmation of reunion, of belonging, of love.

Rosaleen felt him catch his breath and slow his pace. As fear of the future permeated the haze of her passion, his caresses gentled, grew languorous. It seemed as if he meant to draw from every touch the last possible ounce of pleasure. The tenderness in his lovemaking was heart-breaking, so drugging, so addictive that Rosaleen knew she would die the day she had to turn her back on him.

But he was still here. While he remained inside her, she would live each second to the fullest. She pulled him down for another kiss, their tongues darting, tasting, savoring a banquet of passion and love.

Eamon again rose on his arms, seeming never to tire of gazing at her. Rosaleen ran her hands over his corded biceps, down his sinewy chest, to his lean hips. He was indeed still with her, and she wanted him now.

As if he had read her mind—or perhaps her inner caresses—Eamon relinquished the last of his control, riding her hard and fast. Her body answered, shuddered. She cried out his name.

When completion wracked her, Rosaleen spun into a shower of stars more brilliant than the ones sparkling against the night sky outside. Waves of joy crashed through her, and she clung to Eamon. As the final spasms of her climax ebbed, she felt him swell and explode deep inside her.

"Rosaleen . . ." Her name escaped his lips in a sound so ragged, so broken she wondered if he would survive the violence of their passion, or if he had already begun to suffer the death their inevitable parting would surely bring.

For long seconds, the only sound in the room was that of rough breathing and thudding heartbeats. Knowing the moment wouldn't—couldn't—last, Rosaleen took advantage of Eamon's exhaustion to caress him as she knew she soon would not be able to do.

She ran her hands over his taut, silky skin, warm and damp from the exertion of their lovemaking. She tested the strength of the lean muscles in his back, his shoulders, his arms. She ran her foot over his calf as it lay between her legs, feeling the crisp hair that made it so different from her own. She kissed the erratic pulse in his neck, tasting the salty tang of his perspiration on the tip of her tongue.

With infinite sadness, he murmured, "Ah, *cailin* . . . ," then withdrew from her depths, making her heart quake. Every instinct urged her to hold on to him, but Rosaleen acknowledged the futility of fighting fate.

They weren't of this world. Soon they would return to theirs, and love didn't belong there. It was best if the parting didn't come too abruptly . . . although it would inevitably come.

In silence, each rolled away from the other. Rosaleen pulled the light cotton blanket around her, as if its comfort could make up for the loss of Eamon's warmth. She heard him sigh, resignation in the sound. He didn't use his portion of the coverlet, and she felt more alone than ever.

Their good-byes had begun.

Without exchanging a word about their imminent separation, Rosaleen and Eamon rose the next morning and dressed. A weight so heavy she swore it would crush her settled over Rosaleen's heart as she descended the stairs in Annie's house.

True, it seemed she had accomplished what she came to the mortal realm to do. Patrick was no longer in danger of marrying Serena Keller; instead, he showed all indication of marrying his true love.

Despite that success, and the probable attainment of her wand, Rosaleen found nothing to buoy her spirits. Each time she heard Eamon move or caught sight of his dear face, she felt as if her heart would break.

She wanted him. Forever. Far more than she wanted that blasted wand. But they didn't belong here, and their futures were meant to be lived apart.

" 'Twas lucky I arrived on the scene when I did last night," Eamon commented as he retrieved his socks from where he'd dropped them last night in front of the stairs. "I made sure Annie's pot o' gold remained safe."

A FAERIE TALE

Luck and magic were the last things Rosaleen wanted to discuss. Especially Eamon's luck. "Faith, and I can't believe you're after saying that," she muttered, sitting on the parlor sofa. "Why, I doubt Patrick would have ended up on the floor if you hadn't meddled—as usual."

"Sure and you're not telling me you cast another spell?"

"I've told ye many times not all me spells go wrong."

"Did you or did you not cast a spell, Rosaleen Flynn?"

Sitting tall, she said, "I cast a spell, I did. And everything worked out fine. Annie and Patrick are together, and the mayor is warming a jail cell."

Eamon sent her a superior smile as he slipped a leather belt through his trouser loops. "You're forgetting Serena and her friend."

"I'm not forgetting a thing!" Rosaleen exclaimed, peeved. "They weren't breaking into the bank, and when Patrick dumped her, Serena became unimportant."

Eamon waved impatiently. "Not according to Annie. Serena and her new beau were helping the mayor in his nefarious deeds. They just managed to slip past your poor spell. Shows a marked lack of attention to detail."

"Nay, Eamon Dooley, 'twas your bad luck that let them get away. Faith, and I don't know how you've managed to get along this far without me help! I've never known a leprechaun with worse luck."

" 'Tisn't like that a'tall! You're the one with the problem, lass. I've yet to meet a faerie with a worse touch at magic than you."

Rosaleen stood, pride in her stance. "Just look at my results. Patrick found his true love, as I was sent to make sure he did. Me magic worked fine."

"Nay, lass, 'twas me luck that brought them together *and* kept Annie's treasure safe."

" 'Twas me magic that brought them love."

" 'Twas me luck that brought love to them."

She smacked her fists on her hips. "Faerie magic!"

256   GINNY REYES

He did the same. "Leprechaun's luck!"

A pair of horrified gasps made them spin around. The sound of the closing door seemed cataclysmic, final. The look on Patrick's face augured naught but trouble.

The tears in Annie's eyes presaged only pain.

At least they had gathered their belongings from where they'd flung them as they ran to bed in the heat of passion the night before, Rosaleen thought. Her stockings had lain in front of the sofa in the parlor, while Eamon's shoes were still where he toed them off by the front door.

But clothes didn't alter the gravity of the moment. Annie and Patrick had overheard things they shouldn't have. The accusatory looks on their faces led her to believe only ill would come of this terrible morning.

"Allow me to explain," began Eamon.

"Indeed," said Patrick, his anger evident.

Eamon glanced at Rosaleen, then turned to Patrick again. "Why, 'tis simple, me lad. Rosaleen and I have felt all along that we were helping you and Annie realize how perfect you are for each other. 'Tis all there is to it. We were merely celebrating the outcome of our hopes."

A sound akin to a growl escaped Patrick. He wasn't fooled.

He took a step toward Eamon. Eamon took one back, falling onto the sofa as his knees came into contact with the piece of furniture.

"That is *not* what I heard when I came in," said Patrick, his voice deadly. "You and Rosaleen were arguing over magic and luck, and it's not the first time I've heard you talk of these things. What exactly were you two claiming success for?"

"I tell you, boyo—"

"Nay, Eamon, Patrick is right," Rosaleen said, cutting off his ridiculous attempt to distract a man who would not be distracted. " 'Tis time for the truth. Every bit of it."

From the corner of her eye, she saw Annie perch on the edge of an overstuffed chair. A tear rolled down her cheek, and she looked so miserable that Rosaleen had to look away.

"Every bit of it," echoed Annie, her voice breaking.

Rosaleen felt as much a criminal as the crooked mayor, and she feared nothing she said would ever make things right. She had come to treasure her friendship with Annie, the first true friendship she had ever shared. She loved Annie like a sister, the one she'd never had but always longed for.

Patrick's eyebrows crashed over the bridge of his nose. "What was all that nonsense about magic?"

" 'Tisn't nonsense, I'm afraid," Rosaleen said in a soft voice. "I'm a faerie and use magic to help others."

Patrick snorted. "Try again. This time say something I might believe."

Squaring her shoulders, Rosaleen did as asked—without much hope. "I may not always tell the entire truth," she said, "but I never lie, Patrick. I *am* a faerie, and you're me godchild. After you wished at the well to find your own true love, I couldn't let ye marry Serena Keller. Ye can understand that."

He grimaced, as if biting a sour lemon. "I understand I couldn't marry Serena, but I can't see where you had anything to do with it."

Rosaleen smiled, hoping to placate him. "O' course, and ye couldn't. 'Twas up to me to make sure ye found your true love without ye knowing my part in it."

"And you decided Annie Brennan was my true love," Patrick said sarcastically.

"Nay, I didn't choose her. Annie was the right one all along. 'Twas up to me to help ye find your true love. And so I used a dram of magic here and there."

Annie stood, hands shaking, eyes haunted. "So your spells made Patrick fall in love with me. Is that right?"

Rosaleen shook her head. "Nay, I cannot interfere with a mortal's choices, but I can cast spells to draw love to him. That's what I did."

258 GINNY REYES

"You cast spells on me, then," said Annie, fear in her dark blue eyes.

Eamon snorted. "Nay, wee Annie, Rosaleen is making a hash of explaining things. She didn't cast a spell on *you* . . . well, not to make you love Patrick or Patrick love you. She cast spells to bring love into his life. You fell in love all by yourselves."

Patrick shook his head. "Doesn't sound like that to me. Rosaleen tinkered with fate. How real can our love be when it came about as a result of her crazy hocus-pocus?"

"Ah, me lad," crowed Eamon, "because me luck has been on your side all along. Annie wished for a leprechaun, and she got me. You know about our three wishes, don't you?" Without waiting for Patrick's answer, he went on. "She wished for a way to share her feelings, and you turned out to be the answer to that wish. She still has one wish left, too."

"Luck? Wishes?" Patrick asked derisively. "You want me to trust my future to luck and magic and wishes? To idealistic poppycock?"

Annie fell back onto the chair, shaking her head. "Luck and magic and wishes . . ."

Eamon waved expansively. "Why, what is love but a healthy dose of luck and magic? The luck o' finding each other, and the magic o' falling in love."

Annie shook her head. "Love is completion, desire, commitment to another. Love is a promise of forever. Love is choosing one over all others. Love is serious and real. Not luck and magic and wishes."

Rosaleen watched more tears pour down her friend's face. She couldn't believe idealistic Annie, who believed herself destined for a future in the world of art despite her lack of talent, would argue the magic of love. "Annie—"

"No, Rosaleen, don't say a thing. You and Eamon have done enough. It's best if you . . . leave. Go back where you came from, wherever it's permissible to dabble in

A FAERIE TALE 259

people's futures. Especially since it looks as if I don't have much of one, after all.''

''Annie!'' objected Patrick.

Slowly, reluctantly, she faced him. ''You, too, Patrick. Go home. It's obvious we are victims of a cruel joke. You don't love me any more than you loved Serena. It was all a game. I won't hold you to promises made under the influence of such nonsense.''

Rosaleen thought her heart would break. Not only did she have to give up the man she loved and face that pain, but her dearest friend now doubted the joy she had found in a love as powerful as hers for Eamon. ''Annie, please listen. Yours and Patrick's love . . . why, 'tis as real as it can be.''

Betrayal in her gaze, Annie looked at Rosaleen. ''Just tell me this. Did you or did you not play magic of some sort?''

''Yes,'' said Patrick. ''Tell me, *faerie godmother*, did you or did you not ply me with a potion or two?''

When she glanced his way, Rosaleen cringed at the anger in his eyes. Her cheeks grew warm. ''Well . . .''

''See?'' asked Eamon in an overly bright tone. ''Her magic never works. She made you sick that time. This arguing is for naught. Your love is as real as love can be.''

Patrick shot him a glare. ''She hasn't answered my question. Was that damned tea a love potion?''

Eamon sent Rosaleen a pleading look, but she had nothing to offer in their—*her*—defense. Eamon sighed in defeat. ''Aye, lad, 'twas an aphrodisiac she gave you. But it didn't work.''

''Aphrodisiac! Try poison and you might be right!'' roared Patrick.

Rosaleen shook her head. ''I didn't poison ye, I didn't. You're alive and well, aren't ye? I only meant to make ye more appealing to Annie, irresistible—''

''Dear God,'' whispered Annie.

260 GINNY REYES

Eamon tried again. "But don't you see? It didn't work. Besides, me luck was there protecting the two of you."

Patrick rolled his eyes. "Tell me, Eamon, what about your luck?"

"Why, lad, it kept you from being poisoned, it did. And it kept you and wee Annie together until you fell in love, until you shared your feelings, all by yourselves."

"Enough!" cried Annie. "I've heard more than I want to hear. Leave my house. All of you. I never want to see you again!"

Patrick stiffened. His face turned ashen. "Annie—"

"No, Patrick. I want nothing to do with a man whose love springs from supernatural nonsense. I know the real thing—I saw it between my mother and da as I grew up. That's what I want, not some magical spell and lucky happenstance, with a wish thrown in, too. I want a love I can trust, a love that's real and true and lasting. I could never trust what you say you feel for me. Can you?"

For a moment, silence reigned. Rosaleen wished Patrick would say the right thing, but when she saw despair in his eyes, she felt the emotion echo in her heart.

"No, Annie," her godson said. "I have never trusted love at all. I've seen the harm it can do. It can devastate. And since ours has come about through such odd circumstances . . . I just can't."

Rosaleen glanced at Eamon, who looked as miserable as she felt. As miserable as Annie and Patrick looked.

They had failed. They had come to bring these two together, and just when it seemed success was at hand, they failed.

Too, they let themselves indulge in a human emotion and would now suffer for it. 'Twould have been better if they hadn't come a'tall. Matters had never been worse.

Magic had never failed her this badly before.

Twenty

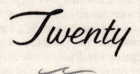

Hours later, in the belly of the night, Annie splashed her scratchy, puffy eyes with water from the washstand in her room. What was done was done, and nothing would change the past. Somehow she had to find the strength to go forward despite her broken heart.

For a moment, she let herself think of the time she spent in Patrick's arms. The tender way he had made love to her. The passion in his touch.

Tears threatened again, so she applied more water to her burning eyes, holding them at bay.

It was hard to believe it had all been a game, nothing more than silly tricks played by two who pretended to possess special powers. Even *she* didn't swallow that stuff.

Her initial instincts about Patrick had been right. He was too stuffy, too businesslike for her. And she was too artistic and spontaneous for him. Still, that didn't mean she believed magic could bring about love.

From what Patrick had said earlier, she felt fairly certain he believed in love even less than in magic. Not her. She had seen love, true love, all her life.

Before her parents died, the Brennan home was filled with joy and happiness. Annie always knew herself loved, just as she always knew the bond between her parents stemmed from the same emotion. She wanted that for herself. Not some crazy faerie-dust illusion.

She had acted heedlessly, as she often did, to her regret. While spontaneity had many virtues, when it came to something as important as one's future, it seemed a measure of prudence and caution didn't hurt. In the future, Annie would consider the possible ramifications of her actions before letting her feelings become deeply engaged. She would never leave herself open to pain like this again.

As if losing her heart to Patrick O'Toole wasn't bad enough, she had also lost her closest friend. She was going to miss sharing secrets with Rosaleen, the womanly companionship she had so missed since her mother's death.

It would be a long time before Annie invited another newcomer in town to stay with her. She would get to know folks better before opening herself to friendship as she had with Rosaleen.

Although the evidence was plain to see, she had trouble accepting the Irish girl's betrayal. Annie had discussed her feelings for Patrick. It hurt that Rosaleen had played silly tricks, used foolish matchmaking ploys, then tried to imbue them with so-called magical powers, supposedly in the name of love. Love—the real thing—went farther than sparkles and giddy games.

Annie had thought love was growing between her and Patrick, the real kind of love. Now, because of Rosaleen's and Eamon's meddling and matchmaking, she couldn't trust the feelings they'd shared.

As of this moment, she was setting aside all thought of romance and concentrating on her artistic goals. Mr. Buntz had agreed to help her with the Haven.

Squaring her shoulders, Annie strengthened her resolve. Yes, she would concentrate all her efforts on the Haven from now on. Although art was a lonely endeavor, it gave her an outlet for the powerful feelings that burned inside her.

Thinking back, Annie realized that since she and Patrick had grown close, since they had made love, she hadn't once brought out her paints. She'd had that outlet for her feelings; she had poured out her love onto him.

If she couldn't have a man to give her love to, or even a friend with whom to bemoan her unromantic fate, then Annie Brennan would use her art to convey her love to the world at large.

Love was love, after all, whatever form one used to express it. Romance and friendship were tricks of magic. And one couldn't trust either.

Early the next morning, heartsore and troubled, Rosaleen headed for the stand of trees outside Woodbury to seek solace in nature.

How could everything have gone so wrong? 'Twas true enough, everyone knew on occasion her spells failed, but this time she had managed to ruin her godchild's life— not to mention her own—in the process.

She'd had assistance in bringing ruin about, she had. Eamon Dooley bore his share o' the blame. Faith, and he had the worst luck imaginable!

Rosaleen smiled ruefully. Ah, but he was a charmer, he was. And she had been well and truly charmed. That charm, however, had distracted her, and she had failed to achieve what she had come to do.

She would never earn her magic wand. To her surprise, that didn't bother her half as much as did the rift between Annie and Patrick—and the rift between Eamon and herself.

She had known all along they would eventually part. But she hadn't expected the pain to be so great. If anticipating the pain hurt this badly, how much worse would actual farewells feel?

Tears filled her eyes, blurring her view of the trees up ahead, but knowing her destination, she kept going. She would never again experience Eamon's kisses or lay sated in his arms, hearing his heartbeat slow down after pounding in ecstasy.

Although she had wondered about love while in *Tyeer na N-og*, she hadn't known what she was missing. It had been simple to do without. Now she knew love's joy, richness, warmth, passion. Its tenderness, too. She would sorely miss it all.

As she would miss Annie's friendship.

The sun had risen enough to dry the dew from the field. Rosaleen sat on a cushion of grass and breathed the fragrance of the earth. Soil and sun. Summer greens. At least this never changed.

For years—nay, centuries—she had longed for a special friend, someone with whom to share confidences. In Annie she had found the best of friends. To her dismay, her magical ineptitude destroyed the closeness that had grown between them, the friendship she already missed.

If only magic could make things right again, she thought, picking through a patch of clover. Mayhap a shamrock's luck . . . but no. It didn't seem there was anything to do.

Hugging her knees to her chest, Rosaleen propped her chin on them and stared at a blue jay perched on a nearby oak, his chatter like a reprimand, a scolding from which she couldn't defend herself.

"Ah, *cailin*, you look much as I feel."

Rosaleen started. "Faith, and you're the last soul I expected to see today."

He lifted a shoulder. "Can't say you seem pleased by me presence."

"No more than ye do with mine."

A wistful look appeared on his face. "Sure and it's hard to see you and not hold you. Even if 'tis for the best I don't."

Tears again threatened. "That's the rightest thing you've said yet, Eamon Dooley. Even if 'tisn't one I'm happy to hear."

He gave her a lopsided grin. "I'm not happy to say so, but 'tis true enough."

Blinking hard, she said, "We've made a mess of things, haven't we?"

"Won't argue with you there."

Rosaleen arched an eyebrow. "Never thought to see the day."

"Once upon a time I offered to stop the sparring, if you'll recall."

"I could never forget, Eamon. Not a thing."

"Nor can I."

Both fell silent, each lost in memories of a love that couldn't be.

Drawing a breath for strength, Rosaleen tried a different tack. "Will ye keep trying for that pot o' gold?"

"Nay, it doesn't matter much now. There's many more important things to think of, to live for."

"Indeed."

" 'Twould seem you won't be chasing that wand, then."

Rosaleen gave him a bittersweet smile. "I've much to occupy me mind, and none of it needs a wand."

"You'll be going back soon, then," Eamon said.

"Aye, but I'd like to bid farewell to Annie before I do." Rosaleen stood. "She's hurting, she is, and she's angry with me. But I can't just leave without a word. I want to say I'm sorry, even though she won't be wanting to hear it."

As she started back toward Woodbury, Eamon fell into step at her side. "I know how you feel," he said. "I can't be leaving, meself, without a chat with Patrick."

Rosaleen glanced his way. "You're after heading to town this soon?"

Eamon shrugged. "I came here since I had nowhere else to go. I can't impose on Patrick's hospitality as things stand. Besides, the faerie burgh is there," he added, nodding toward the small rise near the trees.

266 GINNY REYES

For long moments, the only sound was of their footsteps. When the silence grew uncomfortable, Rosaleen said, "So ye want to speak with me godchild, ye do."

"Indeed. I like the lad and have much respect for him. We're friends, you know."

"As are Annie and I."

They strolled along, the song of birds doing nothing to lift their spirits. Unable to stand the strain any longer, Rosaleen said, "No better time than now, then."

Eamon's eyes widened. "For . . . good-byes?"

"Aye, and more's the pity."

Silence again.

"I'd like to say farewell to the lass, too," he said.

"Come with me."

"You wouldn't mind?"

"Why? 'Tis but farewell I'll be saying."

"Ah, *cailin*, 'twas much we gained *and* lost."

Rosaleen firmed her spine. "Best to put an end to it here and now. I can't bear to let it drag on any longer."

His heart in his eyes, Eamon said, "We've reached the end, then, love."

Knowing he spoke of them rather than their friends or their time in the mortal realm, Rosaleen's throat tightened with emotion. "The end," she whispered.

After trying fruitlessly to work half the morning, Patrick threw his pen down on his turpentine-mottled desk and gave up. He couldn't concentrate.

Well, it wasn't a matter of not being able to concentrate, but that his concentration wasn't where it should be. Right about now it hovered somewhere in the vicinity of Woodbury's would-be *artiste*.

The woman he loved.

No matter how hard he tried, Patrick couldn't convince himself he had no particular feelings for Annie. He *loved* her. He just couldn't trust his—their—emotions. Espe-

A FAERIE TALE

cially not feelings born from some crazy scheme of Eamon's and Rosaleen's.

Faerie magic. Leprechaun's wishes. What nonsense.

He rubbed the ridges on his forehead. Try as he might, Patrick couldn't forget the pain in Annie's eyes last night. It had never been his intent to hurt her, but clearly he had. As had Eamon and Rosaleen. While he couldn't do a thing about their deplorable behavior, he could apologize for the pain he had inflicted.

He had to see Annie again. *Not* at the bank, though. He would have to return to her house, where he had come so close to touching Paradise. Where memories had the power to bring him to his knees.

Still, he knew what he had to do.

No matter how much it hurt to do so. He loved Annie Brennan, heart and soul. But after love destroyed his mother, he couldn't consign Annie and him to the same fate, especially in view of the ludicrous circumstances surrounding their romance.

Love was fraught with enough dangers all its own. It blinded people to reason, led them to disastrous decisions. How much worse would a love sprung from a faerie's crazy spells and a leprechaun's luck be?

Spells. Leprechauns and faeries. Luck and wishes.

Of course he couldn't trust such nonsense. No sane man could. He had to make sure Annie understood his reasons for breaking their engagement. It had nothing to do with her. In fact, she was the one most wronged.

With a grim smile, Patrick took his hat from the cabinet where he always set it and told Pearson he'd be gone for a while. His behavior was unprecedented—until Annie. It wasn't just leaving the office partway through the day twice now that was unusual; he didn't know another man who had tromped so swiftly through two engagements.

Oh, but he was glad he had escaped a future with Serena!

Although danger of a different sort lurked in a marriage

268   GINNY REYES

based on volatile emotions, he couldn't say he was glad
to break off his betrothal to Annie. There was something
about her, something that reached deep and touched him
in a spot no one had reached before. It was as if she
belonged there, where his heart felt so empty right then.

Patrick cursed. He'd begun to think like the lot of them.
If he didn't watch himself, he would start spouting nonsense about magic and spells, luck and romance and
wishes. He might even begin to trust his love for Annie.
That was something he simply couldn't do.

He had to make sure she understood why he had ended
their engagement. And he had to do it right away.

Leaving the bank, he blinded himself to the summer
sunshine, the cheer of the day. Minutes later, he stood
before the Brennan front door, braced for the difficult encounter.

Annie answered his knock while tucking her blue-and-
white-striped blouse inside her royal blue skirt. When she
saw him, her swollen, reddened eyes widened in surprise.
"Patrick! What are *you* doing here?"

Not wanting to give gossips any more fodder, he gestured toward the parlor. "May I?"

She stepped back. Without a word, she led him to the
sofa. "Since you're curious," he said, "I'll get right to
the point. I came because last night ended poorly."

She rolled her beautiful sapphire eyes. "Indeed."

"And I have some explaining to do."

"I don't think so. You made yourself abundantly
clear." She blinked, and he wondered if she was about to
cry again. But then she drew a deep breath and squared
her shoulders. "I thought I made myself clear, as well."

"Oh, you did," he muttered, remembering the pain
he'd felt when she sent him away. "But I still need to
explain why I can no longer marry you."

"I know why. I'm not as stupid as you think."

"I don't think you're stupid! Just flighty and dreamy."

"Criminal faults, I'm sure. At any rate, I don't need

A FAERIE TALE

your explanations." She stood, her bearing regal despite her diminutive height. "Good day, Mr. O'Toole."

He surged to his feet. "Dammit, Annie! I have something to say, and I'm not leaving until you hear it."

Tipping her chin up, she said, "Make it quick, then."

Praying for patience, Patrick sat again. She didn't. He tamped down the urge to yank her into his lap and make her listen, but that wouldn't help, since he didn't think he would do much talking with her in that sensitive position.

"As you wish." Because he didn't often bare his soul, Patrick prayed for courage, too. "Since I didn't grow up in Woodbury, you never met my mother. She died shortly before I took the position at the bank."

"I regret your loss, sir."

"Annie . . ." he said in warning, but she showed no sign of backing down. Fine. He would go on. "As I said, you never met my mother, so you didn't see how a difficult life aged her. She wasn't old in years when she died, just weakened by suffering and pain."

A glimmer of interest flickered in her gaze, but she remained silent. And standing.

He continued. "Back in Ireland, Mother fell in love with Sean O'Toole, my father. Her feelings blinded her to the truth of his character. Sean was a firebrand Fenian, sworn to fight to the death for Ireland's freedom. He took part in every meeting, every rally, every altercation, and soon enough the authorities found an excuse to arrest him. Mother was increasing."

"Oh, dear," said Annie.

Patrick hid the satisfaction her attention brought. "Sean was beaten to a pulp by the prison guards, but he died a true Irish martyr's death. His last words were for Eire."

"And your mother . . . ?"

"Mother hadn't a soul left. They all died during the famine when she was a child. All but a cousin who emigrated to Philadelphia. We followed shortly after I was born, and life continued just as hard and painful as in Ireland. I needn't say much about the feelings of many Americans for the Irish.''

Catching her bottom lip between her teeth, Annie shook her head.

"We went hungry, even though Mother spent eighteen-hour days scrubbing floors. Near starvation and slave labor will wear away a woman's looks and steal her youth.''

A frown pleated Annie's forehead. "But how did you become a banker?''

The memories had dredged up his pain. Patrick stood and paced the room. "Mother was sweet and kind. She also had a wicked sense of humor. A gentle German giant by the name of Guenther Mertz decided he couldn't live without Margaret Mulligan O'Toole at his side. We moved to his farm outside Lancaster, and his profits paid for my education.''

"Then at least her final years were happy ones.''

"I don't know that I'd call them happy. By that time, she had developed a cancer, and it continued to rob her of what life she had left.'' The years seemed to flash through his mind. "Oh, she was content, and Guenther made sure she lacked for nothing, but her heart belonged to Sean O'Toole. The man who damned her to that horrible life.''

With a look of wisdom that far exceeded her years, Annie studied him. "And you decided not to follow in her footsteps.''

Patrick clenched his jaw. "I decided I would never love like that, so deeply, so blindly, so foolishly. Nor could I waste my life loving an ideal more than those who count on me. I will never do to a woman what my father did to her. I could never curse her—and our child—to that kind of misery.''

Annie's blue gaze seemed to pierce his soul. "Even if she chose to support your efforts and spend what time she could with you? For the sake of a glorious love?''

A FAERIE TALE   271

"Pah!" Of course Annie would ask such foolish things. "What's love but a crazy feeling that makes your stomach lurch, your head spin, your heart pound? Taken like that, it resembles indigestion. And it can cause unspeakable pain."

"It can also bring immeasurable joy."

"Joy is fleeting."

"So is pain."

"Not when a man is so caught up in an idealistic cause that he refuses to see what's before him. The pain he inflicts can last a lifetime. Or two."

Annie's eyes widened. "Might this have anything to do with your opposition to my Haven?"

Patrick felt heat in his cheeks. "A bit, I'd say."

"A lot," she shot back.

"Well, I couldn't let you risk your entire future on a crazy dream. Not if I could do something to prevent it."

To his surprise, she didn't immediately respond. She fell silent, an intent expression on her face. "You should have told me this earlier," she finally said.

"I'm a private man, Annie. I don't tell my life story to all my clients."

"Perhaps. But later, when we were falling in love— Oh, excuse me, Mr. O'Toole. That's right. *You* can't fall in love. That emotion is too dangerous, it might cause too much pain."

Patrick's hold on his anger began to wobble.

"Regardless," she went on, "you should have explained why you were so opposed to what was, essentially, none of your business. You shouldn't have had a say in how I used my money."

He ground his teeth. "That's not the way things are, Annie. An executor of necessity *must* make the money and its use his business."

Out came her stubborn chin. "Still, you should have said something. I questioned your intentions and doubted your feelings—"

"It's those feelings we're discussing. Feelings I can't trust. And that is the reason I must break off our engagement."

"Is it your feelings for me you don't trust?" she asked. "Or mine for you?"

Squirming despite himself, Patrick considered her question. "Both. You see, aside from being powerful enough to make me lose sight of what's important, our feelings aren't particularly real. Thanks to Eamon and Rosaleen's meddling, they're nothing more than the result of propinquity."

"What, pray tell, is that? It sounds like some dread disease."

He smiled. "Almost. Actually, it means proximity. I suspect our feelings grew from the constant contact those two misguided matchmakers forced upon us."

Annie glared. "Fine, Patrick. If you want to believe you suffer from an excess of proximity, then go right ahead. I know what I feel, and although I can't trust Irish magic any more than you, I won't be calling my emotions proximity or propinquity or who knows what else."

He gave her a curt nod. "Then we're agreed."

"About . . . ?"

"The engagement, of course."

"What engagement?" she asked archly.

He bit down hard to keep from saying something he might regret. To his enormous relief, a knock at the front door put an end to the miserable exchange.

Annie rushed to respond.

"Who is it?" he asked.

She gave him an odd look. "The misguided matchmakers."

Patrick groaned. Had there ever been a worse day?

Eamon and Rosaleen entered the parlor, their expressions subdued, their steps hesitant. At least they seemed repentant, he thought.

"To what do we owe this visit?" asked Annie.

A FAERIE TALE 273

"We came to say farewell," said the Irish girl in a subdued voice, "and to explain."

Crossing her arms over her chest, Annie tapped a toe. "First Patrick *needs* to explain. Now you." She pursed her lips. "Farewell will do."

Eamon stepped up and dropped an arm around her shoulders. She ducked, then sat on the sofa. Eamon shrugged. "Methinks a wee explanation can't hurt. After that, we'll be on our way."

"On your way where?" Patrick asked.

"To *Tyeer na N-og*, o' course," Rosaleen answered.

"Not again!" exclaimed Annie.

"Hush, Annie, lass," urged Eamon. "And listen. 'Tis all true, if hard to believe."

"Everything about you is hard to believe," muttered Patrick.

Eamon waved toward him. "You, too, boyo. Listen up." He waited only long enough for Patrick to join Annie. "Rosaleen and I may not always tell everything there is to tell," he said, "but we haven't lied to you yet. We *are* o' the gentry, and we came to help you both find your way."

Patrick snorted.

Annie rolled her eyes.

Rosaleen gnawed on her thumbnail.

Eamon continued. "We're o' the *Tuatha De Danann*. We came to Eire and conquered the Firbolgs back in times past. For many years we ruled the land, but then the Milesians came. They drove us underground into the grassy burghs and lands beneath the waters, where we now live."

Annie stood. "You can stop now. I've heard the legends many times. My da knew them all and told them to me over and again. You're no more faeries than Patrick and I are."

"But we are, lass, and we have mastered magic," Eamon insisted. "We are the faeriefolk o' Eire, the ones in the tales and legends, the ones who live in *Tyeer na N-og*."

Patrick gave a short, mirthless laugh. "The Land of the Young, as mother used to say. I suppose you'll tell us you're far older than you look."

"Six hundred years, give or take a few," said Eamon.

"Four hundred for me," offered Rosaleen.

Patrick glanced at Annie, and both shook their heads. Did he, however, see a gleam of interest in her eyes? Damnation! She didn't believe Eamon's faerie tale . . . did she?

Then he laughed inwardly. With Annie, anything was possible, even believing a story as wild and ludicrous as this. Still, just because she did didn't mean *he* had to.

"If, as you say, you have mastered magic, then what was all that about failed spells and bad luck?" he asked.

Eamon colored.

Rosaleen coughed. "You see, Patrick," she said, "I needed more practice to earn me wand, because at times me spells go awry. Since you were all alone in the world, and not even in Eire, at that, King Midhir sent me to help you a wee bit."

"What about me?" asked Annie.

Eamon cleared his throat. "I've been after earning me pot o' gold, lass. But 'tis lucky I am with wishes and such. You wished for a leprechaun on a faerie mound, and here I am. You wished to share your feelings and you found love. You still have one wish left, so take care when you wish."

"I don't believe a word of it," she said. "You've played with our feelings, made a mess of things, and now look at us. Where's the magic? The luck?" They all looked around. No one seemed willing to answer. "For that matter, where are Eamon's pointy ears, the tiny size, Rosaleen's wings?"

"Fie, Annie!" exclaimed Rosaleen, a weak smile putting in a momentary appearance. "Ye can't be believing that?"

Annie arched an eyebrow.

A FAERIE TALE

"*Tuatha* look much like mortals," the Irish lass explained, "sometimes not quite so tall, but otherwise unremarkable."

"The trouble you've caused is *most* remarkable, if you ask me," said Patrick. "Especially the trouble you caused with your miserable matchmaking."

Miserable was a good word, Annie thought. "Go on," she said. "Go back to your Land of the Young and be happy. At least you found each other."

To her amazement, tears filled Rosaleen's eyes. "Nay, Annie, there is no such thing as romantic love in *Tyeer na N-og*. Eamon and I have said our farewells." A sob broke from her lips. "As I must bid ye now. I must be after going."

Despite her reluctance to believe the crazy tale, Annie saw real pain in Rosaleen's gaze. "Have a pleasant trip," she said inanely. Then, because she hurt, too, she added, "Write sometime and tell me more tales."

Tears rolled down Rosaleen's cheeks. "Ye don't understand. 'Tis good-bye, we're saying. For good."

Not knowing what else to say, Annie nodded.

Patrick shrugged, but she saw sadness in his eyes, too. "I should return to the office," he said. "I suppose good-bye is all I can say."

"Farewell, me friend," said Eamon, not even trying for cheer. " 'Tis hard indeed to leave."

"Aye," added Rosaleen, so softly Annie almost missed it.

Then, before anyone began crying in earnest, the alleged magical beings left. Annie turned to Patrick. "I'll miss them."

"There's much I'll miss, too."

Annie drew in a sharp breath. He cared! He really cared for her, but fear held him in its grip. As it did her.

Were their feelings for each other strong enough to someday conquer that fear?

Twenty-one

Annie's heart pounded at the possibilities she suddenly glimpsed, but Patrick's forbidding expression told her she wouldn't soon find answers to her questions. Love wasn't an easy matter, it seemed.

As it certainly wasn't for her Irish friends. Annie couldn't forget the sadness in Eamon's gaze each time he turned toward Rosaleen. The tears Rosaleen shed gave abundant evidence of her feelings for him.

"There really should be something we can do for them," she said.

"Huh?"

She hadn't realized she'd spoken aloud. "I was just thinking there must be some way to bring Rosaleen and Eamon together again."

Patrick arched a brow. "Been casting love spells lately?"

"Don't mock me, Mr. O'Toole! I'm serious. Didn't you see how unhappy they both were?"

"They did look miserable. But they brought it on themselves. All that magical nonsense. No one in their right mind would believe it."

"We certainly don't have to," Annie responded self-righteously, but wishing magic *were* real. "That doesn't

A FAERIE TALE

mean we can't help two friends realize how right they are for each other.''

"How do you propose we do that?"

"Oh, I haven't gotten that far yet. I just feel terrible for them and want to help any way I can."

"Annie," he warned in his banker's voice, "don't go getting any of your crazy artistic notions now. Perhaps a serious conversation with each one will do."

Annie waved a dismissive hand. "I doubt it. Didn't you see how set they were on returning to their Land of the Young—wherever that may be?"

"You may be right. Still, I don't like the thought of meddling in their lives. I certainly didn't appreciate their meddling in *ours*."

Annie bit her bottom lip. "I didn't, either, but there must be *something* we can do."

As if suddenly noting the passage of time, Patrick pulled out his watch. "I must be getting back to the bank. I've been gone longer than I thought."

"But what about Eamon and Rosaleen? Won't you help me help them?"

"Of course," he said hastily. "I have to make sure you don't get carried away. Let's both think about it, draw up plans, consider alternatives and possible outcomes, then discuss everything and decide what to do."

Annie grimaced in disgust. "Very well, Patrick. We can proceed in bankerly fashion. But believe me, I *will* do something, no matter how dreadful you make the process."

"Not dreadful," he said, opening the door, "just careful. We wouldn't want to make a mess of their romance as they did of ours."

As he left, Annie felt a tug at her heart. True, he was a fuddy-duddy, but he undoubtedly meant well. And he cared about Rosaleen and Eamon, otherwise no argument would have made him agree to support her efforts.

Unless it was to keep her from making a fool of herself—*again*. And that brought up another important matter. Patrick cared for her. In fact, he *loved* her, even though he refused to trust that love. If his feelings weren't such, he wouldn't care if she made a fool of herself.

Smiling for the first time that day, Annie called her cat. Fergus usually avoided company, which made his behavior that day with Mayor Keller that much more remarkable. She smiled wickedly. Wise cat, Fergus O'Shea.

With a loud "*Mrreowww*," the tom rubbed against her ankles, and when she picked him up, he began to purr. "I still have you, you unsociable rascal, even though I'd rather hug *him*."

Perhaps things would eventually work out. Perhaps while helping their Irish friends, she and Patrick would find a way to trust their feelings, feelings that for her grew stronger with every passing minute.

Maybe their love was stronger than faulty magic, lousy luck, and a handful of wishes. Maybe it would last longer than a fleeting spell or a fortunate happenstance.

They might even discover that love was love, regardless how it came about.

Annie smiled. She liked that idea, especially since it came so close to her philosophy of art. But she liked the idea of loving Patrick even more. Perhaps he would propose again someday. As he had the last time. In bed. After they'd made love.

Eamon and Rosaleen left the Brennan home in silence. Good-bye was imminent, but neither wished to be the first to say it.

"What is it?" Rosaleen asked when she noticed Eamon's serious expression.

"Sure and there must be something we can do to get those two together again!"

Grasping his arm, she dragged him to a standstill in the middle of Main Street. "Eamon Dooley, don't ye be after

A FAERIE TALE 279

interfering again! Didn't ye see their faces? Why, they're heartbroken, they are."

"That's exactly it, Rosaleen. They belong together as man and wife, not all weepy and gloomy, and fearing magic and all."

She crossed her arms. "Well, I won't be after casting any more spells. 'Twas bad enough seeing Annie's face when she felt I betrayed our friendship by matching her up with Patrick."

"Who said anything a'tall about your magic? It always goes awry, and I'm wanting me friend Patrick to find happiness, not more trouble, as he said."

"All I want is for Annie to look like herself again, smiling at Patrick, and painting to her heart's content."

Eamon rolled his eyes. "Sure and you can't be meaning that about her awful art, *cailin*?"

"Aye, she's a bad one, at that." Rosaleen remembered confidences she and Annie had shared. "Mayhap she *should* find another way to express those feelings o' hers. Mayhap Patrick O'Toole *is* that other way...."

Eamon danced a jig in the road. "Sure and I can't be forgetting this moment. You're saying I'm right, you are!"

Rosaleen glared at the gleeful man. "I only said Annie loves Patrick."

"He loves her."

"They belong together."

"As you were sent to ensure."

"So," she said, hoping to avoid any further discussion of her failed mission, "how do you propose we bring those two together again?"

" 'Twon't be an easy thing, it won't." Eamon headed toward the Square. "Will you be staying long enough to help me see things through?"

Rosaleen hurried to keep up. "O' course, I'll be after staying! Faith, and I wouldn't leave me godchild to your lousy luck.'' She softened the impact of her words with a slow wink.

''Ah, *cailin*,'' he said, his pace slowing, his eyes bright with love. ''You're the fairest magical one ever, you are.''

''You're a fine one yourself, Eamon Dooley.''

''Too bad there's no hope for us. . . .''

Rosaleen blinked hard to keep the tears from falling. ''Aye, 'tis too bad, indeed.'' Firming her spine, she added, ''And that's why we can't be fretting over it. Instead we must bring Annie and Patrick together again.''

''See? I knew you'd say I was right!'' He took one of her hands in his, wrapped his other arm around her waist, and waltzed her down the center walk in the Square.

''Eamon!''

''Hush now, *cailin*,'' he said, swinging her in another intricate set of steps. ''We're marking a momentous occasion. Rosaleen Flynn agrees with Eamon Dooley. Cause for celebration, indeed.'' With a final twirl, he released her, then gave her a courtly bow. ''And we'll be bringing Annie and Patrick together again. Forever, this time.''

''Aye, Eamon Dooley. That we will.''

Suddenly they fell silent. Then Rosaleen said, ''How—''

''How—'' Eamon said at the same time.

They laughed, shaking their heads. Eamon took Rosaleen's hand in his, and they resumed their leisurely walk. The thrill his gesture shot through her caught her off guard, flooding her with memories. Ah, Eamon . . . how she loved the scamp.

''Methinks,'' he said, cutting into her reverie, '' 'twould be best if we took time to think things through. We wouldn't be wanting anything to go wrong this time. We must plan, consider all possibilities, prepare for anything that might go wrong—before it does, you understand. Then 'twill be but a matter of choosing the best plan.''

Rosaleen shook her head. ''Faith, and they'll both be

A FAERIE TALE   281

as old as we by the time ye finish with your thinking and planning and choosing.''

''Ah, but, lass, we must take more care this time. We can't be trusting your magic or even—alas—me luck. We can't just leap up and act so as to *do* something for the sake of doing anything a'tall.''

''Very well, Eamon Dooley. We'll do things your way.''

''Momentous day, indeed!'' he crowed. ''You've said I'm right, not once but twice. And now you're willing to do things me way. Who knows what other marvels might come to pass before the sun sets?''

''Faith, and do ye know what day 'tis?''

''Nay. Haven't paid much attention to the passing of time.''

She chuckled. ''Why, 'tis Midsummer Day! A perfectly wonderful, magical day!''

''Rosaleen . . .'' he said, caution in his voice.

''Nay, nay,'' she said with a careless wave. ''No reason for worry. I'm not after casting spells. Not seeing how they've turned out of late.''

A tender expression filled his face. ''Don't worry, lass. This will turn out splendidly, it will. When we worked together last, they ended up engaged, stopped a robbery, and sent the crooked mayor to jail, where he belongs. We won't fail this time.''

''We can't, Eamon. Their future is at stake.''

Their gazes met, palest jade and deepest emerald, emotions shining bright. Longing filled Eamon's wistful smile, and Rosaleen's heart cracked a bit more.

Even if her future held only bittersweet memories, she would make sure her godchild and her dearest friend had something far better to look forward to. She would do all in her power to ensure they had before them the forever kind of love Annie described.

Rosaleen and Eamon would work true magic on their mortals, the sort that didn't need wands, pots o' gold, or

282 GINNY REYES

wishes. They would help their friends find again the magic of love.

A short while later, as Eamon reclined against the faerie mound on the field at the outskirts of Woodbury, he pondered the events that had led to his being there, alone, yet still not ready to return to *Tyeer na N-og*.

Sure and he'd jumped at the chance to spend more time with Rosaleen, especially since they now had a scrap of hope of helping wee Annie. Patrick, too. But 'twas time with Rosaleen he wanted, all the time he could steal.

As he watched a dragon cloud scud across the true-blue sky, a carriage rolled by. Glancing that way, he noticed the man and woman inside. "Why, if 'tisn't that slippery Serena Keller herself!"

Rising, he dusted off his rear and ran after the vehicle. The gent at Serena's side was likely the beau Annie saw her kissing while the mayor tried to rob the bank. Although he couldn't imagine what they were up to, he knew 'twould be no good a'tall.

Calling on one of the more esoteric powers of the ancient magical beings of the Celtic realm, Eamon invoked a *feth-faidha* to change his form. In truth, he chose no form, as he preferred to once again make himself invisible.

Invisible to all but a sharp-eyed Irish faerie, he thought, remembering how well she'd seen him that one morn at the bank. 'Twouldn't happen this time, as the lass was nowhere in sight. He was free to follow the spalpeens and keep ill fortune away from his wee Annie.

Just in case someone else had powers of vision like Rosaleen, however, he ran from tree to tree, staying hidden while keeping the conveyance in sight.

That was how Rosaleen next saw the man she loved. As she sat on the wall of the well she landed in when she first came to Woodbury, she watched him chase an un-

A FAERIE TALE

283

remarkable black carriage while darting furtively from tree to tree.

"Faith, and he's at it again!"

Fearing for his safety, not to mention his freedom—surely he would be arrested if any clear-thinking soul saw him make such a fool of himself—Rosaleen intoned a protective spell for the man she loved.

Just to make sure, however, she ran in his wake, hurrying in an effort to prevent further disaster. But as she followed, she saw him dodge behind the carriage, catch a stone on the heel of his gleaming black boot, and fall head over heels in the dust. He did have the worst luck.

"Eamon Dooley, you'll be the death o' me yet," she said, running to help.

As he dusted off his bright emerald coat and wine-red waistcoat, he gave her a disgusted look. "You can see me, then?"

"You're not after telling me ye thought ye made yourself invisible again?"

"O' course, and I made meself invisible. I'm a master at the *feth-faidha*, I am."

"Ye don't look like a deer or a dog or a rabbit, ye don't, and you're visible enough for anyone to fear for their silver. Why were ye after that rig?"

"You're the only one who sees me when I change me shape," he argued peevishly. " 'Twas Serena Keller in that carriage, you know. Had a man with her, and 'twould seem to me they're up to trouble again."

"I wouldn't have thought they'd come back after that night."

Eamon stared in the direction the carriage had disappeared. "You know, lass, 'twouldn't come as a surprise if they came back for the money they never got."

"Hmmm . . . you might be right."

Eamon cheered. " 'Tis the third time in one day!"

"No time for that kind of nonsense," she scolded. "Serena and her beau mean trouble for Annie."

284 GINNY REYES

" 'Tis up to me—*us*—to bring the lass the luck she'll need to outwit them both."

"No luck. No magic. Let's just be giving her our help."

Taking her hand in his, Eamon led them off at a fast clip. Sure enough, with the roan gelding tethered to the hitching post, the black carriage stood guard before the Brennan home.

Without a sound, they went up the porch steps and approached an open window. A peek inside told the story. Annie sat on a ladder-back chair, while Serena's friend wrapped miles of rope around her. Her blue eyes shot flames of rage at her former rival. "You won't get away with this," she said.

Serena gave her a superior smirk. "What makes you say something so silly?"

"Just remember the other night. And your father is keeping Officer Riley company in the jail. I expect you'll soon join them."

Serena laughed. "I don't see sign of the fool. Besides, Stephenson's in charge today." She smiled sappily at her accomplice. "He won't let *anything* go wrong, will you, dear?"

As if she were a bothersome fly, Stephenson jerked his head. "Give me your handkerchief, Serena. Your friend here talks too much for her own good."

Annie's eyes widened. "Don't you dare—*mrfnsldn*!"

Running her fingers down her lover's chest, Serena said, "Let me go with you."

Stephenson graced her with an icy glare. "You'll be safer here."

"Oh, darling, how perfectly *sweet* of you to think of my safety," she cooed. "But there's no need. Patrick poses no danger, now that Annie has signed the rental and sales agreements."

Eamon and Rosaleen exchanged worried looks.

Serena continued. "Besides, I might be able to help you

A FAERIE TALE 285

with him. Patrick can be . . . difficult at times.''

''If there was something you could do, you would have done it long ago. Stay and watch *her* while I take care of business.''

Serena winced.

Eamon muttered, ''So there!'' As Stephenson left, presumably to confront Patrick, he waited a few, prudent moments, then followed.

''Wait!'' said Rosaleen. ''Where are ye going? Annie needs help.''

''I need to make sure that crook doesn't take off with her pot o' gold. I must warn Patrick.'' Running down the porch steps, he called back, ''Besides, Serena can't do Annie much harm. The lass is safe enough. You can watch over your godchild's true love. I have to see to wee Annie's treasure.''

Before Rosaleen could object further, he was gone. She was left to pace the porch and occasionally peer through the window to make sure Annie was safe.

In the meantime, Eamon raced to the bank, his heart pounding in his chest. This was his chance. He could help Annie if he did things right. By gum and by golly, he wasn't going to mess things up this time.

But by the time he arrived at the bank, Stephenson had already gone into Patrick's office. Although the door was closed, he could hear the rumble of voices inside. Ensuring that Pearson, Patrick's mastiff of a secretary, was nowhere in sight, Eamon pressed his ear right up to the wooden panel.

''I have Annie Brennan,'' Stephenson said.

A moment of silence followed. Then, in a terse voice Patrick asked, ''Where do you have her?''

''At home. Serena's making sure she doesn't make trouble.''

''And she signed this document?'' asked Patrick, clearly unwilling to trust a word Stephenson said.

''With some persuasion.''

286 GINNY REYES

"You hurt her, dammit!"

"Didn't have to. It only took a mild threat."

A chair scraped the floor. Heavy footsteps crossed the room, then returned to where they'd started. "Does she realize how much she has given up by signing?"

"If she looked at the figures, I'm sure she does. But I didn't point it out."

"It's not just the money," Patrick said. "She won't have the funds for her Haven. She's giving up her dreams!"

Stephenson laughed. "Surely you don't expect me to worry about her dreams, do you?"

"I guess not."

To Eamon's dismay, Patrick sounded defeated.

"Now," said Stephenson, "let's not waste any more time on dreams and nonsense. Do what you must to pay me this month's . . . rent. Then I'll free the girl."

"If I don't . . . ?"

"You wouldn't want her pretty face to look like mine."

"Your flaws run deeper than your flesh," Patrick said, sheathed rage in the words. "But I would rather have her safe than all the money in the world."

"Ah, Mr. O'Toole, that's where you and I differ." Stephenson's words had an oily feel. Eamon longed for a bath. "Women are commodities. Especially if a man has enough money."

"I'll get your damn papers," bit off Patrick.

As the door flew open, Eamon ducked under Pearson's desk. His left foot nearly brought Patrick to the floor.

"What are *you* doing there?" demanded his banker friend in his most unfriendly voice. "And where is Pearson?"

Eamon glanced behind Patrick, but Stephenson seemed happy to wait in the office. "Shhh . . . you don't want the spalpeen to hear us, do you?"

"Where's Pearson?" Patrick growled again.

"I don't know. Hasn't been here since I arrived."

A FAERIE TALE

287

"When was that?"

"When Stephenson told you he had the wee lass."

"So you heard the whole thing."

"O' course. And I'm about to solve your troubles."

Horror filled Patrick's face. "Don't you dare do a thing—"

"Hush now, boyo. Listen to me."

As Eamon explained his plan, Patrick gained a measure of admiration for his Irish friend. Crazy though Eamon seemed at times, his idea was so simple it stood a good chance of working. Something had to, because Patrick couldn't stand the thought of harm befalling Annie.

His hands were shaking like leaves in a storm. Annie had to be petrified. Knowing Serena and her lover were out to steal her dream, she must also be hurting deeply. All this, on the same day Patrick broke off their engagement.

His heart went out to her. He had to make sure she was safe. And her money . . . well, money was only money, after all. Annie was worth more than all of the Woodbury Fiduciary Bank's assets. To make sure nothing happened to her, Patrick was willing to hand the Brennan fund to Stephenson and kiss good-bye to his splendid career, his safe and secure future—everything.

Besides, he was young, hard-working, well-educated. He would provide for Annie. If he worked another job, he might even earn enough to help set up her Haven. Sooner or later, probably later, he would replace the money with which he was about to buy her safety. The money her father had left her.

If Eamon's plan didn't work.

A crooked smile tipped up his mouth. Yessir, he was going to marry Annie Brennan so fast he'd make her head spin. Then he would spend the rest of his life making sure she never lacked a thing, not even that crazy Haven of hers. Even if he had to work himself to a nub.

And they'd always have their love.

288 GINNY REYES

With a nod to Eamon, Patrick went back inside the office. "My secretary will bring the papers for our signatures," he told Stephenson.

With his nod, the silence in the room grew greater, deeper. Patrick's nerves grew tighter.

Annie. He could only think of Annie.

If he thought about the money he might remember the past, and that might make him falter when he had to stay strong. He had to make sure everything went right. He had to outwit Stephenson.

Just when the strain became unbearable, Eamon entered the office, papers in hand.

"Who is he?" asked Stephenson.

With a quaint bow, the Irishman said, "Eamon Dooley, Mr. O'Toole's secret'ry, at your service," Turning to Patrick, he winked. "The papers you wanted."

"That will be all, Mr. Dooley," he said, looking pointedly toward the door. When Eamon left, he signed where needed.

"Strange fellow," Stephenson commented.

"Never mind him," Patrick urged. "Sign here and release Annie."

"*Tsk-tsk*, a romantic in banker's clothes," taunted Stephenson. "Not wise, Mr. O'Toole, not wise at all."

"Just sign the damn papers," he ground out.

Stephenson arched a brow. Then, taking a pen from Patrick's desk set, he scribbled black across the bottom of the page. Waving the paper, he went toward the door.

"Just a moment, Mr. Stephenson," Patrick said.

"Stephenson will do."

Patrick gave a brief nod, then went on. "We need a copy for our records. Sign this one, too."

He did as asked. "Are we finished?"

"Finally," said Patrick. "Let me find a teller who can handle the transaction."

As they walked out the door, the only thing on Patrick's

mind was Annie's fate. He wondered how she was faring across town.

With a gardenia-reeking handkerchief stuffed in her mouth, tears of rage and frustration scalded Annie's eyes again. To think this could happen even after the mayor had been jailed! Of course, it had been naive to think Serena and her scary lover would so easily give up.

But to be trussed like a chicken, unable to help herself or the man she loved, was unforgivable. Knowing how Patrick felt about her money, he was sure to hate her for signing it all away.

At the moment, the last thing on her mind was the Haven, even if after this latest debacle ended she would mourn the loss of her dream. As Mr. Buntz had said, there was that community of artists in Mt. Gretna. As soon as she was free, Annie would find out what exactly they could offer someone like her.

Right now, she would think of Patrick and getting free. He might need her help, after all. What if Serena's accomplice lost his temper when Patrick refused to hand over the funds? What if he hurt Patrick?

The man didn't look squeamish in the least. Annie feared that Patrick might soon sport a matching scar—or worse—thanks to the dangerous crook. She prayed for Patrick's safety; she knew she couldn't stand it if anything happened to him while he tried to protect her.

As if in answer to her prayers, a loud pounding came at the door. "Serena!" cried Rosaleen. "I know you're in there. But I have something to tell ye, I do. Something you'll surely be wanting to know."

"What makes you think I want to know anything you can tell me?" Serena asked.

" 'Tis about that man ye brought to town."

In a flash, Serena opened the door. "Well?"

Rosaleen strolled in, smiling triumphantly. "Well, lass, seems he's not wasting for love of ye. He's leaving

290 GINNY REYES

Woodbury—and *you*—now that he has what he came for."

"You mean . . . ?"

"Aye, Serena, he's leaving with the money."

"No!" cried Serena. "He loves me. I know he does."

"He loves money more."

Serena ran outside, her heels clacking down the porch steps.

In seconds, Annie was freed. The hug the friends shared was sincere and healing.

"Hurry, now," urged Rosaleen. "I'm after thinking Eamon and Patrick will be needing help."

"What kind of help?"

"I can't be knowing for sure. I've been here all this time since Stephenson left with Eamon following."

"Then, Stephenson isn't really leaving?"

Rosaleen shrugged. "I don't know, lass. Thought 'twould be the perfect way to get Serena out of me way so I could set ye free. Hurry now. We must be going before Eamon's lousy luck ruins everything again."

With a nervous chuckle, Annie followed her friend down Main Street. When they arrived at the bank, they heard Serena's cries.

They'd come to the right place.

As they entered the building, pandemonium met them. Serena hung on to one of Stephenson's coat sleeves, while he tried to shake her loose. "No!" she yelled. "You won't get away from me that easily. You promised to marry me."

"In the heat of the moment."

"Doesn't matter when," she countered. "You can't break a promise just like that."

"Seems it's not the first time it's happened to you. You have experience recovering by now." With a violent shake, Stephenson pulled away, and the sound of ripping cloth filled the air. "But I can't waste any more time on you. I must take care of business now."

Serena stomped after him as he approached a teller's window, undaunted if enraged. Stephenson ignored her and handed the clerk a sheet of paper. Patrick appeared behind the bank employee.

With a glance at the document, the teller's eyes widened. He turned to Patrick, who smiled and summoned Mr. Harrison, the bank's guard.

"We have this . . . gentleman's signed confession to attempted embezzlement, Harrison," Patrick announced. The room grew silent. "Handcuffs are in order."

In a kaleidoscopic swirl, movement broke out seemingly everywhere. Harrison approached Stephenson, but curious customers got in his way. Stephenson glanced at Serena, still weeping, then made for the brass-and-glass doors. When it looked as if he would escape, a wild whoop erupted in the back of the room, and flying through the air, Eamon wrapped his arms around Stephenson's legs, throwing the man to the ground.

The downed robber turned the air blue with curses, to no avail. Mr. Harrison shackled his crook.

From the corner of her eye, Annie saw Serena sidle toward the doors. Eureka! Here was her chance.

"Oh, no you don't," she cried, running. In a flash, she clutched a handful of yellow chignon and hung on for dear life, despite Serena's efforts to pull free. "How does it feel to be restrained?"

"How dare you . . . let me go!" Serena twisted and turned, but Annie's smaller stature served her well. She dodged Serena's blows with ease, still holding on to the woman's hair.

"You can't do this to me," said the former mayor's daughter. "Let go! You'll make me bald."

"Would serve you right," Annie muttered, dancing to miss the jab of an elbow. "I have another one for you here, Mr. Harrison," she called.

Moments later, a pair of handcuffs adorned Serena's slender wrists.

Patrick ran up to Annie. "Are you all right?" he asked.

"Of course I am. What about you?"

"I just stopped a swindler," he said with pride. "And I didn't get my head bashed in!"

"I apologized for that. Profusely, as I recall."

Patrick gave her a suggestive look. "Hmmm . . . perhaps not often and profusely enough."

"Patrick O'Toole, how can you say that? After all that time we spent in your be—"

He cut off her revealing words with a kiss. A stunning kiss. A loving kiss.

When he lifted his lips from hers, Annie's head spun.

"Will you forgive me?" he asked.

"For what?"

"For being a fool."

"Which time?"

"Annie . . ." he said in his most reproving voice, "I'm trying to apologize for breaking our engagement. So, do you forgive me?"

"Does this mean we're still engaged?"

"How about a new proposal?"

"Give it a try."

"Will you marry me and be the love of my life? Be my wife, whether we're rich or poor, through all the troubles we're sure to find?"

She met his brown gaze. "And the memories of your mother?"

"When Stephenson said he'd captured you, I realized you were right. My mother lived a powerful love with my father, one that gave her memories to fill a lifetime. I want those memories with you, but I plan to make sure they're good ones." He tightened his hold on her. "I promise you won't lack for anything, even though we'll never be rich."

"Oh, yes, we will," she said. "We'll be rich in love."

"You'll be rich in gold, too, boyo!" said Eamon,

straightening his red waistcoat. "Aren't you forgetting something?"

Patrick gave him a quelling glare. "I was getting to that, Eamon. Why don't you go see to your own romantic affairs. I'll take care of Annie." Leaning close, he whispered, "In every way."

A delicious shiver ran down her spine. "Stay on the subject, Mr. O'Toole. What about the gold?"

"Oh, the Irish madman and I kept Stephenson's hands out of your money."

Annie shot a glance to where Officer Riley was helping the guard lead Stephenson and Serena out of the bank. "Doesn't look as if he could have done anything with it."

"That's not the point, woman!" Patrick placed his palms on Annie's cheeks. "I was ready to give him every cent you owned. In fact, I approved the rental and sales agreements. Your safety meant more to me than all the wealth in the world. I decided I would find the funds for your blasted Haven, if it came to that. But we didn't let it. Your money's safe."

"Oh, Patrick . . ." Annie's eyes filled with tears. Of joy. "You did that for me? You *do* love me . . ."

"Of course I do. Isn't that what I've been trying to say?"

"But you haven't said it."

His gaze grew hot. A sensual shiver again tripped down Annie's spine. "Loving you, Annie Brennan, is the single most magical thing that has happened to me. I intend to keep the rest of my life filled with your magic."

His lips came down on hers.

Across the room, Eamon took hold of Rosaleen's hand. "Well, lass, looks like I finally did what I was sent to do. I made sure no harm came to her pot o' gold. And I didn't even need me luck to do it."

Rosaleen chuckled. "Aye, Eamon Dooley, I did me

job, as well. I brought me godchild his true love, and 'twasn't through magic I did it, either."

Then he frowned. "You could really see me today? Behind the carriage?"

"Aye, just as on that day here at the bank. Ye have no mastery of the old ways, ye don't."

"And your magic never works."

For a moment, both fell silent. Moments later, Rosaleen said, "But I've known magic, and 'tweren't the faerie sort a'tall. There's magic in your kisses, in your arms. There's magic in your love."

Emotion clouded his emerald eyes. "Aye, lass, you're right there. Your kisses are magical indeed. And loving you . . . ah, *cailin*, loving you is . . ."

Their gazes said more than words ever could. Eamon wrapped his arms around Rosaleen, held her close to where his heart pounded hard enough for her to feel.

" 'Twon't be easy, going back," she murmured, her throat tightening.

" 'Twill be lonely, too."

He kissed her temple, her forehead, the tip of her nose, her lips. Then he kissed her again, this time deeply, passionately, with all the love he'd confessed.

Then Rosaleen pulled back. "I can't, Eamon. I can't go through this again. I can't say good-bye, then see ye again, only to say farewell one more time."

"Then why say farewell a'tall?" he asked. "Nothing's forcing us back, is it?"

Rosaleen drew in a sharp breath. He was right. "But what of our ages? Are ye ready to turn six hundred all at once?"

"If you'll turn four hundred at me side."

"Do ye think 'twill happen to us?"

He shrugged. "Only one way to tell. Besides, I've only known it to happen to mortals who come to *Tyeer na N-og* once they leave. P'r'aps it doesn't work that way for us."

Rosaleen's head spun with possibilities. "Do ye really

A FAERIE TALE
295

think we could . . . stay here, stay together? You're willing to be mortal, to face death someday?"

"Ah, *cailin*, if you're no longer at me side, 'twill be death I face the minute I go back." He winked. "Besides, I'd be happy just to live only dozens more years as long as I can sleep with ye."

Rosaleen arched an eyebrow. "Sleep, ye say?"

"Well, lass, p'r'aps not so much sleep."

"You'll give up your pot o' gold?"

"Don't have it, do I?"

Rosaleen smiled tenderly and shook her head. "And your lucky charm?"

"I'm keeping all me charm, lass! I'll be using it on ye often enough. And the luck . . ."

"Aye, ye weren't lucky a'tall!"

He gave her a gloating grin. "No more than your spells are magical."

Rosaleen chuckled. "Faith, and we're a pair! No luck, no magic, and more love than there's ever been in *Tyeer na N-og*."

"P'r'aps that's the truth of it, lass. Our magic didn't bring Patrick and Annie any love, but it sure does seem that love itself brings a world o' magic."

" 'Twould seem that way, no?"

As they left the bank building for the brilliant Midsummer Day sunshine, Eamon exclaimed, "Sure and there's something I'm forgetting!"

"What would that be?"

"Where's Annie?"

"Where she belongs, in Patrick's arms."

"Ah, well, there's no hurry, then."

"For what?"

"For reminding her o' her last lucky wish. Wonder what she'll be wishing next. . . ."

"Eamon Dooley, you'd better stop that lucky wish nonsense, or I won't be marrying ye."

"Did I ask you, *cailin*?"

Rosaleen gave him a sensual smile, knowing how it would affect him. "Ah, but ye will."

He pulled her closer to his side and slipped an arm around her waist. "No more wishes, then?"

"No more."

He kissed her temple. "How about magic?"

"Eamon . . ."

Rosaleen braced herself at the sight of wicked glee in his eyes. Whatever came next would surely be full of mischief.

"So, *cailin*," he said with a wink, "since we're speaking o' love and magic, would you be wanting some more of me magical touch?"

Author's Note

Celtic mythology fascinates me. When I learned that Jove planned to launch a line of Magical Love romances, faeries and leprechauns and Irish tales immediately sprang to my imagination. As usual, I played "what if," and from that *A Faerie Tale* unfolded. My contribution to the legend is the conditions Rosaleen and Eamon must fulfill to attain their magical tools. The background for them and their powers—or lack thereof—is based on the following books:

To Ride a Silver Broomstick, by Silver RavenWolf, Llewellyn Publications, St. Paul, Minnesota.

The Crone's Book of Words, by Valerie Worth, Llewellyn Publications, St. Paul, Minnesota.

A Victoria Grimoire, by Patricia Telesco, Llewellyn Publications, St. Paul, Minnesota.

Celtic Myth and Magick, *Witta, An Irish Pagan Tradition*, *Faery Folk*, by Edain McCoy, Llewellyn Publications, St. Paul, Minnesota.

Magical Herbalism, by Scott Cunningham, Llewellyn Publications, St. Paul, Minnesota.

The Encyclopedia of Celtic Wisdom, by Caitlin and John Matthews, Element Books, Inc., Rockport, Massachusetts.

Irish Fairy and Folk Tales, edited by W. B. Yeats, The Modern Library, Random House, New York, New York.

The Story of the Irish Race, by Seumas McManus, The Devin-Adair Company, Old Greenwich, Connecticut.

As always, I love hearing from my readers. Please write to me at The Berkley Publishing Group, c/o Publicity Department, 200 Madison Ave., New York, New York 10016. You can also reach me online at GINNYAIKEN@AOL.COM.

DO YOU BELIEVE IN MAGIC?

MAGICAL LOVE

The enchanting new series from Jove will make you a believer!

With a sprinkling of fairy dust and the wave of a wand, magical things can happen—but nothing is more magical than the power of love.

___**SEA SPELL** by Tess Farraday   0-515-12289-0/$5.99

A mysterious man from the sea haunts a woman's dreams—and desires...

___**ONCE UPON A KISS** by Claire Cross
0-515-12300-5/$5.99

A businessman learns there's only one way to awaken a slumbering beauty...

___**A FAERIE TALE** by Ginny Reyes
0-515-12338-2/$5.99

A faerie and a leprechaun play matchmaker—to a mismatched pair of mortals...

VISIT PENGUIN PUTNAM ONLINE ON THE INTERNET:
http://www.penguinputnam.com

Payable in U.S. funds. No cash accepted. Postage & handling: $1.75 for one book, 75¢ for each additional. Maximum postage $5.50. Prices, postage and handling charges may change without notice. Visa, Amex, MasterCard call 1-800-788-6262, ext. 1, or fax 1-201-933-2316; refer to ad # 789

Or, check above books   Bill my: ☐Visa ☐MasterCard ☐Amex_____(expires)
and send this order form to:
The Berkley Publishing Group   Card#_____

P.O. Box 12289, Dept. B   Daytime Phone #_____ ($10 minimum)
Newark, NJ 07101-5289   Signature_____

Please allow 4-6 weeks for delivery.   Or enclosed is my: ☐ check ☐ money order
Foreign and Canadian delivery 8-12 weeks.

Ship to:

Name_____   Book Total $_____

Address_____   Applicable Sales Tax $_____

City_____   Postage & Handling $_____

State/ZIP_____   Total Amount Due $_____

Bill to: Name_____

Address_____City_____

State/ZIP_____